''I'd rather be a bully than a fake, like your marquis.

''But, of course, *he's* got money—you can tell from the cut of his clothes.''

''What do you know about clothing?'' Sarah asked, bristling at the way Zeke kept referring to the marquis as hers.

He grinned, delighted as always to have raised her ire. ''Enough to know that this blue you're wearing is perfect for you. It turns your eyes the color of the hills behind Lake Champlain just after sunset.''

She felt herself blushing with pleasure and also with surprise. Men had been paying her compliments since she could recall; mostly she didn't believe them and was offended or bored.

Of course, Zeke noticed. He leaned close to her and murmured, ''Careful, Sarah, you shouldn't look so pleased.''

Dear Reader,

Our titles for June include *The Lady and the Laird* by Maura Seger, a charming story of mischief and mayhem. Forced to occupy a crumbling Scottish castle for six months or lose her inheritance, Kaitlyn Sinclair is ill prepared for the devilment caused by the castle's former residents—one living and one long dead.

Those of you who have enjoyed Julie Tetel's previous novels will not be disappointed with *Sweet Suspicions,* her first book for Harlequin Historicals, an intriguing romance that pairs a well-connected yet penniless woman with a rich outcast of London society on a hunt to uncover the murderer in their midst.

The Claim is the first of two titles by Lucy Elliot involving the infamous Green Mountain Boys. When frontiersman Zeke Brownwell declares himself the owner of the very same land that citified Sarah Meade believes is hers, the sparks begin to fly.

Captive Kathleen James impetuously marries fellow prisoner John Ashford to save him from certain death in *Pirate Bride* by Elizabeth August. This tale of danger and adventure is the first historical for Harlequin by this popular contemporary author.

Four enticing stories from Harlequin Historicals to catch your fancy. We hope you enjoy them.

Sincerely,

The Editors

The Claim

Lucy Elliot

Harlequin Books

TORONTO • NEW YORK • LONDON
AMSTERDAM • PARIS • SYDNEY • HAMBURG
STOCKHOLM • ATHENS • TOKYO • MILAN
MADRID • WARSAW • BUDAPEST • AUCKLAND

Harlequin Historicals first edition June 1992

ISBN 0-373-28729-1

THE CLAIM

Books by Lucy Elliot

Harlequin Historicals

Shared Passions #8
Frontiers of the Heart #24
Summer's Promise #44
Contraband Desire #64
Private Paradise #79
Passionate Alliance #95
The Claim #129

Harlequin Books

Harlequin Historical Christmas Stories 1989
"A Cinderella Christmas"

LUCY ELLIOT

is a happily transplanted Easterner living in northern California with her husband, son, dog and any neighborhood cat who wants an extra meal. She has been making up stories for her own entertainment since earliest memory—full of romance, adventure and, of course, a happy ending.

To Lynn, Sonia and Barbara,
my faithful critique group, whose wit, insight and
whimsy have helped me more than they can guess—
not to mention the pasta and fondue!

Chapter One

Albany, New York, 1773

Sarah couldn't make sense of the surveyor's story, partly because he was stuttering so badly and partly because the farmer and his wife were both babbling at once about a big man and wild Indians and a whip.

"Calm down!" Sarah commanded, holding up both of her hands. "Sit down, all of you, and speak calmly." They were in the hallway. When she gestured to the parlor, the farmer and his wife seemed willing, but the surveyor held back.

"C-c-can't!" he stuttered.

"They whupped him," the farmer explained.

"Who whipped him?" Sarah demanded, trying to hold her temper, which was becoming difficult. It was midnight by the last watch and they'd gotten her out of bed. It didn't help matters when she realized that her father was still out, likely finding new ways to lose money he no longer had.

"Th-the Indians and the b-b-big man," stuttered the surveyor.

"Tied him up," put in the farmer, "and went after him with a cord. Did the same to the chainman—he fainted dead away, and when they cut him free he took off running and he's likely running still. They'd have whupped me, too, if the missus hadn't put up such a fuss. So the big man decided to take it out on our place. Burned the roof and run the stock off—run us off, too," he concluded dourly, while his wife glowered at Sarah as though it were all her fault.

"But why?" Sarah demanded, still trying to understand. Why, when this couple had nothing except a few chickens and pigs. "What could he possibly want?"

"L-l-land," the surveyor answered.

"Land?" Sarah turned to him.

Jerkily, he nodded. "H-he wanted us off h-h-his land."

"*His* land!" cried Sarah with such force that the surveyor flinched. "*His* land? Of all the—that land is mine! I've got deeds for every acre, except the hundred I sold to you," she added to the farmer and his wife.

The wife crossed her arms over her bosom. "That's not what the big man said."

"I don't care about any big man!" snapped Sarah. Her temper was slipping fast.

"You would," advised the farmer, "if he'd come after you with a whip. After what happened up there, Mistress Meade, we want our money back."

"Money!" Sarah muttered, hearing steps on the front walk. This would be her father coming home at last—and most probably too tipsy to be of any help. She closed her eyes in frustration, then jerked them open fast as, to her amazement, he began to shout her name. The shout swelled to a full bellow—and it wasn't exactly her name.

"S. J. Meade!" the voice thundered. "Meade—I'm warning you!"

"It's him, the big man!" gasped the farmer, and his wife gave a little yelp. As for the surveyor, he fainted dead away, bumping down the wainscoting to sprawl on the floor.

The servant, who'd been nodding off during the garbled tale, awoke with a start and goggled in terror at the door.

The knob began to rattle. "Meade!" the great voice boomed. "S. J. Meade! I know you're in there! Open up in the name of the Lord!"

"He swears awfully," squeaked the farmer, backing up toward the parlor door. He tripped over the surveyor and went down in a heap.

"Let me in!" The voice was roaring now.

"Mistress?" The servant quaked.

Sarah alone was not shaking. In the first place, she was still too startled to be afraid. Beyond that, she was thinking of the money the farmer wanted back—money that had long since gone to pay her father's debts. And then there was this scoundrel who was hammering on the door, waking every soul in Albany who wasn't deaf. And the deaf ones would hear of the scandal secondhand; by tomorrow morning it would be all around the town and people would point and whisper when she walked down the street, exactly the way they had in Philadelphia.

She squared her shoulders and gestured the servant toward the door. "Let him in."

"But, mistress—"

"Do as I say. Let him in. Then we'll see just what sort of false claim he's making on my land."

The farmer and his wife slunk back as the servant threw the bolt. No sooner had he done so than the door was flung open by a man who was as big and bigger than the three had said. Leonine head, massive shoulders, black eyes flashing fire: if it hadn't been for the strip of skin showing above his beard, Sarah might have easily mistaken him for a bear. He was so big he had to duck as he came through the door.

He came through it roaring. "S. J. Meade! You yellow-livered coward! You low-down thieving Yorker! I'll teach you to steal from me!" He paused for breath, his great chest heaving, as he surveyed the hall. As he did, Sarah heard a whimper and prayed that it wasn't her. She realized that it wasn't when he glared at the farmer's wife.

But only for a moment, then his eyes swung back to her. "Where is he?" he thundered, glancing up the stairs. "Is he such a coward that he'd send a woman in his place while he trembles beneath the bedclothes! That won't do him any good. You'd best fetch him directly, missy. Tell him Shadrach Zedekiah Brownell is here!"

"Fetch whom?" demanded Sarah, her anger giving her strength. As if things weren't already bad enough without this madman bursting in.

"Fetch your thieving husband, or father—whichever he is. Or better yet, I'll fetch him from bed myself!" Swinging into action, he covered half the distance to the staircase in one stride.

Sarah moved to block him.

"Out of my way!" he roared, clasping one mighty hand around her arm.

"I have no husband," she said coldly, before he could thrust her away. "And though it's none of your business, my father isn't home. There's no one up there for you to drag out of bed. In any event, Mr. Brownell, I'm the one you're looking for."

Her last words stopped him. "You!" His grip slackened and his great beard rippled as his jaw followed suit. "But you're a woman. I took S. J. Meade for a man."

"Whatever you took," Sarah said dryly, "I am S. J. Meade. I'm the one who owns the land. And as long as we're on the subject, if I ever hear of you coming onto my land again, I promise I'll have you arrested and thrown into jail."

In the silence that followed, Sarah could hear the surveyor moaning as he came out of his faint and the farmer hissing for him to keep still. If Mr. Brownell heard them he didn't condescend to turn his head. Instead, his black eyes stayed fixed on Sarah with an intensity that gave her the impression he was making up his mind—though what the decision concerned, she couldn't have ventured the faintest guess. She doubted that reason or logic ever governed this wild man's thoughts.

Whatever Mr. Brownell was deciding he was taking his time, and Sarah had no inclination to wait patiently, at whatever o'clock in the morning, with bodies sprawled in the hall—and with her arm still gripped in the paw of this uncivilized black bear, who seemed to rely upon violence to settle his disputes.

"It's very late," she said firmly. "And I believe I've made my point. If you leave right now and quietly, I give you my word not to bring charges for the damage you've already done. But the next time, I warn you, I won't be so kind. Good night, Mr. Brownell,'' she concluded, looking pointedly at the hand that was still wrapped around her arm.

Mr. Brownell's eyes remained fixed on her face and for another moment his expression didn't change. Then, with no warning, he threw back his head and roared with laughter so loudly that Sarah would have jumped three feet straight up if he hadn't been holding her.

''You warn *me!*'' He bellowed so loudly that the overhead lamp began to swing, casting crazy shadows up and down the hall. ''You warn *me* to stay off! Ho! Ho ho! Well now, missy, I'll tell you what. I didn't come here for a woman—I came for S. J. Meade, but when you talk that way, I guess you'll do.''

''You guess I'll 'do' for what?'' demanded Sarah, but he didn't bother to respond, and in the next moment, to her utter shock, she felt herself being scooped up and flipped upside down over the massive right shoulder of Mr. Brownell. Her face collided roughly with the back of his woolen coat. Too shocked to speak, she sputtered a furious wordless protest as he wheeled around and strode through the front door, which had been standing open ever since he'd burst in.

By the time he reached the front gate, she had found her tongue. ''Put me down!'' she demanded with as much indignation as she could muster while hanging upside down. Finding her hands free, she pounded on his back, but she may as well have been hammering on solid oak.

He'd left his horse tied up to the hitching post in the street. Holding her with one hand, he unhitched the reins, then swung into the saddle with her still dangling over his shoulder.

''What are you doing, damn you!'' she gasped as they began to move. Beyond any fear or discomfort was the unspeakable indignity of a strange man's arm clamped across her thighs—not to mention the night air blowing up her skirts.

''Halt! Who goes there!''

Thank heaven, it was the watch! Sarah heard the reassuring rattle and, turning her head, caught a glimpse of the uplifted and astonished face. "What are you doing?" the watchman demanded. "Put that woman down or—agh!"

His threat ended in a gurgle as Mr. Brownell's free hand swept down to seize him around the throat and raise him until his anguished face was level with Sarah's eyes.

"Or what?" Brownell growled. "Or you'll run through the streets yapping at my heels? You'll lose your teeth if you do that, and you still won't get the girl. So why don't you just shut up before I lose my temper and consider really hurting you!" For another moment he held the gagging man. When he opened his hand to release him, the man crumpled into a heap. "I mean that," Brownell warned him before he rode on.

Sarah twisted around to look after the inert heap that had been the watch. She could feel the cold little prickles of fear at the back of her neck and she knew that if she let them, they'd sweep up and over her. Such fear wouldn't help her deal with this wild man who was carrying her off to who knew where like a sack of meal.

She wondered where he was going. She didn't come from Albany, but she'd been here long enough to know that they were heading out of the city toward the north; once they left town they weren't likely to find anyone on the road in the middle of the night, which meant that any stand she made, she'd have to make right here.

"I'll scream," she threatened. "I'll bring out the whole town." Not waiting for his answer, she opened her mouth and screamed, but she'd scarcely gotten a squeak out when she felt herself being dragged down over his shoulder and into his lap. She'd hardly landed when his hand clamped across her mouth.

"Not that it makes any difference," he growled above her head. "You could scream your lungs out if you pleased, and I'd give a new shilling for every burgher with the courage to leave his warm bed."

Sarah didn't answer; she couldn't because of his hand, but beyond that her ears were ringing as the blood flowed from her head. She was relieved to be right side up, but her present position was no less compromising than her last. She'd traded the hump of his shoulder for the vise of his thighs, which were braced hard against the saddle in order to guide the horse while his hands were fully occupied with manhandling her.

His right hand covered half her face, while his left circled her waist, the tips of his fingers resting so near her breasts that only by arching backward could she keep from touching him. But arching only thrust her more closely between his thighs—the devil or the deep blue sea, as her father would have said.

The thought of Father brought a whole new wave of damning thoughts. For as long as she could remember she'd spent her life trying to keep him out of trouble and bailing him out when he fell. But since he fell faster than she could bail him out, they'd sunk steadily until three months ago, when they'd found themselves on the brink of losing everything, including their home in Philadelphia.

Then, with miraculous if uncharacteristic luck, Father had won six thousand acres of undeveloped New York land in a game of cards. Before he could lose it, Sarah had forced him to deed it to her, and they'd both come up here from Philadelphia to sell it as profitably as they could. Things had gone fairly smoothly until an hour ago, but now they seemed to have taken a distinct turn for the worse—a turn by the unwieldy name of Shadrach Zedekiah Brownell.

She twisted her head in protest against his hand over her mouth, but strength was all on his side and he kept his hand in place till they'd left Albany well behind.

"Scream now if you like, missy," he suggested in a tone that made her much too angry to feel afraid.

"You know what you are?" she told him as soon as she could speak. "You're nothing but a big bully, yelling at people and frightening them in order to get your way."

"It works, don't it?" he retorted, and chuckled deep in his chest.

"You find violence amusing?" She shifted, away from his intimate grasp, and succeeded in evading his fingers, though not his thighs.

"That depends." He chuckled again, shifting easily with her so that his fingers were under her breasts again.

She suspected he'd moved on purpose, so this time she stayed where she was. Mr. Brownell was evidently enjoying himself and she didn't mean to give him the added pleasure of a game of cat and mouse. Besides, she had bigger worries, since with every pace the horse was carrying them farther away from Albany. "Where are we going?" she demanded, trying to make her voice firm.

Her firmness rolled off him like water from a duck's oiled back. "You'll see," he said with a shrug that slid her so close against him that she could feel his heart beating straight through both his waistcoat and his shirt. She wasn't a small woman, yet she felt dwarfed by him. He rose up on all sides around her, blotting out the stars and the sky, and the warmth from his great body overcame the chill from the air.

His gaze wasn't as disturbing as their intimacy, but she had no choice but to ignore that as best she could. Briefly she considered the possibility of appearing weak in order to appeal to his sense of chivalry. But fluttery weakness came as hard to her as speaking French—besides which, she didn't imagine that Shadrach Brownell practiced much chivalry. Which left reason and conviction, for what they might be worth.

"Look, Mr. Brownell," she said in her most reasonable voice. "I believe there has been some misunderstanding about the land, but whatever it is I'm sure it can be worked out. If you'll just take me back to Albany, I'll be more than happy to show you my deeds, and, after that, if you still have a question, I'm sure I can answer it."

There was a moment of silence, then he said simply, "Zeke."

"Zeke?" she faltered.

He nodded once against her, his beard tickling her cheek. "That's my name. Nobody calls me Mr. Brownell—leastways, nobody I trust."

"All right, then, Zeke," she said patiently. "If you'll please turn around—"

"I do have a question." He stemmed the flow of her words. "Will you give up the land?"

"Give it up?" Forgetting his fingers beneath her breast, she straightened and turned to him.

He met her gaze calmly, his eyes two circles of darkness above the darkness of his beard. "That's my only question. Will you give it up?"

That was his only question: would she give up six thousand acres of good northern land, land that she owned free and clear—land that was her only hope for avoiding total disgrace? The impossibility of the suggestion made her forget to be reasonable.

"You must be mad!" she exclaimed. "I'll never give that land to you—I'd rather give up my life!" It was no more than the truth; whatever this giant had in mind wouldn't be half as bad as her future would be without the money from the land. She sat up straight and faced him, fear forgotten now.

Even in the darkness, she saw something change in his eyes. They lit with a new interest. Did he finally realize that she wasn't like the others, to be chased off by his bullying? If so, now maybe he'd change his mind and let her go. At the thought of it her hopes rose, but in the next moment the mighty shoulders shrugged. "If that's the way you feel," he said, "I guess there's no point in me turning the horse around."

"Of course there's a point!" she protested. Really, the man was mad! "You're kidnapping me! That's a crime—you'll be punished!"

"Is that what you believe?" His eyes had lost most of their interest, though a bit lingered as they flicked over her. "If you think so, missy, I guess you're not from here."

"Where I'm from is none of your business!" she snapped. "Turn around this moment! I demand that you take me back!'' Anger and frustration fired her demand, but it made no more impression than her fists had on his back.

"I can't do that, missy," he said almost peaceably. "You see, we're expected."

"Expected?" She tensed. "By whom?"

"You'll see when we get there," he answered easily. "Meanwhile, you'd do better to stop your fussing and settle back. We've got a long ride yet, and if you spend it set up like a ramrod, you'll likely be pretty sore by the time we arrive."

He was referring to her posture, which was still erect so that her bones jarred and rattled with the horse's every step. He wanted her back against him, so he could paw her while he rode. She'd rather be crippled when she got to wherever he was taking her. She'd rather throw herself beneath the horse's hooves. In a moment of desperation she considered breaking free, but the strength of the arms that held her made her give up the idea. And even if she did manage to evade his grip long enough to reach the ground, she knew she couldn't outrun him, not with that stride of his.

She was trapped like a fly in a spider's web for whatever he had in mind, and the only question remaining was how bad that whatever would be. Quite bad, she imagined, but she didn't feel afraid. She felt angry and frustrated; she felt angry not only at Zeke Brownell but at men in general for blithely making messes she had to waste her whole life cleaning up. After years of steady sinking she'd finally found a way to lift herself back up, when along came this total stranger to ruin everything just because he happened to form the notion that he owned her land.

She wouldn't let him. It was as simple as that. He could shout and threaten until the walls shook, and he could heave her around like a sack of beans, drag her off to wherever he wanted, but he wouldn't get her land.

"You'll pay for this, Mr. Brownell," she promised bitterly. "You'll pay for what you're doing now, and you'll never lay your hands on a square inch of my land!"

"We'll see about that, missy," he answered placidly, clicking to his horse and guiding it onward into the starlit night.

Chapter Two

Sarah envisioned a hammock in the trees. High up, near the top where the warming sunlight flowed between the leaves and the breeze was cool and light. The hammock held her gently and rocked her back and forth. It was restful, pleasant. She smiled and couldn't recall when she'd felt so peaceful and free of care. Certainly not these last weeks, which had been fraught with arrangements to come to Albany and have the land surveyed, and attempts to pacify the Philadelphia creditors with the promise of payment to come, all the while trying to keep Father from running up new debts even before the old ones were paid off.

And then there had been last night, waiting for Father to come home, falling asleep only to be wakened by the farmer with his tale of the big man and his whip. And then the man himself appearing and carrying her away.

The man. The warmth of the sunlight vanished along with the coolness of the breeze, carrying with them the vision of the hammock rocking pleasantly in the trees. Peace and security departed as Sarah came sufficiently awake to realize that she was nestled against Zeke Brownell's broad chest. Her body was turned sideways so that she sat across his lap with both of her legs slung across his right thigh. Her forehead was pressed against his tickling beard and her fingers were curled cozily into the thick wool of his sleeve. Worst of all, the position was wonderfully comfortable—so comfortable that her inclination was to snuggle in more closely instead of springing away as instinct warned her to.

Delaying by a minute the moment when she'd have to come face-to-face with him, she cast her mind back briefly to what she could recall. They had reached the river in the wee hours of the night to find the ferry boat tied up and a warning on the ferryman's door about what would befall the traveler who dared to wake him before dawn.

Zeke hadn't waked the man. He'd borrowed the ferry instead, launching them one-handed while maintaining a firm grip on her. She would have risked the ferryman's wrath by shouting for help if Zeke hadn't foreseen the possibility and tied his handkerchief firmly across her mouth. He kept it in place until they'd reached the eastern bank and he'd tied them fast to the mooring there. Then he'd unfastened the handkerchief and used it to hold the payment he left for the trip, as well as something extra for the ferryman's trouble in fetching the ferry back across. He'd left the handkerchief knotted to the pole, then hoisted Sarah back into the saddle and ridden on into the woods. And sometime between then and now she'd fallen asleep and ended up curled like a kitten in his arms.

She didn't want to open her eyes. She didn't want to see how far they'd come, and she didn't want to face whatever was awaiting her at the journey's end. Most of all she didn't want to face Zeke Brownell after she'd disgraced herself by falling asleep in his arms.

Then something changed. Beneath her legs, Zeke's thighs tensed and his body leaned to the right. She realized that he was guiding the horse. The horse realized it, too; in response to his pressure it turned obediently to the right, trotted a few yards forward, then came to a sudden halt. Zeke's body relaxed beneath her and his big hand shook her awake.

"Rise and shine, missy. We're here."

Missy. She hated him calling her that, and she had no desire to be wherever they were. She wanted to keep her eyes shut and make it all go away.

"Missy?" He shook her again.

Reluctantly she opened her eyes and looked around, straightening to put as much space as she could manage between her and Zeke, which, given their situation, was really no space at all—a couple of random inches between her shoulder and his chest. Since she had no choice in the matter, it was the best she could do.

She felt like a sleepy child blinking against the sunlight, whose brightness made her want to shut her eyes again. She raised her hand to shade her eyes and turned her head, and after a few moments she could see enough to understand that they were standing in the yard of a rural inn. It was a square two-story wooden building with three chimneys and the sign of a snarling wildcat hanging outside the door.

"What is this place? Where are we?" She felt ridiculous, completely surrounded and dwarfed as she was by Zeke. She couldn't move forward without falling off the horse, and moving backward only increased their intimacy. Indeed, any movement was embarrassing given the way he had her arranged across his lap. The best she could do was to sit still and try to look dignified, but even that was impossible, because when he shifted even slightly she felt herself sliding and had to grab onto his coat.

"Fay's tavern," Zeke answered comfortably. "It's called the Catamount. See that critter on the sign?" He gestured toward the wildcat, turning her so that she could see. "Catamount's what folks in these parts call a cat like that."

"What are these parts?"

"Bennington. New Hampshire Grants."

"Bennington!" She forgot all about his size and nearness in her dismay. She didn't know exactly where Bennington was, but she'd been in Albany long enough to know that it was the headquarters of the band of outlaws known as the Green Mountain Boys. She'd been too busy dealing with the land to pay heed to the stories and rumors she'd heard, but as she stared at that snarling wildcat, bits and pieces filtered back, suggesting who Zeke Brownell was and why he'd brought her here. It wasn't a pleasant suggestion.

"Zeke!"

The voice calling out Zeke's name was eager and young. Looking up, Sarah saw a boy loping toward them across the yard. He was trailed by a hound dog with long droopy ears and the same ambling loose-jointed lope. The boy, she noticed, was carrying a gun—a long-barreled rifle almost as tall as he.

Before she could notice anything else she felt herself begin to slide. Zeke had suddenly vanished so she grabbed for the horse's mane, and in the next moment found herself sitting in the saddle alone, watching as Zeke strode forward to greet the boy.

"Ho there, Archie!" he boomed as both boy and rifle disappeared into his arms, dwarfed as completely as Sarah herself had been. "How've you been behaving?" Zeke demanded as he set the boy back down.

"Pass'bly," the boy answered with a crooked grin. He was about nine or ten and as unpresentable as any child Sarah had ever seen, with his patched homespun and his ragged thatch of hair caught back willy-nilly and held with a leather thong. He looked no better than the hound at his side, which was wagging its tail slowly and waiting to welcome Zeke.

The dog's tail wagged harder as Zeke tugged on its ears. "Thumper, you old cur! Have you been giving the possums a hard time?"

"We caught us two last night," the boy volunteered, stirring up dust with his bare feet and trying not to look too proud. "I gave 'em to Mrs. Fay. She said she'd cook 'em up."

"Well now, that's not half-bad." Zeke scratched his beard, also struggling to hide his pride, so that for just a moment he looked touchingly like the boy.

But the boy had forgotten the possum and was staring at Sarah instead, his brown eyes more than half-hidden by the shaggy fall of his bangs. "Say, Zeke, who's that?"

"Who?" Zeke turned back to the horse and looked at Sarah as though his interest in hunting had wiped her clear out of his mind. She knew very well that it hadn't, but this way he had an excuse to look her up and down slowly and with outrageous impudence. When he'd finished with his inspection, he ruffled the boy's hair. "Well now, Archie, who do you think that is? Who did I go for?"

"For S. J. Meade."

"And that's who I've got here. Mind your manners and don't stare, and you'd best say your hello politely or she's likely to snap your head off."

The boy heard none of this except who Sarah was. He turned to Zeke wide-eyed. "B-but, Zeke, she's a she!"

At the boy's confusion Zeke's amusement drained away. "Damn it all, boy, don't you think I know! And if you're going to stand there stammering and gawking, you'd best put yourself to good use. The horse has had a long night, he could use some feed. As for you, missy," he said to Sarah, "we'd best get you inside. There's folks awaiting us."

As he spoke he reached up for Sarah but she pulled herself away. "My name isn't 'missy,' as you know perfectly well. If you must address me, you may call me Mistress Meade."

Zeke's eyebrows, which were black and thick, shot up at that, and to her irritation a measure of his good humor returned. He cuffed the boy on the shoulder. "Did you hear that, Archie boy? We may call her Mistress Meade! And what if I choose to call you S.J. instead? What if I choose to call you Sally?"

"You'll get no answer from me." She stared down at him coldly.

He didn't mind—quite the reverse. He threw back his head and let out a hoot of laughter that surprised the horse so that it stiffened as if it meant to shy. But before the horse could shy, Zeke's big hands were around Sarah's waist and he was swinging her out of the saddle as though she weighed nothing at all. It was a giddy sensation and was followed by another all-too-familiar one as Sarah felt herself falling forward toward the rough wool of Zeke's coat. She put her hands out in protest but that did no good: she ended up slung over his shoulder with her face smack against his back.

She heard him call to Archie as he strode across the yard, "See to the horse first, then come on inside."

"Put me down, you devil! Damn you, put me down!" She was seething—livid—but of course he paid no heed. He carried her into the tavern as he'd carried her out of her house, except that this time there were strangers waiting to enjoy her predicament. She heard the door fling open and caught the sharp scent of wood smoke and tobacco and the sweeter scent of punch. She also heard the sound of male voices, which abruptly stopped.

She had no view of the room since Zeke was facing it, which gave the room's occupants a fine view of her rear end. She told herself that by acting this way Zeke was really demeaning himself and she braced for the telltale shifting that would mean she was on her way down. She felt it, then she was sliding until her feet hit the floor.

She stood there, blinking as dumbly as she had in the yard, while her body once more accustomed itself to the change in altitude. She was in the taproom of the tavern, a big room with an enormous stone fireplace. The room was full of tables, several of which were occupied by men who appeared to be cut from the same cloth as Zeke Brownell—homespun, to be specific, and with that same wild look in their eyes. Their eyes were all fixed on Sarah and they all held the same surprise that she'd seen in Archie's out in the yard. She doubted Zeke would like their reaction any more than he'd liked the boy's, and she braced herself against the inevitable noise.

There was a moment of shifting and coughing, then one lanky fellow spoke up.

"Who've you got there, Zeke?"

As she expected, Zeke answered at the top of his lungs.

"Well, Jasper," he demanded, "who in the hell do you think I've got? I went for S. J. Meade and, by God, I brought her back!"

Jasper's Adam's apple jerked wildly in his throat. "B-but, Zeke, she's a woman."

"Son of a whoreson!" Zeke roared. "I've brought her all the way from Albany and don't you think I know!"

"But—"

"But nothing!" Zeke thundered. "There's nothing you need to know except that this is S. J. Meade, and she claims the land is hers! And I suppose you think I ought to let her keep it just because she's wearing skirts?"

"Well, no," Jasper faltered. "I don't guess—"

"No," Zeke interrupted, "I don't believe you do, because if you think she deserves some land, I suggest you give her yours! Any other objections?" He glared around the room. When no one spoke, he nodded tersely. "Good. Because I'm pretty thirsty after all this riding around, and Sally here is likely to need some breakfast before the trial. Jasper, why don't you go see if Mrs. Fay's got something for her to eat, and some of you others had best rouse yourselves to round up the rest of the Boys. As for me, I believe I'll commence with a swallow of ale."

Turning his back on Sarah as though she'd ceased to exist, he strode past the tables on his way to the bar. He hadn't gone three paces when one of the other men spoke, a man with red hair who was almost as big as Zeke. "We never have tried a woman."

Zeke stopped and slowly turned to the red-haired man, who looked less disapproving than dubious. "Well now, Remember, as far as I can recall, we've never had a woman who's laid claim to our land."

Zeke's eyes shifted to Sarah, who'd been doing her best to keep track of what was going on. Her earlier suspicion had all but been confirmed: She'd been delivered into the hands of the Green Mountain Boys.

Albany had been full of tales about the Green Mountain Boys. Roughneck backwoods squatters with more brawn than brain, who had the mistaken impression that they were the true owners of thousands of acres of virgin land lying west of the Connecticut River between Massachusetts and Canada. Land that had in fact been granted to law-abiding folk. Named for the mountains that formed the backbone of that country, the Boys enforced their so-called "title" by terror and by force.

Tales of ambush and midnight ghosts tumbled through Sarah's mind—fantasies she'd discounted as the clacking of idle tongues, but which she now recalled all too clearly as she returned Zeke's look. The surveyor's garbled story— Suddenly she understood that these wild-eyed creatures were the Green Mountain Boys themselves, and Zeke was one of them, if not the leader of the band!

And this trial they were planning? No doubt it meant to determine whether she or Zeke owned her land. She didn't believe for a moment they planned to hold it in a proper court. She guessed they would hold it right here in the Catamount, with themselves as judge and jurors—in which case it wasn't hard to foresee what the verdict would be.

Of all the bloody nerve! She met Zeke's appraising look with a defiant one. She was hungry and disheveled but she wasn't scared. He could have five trials—he could have five hundred, she didn't care. She'd die before she let him and his band of hoodlums bully her out of her land.

The sight of her defiance had a predictable effect on Zeke. To her disgust she saw him smile within the thickness of his beard. "She can handle a trial," he drawled. "I guarantee she won't up and faint, or whatever else Yorker women do. Hell, she's probably got stronger nerves than most Yorker men, yellow-livered cowards and whoresons that they are.

"Besides," he added, turning back to the red-haired man, "if we don't try her here, every Yorker with a Grants claim will get the message loud and clear that if he turns his claim over to his wife or his daughter we'll let it be. Then all the rest of you can say goodbye to your land and spend the rest of your life scratching out a living on what few worn-out acres are left in the Bay colony or in Connecticut. Is that the way you want it?"

The red-haired man—the one called Remember— screwed up his broad face. "Hell's fire, Zeke!" he protested. "You know damned well it's not. We all want our land here just as much as you!"

"Then if you've come to your senses, maybe we can quit this tongue-clacking and get to work. Choose your judge and pick your jury. I need something to drink!"

The door opened and Archie and the hound sidled in. Zeke sent them a quick look before he strode to the bar, where the barman was waiting with a huge tankard of ale. Zeke lifted the tankard and drained it in a single draft, then slapped it down on the counter to be refilled. Meanwhile the man named Jasper had shuffled off, presumably in search of Sarah's meal. A few of the others had vanished out the front in order to collect their missing comrades for the trial. Archie was staring at Sarah as he had out in the yard, and those of the Boys left in the room were staring at her, too.

Zeke, by contrast, seemed to have put her out of his mind and at this moment was waiting for the barman to refill his mug. Sarah fixed a disdainful look at the back of his coat, then turned her head purposefully to spread that same look around the room. Were these to be her judges? she thought scornfully. They were no better than Zeke—a pack of ignorant backwoods oafs. Let them fetch her breakfast. She wouldn't demean herself by eating their food or even sitting in their chairs. She'd fall down dead from exhaustion before she'd deign to sit.

She'd almost completed her scornful survey when she saw the man sitting alone at a table in the back. The first thing that caught her eye about him was that his dress was different. He wasn't wearing homespun but rather English wool—not fancy but decent. And though he wasn't wearing a wig, his dark hair was neatly pulled back in a queue and tied with a black silk ribbon whose ends were tucked away. His expression was thoughtful, his manner reserved. In dress and manner he looked completely out of place, and she couldn't help but wonder what he was doing here.

Zeke, who'd finished his second tankard, wiped his mouth on his sleeve and turned. Catching the object of Sarah's attention, he slapped down his mug and boomed, "Well, Eli, I suppose you've got an objection, too!"

The question was a challenge and Zeke's tone was belligerent, but the man he'd called Eli didn't seem to take offense. His eyes still on Sarah, he said reflectively, "I'm not sure that bringing her here was a good idea. Her being a woman may shame the Yorkers out of their cowardice. They may feel obligated to come here after her. They may think chivalry demands some sort of revenge."

Zeke snorted in derision. "Poppycock! There aren't a half dozen chivalrous men in all of New York—and if they do come, so what? We'll turn them back just like we've turned back every other Yorker who's set his flat foot down in the Grants!"

"What if they send the army?"

"For Mistress Meade?" Zeke turned to give Sarah yet another appraising look. Derision faded and he smiled. "She is pretty enough, isn't she—all those golden ringlets and those big blue eyes, and her mouth looks like a flower when she purses it up that way. If I were the governor I'd send my troops right away. Hell, I wouldn't send my army, I'd go after her myself!"

His eyes lingered on Sarah and subtly his expression changed. As if his mind were speaking to hers, she watched as he envisioned himself claiming her as the spoil of war. His eyes darkened and heated with a fierce virile joy that sucked her to them with a force equal to that of his arms. Too startled to resist him, she felt herself being drawn in: her breath caught, her lips parted—she could feel the heat on her skin just as she'd felt his heat last night. The experience was amazing, overwhelming. Frightening. People were watching and she couldn't look away. She was beginning to panic when his eyes changed again, focusing as he realized what he was doing to her.

Before she could drag her gaze free, he broke into a broad grin. "Don't get your hopes up, Sally. No matter what Eli says, the governor's a fool. He won't send the army. Neither will His Majesty's commander, General Haldimand. They're both afraid to cause trouble with the Green Mountain Boys—they're afraid we might start a general revolt in the colonies. Isn't that right, Eli?" His eyes moved back to well-dressed, reflective Eli, who'd been watching the exchange.

Eli inclined his head briefly. "Maybe so," he agreed. "So long as we treat her well and don't give them anything they believe they need to avenge."

"Well! Why wouldn't we treat her well?" Zeke flung out both arms to embrace the entire room. "Haven't we brought her to our finest hostel on our finest horse—not to mention her being in the care of our bravest knight. We'll give her Mrs. Fay's best breakfast, then we'll give her our finest trial—a much finer trial than they'd give any of us in New York, if I do say so myself.

"How could we treat her better?" Zeke challenged the room. Nobody answered, including Eli, to whom Zeke's eyes returned and upon whom they dwelled as they lightened with a new idea. He held up one finger. "We'll do even more. We'll give her representation."

"Representation?"

"A lawyer, and not just a lawyer but the best lawyer in the Grants." Zeke's eyes settled on Eli.

"Oh, no," Eli said.

"Why not?" Zeke demanded, his eyes sparkling now. "You're the one who's worried about things being fair. What could be fairer than you representing her?"

"Listen to what you're saying. I'd be doing it against you!"

Zeke seemed delighted. "All the better! You know there's nothing I relish more than a good fight with a worthy adversary, and you and Mistress Sally here, together, are about as worthy as they get. I'm sure the rest of the Boys would approve. Isn't that right, Boys?"

As the Boys mumbled their acquiescence, the kitchen door bumped back to admit a stout woman carrying a ladened tray. Stepping into the room, she announced, "Here's the mistress's breakfast if she'd like to eat."

"I'm sure she would," Eli answered before Sarah could reply. "Why not show her into the parlor. She'd likely enjoy the privacy, and in the meantime we can settle this point out here. If you have no objection?" he said to Zeke.

Zeke looked from Eli to Sarah and gave a dismissive shrug. "You go with her, Archie. Keep an eye on her, and if she tries to escape, shoot her with your gun."

Archie swallowed so quickly he began to cough. "Yes, sir!" he muttered, and moved swiftly to obey.

The woman with the tray also moved, but Sarah stood her ground. She was still smarting from all of Zeke's earlier abuse, and added to that was her fury at the way she'd melted just now when he'd looked at her. Her fury was far more with herself than it was with Zeke, but she felt no compunction about taking it out on him.

"Thank you for all your kind permission," she said icily, "but I'm quite capable of deciding where and when I'll eat. And as for your offer of a lawyer, I refuse that, too. All this talk about a trial is nothing but mockery. This is a tavern, not a courtroom, and nobody here has one shred of legal authority."

"Of course we have," said Zeke. "We've got the full authority of the New Hampshire Grants!"

"New Hampshire?" Sarah slapped the words down with disgust. "We aren't in New Hampshire here, we're in New York! New York owns everything west of the Connecticut River, and this is to the west!"

Far from protesting, Zeke smiled maddeningly. "So you believe, Sally, but we here in these parts don't happen to agree, and while you're in these parts you'll have to answer to our authority."

"*Your* authority!" She practically shouted, she was so fed up with him. "This isn't New Hampshire and you know it! The king said so himself. The governors wrote and asked him and he said this was New York and you can't make it New Hampshire just by saying so, any more than I can make it Pennsylvania. This whole thing is preposterous and I refuse to participate." She was shaking when she finished, and if her hands could have fitted around it, she might have tried to wring his neck. Talking sense to Zeke Brownell was like banging into a stone wall.

Zeke turned to Eli. "Maybe you were right. Maybe she doesn't need a lawyer. She can speak well enough for her-

self—with or without breakfast,'' he added with a glance
toward the tray. ''If you try to make her eat it, she'll probably tell you that Grants food will stick in a Yorker craw.''

Sarah would have retorted but again Eli intervened. ''She
doesn't have to eat the food but she could use a cup of tea.
At the very least, I imagine she could use a break from
you.'' He gave Sarah a sympathetic look, then said to the
woman with the tray, ''If you'll take it into the parlor,
Mistress Meade will have it there.''

''She won't either,'' Zeke maintained. ''You heard her,
she said so herself. She makes up her own mind about when
and where she eats and she's just ornery enough to—''

''Thank you.'' Sarah addressed Eli as if Zeke weren't
even there. ''A cup of tea in the parlor would be very nice.
Shall we go?'' she said to the woman.

The woman led the way with Sarah following and Archie
and his faithful hound bringing up the rear. They left Zeke
behind them, for once silent with surprise.

Zeke didn't stay silent for long. From the sounds reaching Sarah through the parlor's closed door, he and Eli were
continuing their discussion with more spirit than before.
She faced Archie across the untouched dishes of smoked
fish, roast mutton, baked apples, bread and cheese and listened to Zeke's familiar booming bass. She couldn't hear
his words from here but she recognized his tone, and the
lulls of relative silence must be Eli's replies. For the second time she wondered what Eli was doing here, and why
he alone seemed prepared to stand up to Zeke.

Archie fiddled with his rifle's stock and gestured to the
tray. ''Might's well eat them vittles. Mrs. Fay ain't too bad
a cook.''

She fixed him with a frigid stare, which she regretted instantly. After all, he was only a child and couldn't help
where he'd been born or the adults who controlled his life—
to such an extent as his life was controlled, which didn't
strike her as much. Relenting, she poured a cup of tea and
stirred in a spoonful of sugar. Archie watched her stirring,
still fiddling with the stock.

She set the spoon next to the saucer. "You can put the gun away. I'm not planning on running away and I can't very well enjoy my breakfast with a gun pointing at my face."

Archie looked apologetic but he didn't move the gun. "Zeke wouldn't like that."

"And you always do what Zeke likes?"

"Mostly. You've seen for yourself what he can get like when he ain't pleased. Bellows louder'n a goddamn bear with all four feet in a trap."

She tried not to shudder at his use of profanity. "Is Zeke your relation?"

"He's my father," Archie said, sitting up straighter and speaking the word with pride.

She should have guessed it. He had the same dark eyes, though his hair was lighter, flecked with streaks of blonde. It might even be mainly blonde if it were ever washed. "What about your mother?"

Archie's shoulders slumped a bit. "She died, back when I was born."

"So did mine," said Sarah. "She died when I was five years old."

Archie looked interested. "Then it was just your father and you?"

She nodded grimly. "That's who it was. Sometimes there were governesses but they never stayed long." Her father had fired the ugly ones and scared the pretty ones away. "What about you, Archie? Do you go to school?"

His hair hid his eyes briefly as he shook his head. "Zeke and me, we don't believe in that sort of thing."

She opened her mouth to comment before she thought the better of it. Instead she asked him, "How often do you have these trials?"

He shrugged. "Whenever."

"Whenever what?"

"Whenever some Yorker tries to steal our land."

She told herself to ignore his choice of words. He was just repeating a lesson he'd learned and she didn't have to tax her brain to guess who had taught it to him. "What makes you think the land is yours?" she asked evenly.

"I don't think it, I know it." He looked her in the eye. "Zeke paid for every acre fair 'n' square. He's got the deeds to prove it."

"So have I."

His young mouth tightened and he muttered, "Yorker deeds."

She made a sound of exasperation. "Yes, Yorker deeds, because it's Yorker land. It's always been Yorker land and it always will be. I know the governor of New Hampshire once pretended to own the land and granted it to unsuspecting buyers before the king told him to stop. I'm sorry if he sold some of that land to your father, but he had no right. My deed is the legal one because it was granted by New York. The king says so," she repeated. "Don't you believe your own king?"

Archie stiffened at the question, his jaw set with a resolution that told her that if given the choice between believing Zeke or the king, he'd probably believe Zeke. Instead of feeling angry, she envied him. She'd stopped trusting her father long before she was ten and she imagined it would be lovely to have that much faith.

"Never mind," she said kindly. "It's not for you to decide. Or me," she added, thinking of the trial ahead. "After they find people guilty in these trials, what do they do to them?"

"That depends."

"He whipped the surveyor I sent up to the land."

Archie's expression turned to horror. "He'd never do that to you! Zeke'd never whip a woman!"

"That's a comfort, at least."

"Yes'm," Archie agreed. "All the same, Zeke sets a powerful store by that land. He'd sell his soul to the devil before he'd give it up."

Sarah sighed deeply. "So would I, Archie. So would I."

It wasn't until the knock came on the door that Sarah realized Zeke's shouting had stopped. The knock was Eli, who told Archie he could leave. Archie went back out into the taproom, followed by the dog. When they'd gone Eli sat down in Archie's vacant chair.

"There's no point in not eating." He glanced at the untouched meal. "An empty stomach won't make anything easier."

She ignored his comment but not his tone, which was the opposite of Zeke's. Zeke would have bullied and browbeaten her, while Eli suggested in the mildest of ways.

"I suppose he won the 'discussion.'"

Eli smiled briefly. "Yes, he won. You've got a lawyer for your trial—if you want one."

"I don't."

"That's your decision."

"Thank you for seeing as much." She wondered if he would leave then, but he stayed where he was.

"Zeke will find some way to tease you whether or not you eat. You can't stop him, so you may as well suit yourself, and you'd do better to keep your strength up if you mean to match wits with him."

"I haven't noticed he's so sharp-witted. Just loud," she said, but she knew Eli was right. Besides, the longer she sat here the hungrier she got, and if she didn't eat now she wasn't sure when she'd get another chance.

Eli showed no reaction when she picked up the fork. For several minutes he watched her in silence, then he said, "I suppose you don't want a lawyer because you the think the trial's a farce."

She set down her fork and looked at him hard. "Of course I do. What else would you call Zeke Brownell bullying everybody here to agree that my land really belongs to him? You may want a circus, Mr. Whoever-you-are, but you won't get one from me, and in the end I'll hold on to that land against Mr. Brownell and anyone else who tries to take it away!"

Zeke would have retorted, but Eli only regarded her with the thoughtful expression she'd seen before. "There's another side to Zeke from the one you've seen so far."

"Zeke Brownell could be a hexagon for all I care, but that doesn't change a thing. You can have your trial but I won't participate."

"If you don't try you can't win."

"I can't win anyway. You're only trying to trick me into taking part in the trial because you know it won't be as much fun if I don't."

Eli shook his head slowly. "That's not necessarily true. We once had a defendant who hollered so much they shut him in the cellar while we held court. That was probably the best trial we've ever had." His face was deadpan but his eyes were amused.

Her eyes were unyielding. "That doesn't change the fact that I can't possibly win. What other reason could there be to risk being made a mockery of?"

"Pride, maybe? Or just plain cussedness? And if you don't, Zeke will call you a quitter. And," Eli added, "if you get him worked up, you can lead him into traps."

"I don't care what he calls me." She picked up her fork and began to eat again. But Eli's last statement had planted a seed in her mind. She chewed slowly. "You didn't want to do this when he first brought it up."

"Maybe I've changed my mind."

"Why? What made you change it?"

He shrugged. "I don't know. Pride? Or just plain cussedness."

"Did he call you a quitter?"

"He might have done."

This time, when he smiled, she couldn't resist smiling back. Eli watched her eating for several minutes before he said, "I'd like you to tell me how you got the land."

That touched her temper. "I got it legally."

"From whom?"

"My father."

"Who did he get it from?"

"He won it in a game of cards in Philadelphia—which is where we come from, despite Mr. Brownell's assumptions that I come from New York."

Eli ignored her comment. "Why did your father sell the land to you?"

"Why not?" She went back to eating but she could feel him watching her.

"Because it's an unusual thing to do. Were you getting married? Was it part of a dowry?"

That made her want to laugh, but the laugh would have been bitter so she kept it to herself. Eli kept waiting, so finally she set down her fork. "He was forced to transfer it to me by his creditors so he couldn't lose it the way he's lost everything else we've ever had—including our house in Philadelphia, which is mortgaged and will be sold unless we can redeem it within the next six months. The creditors agreed to give us six months' grace if he transferred the land to me, so he did."

If she'd expected a strong reaction, she was surprised. "Then why not transfer the title to the land to your creditors? Why go to all the trouble of having it surveyed?"

"Because if I subdivide it and sell it in lots I'll make more than twice as much as I would if I sold it whole. That way we'll end up with something after we're through."

"What then?" asked Eli.

"Then I will do my best to hang on to what I have. I don't see the purpose in these questions. How do they prove that I own the land?"

"They don't, necessarily. On the other hand, they may show that you deserve it more. What about your mother?"

"My mother is dead. She died years ago, in England. That's where I was born." She stopped. Eli waited. Finally she sighed. She'd told him the worst already and she couldn't see what harm it would do in telling him the rest. Besides, it was a relief to be telling her side of the story instead of listening to Zeke hurling accusations at her.

"My mother's family was very wealthy. When she married my father they gave her a large dowry, but they must have regretted that almost immediately. There was still a good deal of money left when my mother died. I remember grand houses, coaches, jewelry—first in England and then in Philadelphia. I also remember men knocking at the door with that particular look in their eyes."

"What look?"

"I can't describe it—hard and embarrassed at once. The look of a man who's owed money and hates to ask for it, especially of the daughter her father sends to speak to them. The older I got the more men there were, until finally everything was gone.

"Everything," she repeated, her eyes on her half-finished meal. "Then, by some miracle, my father won this land. Left to his own devices, he would have staked it on the next game and lost, but I managed to get it from him before he did. Then I rushed around the city using it to hold our creditors off. They gave me six months to come back and pay them off, and if I don't do that, as sure as I am sitting here, we will lose everything."

She looked at Eli. "So you see that whatever Mr. Brownell has in mind to frighten me, it can't be any worse than giving up that land. Short of killing me."

"We won't kill you," Eli answered as swiftly as Archie had. "We don't kill people."

"Then you won't get my land."

Someone knocked on the door just then. "Eli? You ready in there?" Before Eli could answer, the door opened and Jasper stuck in his head. "Remember's judging. I'm bailiff and I'm supposed to call for you."

Eli looked at Sarah. "Would you like to finish your meal?"

She shook her head briefly. "Thank you, I've had enough." She put down her fork and wiped her mouth. As she stood she realized there was something she hadn't asked.

"Your name," she said to Eli. "I don't know your proper name."

He paused, his hands on the table, and a familiar spark lighted his eyes. "Brownell," he answered. "Elijah Jehail Brownell."

"Brownell!" She reached for her napkin as she began to choke. "You can't be related to Zeke!"

"He's my older brother. But rest assured, I won't let that interfere with your case."

Sarah gaped at him, not knowing whether to laugh or to cry. "This changes everything. I can't go ahead with this."

"You can and you will," said Eli, as calmly as before, and she must have believed him, because the next thing she knew she had pushed her chair back and was allowing him to guide her out through the open door.

Chapter Three

There had been changes in the room since she'd left. For one thing, the furniture had been moved around to approximate a court. One long table now served as the judge's bench, with twelve chairs for the jury set off to one side. Two smaller tables had been set opposite and Zeke was already seated at the one on the left. He turned, along with everyone else, when Sarah and Eli came in, and Sarah could tell from his expression that he was pleased to see she hadn't managed to fire Eli and was prepared to enjoy himself thoroughly.

After Eli's revelation she was in no mood for Zeke's look, and she stopped, wondering if she wouldn't be wiser to turn around and walk straight out as she'd threatened earlier. Eli must have guessed what she was thinking because he murmured, "Ignore him. He's nothing but a layman, and as he said before, you've got the best lawyer in the Grants."

"Are there any others?"

"Two besides me, only one's a hopeless drunk. Since you've come this far you ought to go through with it all the way." Stepping forward, he pulled out her chair for her.

This action brought a pointed chuckle from Zeke. "Prefer that, do you Sally, to my brand of gallantry?"

Her impulse was to answer but she recalled Eli's advice; instead of whirling on Zeke, she took her seat with a flourish before she turned around to take her first good look at her audience.

The sight was far from encouraging. Whereas the room had been mostly empty when she had arrived, now every table was almost full and most of the men were looking every bit as rambunctious and ready for fun as Zeke. She didn't notice the sprig of greenery in each one's buttonhole until Jasper stopped at their table to give one to Eli.

She watched as Eli slipped it on. "What's that for?"

"The official emblem of the Green Mountain Boys."

The entire jury had one. And when he strode in a moment later, so did Remember the judge.

"All rise!" bawled Jasper, a little bit after the fact, so that most of the Boys were still easing themselves up when he bawled, "Sit down! Court's in session. Anyone with business, draw near and listen close. God save the king!"

"Thanks, Jasper." Remember looked from side to side. For a robe he was wearing what looked like somebody's old cloak, and for a wig he sported his own flaming red hair. "You ready, boys—Eli? Zeke? Seeing's how Zeke's the plaintiff, he may as well begin."

"Thank you kindly, Remember. I don't mind if I do." Hitching up his breeches, Zeke came to his feet and stepped around the table in order to address the crowd. "Gentlemen of the jury, Remember, Jasper. Boys. What we've got here is another Yorker trying to steal our land."

He gestured to Sarah, who was once again struggling to hold her tongue. "As you probably all know, this here is Mistress S. J. Meade, and as you can see for yourselves, Mistress Sally ain't a man. Now some of you may think that makes a difference. Eli here does. He thinks if we don't treat her kindly the Yorkers may take offense and decide to storm Bennington or send in the army or some such thing. He felt so strongly about it he volunteered to represent her in this trial. If you ask me, the truth is that Eli's fallen in love with our Sally here. Not that I blame him, since she's pretty enough. But pretty or ugly, she says she owns my land and that makes her as dangerous as any Yorker man."

He paused to grin with amusement as Eli's hand, planted firmly on Sarah's shoulder, restrained her from jumping up. "Later, Sally," he admonished. "You'll have your turn when I'm done. That is, if your lawyer will let you."

"Your Honor, please." Eli appealed to Remember to reprimand Zeke, but Remember was too busy enjoying the spectacle to recall that he was the judge. So Eli said, "Remember, would you please instruct the plaintiff to stop harassing the defendant and to get on with his case."

Remember stopped grinning and showed the good grace to flush. "He's right, Zeke," he said sternly. "Get on with your case."

"Where was I?" Zeke's eyes lingered on Sarah. She met them and looked away, suddenly afraid that he would do to her what he'd done before. To her disgust, she heard him chuckle as if he'd read her mind.

"Oh, yes. I was talking about Sally here. I was just about to tell you what she did. She sent a damned Yorker surveyor up there to mark out my land, and he'd be up there at this very moment, rattling his chains, if I hadn't heard about it, gone up there and suggested that he leave."

This was too much for Sarah. Shaking off Eli's hand, she leapt to her feet and cried. "Suggested! You suggested, my foot! The truth is, Zeke Brownell, you frightened the man half to death!"

Zeke grinned, delighted to have gotten such a rise out of her. Then he nodded. "You bet I frightened him. He's lucky I didn't kill him. The next time I catch him, I may. When you see him you can tell him so for me."

"I most certainly will not! And I'm warning you that the next time you set foot on my land you're the one likely to get killed!"

Zeke hooted and all of the Boys whistled and clapped. Through the noise Eli said to Sarah, "You've made your point. Sit down."

"And let him tell more lies?"

"Real court or pretend, telling stories is what a trial's all about. You'll have your turn when he's through."

But no sooner was she seated than Zeke hooted again. "Keep it up, brother Eli, and pretty soon you'll have her eating from your hand!"

"All right, all right," said Remember before Sarah could respond. "Zeke, you stick to your subject. What else have you got to say?"

"I've got to say what's the point of this trial? There's six thousand acres of land east of Lake Champlain and the point of this trial is to say whose it is. It's mine, I can prove it, and that's just what I mean to do—for all lawyer Eli'll try to dazzle you with his fancy talk and Mistress Sally will dazzle you with her good looks.

"I don't talk fancy, and as for looks, they used to say I was so good at trapping because I could kill muskrat without a gun. I may talk plain and look ugly but that land is mine, and if you sit tight and listen I know that you'll agree. That's all for now, Boys. It's Eli's turn." He grinned at the other table as he took his seat.

"We reserve our opening statement."

"Reserve it for what?"

"For later." Eli answered Zeke without getting up.

Zeke turned to Remember. "Remember, can he do that?"

Remember gave a sheepish shrug. "How'n the hell do I know? Eli's the lawyer. If he says he can, he can."

"I can," said Eli, and Sarah shut her lips, battling the temptation to stick out her tongue at Zeke. After the drubbing he'd given her, any triumph tasted sweet.

"All right," said Remember. "Let's go ahead. Zeke, call your first witness."

"He's afraid," goaded Zeke. "He won't give his opening statement because he's got nothing to say. He knows damned well that Sally has no right to the land."

"Zeke," Remember repeated, and his voice held a warning note.

"All right, all right," Zeke grumbled and came to his feet again. "Seeing's how my only witness is myself and I can't both ask questions and answer them, I'll have Sam Crawford ask them while I take the stand. Sam?" He paused, then added, "Unless brother Eli objects?"

"He doesn't," said Remember before Eli could respond. "Give Zeke the oath, Jasper, so he can take the stand."

Jasper had misplaced the Bible, but they found it behind the bar, then Zeke covered it with his big hand and swore that he would tell the truth by the solemn honor of the Green Mountain Boys.

"What about God?" Sarah whispered in Eli's ear.

"He's got peculiar beliefs. Take my word, it's easier this way."

Sam Crawford was a short man in farmer's breeches and brown coat. He was also short on words. Marching up to Zeke's table he told him to show the court what he had to prove he owned the land.

Zeke preferred things slower. "What about my name and address?"

"We already know all that," Sam said. "What about the proof?" He held out his hand for the deeds, which Zeke produced from his coat.

Sam looked them over. "I see that these here deeds were granted by Benning Wentworth. Can you say who he was?"

"Governor of New Hampshire."

"But what about the folks like the defendant here who claim that the land wasn't New Hampshire's to give? What about the people who claim that the king gave all the land west of the Connecticut River to New York?"

"That's two questions you're asking and I'll answer the second one first. The king did give the Grants land to New York."

Sarah's mouth dropped open. Zeke saw it and grinned. "Hold your horses, Sally. I'm not giving in. The Grants have only been New York's for the past nine years. Before that they belonged to New Hampshire, but for the most part no one cared because they were full of Indians who'd get ten pounds of French gold for every English scalp they brought to Montreal. But all that changed in 1760 after we'd beaten the French. Then there were a lot of men who wanted to live up north, and that's when Governor Wentworth began to sell off the land.

"The first time I saw that land was during the war. I passed through it on my way to Canada and as soon as I saw it I knew it was for me, so when I heard that Wentworth was selling, I made up my mind to buy. I trapped and sold furs and every other damn thing I could, and every cent I got a hold of I put into that land. I bought about six thousand acres over the next three years.

"Meanwhile the governor of New York heard about what was going on, and he decided that if the land was so desirable he wanted it for himself. So he wrote to Governor Wentworth and told him that he believed everything west of the Connecticut belonged to New York, so he'd better stop granting it right away. Well, Governor Wentworth wasn't about to give up his land just because the Yorkers wanted it for themselves, so the only way to settle the question was to put it before the king."

"They sent the king a petition?"

"Yes, sir, and the king answered in 1764."

"What did he say?"

"He agreed with Governor Wentworth, that the Grants were New Hampshire land and had been all along, but for one reason or another, now he was taking it away from New Hampshire and giving it to New York. All I can say is those Yorkers must have had some damned good friends at court!"

Eli made a motion to Sarah to keep her in her seat and Sam asked, "What about the land Governor Wentworth had already granted? What did the king say about that?"

"Those grants were all still good, because when Governor Wentworth made them, New Hampshire owned the land."

"So New York is bound to honor them"

"That's right." Zeke nodded. "As far as New York is concerned that land isn't hers to sell, which means that Sally here can't prove she owns the land unless she's got a deed for it that's dated before mine. Speaking of deeds, Sam, you best show those to the jury before you sit down." Winking at Sarah, he prepared to leave the stand.

"Not so fast, if you please." Eli came to his feet. "I've still got to cross-examine you."

Zeke stopped and turned back, looking startled. Then he grinned. "Well, of course you do. Ask away, little brother. I've got nothing to hide. And we want to give Sally here the trial she deserves."

Eli returned his smile. "Indeed we do. So would you please tell me how New York got her name?"

"What?" A sudden wariness wiped away Zeke's grin.

Eli repeated, "How did New York get her name? Wasn't she named for the Duke of York?"

"I guess so," Zeke admitted. "But I don't know why you ask."

"You don't have to," said Eli. "That's not your affair. Can you tell us why she was named for the Duke of York?"

"I can, but I won't. This isn't a damn history lesson! What are you getting at?"

"You'll see if you answer my questions—unless you're afraid."

"Afraid!" Zeke bristled with scorn at the very idea. "All right, little brother, she was named for the Duke of York because she was his colony. He got it from his brother, King Charles, the year the English defeated the Dutch."

"In 1664," Eli agreed, reaching into his pocket for a piece of paper Sarah had never seen. He unfolded it carefully and held it up to the light. "I want to read you something and then I want you to tell me if you know what it comes from. 'To my brother, James Stuart, Duke of York, is hereby granted all the land from the west side of the Connecticut River and to the east side of Delaware Bay.' Do you know what that comes from?"

"I couldn't begin to guess."

"I don't believe you have to guess. I believe you know. Isn't that the grant we were just talking about—the grant of New York colony made in 1664? Isn't that the definition of the boundaries?"

Zeke didn't answer but he turned very red in the face and he folded his arms across his chest. Sarah settled back in her chair, beginning to enjoy herself.

Eli continued, "You've testified that in 1764 the king took the Grants away from New Hampshire and gave them to New York. According to you he did this for 'various reasons.' Can you say what those reasons were?"

"If I don't I suppose you'll tell me."

"Not all of them. Just one. Isn't it true that the king's decision really said that the land Benning Wentworth had been selling had always belonged to New York, ever since it had been granted to James Stuart, the Duke of York, by his brother King Charles—a full hundred years before the king issued his decree?"

Zeke's eyes were flashing fire. "Why, you... you traitor!" he roared. "How can you stand in this courtroom and say such things? If you weren't my own damn brother, I'd say you'd gone over to New York! You ought to be tried for treason!"

Eli shook his head. "I'm only doing what you wanted me to do. No more questions," he added, and sat down.

But Zeke's anger didn't end so easily. He pointed his finger at Sarah. "She put you up to this! She may look like an angel, but she's done the devil's work!"

The room had fallen silent. Remember cleared his throat and said, "If Eli's finished, Zeke, you'd best stand down, and if you have more witnesses, now's the time to put them on."

"I don't need more witnesses!" Zeke said angrily. "You were here, you heard me. I already made my case." Turning back to Sarah, he said, "Let's see you do the same."

This time she met his eye without any fear of him melting her away. For the first time since the trial had begun, she was glad she'd taken Eli's advice and decided to stay. The air between them crackled; she felt strong and alive, as though a measure of Zeke's power had flowed into her. It was an amazing feeling and Zeke must have felt it, too, for his eyes widened and he raised his head and their eyes blazed into each other's, fire into fire.

Hers were still blazing when Zeke took his seat and Eli stood to give the opening he'd reserved, his calm voice almost lulling after the force of Zeke's.

"Just about every question in law has two sides to it. One side has to do with facts. For example, either Tom punched Will or he didn't. Open or shut. It's when you start looking at why he punched him that the real problems begin.

"That's what I call the human side of the law. Every case has one, and more often than not it's the side that matters most. Maybe Will was a bully and he'd been taunting Tom for years and finally Tom couldn't take it any more. Or maybe Will was an honest God-fearing man and he'd just found out that Tom was the one who'd stolen the plate from the church, and when he told Tom he meant to report him, Tom punched him in the nose. In both cases someone was punched, but in one case we may believe that that punching was deserved.

"We all know the story of how Zeke got his land—how hard he worked to buy it and how much he thinks of it. Right now, on the human side, you'd most likely hold for Zeke, but there's another side to the story. There's Mistress Meade's, and when you hear it you may find that she's got every bit as much right to that land as Zeke. After you hear her story, you may decide that she's got more."

When he paused Zeke snorted, but Eli only smiled and said to Sarah, "Would you please take the stand?"

To her surprise, she felt nervous, standing next to Remember's table behind the pulpit they must have borrowed from some church. Or more likely stolen, she thought, looking out at the roomful of Boys. As for Zeke, he was sitting with his legs stretched out and his arms folded across his chest. Go ahead, his stance was saying, try to change their minds. She stood up straighter. Just watch me, her stance replied.

Eli said, "Please state your name and address."

"Sarah Jane Meade. One hundred sixty-seven Cherry Street, Philadelphia, Pennsylvania colony."

"Then you're not from New York?"

"No."

"But you are currently residing in Albany?"

"Yes, I am there with my father, staying at the house of a friend."

"What brought you to Albany?"

"I wanted to sell some land. More or less the same land Mr. Brownell says is his."

"Will you please tell the jury how you came to own that land?"

Zeke snapped to attention. "She doesn't own it! That's the whole point of the case."

"Yes, I do!" she retorted.

But Eli raised his hands. "Never mind. Tell us how you took the title that you hold. Please," he added.

She stopped looking at Zeke. "I got it from my father."

"And why was that?"

"Because—" she said, then stopped. Until this moment she hadn't considered Eli's strategy. She'd been too busy holding down her temper and exchanging barbs with Zeke. From Eli's opening statement she should have realized that he intended to play on the jury's sympathy, but she hadn't until now, and now that she did realize she knew it wouldn't work. She couldn't beg for the pity of this outlaw horde, and she wouldn't expose her shame in front of Zeke Brownell. She wouldn't win on weakness if she couldn't win on strength—especially when the odds were that she wouldn't win at all.

"Why?" repeated Eli. When she shook her head, he said, "Wasn't it because you were afraid that if the land wasn't transferred to you, your father would gamble it away as he'd gambled away everything else?"

Sarah's back stiffened as Zeke's eyes swung to her. In them she recognized surprise, pity and disbelief. Her stomach constricted and her cheeks began to burn.

"Isn't it true," said Eli, "that your father's creditors have given you six months to sell the land, and if you don't sell it in that time they'll take everything a—"

"Please—" she interrupted, but Zeke's roar drowned her out.

"Now just hold on a minute!" Pulling in his long legs, he came surging to his feet. "I don't see what all this has got to do with anything! I heard what you were saying about the human side of things, but this case is about who owns six thousand acres of land, not about whose father has a weakness for cards. Besides, we've all heard enough of rich Yorkers crying poor while they're living in their fine houses and wearing their fancy clothes. So if you please, brother Eli, let's forget the sob stories and keep to the facts.''

''If you—'' Eli began to answer, but this time Sarah was there first.

Her cheeks still flaming, she spoke to Zeke. ''In the first place I'm not a Yorker, and in the second place I wasn't crying poor. My reasons for buying the land are none of your affair. I don't want your pity or your charity and what I do want you can't give me because it's already mine.'' She turned back to Eli. ''I told you there was no point. Thank you for trying but I have nothing more to say.''

''Not so fast!'' Zeke said, as Eli had said to him earlier when he'd attempted to leave the stand. ''I've got a question to ask you, Sally, before you run away. You say that you own the land, but can you show us your deed? Have you got it with you?''

''You know I don't. I didn't have time to get it before you kidnapped me!''

Uneasy laughter rippled through the room and for the first time in a long while the watching Boys relaxed.

Zeke addressed the jury. ''It's just like I said. She hasn't got the proof.''

Eli shook his head. ''Not hard proof, maybe, but she's got circumstantial proof. You rode all the way to Albany and brought her all the way back, then you insisted against opposition that we go ahead with this trial. Why would you have done that if you didn't believe that she held the New York title to the land? Not because the two of you hit it off so well.''

The laughter that followed this statement was loud and unrestrained. Sarah and Zeke were the only ones not smiling. Zeke was glaring at Sarah and Sarah was glaring back as if it were only a matter of time until one or the other lunged.

Seeing this, Remember said hurriedly, ''I believe we've heard enough. I don't think we need closing statements.

The jury knows what's what, so, Jasper, why don't you take them out to deliberate. Take them into the parlor.''

Jasper did as he was told and the rest of the Boys stayed seated until the jury had filed out. Then most of them got up and began to mill around, shooting glances at Zeke and Sarah and cracking half-audible jokes.

Zeke continued to glare at Sarah as she walked back to her table and sat. His glare encompassed Eli briefly, then he turned away and began talking to some of the other Boys.

"He's angry at you," said Sarah.

Eli shrugged. "He'll get over it. He always does. His temper burns high but usually it burns short, and when it burns out he's usually ready to laugh at himself. In the end he'll admit that he got no more than he deserved. He was the one who wanted me to be your lawyer, after all."

"You did a good job. I'm sorry if I insulted you before."

He gave her a crooked smile. "I'm used to having to prove myself. It adds to the challenge," he said, and in his voice she heard more than a trace of bitterness, though something about his expression warned her not to probe.

"Do you think there's any chance that they'll hold for me?"

"Maybe one in a thousand. Maybe even less. I'm sorry I embarrassed you by asking about your father."

"That's all right. I should have known you would, but I didn't think..." She let the sentence trail off, then she thought of something else. "How did you happen to have a copy of King Charles's grant to the Duke of York?"

"What?"

"That paper you read from to Zeke."

"Oh, that." Eli grinned again. Reaching into his pocket, he took it out and showed it to her. It was a letter to him from someone in Boston dated three weeks before. "I was hoping he wouldn't ask to see it. I figured you had him too distracted to ask."

Her smile faded and she looked away. She saw that Archie had joined the group around Zeke and was watching his father with the same pride she'd seen before. She turned back to Eli. "What about the boy?"

"What about him?"

"Why doesn't he go to school? Hanging around in taverns and learning to curse like a sailor hardly strikes me as a proper bringing up."

"Zeke's not much of a believer in a proper bringing up."

"So I gathered. But doesn't he see that in the end the boy will pay the price? He'll never be good for anything but this." She gestured around the taproom with a look of disgust.

Eli also looked, but more thoughtfully. Then he said, "Here comes the jury."

She straightened. He was right. The parlor door was open and they were coming back, led by Jasper like a dozen ducklings following the mother duck. There was a great deal of scuffling and scraping as everyone sat down and Remember made his way back to his bench.

Remember asked, "Have you reached your verdict?"

"We have." The foreman passed a paper to Jasper, who passed it to the bench. Remember unfolded it and read, then he read again. He looked at the jury, who were all looking straight ahead. None of them was looking the slightest bit amused.

Neither was Remember. In fact, he looked so perplexed that finally Zeke demanded, "You've got the verdict—let's hear what it says!"

Remember looked back from the jury to Zeke. Then he folded the paper and carefully put it away. "The jury finds for the plaintiff. Congratulations, Zeke."

A broad grin broke across Zeke's face as he turned to where Sarah stood. But Sarah wasn't looking at him. She was looking at the jurors, who, to a man, were staring at Remember with expressions of total shock.

Remember also saw this and quickly cried, "Winner pays for drinks all around!"

That was enough to bring every Boy to his feet and send all but one of them surging toward the bar. The exception was Sam Crawford, who called out, "Say, Remember, what about the penalty?"

Remember was in the midst of divesting himself of his robe when he heard the question. He stopped and looked blankly at Sam.

"The penalty," Sam repeated. "After all, what's the point of a trial if there's no penalty?"

Remember shook his head. "There's the lesson to be learned from the experience, and I believe that Mistress Meade has learned hers about asserting a Yorker claim to Grants land. I'll leave it for Zeke to see her safely home. Court adjourned," he added as an afterthought. "Now, Mr. Fay, what about those drinks?"

"That was fixed!" Sarah fumed to Eli as the rest of the Boys swarmed the bar. "I'll bet you a hundred pounds that the jury said that the land was mine. He bullied the judge into lying—just like he bullies everyone!"

"Who bullies?" inquired Zeke, looming over them. Without waiting for her answer, he slapped down a mug of cider. "Drink up, Sally girl. You heard the judge's order. We've got a long ride ahead of us."

"Us!" Sarah regarded the mug with disgust. "I wouldn't ride across the street with you if it was full of serpents and you had the only gun!"

Zeke chuckled, his spirits completely restored. "You don't shoot serpents, Sally. You stab 'em with a spear. Good work, Eli. I guess I made the right choice when I put my money on you. Better luck next time." He clapped Eli on the shoulder and went off chuckling.

"He is a bully," Sarah said, watching as someone thrust a mug into Zeke's hand, which he drank off quickly and raised to be refilled. "What did he mean about putting his money on you?"

"He gave me money so I could go to school."

She turned sharply. "I thought you just told me he doesn't approve of school."

"He doesn't. But he knew it was what I wanted so he supplied the means. You see, he's not a bully all the time."

"Just mostly," Sarah answered.

Eli shook his head. "Drink your cider and I'll tell you about something that happened a long time ago. I was eleven at the time and Zeke was fourteen. I'd just had a fight with my father—also about going to school. I wanted to go on but he was against it, so in typically Brownell fashion I decided to run away. Only I happened to pick the wrong day to leave. I hadn't gone two miles when a blizzard hit. It was so bad I doubt I could have found my way back if I'd wanted to, and by the time I did want to, it was too late. It must have been ten below and the snow was blowing so hard I couldn't see a thing. I kept looking for shelter but I was in the middle of a field and going around in circles so I never reached the trees. That's where Zeke found me.

"He'd come in after the storm had begun, and when he heard that I'd gone off he went straight back out again. My father tried to stop him—the storm was so bad at that point he figured we'd both be lost—but Zeke went anyway. By the time he found me we were both half-frozen to death. My feet were so frozen I could barely walk, so he slung me across his shoulders and somehow he managed to get to the trees and dig us out a cave. He spent the rest of the night lying on top of me to give me the warmth from his body to keep me alive. We stayed there until the storm stopped, then he carried me home."

Sarah blinked as he finished, then she shook her head. "I have no doubt that there are moments when Zeke puts his strength to good use. But that doesn't excuse the rest."

"I wasn't trying to excuse him. I was trying to explain. Understanding a person is more than a morning's work."

"And what makes you think that I want to understand him at all?"

Eli regarded her long and thoughtfully, so long that she began to feel ridiculously afraid—as though he were looking into the future and studying her fate. Finally he answered, "Because I believe you could. And because I have the feeling you haven't seen the end of him yet."

She shivered at his tone of voice as well as at his words.

"Got a chill, Sally?" Zeke's voice boomed at her side. "Probably nothing exercise won't heal. You'd best thank your lawyer so we can be on our way. Keep an eye on Archie, Eli. I'll be back late tonight."

"Will do," Eli answered. He stood and shook Sarah's hand. "Good luck, Mistress Meade."

"Thank you." With regret Sarah watched him walk away.

"Time's a-wasting, Sally."

Sarah turned back to Zeke. "I told you, Mr. Brownell, I'm not going with you."

"That's right," Zeke agreed. "You're not going with me—I'm going with you. Judge's orders."

"Your judge was no judge at all, and I'm not going." She set her jaw.

Zeke was silent for a moment, then he said, "The widow Williams has a spare room upstairs. Mistress Morgan has a room, too, but Ida Williams is a better cook. I'm not sure about the charges. You'd have to ask yourself."

"What charges? What are you talking about?"

He shrugged. "If you're not going, you'll need a place to stay. I was just making suggestions. If you don't trust my word, you might prefer to ask Eli or somebody else."

In her lap Sarah's hands were clenched into fists, and it was all she could do not to swing one of them up at Zeke's face. Instead she forced herself to unclench them and stood and walked out of the taproom with all the dignity she possessed. She knew everyone was watching but she kept her eyes on the door and tried to take comfort in the fact that at least she was leaving on her own two feet and not slung across Zeke's back.

Archie had their two horses ready and waiting outside. Sarah allowed Zeke to hold hers as she swung up. When she took the reins from him, she told him goodbye.

"You're not going with me. I don't care what your friend said. You may give me directions and I'll get there on my own. As far as your being responsible for what happens to me on the way, I'll absolve you in writing if you'll bring me a paper and ink. As for the horse, I'll arrange to have him sent back.''

Archie was wide-eyed but Zeke only looked amused. ''Left outside the gate and straight on down that road. It'll take you to the river if you stick to it and don't wander off on any of the paths leading in.'' He fished in his pocket and handed her a coin.

''What's that?''

''For the ferry. Unless you plan to swim.''

She hated to take it from him but she had to, so she did.

''Have a good ride, Sally,'' he bade her, stepping back and watching as she turned the horse out of the yard. ''Sorry about the verdict. Better luck next time.''

''You're the one who'll be sorry!'' she snapped despite herself, and she gave the horse a brisk slap to send them on their way.

Chapter Four

As Zeke had predicted, it wasn't difficult to follow the road, which passed through forests and, less frequently, cultivated fields, green with rows of new corn or with the stubble of winter wheat. The day was fair and pleasant, and Sarah might have enjoyed the ride if it hadn't been for her worries and her anger at what she'd been through.

All of her anger was directed against Zeke Brownell. Red-haired Remember believed she'd learned her lesson about the land. Did Zeke believe the same? Did he think that she'd been browbeaten or even frightened into abandoning her claim? She burned with indignation that he might think so little of her as to imagine she'd give up so easily. Of course she wouldn't. She wouldn't give up at all. One way or another she meant to beat Zeke Brownell, and a part of her was even relishing the fight, though another, more practical part was concerned that the struggle with Zeke might waste precious time.

That practical part also wondered where her father had been last night. Albany had the reputation of being a quiet conservative town, and what she'd seen of it thus far attested to that. On the other hand, even the quietest town had a few errant souls, and if there was even one in Albany, her father would sniff him—or her—out. She hoped that he hadn't tracked down a game of cards. If he had, she hoped these Albany Dutch were too canny to give him credit on his note.

She wished that George Mason would come home from his business trip. Mason was the friend in whose home they were staying until they sold the land. Mason had known Sarah's mother's family in England before he'd immigrated to New York, and when Sarah and her father had moved to the colonies he'd done his best to look after her. George Mason had always been a friend to her, but living so far from Philadelphia there had been a limit to what he could do.

It had been Mason who had advised her about selling the land. As soon as her father had signed the deeds over to her, she'd written to him and Mason had suggested that she have the land subdivided and sell it off to individual settlers rather than find a buyer for the whole. He'd insisted that she and her father come to Albany and had offered her the use of his house for as long as she wished. She had accepted gladly and had looked forward to his company and steadying influence, but unfortunately, several weeks before they arrived, business had taken Mason to Bermuda and he'd been gone ever since.

She wondered what the servant had told her father when he'd finally come home last night, and she wondered what he'd done. One thing was certain: he hadn't rushed off in hot pursuit of his daughter, especially not after the servant had described Zeke. Henry Meade could be charming but he'd never been brave. Not even money could convince him to take a physical risk. Having learned that his daughter had been kidnapped he wouldn't have leapt on his horse— he'd have gone to the sheriff and convinced him to leap on his. Her father could be persuasive, as she knew all too well.

She recalled Zeke's declaration that New Yorkers were all afraid to ride after the Green Mountain Boys. She suspected that he'd been exaggerating as usual and she perked up at the thought of the sheriff and a posse possibly riding this way right now. If they were riding, she'd probably meet them on the road, then she could tell them what had happened and direct them to the Catamount. She could just imagine the look on Zeke's face when she rode up with the sheriff and watched him placed under arrest. She was tired and sore from the saddle, but even so, if she met the sheriff she'd definitely ride back just for the satisfaction of being there when they arrested Zeke.

A wet splat on her forehead made her look up. She'd spent the whole last hour thinking so hard that she hadn't noticed the weather changing as she rode. The sun had been shining brightly when she'd left the Catamount but now the sky had filled with clouds. The high ones were white and filmy but the low ones were dense and gray and the air was damp and heavy with impending rain.

"Perfect—a storm!" she muttered, and immediately blamed it on Zeke. Why not? She wouldn't have been here if it hadn't been for him. Worse, what few farmhouses were scattered among these woods most certainly belonged to the Green Mountain Boys, and she'd rather perish from exposure than seek shelter from one of them. Besides, if she left the road she'd miss the sheriff. If he was on his way.

She rode on doggedly, trying to ignore the rain, which steadily increased from big fat random drops to a drenching downpour that plastered her clothes to her body and turned her hair into a sodden streaming weight. Just when she was feeling that things couldn't get any worse, the wind began to blow and suddenly she found herself in the midst of a full-fledged storm.

It was hard to say which was more miserable to endure, the rain, which fell in torrents, or the wind, which came in gusts, flinging the rain against her in solid sheets, then pausing to change direction before lashing out at her again. The force of the storm's fury shoved horse and rider this way and that, blinding and terrifying both. Beneath the savage howling came a dull rumbling—a warning that the storm's real climax had yet to be seen.

The rumbling grew louder, then suddenly lightning flashed with lurid brightness, seemingly right overhead. Terrified, the horse shuddered and tossed its head, very nearly yanking the reins out of Sarah's hands. She managed to hang on grimly but her hands had begun to shake.

She was a decent rider but by no means exceptional, and she knew that at any moment she could lose control.

She knew she had to stop. Better to endure this hell in one place than to stumble and crash about—and very likely end up by laming the horse. She pulled up hard on the reins, but just as she did a terrific clap of thunder split the earth in half. The sky turned white, the ground shook, the horse gave a piercing scream; it reared up, then plunged forward into the storm-tossed woods.

Sarah couldn't see anything but pouring rain and streaming hair and leaves flying everywhere. The storm's fury seemed to be pointed directly at them, ripping loose whole branches and flinging them through the air. She heard an awful roaring but she couldn't see if it was a tree falling or only the punishing wind. A branch, torn loose, grazed her shoulder, then struck the horse, which jerked its head so sharply she lost hold of the reins.

"Stop! Oh God, please stop!" she screamed, but her words were torn away by the storm. Her fingers stiff with terror, she grabbed for the flying mane and flung herself forward, clinging for dear life and expecting at any moment to be jolted off and crushed beneath the lashing hooves or a falling tree.

"No! No!" she was screaming—to herself more than to the horse—hunched down, eyes squeezed shut, far too terrified for tears. Only once in her life had she been this afraid, on the ship to America when she'd been a child. They'd run into an awful storm that had almost sent them down. She remembered waking up in her cabin all alone because her father had been out playing cards. She'd lain there rigid with fright until the storm had tossed her to the floor. Shrieking with panic and completely beside herself, she'd remained there, eyes shut tight, feeling lost and abandoned and utterly alone.

She'd never forgotten that feeling; until right now she'd never experienced anything as frightening. But hurtling wildly through this blinding storm was almost exactly the same, except that this time there was no captain and crew to save her life. There was no one here to save her—no stranger and no friend.

She scrunched down farther, trying to disappear, but she couldn't make herself small enough to escape the pounding rain. She was so frightened she imagined the horse had calmed. She imagined she heard a man's voice calming it. She imagined she felt something warm and solid nudge against her leg.

It was true, the horse was slowing. She took a quick breath and opened her eyes, but she could see nothing through the tangle of her hair until she unclenched her hand and pushed her hair away. Then, to her amazement, she saw that she wasn't alone but had been saved by another rider, who held her horse's reins and had almost managed to curb his headlong flight. In the wet and the confusion she couldn't see his face but from the spread of his shoulders she knew it was Zeke Brownell.

"Whoa!" he called hoarsely, and finally the horse stopped, its flanks shuddering and its head down against the rain.

Sarah was also shuddering with spasm after spasm of fear. Leaning forward through the chaos, Zeke shouted, "Are you all right?"

"Yes, I think so," she answered, except that no words came out. She opened her mouth to try again but did no better than before. Holding the reins of both horses with one hand, Zeke reached out to push back her hair. She felt the rough warmth of his fingers graze against her ear. When his hand gripped her shoulder, she took one long ragged breath; then she released it and began to cry.

That was the last straw in her humiliation but she couldn't stop. She couldn't stop, despite the knowledge that her bawling like a baby was the last thing that either of them needed now, with the storm still raging and dislodged branches flying everywhere. She knew she should pull herself together, but she couldn't even try, and when Zeke reached out for her she went to him willingly.

With one arm, as he'd done the last time, he scooped her onto his horse. She felt his thighs beneath her and the rampart of his chest and his shoulders keeping out the rain. He put his lips to her ear and murmured gentle things, calling her a brave girl and swearing she'd be all right. That night on the storm-tossed ship, her father hadn't come, but finally one of the passenger's wives had thought to look for her and had taken her back to her cabin where her husband was being sick, and Sarah had spent the rest of the night helping to care for him. But all the time she'd been wishing for her father to come and put his arms around her and promise everything would be all right.

Lightning turned the world white and thunder cracked so near that the ground shook beneath them and both of the horses reared. Zeke managed to hold on to all the reins and to keep his seat, but after he'd brought the horses down he shouted, "We've got to get out of here."

"To where?" Sarah shouted, but he hadn't heard. Tying her horse's lead to his saddle and keeping her on his lap, he urged his horse forward into the woods. She guessed he had a destination and it turned out that he did—but before they reached it the thunder had panicked the horses again and a tree had crashed down so close she knew that only God himself could have kept them from being killed.

Zeke's goal was a little cabin, not much more than a shack whose windows were shuttered, though one of the shutters had broken loose and was banging wildly against the wall.

"Get inside!" he shouted as he swung her down. He gave her a push toward the cabin and she battled her way to the door while he tied the horses to the solidest tree he could find and refastened the shutter as best he could. She was still struggling to open the door against the wind when Zeke loomed up behind her and gave it a single firm shove. Darkness yawned before them, then they were inside, the door slamming shut behind them, in blessed relief from the storm.

Or rather in partial relief, for though the cabin had a roof and four walls, none of them was snug. The wind howled through the crevices and the rain dripped through the roof.

Still, compared to what they'd been through, it was paradise.

Zeke's hands held her briefly. He repeated, "Are you all right?"

"Yes. Fine." When she nodded, he let her go and went to kneel at the fireplace, where someone had thoughtfully left a stack of wood.

The wood was partly damp from the leaking roof but Zeke got it to burn and even found a candle to give them light. She went to stand by the fire but she was shivering.

"You're soaked to the skin." His hands moved up and down her arms, chafing them roughly and bringing a measure of warmth. Looking around behind her, he spotted a blanket on the wooden pallet that served as a bed. He let her go to retrieve it.

"You'd best get out of those wet things and wrap up in this."

Wordlessly she nodded. She was too chilled to protest. She reached for the buttons of her bodice, then she thought of him less in modesty than in frank concern.

"What about you? You're soaked, too."

His beard parted in a crooked grin. "My mother used to say that I must be half-wild. A little wetting now and then never bothered me, and once this fire catches hold I'll dry out soon enough. You get yourself cozy and I'll see what we've got in the way of food."

He left her at the fire to change her clothes and went to open a trapdoor at the far end of the room. As he rummaged with his back to her, Sarah peeled off her sodden clothes. She left her chemise on and wrapped the blanket over that. By that time Zeke was back again, not with food but with a rope, which he strung across the room.

"Those wet things will dry before you know it if you toss them over this. There isn't much in the way of provisions, but I can make us a pot of soup good enough to warm you if you're not too particular."

"Not in certain circumstances," she replied through chattering teeth, and saw him glance at her to see if she was joking or not.

When he saw she was, he smiled a brief friendly smile that crinkled the laugh lines at the corners of his eyes. Then he said, "Best hang those things up," and stripping off his own coat, he slung it on the rope. He added his waistcoat, then got back to the food.

He opened the door briefly for water for the soup, then rustled and clattered with whatever he'd found in the storage space beneath the floor. By the time she'd hung her things up he was crouched at the hearth, hanging the kettle on a fire hook and stirring its contents with a roughly whittled spoon. Without his coat and waistcoat he looked even bigger than before, massive in the shoulders though less so through the hips, well proportioned on an impressive scale.

He looked like the gods from Greek mythology she'd read about. Like Zeus or Apollo or mighty Mars, the god of war—which made it almost comical to see him stirring soup. Comical and touching, Sarah thought, watching him, and she also remembered what Eli had said about understanding being more than one morning's work. Then she realized something she hadn't thought of before.

"You followed me, didn't you?"

"Of course I did," he answered promptly without turning around. "You didn't think I'd let you ride all that way yourself? You might have gotten yourself into trouble."

"Might have!" she said ruefully, but he made no response—none of the bombast or bravado she would have expected from him. It was as though all that had washed away in the storm. Hugging the blanket around her, she came to crouch by his side and looked up at his face in the flickering light of the fire. His eyes were clear and steady as he tended to his soup and the brows above them dark and definite. The rain had wound his beard into tight little curls, through which she could see the generous curve of his lips.

The sight of his lips, the curve of them, did something strange to her. She shifted her eyes to the fire. "You saved my life. Thank you."

Zeke shook his head. "If I hadn't been there, you'd have thought of something else."

"I wasn't thinking at all when you found me."

"Maybe not just then but you would have pretty soon."

"If the horse hadn't thrown me first and broken my neck."

Zeke took the spoon out and slid the kettle's cover on. Still squatting, he turned to her with some of the old sparkle in his eyes. "That doesn't sound like Mistress S. J. Meade. Scared or not, she'd have kept her saddle and she'd have gotten home—maybe just a wee bit worse for the wear."

"If you believe that, then why did you follow me?"

"Because—" he began. Then he broke off and grinned broadly at her. "Now that sounds exactly like Mistress S. J. Meade. You warmer now, Sally?"

"Yes, thank you. I am," she said, but as she said it she shivered from head to toe.

Zeke put the spoon down on a stone beside the hearth and stood up, holding out his arms. "Come here, Sally. I'll rub you warm."

"I'll be fine, really," she protested, but he paid her no heed. Reaching down to where she was still crouching, he pulled her to her feet. He turned her to the fire and moved around so that he was standing behind her, his hands rubbing her arms the same way he'd rubbed them before. She felt the warmth of the fire heating her cheeks and Zeke, like a giant fire screen, warming her from behind. Relief seeped through her like liquid heat; her body stopped shaking and her eyelids fluttered shut. She felt pleasantly drowsy and absolutely safe. She heaved a long contented sigh as Zeke's rubbing stopped.

Her eyes flew open as his voice startled her. "No wonder you're still freezing, your hair's soaking wet! You stay here by the fire while I find something to dry it with."

She stared into the fire, the hypnotic oranges and blues, and he was back before she knew it with something in his hands. A length of sacking.

"Most likely not what you're used to but it'll have to do." He turned her sideways and slid the cloth over her head to gather up her wet hair, then he began to rub. He worked methodically, starting at the top, then making his way down each side. He was also more gentle than any maid she'd ever had. She stood, obedient as a fresh-bathed child, letting him do his work and watching his expression when the cloth didn't cover her eyes.

He worked with such concentration he didn't know she was watching him. Despite his beard she could see his tongue tucked in his cheek, and the sight of that filled her with the urge to laugh. Warmth drifted to her from the fire and drifted to her from him. Little by little, as they stood there, the warmth of the fire ebbed as the warmth coming from Zeke's body steadily increased. The urge to laugh receded and something else took its place, something stirring and mysterious.

"That's better," Zeke murmured, dropping the now sodden cloth and using his fingers to fluff out her curls. His fingers grazed the blanket that covered her arms and her breasts. At his touch she shivered.

His gaze swung to her. She knew that he'd been about to ask if she was still cold, but as soon as he saw her expression he knew it wasn't that. All his concentration suddenly fell away, replaced by a sort of wonder that made her shiver again.

"Sally," Zeke murmured. His fingers touched her chin, lifting it until her face was tilted up to his. His eyes were as liquid as they'd been at the Catamount. They were also as full of joy, but instead of a fierce joy, this was soft and new and it held her as gently as his arms had done. She didn't know if she was breathing. The whole world seemed to have stopped—no cabin, no leaking roof, no storm raging overhead, just Zeke's hands resting on her and his eyes full of wonderment.

"Sally," he repeated, and his eyes flickered shut as slowly, very slowly, he bent to kiss her lips.

She held her breath until his mouth reached hers. His lips were as warm as the fire and unbelievably soft, and when he moved his head even slightly his beard tickled her chin. When he moved his body the warmth of it rose up to envelope her. It felt wonderful; she had no urge to pull away.

She only wanted to shut her eyes and slip deeper into his kiss. When his arms slid around her they felt familiar and wonderfully sure. She sighed with pleasure and felt his lips curl in a smile.

He didn't kiss at all like the Zeke that she'd first met. That Zeke had been imperious but this one was patience itself: tasting, savoring as though they weren't in a leaky cabin in the middle of a storm but lazing in the sun in a summer meadow. That's what his kiss made her think of: meadow grass and warmth, the sweetness of wildflowers and the satisfied droning of bees. She snuggled against him as his lips parted hers and his big gentle fingers stroked back her tangled hair.

His hands slid down her shoulders and her hands slid up his chest, over the damp cloth and the hard muscle beneath. She'd forgotten the blanket, which his hands had been holding up, but as he caressed her the blanket began to slip.

She jerked by instinct and he responded instantly. Catching the ends of the blanket, he held them together beneath her chin the way a nanny would hold a towel after her favorite charge's bath. Gently he kissed her forehead, the tip of her nose, her lips, one ear then the other, the side of her jaw. They were lovely, lovely kisses that warmed her like the fire, but instead of warming just her skin, these warmed her all the way through.

"Sweet Sally," he murmured, returning to her ear, nibbling then licking, a quick flick of his tongue that made her shiver with a different kind of warmth. The warmth reached deeper as his tongue flicked again. By the time she'd gotten over her shiver, he'd returned to her lips for a kiss that started at the top of her and reached all the way down, leaving her as breathless as if she'd been battling the storm. When the kiss ended, his head drew back, then the blanket parted and his lips found her throat.

She meant to protest, but her protest came out a sigh because his lips were too warm and comforting to wish away. He smelled of smoke and wet wool but the smell was nice. So was the tickling sensation of his beard against her skin as he did secret things between the ends of the blanket, still in his hands. It was hard to think that she scarcely knew him when he seemed to understand how to delight her better than she did herself. All her life men had been disappointing her, but this moment seemed to give her everything she had ever lacked. She had never imagined that a man could be so gentle, yet possessive and utterly masculine.

She felt dizzy in a lovely way. When she put her hands out for balance the blanket slipped away, then Zeke's strong arms were around her, pressing her to his chest, the warm dampness of his cotton shirt stealing through her thin chemise.

He murmured, "Mmm, sweetness," and rubbed his cheek against her hair, and she rubbed herself against him, feeling wonderful—warm without the blanket, soft and feminine. He framed her face with his big hands and tilted back her head. She thought he meant to kiss her again. When he didn't she opened her eyes and found his eyes moving all around her face with an intensity of expression that made her feel something new, something sharper and stronger than she'd felt before—the same thing she'd felt at the Catamount when he'd started melting her.

Still holding her head, he kissed her, his fingers twined in her hair. This kiss was deeper than what had come before. It struck a chord of urgency to which she felt herself respond, straining up on tiptoe with her arms wrapped around his neck. They stayed that way for a long time, and when his hands left her hair and slid down along her ribs, she could feel every cushion and callus on his palm as if she weren't even wearing her chemise.

This time he whispered only a wordless "Ahh!" and she was no longer dizzy but vividly attuned to the smallest nuance of everything he did—to the flexing of his muscles and the shifting of his hands. Her whole body was vibrating as though something dammed up too long were about to break loose. Then suddenly it came to her what that something was.

"No," she whispered. Then louder she said, "No, Zeke."

"Why not?" he murmured, stroking her body in an even more intimate way.

She felt herself responding and tried to pull away. "Because we mustn't," she pleaded. She meant to add, "And it's not what I want," but she couldn't because that wasn't the truth.

She felt him react to the pleading tone of her voice. She could feel his reluctance and she could also feel the depth of the effort it took for him to stop. Ironically, though she was grateful when he raised his head, there was a part of her that wished he hadn't but had gone on kissing her.

They stood together, Zeke looking down at her, and she could feel the heat from his body breaking against her in waves. By the dim light of the fire his eyes were a bottomless black. His hands on her shoulders slowly loosened their grip.

The fallen blanket was lying at her feet. Zeke bent to retrieve it and handed it to her. When she took it their fingers touched and that stopped them both. Then Zeke muttered, "I'd best see to that soup."

She stood where he had left her, clutching the blanket with shaking hands. Her whole body felt like jelly and she was surprised she could even stand without his support. She knew that if she closed her eyes she'd be able to feel every spot his lips or his fingers had caressed. For one bewildering moment she thought that she might start to cry.

Then Zeke spoke from the fire. "Soup's just about ready. You'd best fetch us some bowls from the shelf above the bed."

Stilling her shaking fingers and wrapping the blanket around her again, obediently Sarah turned to do as he said.

The soup was very good. After what had just happened between them, she had thought that it would be difficult to sit at the table with Zeke, but after her first spoonful she found that she was far too hungry for embarrassment. When she complimented him on his cooking, Zeke stopped eating long enough to reply that his skill as a cook was roughly equal to the hunger of his guests.

"You're modest."

Zeke laughed. "I am, once every year or so. You just happened to catch me on the right day." She was staring at him: he gestured to her bowl. "It won't taste half as good cold so you'd best eat up while it's still hot."

The heat of the soup and the heat of the fire and the shock of the day's events swooped down on Sarah as they finished the meal. Suddenly she was so tired she could hardly sit in the chair. Zeke noticed and nodded to the pallet against the wall.

"Time for bed, Sally." He rose to collect the bowls.

"You cooked, I should clean up," she protested, but so feebly Zeke only smiled.

"I'll just put these outside in a bucket and they'll clean themselves. You'll fall asleep where you're sitting if you don't get to bed."

It was true. Sarah stood up and took a step toward the bed. Then she stopped as she realized it was the only one in the room. "What about you?" she asked Zeke.

"I'll sleep by the fire."

"On what. There's just one blanket."

"I've slept with less. Go on now, Sally. Don't worry about me—I'll be fine."

She did what he said. Wrapped snugly in the blanket, she lay down on the straw, closed her eyes and listened as Zeke lay down by the fire. She was just drifting off when she heard him mutter "Damn!"

"What's the matter?"

"Nothing. Go to sleep."

But when she turned her head to the fire she saw what the problem was: the roof leaked in so many places he couldn't keep all of himself dry. There were no leaks where she was lying.

"Why don't you sleep on the bed?"

He raised himself on one elbow to look at her and even across the room she could see the glint in his eye that was part amusement and part something else. That something else prompted her to add hurriedly, "We can sleep head to foot."

"You sure about that, Sally?"

"Of course," she lied, no longer half as sleepy as she'd been before. "It's only the fair thing after all you've done for me."

"All?" His amusement deepened as he regarded her. "Like taking you riding in the moonlight last night and treating you to breakfast at the Catamount?"

When he brought it up she realized she'd forgotten all that, but now that she remembered she found that her anger was gone. It was as though those things had happened to somebody else and she could hardly associate this Zeke with the man who had practically broken her door down, flung her over his shoulder and ridden off into the night.

"Sally?" Zeke was waiting.

"Yes," she said. "I'm sure." She lay back, staring at the ceiling as he padded across the room.

The bed creaked in protest as Zeke lay down. He was so big that his feet hung over the end and his warmth enveloped her instantly, blocking out everything else. She felt her body responding to his presence with a will all its own, and she guessed that Zeke must have sensed it, or must have been feeling the same, because he said quickly, "I can always go back to the floor."

"I'm fine," she said, too quickly, then added, "Good night."

"Good night," Zeke answered, and she felt him shift. She jumped half out of her skin when he touched her foot. His lips grazed her ankle, then he gave her big toe a pinch. "Get some sleep, Sally." He chuckled and let go, and as he settled himself in the straw she found she was smiling. She sighed deeply and felt her body relax. Less than a minute later she was also fast asleep.

Zeke lay in the darkness listening to the evenness of Sally's breathing and enjoying the feel of her beside him in the bed. It wasn't often he had the pleasure of a woman in his bed and a woman like Sally was an even rarer treat. There weren't many women like Sally. Now that he thought about it, he doubted if he could name even one with her spirit and beauty both. If he had to choose between the two in a woman, he'd pick spirit over looks, but it didn't hurt a bit if a woman happened to look like an angel sent down to earth.

Sally looked like an angel: she was downright beautiful. Shifting slowly so as not to disturb her, Zeke raised himself up until he could see her face. She lay curled up with the blanket tucked beneath her chin and the masses of her golden hair mingling with the straw. Her lashes were also golden and curled down so far that even from here he could see the shadows of them on her cheeks. He missed having her eyes open so that he could see the blue that was as dark as a winter twilight without a moon. On the other hand, if her eyes were open she wouldn't look so innocent—smooth-browed as a child without a care in the world. He grinned. If her eyes were open she'd most likely be sassing him.

Her forehead wrinkled as she stirred and muttered in her sleep. The blanket shifted, exposing the line of her throat, until her hands drew the cover close again. But it only took that one peek for him to recall just exactly how sweet it had been kissing her. Damn. He was sorry they'd had to stop, even though he knew that it was for the best. Sally wasn't the kind of woman you made love to at night, then kissed goodbye in the morning with only a fare-thee-well. Not by a long shot, he thought, and grinned again. Slowly and with reluctance, he settled back into the straw.

His thoughts shifted to the trial and he remembered what Eli had said about her father and how, when he'd objected, she'd given him a piece of her mind. It was too bad that a woman like Sally had to have a father like that. On the other hand, having that kind of father had probably taught her to stand up for herself.

He didn't feel too badly about her not having that land. In the first place she couldn't appreciate it. To her it was only a way to pay her debts, and if she was that hungry for money he had no doubt she could find it somewhere else. There must be dozens of rich Yorkers dying to marry her—or rich Philadelphians. Most likely there were plenty of both. Women married for money all the time, and with her looks, Sally could have her pick. No, he didn't feel bad about the land. It was his and he deserved it. He'd take good care of it and not go selling it to a bunch of damn Yorkers who'd be content to accept that colony's aristocratic rule.

A log fell on the fire. Turning his head, Zeke watched the flames shoot up, then fall. He wondered if he ought to get up and feed it more wood before he fell asleep. He guessed he wouldn't because he might wake Sally up. Besides, him being here would keep her warm all night. In the morning he'd build it up again.

Outside it was still raining but most of the wind had died. He'd been close to Sally when the storm had come up, and after that he'd done his best to keep her in sight. After the first clap of thunder he'd made up his mind to ride up to let her know he was there, but before he could reach her her horse had taken fright. He looked at her skirt and bodice hanging up on the line and remembered how she'd curled against him and trembled as she cried.

That wasn't a wise thing to think of, not with her so close. Better to stop thinking and go to sleep. He'd been up for two days and he could use the rest. Folding his arms across his chest, Zeke closed his eyes, and within the space of three breaths he, too, was sound asleep.

Chapter Five

"Rise and shine, Sally—it's a whole new day!"

Zeke's greeting caught Sarah in the midst of a dream about swimming upstream in a river with patterned calico banks. She opened her eyes too quickly and groaned at the light of the sun, trying to remember where she was and why. That took her a full minute; when she remembered, she groaned again.

Zeke chuckled. "Sleep well?" he asked. Before she could answer, he added, "Your things are dry. Best put them on before you eat. I'll be outside with the horses. If you need anything, just call."

After the door slammed, Sarah opened her eyes. She was still coming out of her dream but she was enough awake to understand that he'd left the cabin to give her privacy to dress and that if she didn't get up and do it she'd lose her chance.

A kettle was steaming at the hearth where he'd built up the fire. He'd taken down the clothesline and her things were folded on a chair. He must have shaken them and smoothed them because they weren't as stiff as they would have been when he'd taken them off the line. She dressed as quickly as she could, considering her state of mind.

She felt very strange, very unlike herself. The Sarah she'd been all her life wouldn't have spent the night in a cabin in the midst of nowhere with a man like Zeke Brownell, and even if that Sarah had been forced to, she wouldn't have done what she'd done, especially after everything that had come before.

The problem was she didn't feel like the Sarah she'd always been. She felt as though she'd awakened still halfway caught in a dream and she found that she was wondering what would happen next. She was embarrassed and a little scared, but she was also very curious. Even thinking about what people must be saying in Albany didn't help. Albany seemed far away and she found that she didn't care what its residents thought. She found she cared what Zeke thought, which was the strangest thing of all.

She was dressed and had folded the blanket by the time Zeke returned, bringing in a flash of sunlight and the smell of fresh air.

"Feeling better?"

"Yes, thank you."

"How's the clothes?"

"See for yourself," she answered, then wished that she hadn't, as his eyes made a slow careful inspection that finished with her face and held her eyes for such a long time that she felt her legs going weak.

He finished with a shake of his head that seemed to match what she'd been feeling almost uncannily. Reaching into his pocket, he handed her a comb. "I found it this morning. If I'd recalled that I had it, I could have used it last night. I guess now is better than never."

He turned aside to the fire, leaving her holding the comb, stunned by the way he'd looked at her and by his mention of last night. Images rose before her with startling clarity—his hands fluffing her damp hair, his fingers grazing her breasts, his lips stealing softly down along her throat.

"Breakfast is pretty near ready."

His voice brought her back to earth. She'd been clutching the comb so tightly that the tines had dug a little pattern across her palm. Zeke was crouched down to stir the kettle, his back to her. She sat at the table and began to comb her hair.

Despite Zeke's ministrations, her hair was a mess. Wherever she pulled the comb she encountered a dozen snarls. She could imagine what she looked like—no wonder Zeke had shook his head.

"Whose cabin is this?" she asked, flipping the tangled mass forward to launch a full-scale attack.

"Nobody's now." Zeke's voice came from the hearth. "The man it used to belong to moved on a couple of years back so now the rest of us that use it sort of keep it up."

"What do you mean 'moved on'?" she asked, already breathless from the pain of pulling out the snarls, which she was accomplishing with less patience than brute force.

"These parts were beginning to feel too crowded to him, and I guess he knew it would only get worse. So he pulled up stakes here and moved on to the West."

"Too crowded!" She gritted her teeth and pulled. "Why, these parts are practically deserted!"

"I guess that depends on what you're used to and what you want."

She heard the kettle clatter as he replaced the lid. Her eyes were tearing and her comb was snagged between two snarls, neither of which would give in when she tried to jog it free. Frustrated, she yanked hard.

"Ow!" she yelped, and bit her lip as a good-sized clump of hair tore free at the roots. She yelped again, in surprise, as Zeke's hand touched hers. She hadn't heard him approaching.

"Here. Give me the comb."

"That's all right. I can do it myself."

"You'll scalp yourself, that's what you'll do," he said as his fingers parted hers and claimed the comb.

"No, really..." she protested, but then she gave up. It didn't hurt when he did it. She hardly felt the comb, he worked it through so gently, teasing out the snarls one by one.

"You've got a lot of patience."

"I guess with some things I do."

"But not with others?"

He chuckled. "What do you think? I've got no patience with fools or liars—or Yorkers, as you know. There, that's better." He ran the comb from her crown to the bottom of her curls. "Like gold," he murmured. "Like the sun was shining on it even when it's not. The Bible says if a woman has long hair it is a glory to her and I guess the Bible's right. You've got a glory here, Sally."

That set her heart off again, plunging along as crazily as her horse in the storm last night—that, and his fingers drifting through her hair, and the way he was standing with his thighs brushing against her back. All of last night's sensations came rushing back. She swallowed, seeking distraction, and found it in what he'd just said.

"When you swore on the Bible yesterday you didn't mention God. Eli told me you don't believe in Him."

The comb stopped briefly, then began again. "Sometimes brother Eli says a sight too much."

"Is it true?" she persisted.

"I guess you might say so."

"Why?"

He stopped combing and she felt his hands lifting her hair and letting it drift through his fingers onto her shoulders and back. A thrill fanned through her. "It's a long story," he said. "Sometime back there we had a sort of falling out. I put my faith in him and he let me down. With a small *h*," he concluded, dropping the comb on the tabletop. "Hope you think as much of that soup this morning as you did last night."

She opened her mouth in protest—as much at his withdrawal as at his response to her question—but he was already at the fire, ladling out the soup.

She did like the soup this morning as much as she had last night. They ate in silence, and when they were through Sarah washed the dishes and put them away while Zeke put out the fire and prepared to leave. She noticed he cut more wood and stacked it on the hearth—she assumed for the next bedraggled travelers seeking shelter from a storm. Watching him, she felt a wave of bittersweet nostalgia. She didn't imagine she'd ever see this place again, and though she knew she'd never forget it, she guessed she'd remember the night she'd spent here with disbelief.

They didn't discuss whether or not Zeke would be riding with her. In any event he had to guide her out of the woods, and when they reached the main road they simply rode on side by side. The road was badly littered with debris from the storm, but aside from that and the puddles, the morning through which they rode bore no resemblance to last night's chaotic world. The only wind to stir the trees was a gentle breeze, the sky was pure blue, and every leaf sparkled as though it had been freshly washed.

The sun was warm and the shade pleasantly cool; they rode in a companionable silence punctuated only by the morning songs of the birds and an occasional droning bee. From time to time Zeke whistled or hummed a melody, looking like a man without a care in the world. His mood was infectious, and although Sarah knew she had plenty to think about, she found herself riding along in a pleasant haze. Am I dreaming? she wondered, blinking up at the trees. Will I wake up and find myself back in Albany and listening to Father climbing up the stairs slowly, the way he does late at night?

That seemed about as likely as anything that had happened in these past two days. Before she could stop herself, she released the reins with one hand and gave her arm a pinch.

Of course Zeke noticed and immediately understood. "Trying to wake up, Sally? Surprise—you're not asleep!"

She gave up pinching and turned to look at him. "Where do you come from? Not from Bennington."

"Not likely. No one lived in Bennington until after the war."

"Where were you born, then?"

"Over in New York. Along the Hudson River south of Albany."

Her jaw dropped open, which made Zeke grin. "Close your mouth, Sally, before you swallow a bee."

"You mean you're a Yorker!"

His grin disappeared. "Don't call me that, Sally. Don't ever call me that."

"But if that's where you come from—"

"Come from. That's all. As soon as I could, I got out of there. Me and Eli both. He went off to college and I went to fight the war."

"Where did he go to college?"

"Yale University." He sat up straight when he said it and spoke the name with pride. "Then he read law up in Northampton, in the Bay colony."

"You're proud of what he's accomplished."

"Maybe I am. I wasn't proud of him yesterday when he lit into me."

"I think you were," said Sarah.

He shot her a sideways glance. "What makes you think so?"

"Weren't you?"

"I don't know." After a minute he chuckled. "He was pretty good, wasn't he—the way he got me to chasing my tail?"

"Very good," agreed Sarah. "And Archie could be good, too."

Zeke's smile faded. "What are you getting at?"

"Just that you'd be proud of Archie if he were able to make something of himself."

"I'm proud of Archie just the way he is."

"But you wouldn't be any less proud, would you, if he went to school? He seems to be a bright boy."

"Damn bright," Zeke agreed.

"Then that's all the more reason he should be given a chance to get ahead."

Zeke's eyes narrowed. "This 'getting ahead' of yours—just what does it entail?"

"Going to school, for one thing, and learning not to curse. Learning his manners—"

"In other words, learning to live in civilized society!" He spoke the last words sharply and with a bitter irony, and when she turned in surprise she saw that his eyes, normally so vibrant, had turned flat and cold.

Zeke shook his head shortly before she could reply. "Archie doesn't need improving, he's fine just as he is. Time's a-wasting. No need to dawdle here."

She sighed with frustration and spurred her horse after his, wondering at the reason for his sudden change in mood. But almost as quickly as he'd turned cold, he warmed back up again, slowing his horse down and resuming his whistling and pointing out the various birds and flowers that they saw.

Sooner than Sarah had imagined, he pointed straight ahead and she saw the river glittering in the sun.

"You're in luck, Sally. There's the ferry just coming across."

Squinting to see more clearly, Sarah realized that he was right. The ferry had just pushed off from the opposite shore and she could see the distant forms of the passengers. She tried to count them but she couldn't because the sun's reflection was too bright. Then all of a sudden she had a chilling thought. What if this was the sheriff coming to rescue her? She hadn't given her rescue a thought since the moment her horse had panicked and bolted into the woods, but now that she did think of it, she realized that unless the posse had passed her in the storm, this could be them now. Perhaps their departure had been delayed by the storm.

She glanced at Zeke, who didn't seem alarmed. Perhaps he really believed that no one would come after her. Or perhaps he hadn't considered the possibility. Perhaps what had happened between them had put him off his guard. What if she kept him here talking and the sheriff arrested him?

He'd stopped looking down at the river and was looking at the western hills, the corners of his eyes wrinkled from squinting into the sun. His eyes wrinkled the same way every time he smiled. For some reason that made her remember the way he'd pinched her big toe last night, and as she did, she knew that even to safeguard her title to the land, she couldn't plot his arrest. She'd keep her land some other way and not by tricking Zeke.

"Zeke," she said quickly, "thanks for getting me to the river. Why don't you head back. I'll go on alone from here."

His dark brows lifted as his eyes swung back to her. "What's the matter, Sally, in a hurry to get home? You sound like a woman who's got a beau waiting for her—'course, he couldn't be much of a beau not to have come after you."

She frowned with impatience. "Of course I don't have a beau! I just want to be sure the ferry doesn't go back and leave me here."

"It won't," he said easily. "He'll wait over on this side until he gets a paying fare or until it's dinnertime. If I had a wife like his, I reckon I'd do the same. Either way, it gives us time for a proper goodbye." As he said this he started to climb down from his horse.

"No!" She practically shouted. "That is, I think you ought to get started back. What—what if you run into another storm?"

Zeke looked up at the sky, which was bright blue and cloudless, before he looked back at her. "What's got into you, Sally? You're acting skittish as a colt. Are you afraid I'm going to kiss you?"

"Of course I'm not!" She hadn't even thought of it until he brought it up; she'd been too busy imagining the sheriff dragging him off to jail. But not Zeke—he'd dismounted and was reaching up to help her down.

She glanced back at the river, desperate by now. "Zeke, you'd better go. What if the sheriff is on the ferry and he catches you here?" She expected him to mock her, but he proved her wrong yet again as his eyes filled with the same wonder she'd seen in them last night.

"Why, Sally," he said softly. "I do believe you're watching out for me."

She felt herself flushing. "Zeke, you ought to go."

He shook his head. "It's not the sheriff, Sally. I wasn't boasting yesterday when I told you he wouldn't come. You've got time to come down here and tell me goodbye."

Before she could protest, he'd lifted her down and he had his hands on her shoulders and her body was turning to jelly again.

"I don't think . . ." she murmured as Zeke's lips covered hers.

His lips lingered for a moment before he withdrew them. "Goodbye, Sally," he said. "I can't remember when I've enjoyed a kidnapping more."

He stepped back and offered his hand to help her mount. She stared at it blankly. "You mean that's all?"

She'd said it without thinking and Zeke threw back his head and laughed. "That depends, Sally. What else did you have in mind? We've got another good ten minutes until the ferry lands—more if you don't mind retreating to the woods."

He reached out to her. Instinctively she moved back, knowing how easy it would be to succumb. Invisible strings from his hand seemed to be attached to her. When he pulled, she followed. She shook her head. "There's something," she said without thinking. "There's—there's the land."

"The land?" That stopped him.

It stopped her, too. What was she thinking of, bringing up the land, when she knew it was the very thing that made them enemies? Except they weren't enemies at this moment. Hadn't something changed? Hadn't they spent the night together? Hadn't Zeke cooked her soup and dried her clothes and combed her hair? How could they have done what they'd done together and still not be able to discuss the land?

She looked at Zeke uncertainly. He was waiting for her to speak. "Yes, the land," she said slowly. "I thought that in—uh—view of what's happened, we might be able to reach some sort of settlement."

Zeke let his hand drop. "What sort of settlement?"

"I don't know," she said, licking her lips from nervousness. "Something that would be fair to both of us. I know that you've invested your time and money in the land, so I believe it would be only fair for me to pay you something to compensate you for your loss."

Zeke's left eyebrow rose. "Compensate me?" he repeated. "Weren't you there yesterday? Didn't we have a trial?"

"Of sorts," Sarah said. "But it wasn't legal, and even if it was, you didn't really win."

His brow dropped abruptly. "What are you talking about?"

"The verdict. The jury held for me, but when they gave it to Remember, he said it was for you. You were looking at him. You know it's true."

"Are you accusing him of lying?"

"N-no—or rather, yes. It doesn't matter. Even if the jury held for you, that doesn't make any real difference, since we both know that your title would never hold up in a proper court. Oh, Zeke, please don't look like that. I know what this must mean to you. I know what it means to me and I'm sorry you can't have what you thought you got. But seeing how things have—have changed between us, I'd like to do whatever I can to help you out. I can't say right now just how much I could do. That would have to depend upon what I got for the land. But I promise I'd be as generous as I could, and if you gave me your word that you wouldn't interfere..."

She trailed off, searching for his reaction in his eyes but only seeing the reflection of the sun.

"Have things changed between us?"

"You know what I mean."

He nodded slowly. "I believe I do. You're saying that you think that I've gone so sweet on you I may be willing to give up my claim to the land. You're a fine-looking woman, Sally, but you're not quite that fine."

She hadn't expected that and she clamped down her jaw fast before she could respond, knowing that it wouldn't help to get into a fight with him. She counted to ten slowly, loosened her jaw and said, "Zeke, the king himself has declared that the land belongs to New York—and has all along. Eli himself admitted it."

"No he didn't. He only said that was the opinion of certain folks, mainly New Yorkers and some Philadelphians.

Other folks hold different beliefs—including Eli. He owns Grants land, you know, and he'd never give it over to a Yorker, no matter what you think.''

She felt her temper rising but she tried one last time. ''Zeke, I need the money that the land will bring.''

She must have said the wrong thing, because instead of showing understanding, Zeke's face slammed shut. ''If it's money you want, Sally, why not marry a rich man? I thought that's what 'civilized' women did.''

This time she didn't care about his bitterness. He'd insulted her, abused her, and he'd refused to admit the truth. He might have cooked her breakfast, but nothing had really changed.

''I've tried to reason with you but I can see there's no point. You won't even listen. You're the stubbornest man alive! You know the land is rightfully mine and you're pretending that you don't. Pretend all you like, I'll have it in the end. You may frighten away the Yorkers, but you won't frighten me. If I have to send an army with my surveyor to protect him, then I will. One thing's for sure, Zeke Brownell, you haven't seen the last of me!''

Whirling away from him she tried to mount her horse, only her skirt caught in the stirrup and she couldn't get up or down but stood hopping on one foot, showing Zeke as much bare leg as he'd seen last night. *If he laughs at me, I'll kill him,* she swore to herself.

''Need a hand, Sally?'' Zeke asked mildly. Before she could answer he'd freed her skirt and boosted her up to the saddle. ''I'll look forward to our next meeting,'' he said, stepping clear as she lifted the reins and pulled the horse around. ''Watch out for the horse. You can return him to me then.'' But by the time he said that, she was already riding away.

Zeke stood watching after her. So she intended to fight him for the land. He'd been right about her spirit; she was as spunky a woman as he'd ever met, and it almost made him sorry to know that she wouldn't win. Almost, but not quite. She might have the lushest hair and darkest blue eyes he'd ever seen, but no pair of pretty eyes could make him forget what it felt like to live on another man's land and to live at another man's mercy the way common men lived in New York. He wouldn't let those Yorkers turn the Grants land into that; not so long as he had an ounce of strength left to fight. He had a good many ounces left; what was more, he had a vision of what the Grants could become, and for better or worse that vision didn't include Mistress Sarah Meade.

Down below on the river, the ferry had come close enough for him to be able to see the passengers. Two Yorker farmers, one with his family. So much for the sheriff coming after him. He felt a stab of pity for Sally, having a coward of a father who wouldn't come after her. Well, maybe she'd find a husband who'd make up for it. Maybe she'd find a man rich enough to pay her debts and brave enough to make up for what she'd missed. Whoever she found would be lucky, he thought, recalling last night.

His eyes closed and he drew a long slow breath. By the time he'd let it out, Sally had reached the shore and was waiting for the ferryman to lead her horse on board. He watched her another moment, then he turned away. Maybe it wasn't such a good idea to see her again. Maybe he'd do better to leave this matter to the Boys and confine his thoughts of Sally to the memory of last night. With one last look toward the river, he swung up on his horse and set off at an easy trot back toward Bennington.

Chapter Six

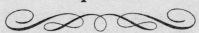

"Mistress Meade!" The servant who opened the door to Sarah's knock practically embraced her with relief. So had the groom in the stable with whom she'd left her horse.

"That man!" gasped the servant. "Then he let you go? We were so worried, we didn't know what to think! And then with Mr. Mason and his lordship coming home—"

"Mr. Mason?"

"Yes, mistress. He came in an hour ago and, oh, my, what a to-do when he heard that you were gone! He's already gone to the sheriff, both him and your father. Not his lordship—he was tired so he's lying down. But you're safe, mistress. That man didn't do you harm?"

"No, he didn't," Sarah said firmly but wearily, and heard just a hint of disappointment in the servant's gusty sigh. Scandal was rare and thrilling in conservative Albany and evidently he had been hoping for a little bit of excitement. Briefly she thought of Zeke, then pushed him from her mind. All the way back from the river she'd been furious with him.

"You said Mr. Mason and my father have gone to the sheriff? Then you'd better send word after them that I'm home, and when that's taken care of I wouldn't mind a hot bath and a change of clothes." With real feeling she added, "It's been a long two days."

"Yes, mistress, of course. I'll set the maid to heating water and send it straight up. Shall I send up tea, too?"

"That would be lovely." Sarah turned to the stairs. Hot bath, hot tea, clean clothes…it sounded like heaven to her, but as she put her hand on the newel post she recalled something in the barrage of exclamations with which the servant had greeted her. She tried to ignore it but it lingered in her mind. Reluctantly she turned back. "His lordship who?"

"The Marquis of Haddom." The servant pronounced the words with crisp formality, though whether his deference was to the man or to the title Sarah could not tell. "His excellency, the royal governor, introduced Mr. Mason to him in New York. His lordship has business in this area."

"What sort of business?"

"I don't know. No one had time to explain, what with all the to-do over your being gone. His lordship found all the bustle wearying, so when your father and Mr. Mason went to the sheriff, he went up to his room to lie down. He left instructions he should not be disturbed."

"I see." Sarah turned back to the stairs. Her hand still on the newel post, she stood there looking up. The staircase seemed unmanageably steep. It was clear the turmoil of these past days had exhausted her; she felt every bit as weary as she had last night when she'd practically nodded off over her bowl of soup.

Zeke's soup. She stood looking up the flight. The servant was watching; she had no choice but to climb, so she lifted one foot and placed it in the center of the lowest stair. Then she lifted the other, then the first again. In her mind she fixed the image of the hot bath awaiting her—and clean clothes, and a long rest in a nice soft bed.

Soft beds made her think of pallets and pallets brought her back to Zeke. Thinking of Zeke made her angry and also disturbed. Tired, disturbed and angry, she arrived at the landing and turned to conquer the second flight. She was five steps from the summit when a voice, very proper and English, addressed her from above.

"I say—this isn't the purloined Mistress Meade miraculously returned?"

The voice not only was proper but spoke with the sort of lisp one didn't associate with the colonies. Most Englishmen who arrived lisping soon learned that it earned them far more ridicule than respect, and those who refused to curb their style didn't last very long.

Tired, angry, disturbed and reluctant, Sarah stopped climbing and looked up. The face studying her from above the balustrade was distressingly well matched to the voice: archly aristocratic and fussily framed by the curls of a powdered wig and billowing lace at the throat.

Pale blue eyes surveyed her, powdered eyebrows rose and the voice lisped, "Strike me blue! Nobody happened to mention that the damsel in distress was also a damsel so beautiful. If they had, I would have rushed off to your rescue myself, though Mr. Mason and your father gave me to understand that my accompanying them to the sheriff would add nothing but confusion. Even so, I hope you will pardon the lack of chivalry. For my part I hereby solemnly vow that I shall exhaust myself in atoning for my most unfortunate lapse."

The speech left him breathless and Sarah unimpressed. "Don't bother," she said briefly, continuing up the stairs.

He took her reply as politeness and ignored it, as she'd feared, moving around from the balustrade to meet her at the top of the stairs, where he stood with one leg thrust out like the court dandy he was. After the homespun she'd been looking at for the past two days, his violet silk breeches and canary yellow coat looked lurid to her eyes.

He executed a flourish that finished with the lace of his right cuff draped over the buckle of his left shoe. Red in the face, he straightened. "Allow me to introduce myself. I am Edward Settfield Bliss, Marquis of Haddom and second in line to the title of the Duke of Wilbershire."

"Pleased to meet you," sighed Sarah as Haddom inspected her even more carefully than he had before, from her wrinkled bodice to her dusty skirts. After all the riding she knew her face must be dirty, too, though thanks to Zeke's efforts at least her hair was combed.

"I say," he ventured, "you're not injured in any way?"

"No, not injured."

"Mistreated? Abused? From what the servant told us the man who came here was completely crazed. I understand he'd killed a farmer and—ahem—abused the wife."

"He did no such thing!" snapped Sarah, her patience wearing thin. The marquis was as starved for scandal as the servant who'd answered the door. "He whipped the surveyor—he only threatened the other two."

"Only!" Haddom's eyebrows inched up toward his wig. "But you—he carried you off by force. Where did he take you?"

"To Bennington. He took me to Bennington and then he brought me back." She tried to step around him so that she could go to her room. "As your lordship so kindly noted, I have been through a trying experience. So if your lordship will please excuse me, I'll just go to my—"

"Bennington!" he exclaimed, completely ignoring her request. "I may be new to this area but I am familiar with the maps. Isn't Bennington one of the towns in the disputed area!"

"It's New York," she said tersely. He was as bad as Zeke, or worse. At least when Zeke saw she was tired he suggested she go to bed. "Please, I really would like to go to my room."

For a minute she wondered if he were deaf since he gave absolutely no indication of even having heard her request. To tell the truth, he looked as though he'd forgotten she was there; he just stood staring at her, preoccupied. She was about to repeat her request more loudly when suddenly he blinked and was instantly transformed back into the gushing model of extreme courtliness.

With another flourish, he cried, "Strike me dead! What am I thinking of—you must rest and right away!" He reached out to seize her arm to help her to her room, but she was faster and managed to dodge his hand.

"Thank you very much, but I can manage myself. I'll see you later," she murmured, edging past him toward her room.

Haddom edged with her. "Yes, yes, most assuredly. I shall look forward to hearing the full account of your ordeal, as I am sure Mr. Mason and your father will when they hear you are safe. Speaking of whom, they must be advised that you are back." He stopped then and thrust one finger in the air. "I shall go this instant to tell them myself. No doubt your father will be immensely relieved."

"No doubt," Sarah said dryly, "but there's really no need, since I've already sent a servant to tell them."

"Ah, but I have made my solemn vow to serve you in every way. I will go find them and inform them myself. Rest yourself, my lady, and leave everything to me!"

"Thank you," she murmured, because she knew she had no choice and because anything was better than having him follow her.

She pulled her door open.

"*Au revoir!*" Haddom trilled.

She closed the door behind her and was blessedly alone.

The maid had long since brought up hot water and Sarah was still soaking in the bath when her father knocked on the door. "Are you awake, Sarah?"

"Just a minute," she called. She got out, dried off and slipped on a dressing gown. When she opened the door she found him standing in the hall, staring at her goggle-eyed as though he'd just had a shock.

He wasn't shocked at all. He'd just taken a pinch of snuff and was about to sneeze. Sarah stepped back to put herself out of range and waited until he'd finished sneezing and blown his nose. He looked her up and down as he put his handkerchief away. "Haddom says they didn't harm you."

"They didn't. Haddom's right."

"You're sure?"

"Absolutely." He, at least, looked relieved, though she knew that had as much to do with his cowardice as with fatherly concern.

He glanced past her and through her open door. "May I come inside?"

"Of course." She stepped back to let him pass.

"Haddom says he took you to Bennington." He chose a chair near the window, pausing on the way to check his reflection in the looking glass.

She nodded. "To a tavern called the Catamount. It's the stronghold of the Green Mountain Boys. They put me on trial."

"For what?"

"For owning the land. One of them—the one who came to get me—claims that the land is his under a grant from the New Hampshire governor. He claims that the land belonged to New Hampshire when his grant was made and then in '64 the king gave it to New York. So they had a trial and afterward the judge said that the land was his."

For the first time since he'd come in, Henry Meade looked distressed. "They didn't force you to agree to anything?"

"No, don't worry. That wasn't the point. The point was to scare me into giving up my claim."

"Did they?"

She shook her head, recalling her parting words to Zeke. "No, they didn't. If anything the experience only reinforced my resolve to go ahead and sell the land."

Her father was silent for a moment, then he asked, "What did they say they'd do if you didn't give up?"

She looked at him. He was older than Haddom, but despite their reduced means, he was equally well dressed in a cherry red silk coat with lace at the throat and cuffs. In his youth Henry Meade had been a remarkably handsome man, and though his looks were no longer remarkable he had aged well through the years.

But when Sarah looked at her father, she didn't see his finely drawn brows, his high cheekbones and long aquiline nose. Instead she saw the watchful sharpness in his eyes and the fine lines of selfishness etched around his mouth. She didn't see the slenderness of his fingers or the shapeliness of his calves but rather the nervous way he was toying with his lace, and she knew that in a minute he'd reach for his snuff. Henry Meade had never cared for the tedious side of life; he preferred to ignore problems and hope they'd disappear. In their life together, the disappearing of problems had been Sarah's role.

She set her jaw and answered, "They didn't say. I imagine they will try whatever means of intimidation they believe will frighten me off."

Her father's brows contracted and he reached for his snuff. After he'd sneezed he felt better. He stowed his box away and smiled. "Haddom likes you. He thinks you're beautiful."

"Father, please! I've just been kidnapped and put to trial by a horde of ruffians. I'm in no mood for your schemes, and for your information I don't like the marquis. He's ridiculously pompous and he lisps."

"Poor Sarah," he said calmly. "You're tired and upset, and you're probably hungry. I can only imagine how they housed and fed you there."

"They housed and fed me well enough," she answered, thinking about last night and feeling a stab of longing so sharp she brought her hands to her breast to press against the spot.

Her father, alert to nuance, caught the movement of her hands. "Is something wrong, Sarah?"

Quickly she shook her head, thinking how strange her name sounded after Zeke had called her Sally for two days. "No, Father, nothing's wrong. When you came home and found me gone, what did you do?"

"I went straight to the sheriff."

"But he didn't come after me?"

"He assured me that he would, but he said it would take time to collect enough men."

"And naturally you volunteered to go with them?"

"Me?" He looked alarmed by the very idea. "You know how I feel about violence. I wouldn't have been any use. In any event, here you are so there was really no harm done."

"No harm," she said dryly, thinking again about Zeke. Before that longing could stab again, she pushed the thought away and murmured, "Poor Mr. Mason. I hope you apologized."

"I did," said her father, relaxing, "and quite elegantly, if I do say so myself. He's looking forward to consoling you himself—he's had them wait dinner until you're ready to eat."

"Mr. Mason is waiting for me? Why didn't you say so before? No, never mind. Leave me so I can get dressed. You'd better send the maid up when you go down, and please tell Mr. Mason I'll be as quick as I can."

"Take your time," her father advised, checking his reflection again. "It always pays to make a good impression on new acquaintances."

Sarah opened her mouth to point out that she'd known Mason all her life, but then she realized he was talking about the marquis. By that time her father was already out the door and she could hear him humming a tune in the hall. More problems and no solutions, she thought with a gusty sigh, pulling open the doors of the cupboard to survey her clothes.

She chose a dark gray overskirt with a deep blue petticoat and bodice that brought out the blue in her eyes. As she dressed she thought less of Haddom than she did of Zeke. Specifically she was thinking of what she meant to say to Mason and the others about her trip to Bennington. She hadn't really considered the question before; things had been moving too fast. But now that she considered it, she realized that there were parts of her story she didn't mean to share.

Last night, for instance. She knew what people were bound to conclude if they found out she'd spent the night in a cabin with Zeke Brownell. Haddom, for instance, and the servant who'd answered the door when she'd come home would both conclude the worst. What was more, their conclusions wouldn't be far from the truth. She ran the silver-backed brush through her hair and recalled how Zeke had called her hair a glory and had held her in his arms and kissed her with kisses that had made her feel—

She slapped the brush down on the dressing table and firmly tied back her hair. She wouldn't think of Zeke

Brownell and she'd steer clear of the things that would make her remember last night. Such thoughts would only distract her from the task at hand, and between the marquis and her father she was likely to have distractions enough.

"You look very pretty, mistress," said the maid who had helped her dress and was now in the process of emptying the bath. The maid paused with a bucket of water dangling from her hands. "You must have been scared when they took you over there—I'd have died of fright. They said those Green Mountain Boys will do anything to frighten a Yorker. *Anything*," she repeated, her eyes growing very large.

"Watch out, you're spilling water." As she rose, Sarah nodded to the rug. She hadn't meant to say more, but at the door she paused. "To answer your question, I wasn't one bit scared, and as for what 'they' say, I believe people make up those stories to amuse themselves. If you want my opinion, the infamous Green Mountain Boys are nothing more than a bunch of backwoods farmers who could use a good tailor and just about any barber at all!"

"But they say—" the maid persisted, but to no avail, since Sarah was already halfway down the hall. "They do say," she grumbled to nobody but herself, and shivered so that the water slopped over the bucket's edge. She didn't believe for a moment that those stories were made up. Mistress Meade didn't know just how lucky she was.

Sarah found the three men waiting for her in the drawing room, and from the way they stopped talking and turned when she came in, she guessed that they had been discussing her trip to Bennington. All three rose to greet her and George Mason took her hands.

"Sarah, my dear! Let me look at you—you grow lovelier every year. And what a relief to have you back and safe. You can't imagine the shock I had returning home, only to be told that you'd been abducted to the Grants. I would have never forgiven myself if you'd been harmed."

He squeezed her hands as he said this and Sarah was touched by the genuineness of his concern. Although Mason was her father's age, the difference between them was vast. If asked to define it, no doubt Henry Meade would have said that Mason had had better luck in his dealings than he, but Sarah understood that luck had nothing to do with it. Her father was still a child, while Mason had grown up and accepted life's responsibility. It was a difference she had distinguished at a very early age and she'd always looked forward to Mason's visits as intervals of reason in an otherwise uncertain life.

"Then you were abducted by the Green Mountain Boys? That was my first thought when I heard what had happened." Still holding her hands, Mason shook his head. "I should have known something like this might have happened when you first told me about the land. I shouldn't have gone off and left you here alone, but I had no idea that your land was part of the area granted by Wentworth after the war."

"How could you have?" Sarah replied. "And as for your feeling responsible, I won't hear of it! If anything, Father and I are the ones who should apologize for having brought all this upon you, upsetting your household and giving you such a frightful welcome home."

"But in fact," Henry Meade said smoothly, "here we are all safe and sound, so doesn't it make more sense to forget what's past and enjoy each other's company—and the doubtlessly delightful dinner awaiting us?"

Mason smiled at Sarah. "Your father is absolutely right. Given what might have happened, we have plenty to celebrate, and goodness knows that the cook is most eager for us to go in." Still smiling affectionately, he offered Sarah his arm.

Haddom, who had been chafing for an opening through which to plunge, stepped forward with an arch look at Sarah's hand resting on Mason's arm. "If Mr. Mason wasn't such a perfectly gracious host, I would certainly challenge him for the honor of escorting Mistress Meade. Today I shall submit, as is my humble duty as a grateful guest, but perhaps tomorrow Mistress Meade will so honor me.''

Mason said simply, ''Perhaps she will,'' and patted Sarah's hand, but when they had passed Haddom, he gave her a sympathetic look, to which she responded with a grateful smile.

As Meade had predicted, the dinner was excellent. Sarah, who'd had nothing but soup since the morning before, ate with a good appetite. She'd been dreading Haddom quizzing her on her trip to Bennington, but Mason must have understood and tactfully diverted the conversation to such subjects as conditions in England and the marquis's business in America.

''You might say I've come here on an educational trip,'' Haddom explained, his hands and lips in constant motion sipping wine and cutting meat. ''Excellent beef, Mason. As good as we get at home.''

''Very kind,'' Mason said politely.

''Education about what?'' asked Meade.

Haddom put down his wineglass and blotted his lips three times. ''You might say education about the condition of the colonies. We hear the wildest sorts of rumors in England—you wouldn't believe what sort of things—so finally I decided to come see for myself.''

''Very enterprising.''

''You might say that I am an enterprising man.''

''Where might we say you've been so far?'' Sarah asked, earning a warning look from her father and from Mason a smile.

She also earned Haddom's attention, and more of it than she would have wished. He blotted his lips again as his eyes flickered over her, and he addressed his response to her eyes, her mouth, her breasts.

''Thus far I have visited the Bay colony and New York. I landed in Boston, but I can't say I liked it there. Not a very gay society and the people are very rude. I much preferred New York—and I am prepared to like Albany best of all.''

"No doubt the city fathers will be glad to hear that," Sarah said.

"I wasn't speaking of the city fathers. I was speaking of you, Mistress Meade. Any city in which you were staying would be enjoyable to me. Although I cannot imagine beginning to truly enjoy myself until I know that the villains responsible for your ordeal have been caught and punished!" He said this with a look at the other men, as if he were expecting them to spring to their feet and shout, "Hear, hear!"

They did not. Meade looked apprehensive and Mason said, "I think Mistress Meade would prefer not to think of such distressing events, at least until after dinner."

"That's all right," Sarah said, putting down her fork. "I'd rather speak about it now and get it over with. I suppose my father has told you what I told him upstairs, and beyond that there isn't too much to add. It's a case of two people asserting their claim to the same land, one by legal right and the other with brute force."

"Brute force is for animals," Haddom pointed out.

"Animals, men and armies," Sarah replied, envisioning Zeke's reaction to Haddom's pompous tone. Facing Mason, she continued, "Mr. Brownell is determined to hold on to his land, so when he heard I was having it surveyed he rushed straight up there to scare the surveyor off, and when he discovered the couple to whom I'd sold a small portion, he scared them off, too. Then he came down here to convince me that, legal or not, he'd never let me or anyone else assert the New York claim." She paused, then added, "While I may not agree with his approach, in his defense I'd have to say that he genuinely believes that the land is his."

"In his defense!" Haddom erupted, a volcano of silk and lace. "My lady, you are too kind-hearted and in this case your kindness is sadly misplaced! This creature doesn't deserve your sympathy, he deserves our revenge, and he shall receive it. I give you my word that he shall!"

"A noble thought, my lord," Mason said mildly. "What about this trial?"

"That's why he took me to Bennington." Sarah retrieved the thread of her story as Haddom subsided, still sputtering. "As no doubt the servants told you, he arrived here thinking that I was a man, but when he discovered I was a woman, he took me anyway. He took me to a tavern called the Catamount, where the rest of the Boys were waiting to put me on trial. Some of them were nervous about trying a woman. They were afraid that the sheriff or even the army would come after them, but Zeke—that is, Mr. Brownell—assured them that all the men in New York were too afraid of the Green Mountain Boys to come to Bennington."

"So they tried you?" Mason said, before Haddom could recommence.

Sarah nodded. "That's right. Mr. Brownell's brother represented me. He's a lawyer, and he did a very good job—so good I believe we actually won, but then the judge reversed the jury's verdict and held for Mr. Brownell. After that I spent the night, then first thing in the morning they sent me back," she finished quickly and in a matter-of-fact tone of voice.

Haddom, whose outrage had been building, erupted once again. "Kidnapping defenseless women! Conducting mock trials! Thumbing their noses at every lawful authority—these outlaws must be punished and as swiftly as possible! I cannot understand why the sheriff did not send a troop after Mistress Meade when he first heard what had happened, since if he had, he might have spared her a good portion of her ordeal. I assume he will send his troop now to apprehend these men. He will, won't he, Mason?"

"I don't think so," Mason said, turning to Sarah with eyes full of troubled regret. "Sorry as I am to say so, I'm afraid that Mr. Brownell is right. Most of the men in this area have heard enough about the Green Mountain Boys not to want to venture into their territory."

"Not to want!" snapped Haddom. "This has nothing to do with want! If they don't want they must be ordered! This is the sheriff's job! These men are nothing but cowards."

"Cowards or realists. The Boys know that whole area like the back of their hands, so it's easy for them to take unwanted visitors by surprise. And although their farms are widely scattered, they've apparently worked out a signal system that lets them turn out large numbers of men faster than you would believe. If the sheriff rides with twenty men, he'll find fifty waiting for him. If he rides with fifty, he'll fine one hundred and so forth. Short of starting an all-out war, they seem invincible."

"Then perhaps a war should be started!"

Mason looked at the marquis. Quietly, he said, "I don't believe starting a war would help anything. It would only fuel resentments and these days resentments are running high enough. If you've been in Boston, you know what I mean."

He went on. "But that's not all. The Green Mountain Boys aren't only numerous, they're also ingenious—rather diabolically so. Take what happened to a surveyor and his chainman six months ago. The Boys caught them on land they considered theirs, so they bound them and took them down to Bennington, where, after the usual trial, they were found guilty of trespass and who knows what else. As it was late by that time, sentencing was deferred till the next day and the two were locked up in separate rooms for the night.

"Just as dawn was breaking the key turned in the chainman's door and one of the Boys appeared. To the chainman's surprise, the Boy whispered he'd come to help him escape before they could do to him what they'd done to the surveyor. When the chainman asked what they'd done, the Boy led him to the window and pointed to a tree from which the chainman could just distinguish something swinging from a rope.

"'That's him,' the Boy said. 'You've got to get away. I'll leave the door unlocked, and when I'm gone, you leave. Go out the back way—you'll find a horse behind the barn. Don't stop riding till you're back in New York.'

"The Boy left," continued Mason, "and the chainman took off. He didn't stop riding until he was safe back in New York, and then he was so frightened he stayed in his house for two weeks. So it wasn't until several weeks later that he ran into the surveyor in Albany.''

"They hadn't hanged him!'' said Sarah.

Mason shook his head. "What the chainman had seen was a sack dangling from the tree. They'd shown the same sack to the surveyor an hour or so before and he'd run off as fast as the chainman did. The Boys have a knack for blending fear and humiliation in a way that makes most men unwilling to lock horns with them at all, and certainly not more than once.''

"I'd have gone back if I'd been that chainman,'' she declared with a toss of her head. "Why, there must have been Boys at all the windows, splitting their sides with laughter, as those men rode off! If I'd been that surveyor I'd have paid them back!''

"They must be paid back!'' Haddom jabbed his finger in the air. "In London you'd never hear of such a thing, and there is no reason that it should be tolerated here. This is the king's jurisdiction, as those highwaymen will learn. First thing tomorrow I will go the sheriff myself and tell him that if he refuses to respond he will have to answer to the royal governor. The perpetrators of this outrage will be brought to justice. Mistress Meade, I give you my solemn word.''

Shaking the lace back from his cuff, he laid his right hand grandly upon his heart. As she looked at him, all Sarah could think of was that, if he were here, Zeke would roar, "Go ahead—bring me to justice, you goddamn popinjay!'' And if Zeke roared that at Haddom, Haddom would probably faint dead away. No wonder the Boys got away with as much as they did.

She shook her head slowly. "He won't have my land. If I have to hire a private army, I'll have that land surveyed and I'll sell it the way I started out to do, and if Zeke Brownell thinks he can stop me, he'll find out he's wrong. He's about to discover that courage doesn't stop at the Hudson River and it's not confined to men.''

"Sarah,'' murmured Mason.

At the sight of his concern, Sarah's expression softened and she reached out to take his hand. "Mr. Mason, you've always been a good friend to us, but there's no reason for you to share the trouble this is likely to bring. I know what your neighbors are probably saying about what happened two nights ago and I don't want to give them anything more to talk about. Until this problem is resolved I think it would be better if my father and I moved to rented rooms."

"Rented rooms!" For the first time her father looked truly alarmed.

So did Mason. "My dear, I won't hear of it. Your moving is out of the question. You must both stay right here. I agree with you that it's time the Green Mountain Boys were stopped, but if you mean to stop them you must remain here where I can offer you protection and help. There's no point in your protesting. My mind is made up."

"You are too kind," murmured Sarah, blinking back a sudden rush of tears of gratitude.

Mason smiled and squeezed her hand. "My dear Sarah, what a two days you've had. You may stay on the condition that we will not discuss these matters anymore today. Tomorrow will be soon enough to begin plotting strategy—for now we will relax and enjoy ourselves. Speaking of enjoyment, I happen to know that the cook has prepared her special chocolate cake. I hope you have room to try some."

"I certainly do." Sarah smiled, glancing at her father, who looked almost faint with relief. As for Haddom, he didn't seem to have heard. He was sipping wine again and looking preoccupied.

The sun had just disappeared behind the western hills when Zeke turned into the yard of Eli's farm. Eli's farm—calling it such held more than its share of irony, since Zeke worked it at least as much as Eli did and had built the house and barn. But that was another story, and not one to be discussed except when Eli got himself into one of his ornery moods and set about goading Zeke to face his ghosts. Then Zeke would holler and Eli would holler back and

Archie and Thumper would take refuge in the barn, and
when the dust had settled Zeke would still be there instead
of up north living on the land he loved—the same land that
Mistress Sally Meade had just promised to survey and sell.

Zeke led his horse to the barn, fed him and brushed him
down. Archie had already milked the cows, who were
chewing their cuds peaceably. Eli's horse and the goat were
chewing, too, and Zeke could hear a hen up in the loft
worrying over an egg. Comfortable home sounds; he leaned
against the horse and remembered the way the pulse beat at
the base of Sally's throat and the silkiness of her hair sliding between his hands.

"Damn!" he muttered, then gave the horse a final pat,
put the brush back on the shelf and walked across to the
house.

Archie and Eli were both in the kitchen, which they'd
always used as the main living room. Archie was picking
burrs off Thumper and Eli was writing a brief. All three
stopped and looked up when Zeke came in.

"You get her home safe?" Archie asked.

"I took her as far as the ferry. I guess she won't have
much trouble finding her way from there." On the fire was
a kettle, which contained the remains of a stew concocted
by Eli, who was a fine lawyer but not much of a cook.

"There's possum," Archie offered when Zeke replaced
the kettle lid. "We left you your share. It's over there on the
table." He pointed to a covered dish, and when Zeke moved
in that direction he got up to join him, straddling his chair
backward with his chin resting on his hands. He watched as
Zeke helped himself to possum and a chunk of bread.
"That sure was some storm we had yesterday. I guess you
and Mistress Meade must have got caught in it."

Zeke glanced at Eli, who had gone back to work and appeared to be completely absorbed in his brief. Archie was
waiting in bright-eyed innocence so Zeke said, "Her horse
took fright and bolted but I managed to calm him down."

"Was she scared?"

"A little." Zeke chewed slowly, remembering the look on Sally's face and the way she had started crying and curled herself into his arms like a new born kitten.

"Where'd you find shelter?"

"Teb Howlan's old place."

"That old shack!" Archie leaned back and made a face. "I didn't think it even had a roof left to keep out the rain."

"It has a roof." Zeke looked over at Eli again and this time he was quick enough to catch his brother's eye. He put his knife down and demanded, "What are you looking at?"

Eli grinned. "What do you think? At your handsome face. You didn't meet the sheriff?"

"Not a sign. I told you he wouldn't come. When we got to the river the ferry was coming over with some men aboard and Mistress Sally got all excited thinking it was him."

"She was hoping he'd arrest you?"

"Not at first. At first she was still feeling grateful for me having saved her in the storm. But afterward she happened to bring up the land again, and after we'd discussed it I think she changed her mind. But it wasn't the sheriff on the ferry, so it didn't make any difference."

Eli was no longer grinning. "What did she say about the land?"

"I don't recall her exact words but the general drift was that she wasn't too happy about the idea of giving it up."

"In other words, she means to fight you."

"Something like that," said Zeke.

Eli said nothing. For a few minutes the room was still, with Eli once again working, Zeke eating his possum and bread and Archie, his chin resting on his arm, staring off into space. Then Archie gave a long sigh and shook his head. "Damn! She sure was pretty, wasn't she? I never did see a prettier woman—did you, Zeke?"

Zeke stopped chewing and felt Eli look up. "Maybe," he said shortly. "Then again, maybe not. Pretty or not, she's a Yorker and she's after our land." He pointed his knife at Archie. "Don't you forget that, boy."

"I won't forget," said Archie, and he sighed again. Eli and Zeke said nothing. They didn't have to speak or even look at each other to know they were each recalling things that had happened long ago. Things best forgotten, Zeke thought to himself.

Later that night, after Mason had retired to his office and Sarah had gone to bed, Henry Meade and the Marquis of Haddom sat over a bowl of punch in an Albany public house. Coming to the pub had been Meade's idea, but Haddom had accepted the invitation willingly. Meade trusted he'd be just as willing to pay for the punch, since these days he was chronically short of funds.

This bowl of punch was their third. They'd reminisced about life in England over the first, and over the second they'd discovered a common acquaintanceship. By the time they'd finished the second, Haddom was pleasantly drunk and Meade had begun to quiz him on the purpose of his trip.

"You said you were here for educational reasons but that sounds rather vague. In my experience a man doesn't come all this way without a more, shall we say, specific purpose in mind. Especially not a man of action such as yourself."

Haddom's chest inflated at Meade's flattery. "To tell the truth, I do have something more definite in mind."

Meade raised his brows in anticipation, but Haddom waggled his head. "Can't, old man. It's a secret." He put his finger to his lips and winked. "But I can tell you this much. There's a chance I might make an offer for your daughter's land."

Meade, who'd been about to drink, slowly set down his cup, then he reached into his pocket and offered Haddom snuff.

"Most gracious of you," Haddom murmured, dipping a generous pinch. "Capital stuff!" he wheezed a minute later, after a thunderous sneeze.

Meade smiled. "I'm glad you like it. I got it here, on Market Street. I'll take you there tomorrow. Now about this land..."

Haddom dabbed at his eyes, which were tearing. "What about the land?"

"My daughter Sarah's. The land she has for sale. You just said you might want to buy it."

"Ah, yes, but that depends."

"On what?" Meade asked, ladling Haddom more punch.

Haddom frowned. "On circumstances. This Zeke Brownell, for one. What's the point in owning land that you can't even claim?"

"Ah, but you could claim it if anyone could, my lord. As you yourself have pointed out, you're a man of great influence. You have powerful connections, such as the royal governor, and no doubt you can prevail upon him to send a troop against this outlaw element. Then, once these brigands had been wiped out, you could not only buy the land—you'd also be my Sarah's hero. I can only imagine how she'd melt with gratitude. You know what they say about women like Sarah."

"No, what do they say?"

"They say that the strongest willed women are the sweetest when they melt. More snuff, my lord?"

"What? No, thank you." Haddom stared into his cup, conjuring up the image of Sarah Meade with her blond hair and blue eyes and body lush enough to make any man a fool. The idea of her melting was a most appealing one. Normally the thought of marriage gave him some shortness of breath, but tonight, through the fog of rum punch, it seemed appealing, and he imagined strolling the Pall Mall with Sarah on his arm wearing something light and fluffy and cut low on her breasts.

"You like her, don't you," Meade murmured, reading Haddom's mind. "Shall I tell you a secret? She already likes you, too. It wouldn't be hard to make her love you."

"What—by buying the land?"

Meade shook his head slowly. "No, not by buying it— not at first, at least. I believe you would make her love you by getting rid of Zeke Brownell. You heard her tonight at dinner. She's as determined to beat him as you are yourself, and if you were to do it for her you'd earn her eternal gratitude. You'd not only get the land, you'd get my Sarah, too."

"You really think so?"

"I know so," said Henry Meade. "After all, she's my daughter and I've known her all my life."

"You'd want me to marry your daughter?"

Meade smiled in response. "What a modest man you are to ask me a question like that. What father wouldn't feel lucky to give his daughter to a man like you. A man of wealth and vision, truly a man among men! I would consider it the happiest day of all of our lives."

Haddom didn't answer, he sat and stared at Meade. He stared so long and silently that Meade finally murmured, "My lord?"

"Hmm?" Haddom blinked repeatedly, focusing on Meade's face, which required a determined effort after so much punch. Finally he succeeded. Leaning forward, he said, "Meade, can you keep a secret?"

In answer, Meade raised his right hand and laid it across his heart. Haddom raised one finger and crooked it, beckoning. "All right, then, come closer, I don't want to be overheard."

Meade leaned forward until he could smell the rum fumes on Haddom's breath and see the specks of snuff still clinging to his upper lip, whose rosy color he more than suspected was the result of paint.

Haddom said, "I'm going to tell you the real reason why I've come, but you mustn't repeat it to anyone. Not even His Majesty knows at this time—though of course if anything comes of it, he'll be told right away."

"Told what?" Meade asked.

"About the colony. The colony to be created from disputed land. Don't you see, it's the best way to resolve the dispute. The king won't give it to New Hampshire and the people of New Hampshire won't let it go to New York, so why not create a completely separate entity that doesn't belong to either one?"

Meade's mouth opened. "How do you fit into this?"

"As you have noted, I have powerful friends, including the members of the Privy Council who first came up with the idea of the new colony. Knowing I had an interest in visiting America, they urged me to gather as much information as possible about the area. They also suggested that I might consider taking a personal part in the plan."

"How personal?" Meade asked. His eyes were beginning to glow. Sarah would have read that glow correctly, but Haddom didn't know Meade and in any event he was too drunk even to notice.

"Very personal." Haddom slurred the *r*'s. "My friends in Privy see me as governor. Of course I told them I'd have to see. I mean, really, who wants to jump into the middle of a bloody mess? But if things could be settled . . ."

"Settled? Of course they could!" Meade reached out one hand to clap Haddom on the shoulder. "You could settle them, my lord! You could be the guiding force behind defeating Brownell and his gang, and after that, what would be more natural than to make you the leader of the colony that owed its birth to you?"

Meade beamed at Haddom, hardly able to contain his joy. The possibilities presented were almost too good to be true. Once Haddom had gotten rid of the Green Mountain Boys, Sarah's land would shoot up in value and they could sell it, pay their debts and have plenty left to spend. Better yet, if Haddom did defeat Brownell, maybe Sarah would change her opinion and agree to marry the man. Then they'd be even richer.

Meade seized the ladle and filled both their cups. He raised his. "To the future!"

Haddom lifted his in response. "To New Sussex!" At Meade's expression, he explained, "It's the name I would choose—after the site of Haddom Hall."

"Of course. To New Sussex—and to victory! Drink up, my dear Haddom, then we'll have more snuff."

Chapter Seven

⤨⤨⤨

The next day at ten minutes past noon, Sarah walked up the front steps of George Mason's house. She walked slowly, thinking of the interview she'd just come from and hoping that Mr. Mason was at home, since she needed some good advice. But as luck would have it, George Mason was out, whereas her father was waiting for her in the front hall.

"If you have a moment, Sarah, I would like to speak to you." He looked at her more closely. "Tut-tut, you look tired. Shall we send for a glass of wine or a cup of tea?"

Wordlessly she shook her head, bracing herself against what was to come; whenever her father asked about her health, she knew he was plotting something. He'd been out with Haddom the night before and she could only imagine what he had in mind.

He waited while she unfastened her cape and gave it to the servant. Then he led the way into the library.

"Where is Mr. Mason?" she asked as he shut the door.

"He and Haddom have both gone out. Haddom's gone to see the sheriff about arresting Brownell. He's also written a letter to his friend, the governor."

"My, my. How lucky for us that he's here." Sarah sank down into a leather chair and watched as her father chose a sofa opposite and helped himself to snuff.

"Haddom's a capital fellow," he said when he could speak. "Rich, well connected and almost a duke."

"Second in line," she pointed out.

"Yes, but I happen to know that the first is a doddering old fellow who could be swept away by nothing more than a bad cold. Haddom will have the title before you can turn around. I doubt you'll be surprised to hear he also thinks highly of you. There is also a possibility that he might buy the land—at a good price, of course."

She looked at him for a moment, then leaned back and closed her eyes. "Let me guess. You want me to be nice to the marquis so he'll buy the land. No, wait, that's too straightforward. Let me guess again. You want me to be nice to him so he'll get rid of Zeke Brownell. Then I'll be able to sell the land at the price I name, either to the marquis or to someone else. Is that it, Father?" She opened her eyes.

He was sitting with his legs crossed and his lips pursed admonishingly—an expression that informed her that she'd been right. "You object to Haddom's manners? I suppose you prefer a man who'll sling you over his shoulder and gallop about in the night?"

"Of course I don't prefer that!" She stiffened defensively. "I just don't want you plotting with Haddom behind my back."

"Plotting? I'm not plotting. I just happened to mention that Haddom liked you, and you, in your suspicious way, inferred the rest." He waved his hand. "Well, never mind, there's nothing to argue about. Mason told me he'd sent you to another surveyor. Did you find him?"

"Yes, I did."

"And, how did it go?"

"It went just fine, that is, until I identified the land."

"And then?"

"He laughed in my face. He'd heard the whole story— along with the rest of the world—and he advised that I do what everyone else with land in the Grants is doing right now."

"Which is?"

"Holding on to it until the trouble's over or else selling it cheap." Pushing herself up from the chair, she said, "All right, Father. You win. I'll be nice to Haddom because you're right about our needing his help to sell the land. But that's all. As far as any further plots are concerned, I'm telling you here and now you can count me out. I'm not going to marry Haddom as a marquis or a duke, and I'm not going to pretend that I mean to marry him."

"Really, Sarah! You're being completely unfair. Have I even mentioned marriage?"

"You didn't have to. I've known you all my life and I know how you work. The Marquis of Haddom is a pompous fop and I'd rather drown myself in the river than spend my life with him, but that wouldn't stop you from doing your damnedest to tie me to him for life if you believed that it would benefit you in any way."

"Sarah, listen—"

"No. For once you listen to me. Here's what I'm going to do. I'm going to sell the land and when I've sold it I will pay off all your debts. Whatever remains after that we'll divide in half, then we'll each take our halves and go our separate ways. That might sound cruel and unfeeling but it's the best I can do. I spent the first half of my life waiting for you to take care of me, and I've spent the last half taking care of you. But now the time has come for me to take care of myself, and when we leave Albany that's exactly what I intend to do. Alone," she added as she turned to the door.

"Wait, Sarah! Please!"

She stopped, and after several moments she reluctantly turned back to find him standing with his hands hanging limp at his sides.

"You're right," he said slowly. "I haven't been a very good father to you. Maybe I was wrong even to try. When your mother died they tried to take you away, but I wouldn't give you up. I took you to America because I believed they only wanted you for revenge and also because I believed that you belonged with me. Now I wonder if I should have given in and given you up to them. Chances are they would have given you a better life."

He said this with utter sincerity; he wasn't telling her anything he didn't believe himself. That had always been the problem—his willingness to fool them both.

Sarah's shoulders sank gently. "Oh, Father, you did the best you could. I don't hold the past against you. What's done is done. It's the future I care about. I want to know what it's like to walk down the street without trying to spot our creditors before they spot me first. I want to know how it feels not to dread every knock on the door. And men," she continued. "I want to know how it feels to meet a man without wondering what he's heard about me. What you've told him, Father," she added as gently as she could. "I want to know how it feels to trust. Can you understand that?"

He bowed his head in response.

They stood in silence for a moment, then Sarah sighed. "Listen. I give you my word that I'll be nice to the marquis. But I want a promise from you in return. I want you to promise that you'll leave everything concerning the land up to me. Everything," she repeated.

He nodded once. "I do promise, Sarah. I won't interfere."

"Not even with Haddom."

"Not even with him."

"Thank you, Father," she said, meeting his eye. She didn't quite believe him but she'd done the best she could. All she could do now was to hope for the best—and try to ignore that at this moment he was searching for his snuff.

"Outrageous!" Haddom was pacing back and forth behind the dining room chair, too overwrought to sit down even though they were having fresh spring greens for dinner, with sturgeon in a cream sauce and very tender lamb. "To think of a sheriff admitting his impotence that way—to a virtual stranger. I couldn't believe my ears!"

"Did he refuse to issue the warrants?" Sarah asked. Unlike Haddom, she was sitting, but she hadn't touched her food. Her father and Mason were eating but Mason looked preoccupied. She knew he was feeling badly that the surveyor had turned her down.

"He might have refused," Haddom answered, "had I not identified myself as the governor's friend and had I not told him that I had already written explaining the situation and requesting the governor's support. And then, when I offered to put up a reward, do you know what he said? He said he wasn't sure he could get someone to post the broadsides anywhere in the Grants. He was speaking of merely posting them, not putting them into effect! In England a sheriff who spoke that way would very quickly be out of a job!"

Meade paused, his fork hovering. "How big a reward?"

"Twenty pounds for the riffraff and one hundred for Brownell, though even the amount I offered didn't impress our guardian of law and order." Haddom's lip curled with disgust. Today he was wearing a coat of emerald green and a waistcoat embroidered with birds and flowers that waved and rippled as he puffed out his chest. "In the end he issued the warrants because he had no choice. After dinner I shall write the whole sordid tale to his excellency, my friend the governor."

"Twenty pounds for whom?" asked Sarah.

"I can't recall their names. Brownell's brother and a half dozen others. I repeated what you'd said to the sherrif and he knew who they were. When the broadsides are ready, you can see them. I'm paying for those, as well."

"Thank goodness we have you to help us," said Henry Meade.

Sarah shook her head. "But Eli Brownell was the one who defended me. I told you he did a good job."

Haddom gazed down at her, his lips pursed with sympathy. "My dear Mistress Meade, I believe you are still suffering from shock. That man's very participation in such a travesty of justice ought to get him disbarred—if he is a real lawyer, which I tend to doubt. When he is captured, I will see that he is disbarred. You needn't concern yourself with the matter."

"But I am concerned. I don't think it's fair to punish him when he did his best to help me. Besides, practicing law is his livelihood."

Haddom smiled. "As are most women, you are too softhearted, worrying about your enemies instead of yourself."

"I am not softhearted," she said as calmly as she could. "And I'm not worried about anyone. I am talking about justice and fair play."

"Fair play?" The silly smirk vanished from Haddom's face and his pale eyes bulged. "These men are thieves and murderers. They don't deserve fair play. The harshest punishment you could imagine would be too mild for them."

"That not true!" she shot back, recalling what Eli had said. "You can't call them murderers. They've never killed anyone, and as far as their being thieves, I've already told you that Zeke and the others honestly believe the land is theirs. They may be mistaken, but I don't believe they're the villains you make them seem."

"Sarah!" warned her father.

Sarah shook her head. "Please, don't stop me. What I say is true."

"No, it's not!" said Haddom in a different voice; he was no longer lisping and his eyes were somber. "I'm sorry to say so, Mistress Meade, but you don't know half the truth about these men. This morning, after I spoke to the sheriff, I made some inquiries and I learned something shocking about Zeke Brownell. I hadn't intended to tell you because I believed it would upset you unnecessarily, but now I believe that you ought to know the sort of man we're dealing with."

He paused, looking at Sarah as if he still weren't completely sure. Though her mouth had turned to cotton, she said, "Please, tell me what you know."

Haddom glanced at the other men before he replied. "Ten years ago Zeke Brownell murdered his own wife."

There was a terrible silence during which the room seemed to tip, so that Sarah had to grip the table with both hands to hold herself in place. After a moment everything steadied, but now it had turned freezing cold, so cold she had to tense her jaw to keep her teeth from chattering. Words seemed beyond her so she shook her head. She couldn't believe it, she wouldn't believe it about Zeke.

Suddenly Haddom was beside her, holding her hand between his. "Good God, she's freezing. I believe she's had a shock. Stab me, I shouldn't have told her—I'll never forgive myself. Quick, a glass of wine!" He raised the drink to her lips and she managed to forestall him before he spilled it down her front.

"Please! I'm fine," she protested, trying to wriggle away, which was impossible. Haddom was holding her hand too tightly for her to wrest it free, so she gave up trying and turned to Mason, her eyes full of mute appeal. "Did he?" she asked him. "Did he kill his wife?"

"I don't know," Mason said slowly. "Nothing was ever proved. I'm sorry to say I don't recall the details now, but I know that he was arrested and held for some time in jail. He never came to trial. I believe that in the end the charges were dismissed."

"Knowing Brownell, it's not hard to guess how that happened," Haddom muttered, half to himself. "They probably paid the judge a midnight visit and threatened to kidnap his wife." Aloud, he said to Sarah. "Please forgive me, Mistress Meade. I should have kept this distressing story to myself, but I didn't like to hear you wasting your sympathy on that man. I will never forgive myself for upsetting you, but I give you my word that before this is over Brownell will have paid for every wrong he's done. Mason has offered you his protection and you shall have mine, too. Both you and your land will be safe from Zeke Brownell."

"Well put!" Henry Meade said, but shakily. The idea of murder didn't sit well with him. It was one thing to deal with blackguards but this was something else, and he didn't like to think of Sarah having been in the grips of a man who'd killed his wife and gotten away with it. If Brownell had come to the house once, he might come again, and Meade didn't like the idea of coming face-to-face with him.

He glanced at Sarah and thought she must be thinking the same, as her eyes were enormous and her lips were almost white. At her side Haddom was still chafing her hand: as Meade watched, he wondered whether it might not be wiser to try to convince the marquis to buy the land right away. He and Sarah would make less money, but at least they'd be safe. They could go back home to Philadelphia and let Haddom take on Brownell. He raised his wineglass and drank deeply for sustenance.

Sarah stared blankly at Haddom's hands rubbing hers, but she wasn't thinking of Haddom: she was thinking of Zeke. She was remembering the Zeke who had saved her and comforted her during the storm, who had cooked her dinner and dried and combed her hair, and who had caught the ends of the blanket and held them at her throat. Haddom's hands were white and narrow but Zeke's were powerful and wide, tanned and callused from a life of outdoor work. She remembered how she felt his calluses through her chemise, but the memory disturbed her and made her want to cry.

Had he killed his wife? She thought of those big hands closing around a throat and squeezing—it would be so easy. He was so terribly strong, and he had a temper, and he acted before he thought. Later he would be sorry, but by then it would be too late. She remembered how swiftly both Archie and Eli had assured her that Zeke would never hurt a woman—too swiftly perhaps, as though they were both recalling something tragic and regrettable that had happened in the past. She was filled with a longing to get away, to sell the land to whoever would take it and flee these memories.

"Sarah," said Mason. "Sarah, are you all right?"

She turned and nodded blankly. "Yes, thank you. I'm fine."

"You don't look at all well."

"I am." She roused herself. Freeing her hand from Haddom's, she reached for her wine. A swallow of wine helped her and she managed a sort of smile. "It was a shock, that's all."

''It was my fault,'' Haddom said. ''You may forgive me, but I'll never forgive myself.''

''Nonsense.'' Feeling better, she took another sip of wine. ''I was shocked, that's all. But now I'm over it.''

It wasn't completely untrue. The first wave of shock had receded and left her wondering why she should react so violently to the story about Zeke. Was it delayed fear about what he might have done to her—or was it also dismay that the story might be true?

Did it really matter? she wondered, sipping her wine. Right now Zeke's image was vivid in her mind, but over time it would fade until she hardly remembered that she had known him at all. The night they had spent together would be the only one; for a time they would be adversaries, then they would be nothing at all to each other.

She set her glass down. The urge to flee had also passed. She wouldn't let this story upset her plans. She'd stay here and sell the land just as she had planned. The surveyor she'd talked to today wasn't the only one. She'd get other names from Mason, and meanwhile Haddom would offer his rewards and continue to make a fuss, and between the sheriff and the governor maybe he'd raise a troop. It wasn't like her to panic and she still had ample time left in which to sell the land. She wouldn't let herself be distracted by memories and rumors of Zeke. She'd keep her mind on her business and in the end she'd succeed.

She smiled at Haddom, who was still sitting at her side. ''You haven't touched your dinner. It would please me if you would eat.''

''If you promise you will join me.''

''Yes, of course,'' she said, and lifted her fork as though she had the slightest appetite.

Chapter Eight

The Van Kalm mansion was on Thatcher Street; it was south of the Van Rensselaers', though every bit as gracious according to Albany's lights. But Albany's lights were not Haddom's.

"It's a house, that's all," he said with a shrug as he and Sarah's father escorted her up the front steps. "And a modest house at that. Meade, you're from England. You know what I mean."

"To be sure," Meade agreed, "From what you've said, this place doesn't equal the guardhouse at Haddom Hall. Isn't that so, Sarah?"

"To be sure," Sarah agreed. "And by all means let's tell the butler so he can repeat it to the Van Kalms."

She was referring to the servant who had opened the door and was standing at attention as they came up the steps. Haddom stood at attention while Meade gave their names so that the butler could announce them to the company.

Once inside, Meade acted as Haddom's unofficial host, introducing him to the Van Kalms and everyone else he could buttonhole.

"Do you know the Marquis of Haddom? His lordship is the one responsible for posting the broadsides against Brownell and his gang from here to Bennington. He offered the reward himself. He's taken it upon himself to clean the Green Mountain Boys out of New York—and he'll do it."

"With the help of my friend the royal governor," Haddom added modestly.

The musicians were playing. Haddom asked Sarah to dance. "Unless Father would like the first dance," Sarah replied with a sarcasm that only her father caught.

"What an affectionate daughter!" Haddom exclaimed. "I only hope that my own daughters will be half as devoted to me as you are to your father, Mistress Meade. And half as lovely," he added as he took her hand and led her to the floor.

"Your father's a capital fellow," he told her as they danced. "We know so many of the same people at home. I don't suppose you remember England."

"Not much. I was very young when we came here."

"Well, never mind. You'll see it again. You must. There is no comparison between the two societies, though I am the first to admit that this one has its charms—the present company most specifically included."

"You are too kind," she murmured automatically, glancing around for her father, who had disappeared—most likely to wherever the men were playing cards. "I am considering a trip to England, after I sell my land." She said this last with an unconscious sigh. She'd spoken to three more surveyors during the past week and every one of them had told her the same thing the first one had: she could hold the land or sell it cheap, but they wouldn't go up there and risk running into Zeke and the Green Mountain Boys.

"Don't despair," said Haddom as though he had read her mind. "We'll get rid of Brownell and his gang in the end. If the sheriff is too frightened to go after them, we'll send the army. I've already suggested as much to his excellency and I am expecting his answer any day. I'd like to see the expression on Brownell's face when a company of his majesty's regulars come knocking on his door."

The marquis smiled to himself and Sarah smiled, too, but at a rather different image from the one Haddom had drawn. In his, no doubt he stood with a drawn sword while the soldiers deftly put Zeke under arrest. In hers, Zeke swung and bellowed, and scarlet flew everywhere as the redcoats scattered before Zeke's furious assault. Then she remembered the story about his wife and her smile disappeared.

"Do you think the governor will give us men?"

"I don't see why not," replied Haddom. "And if he insists that I lead the men, I won't refuse. When my country needs me, I am always glad to serve."

He said this at the moment the dance called for a bow, which he executed with exaggerated grace while Sarah curtsied demurely. All around them people were doing the same, moving in set patterns like a bunch of pretty, mechanical dolls. Sarah had been to these dances for as long as she could recall; roomfuls of silk and satin, buzzing with gossip and lies. Suddenly the evening stretched out endlessly and all she wanted was to get away from Haddom, from the party, from everything.

Haddom was chatting on, completely oblivious. "When you do go to England I hope I have the honor of showing you Haddom Hall. At the risk of sounding immodest, I must confess that it is generally considered one of the showplaces of the country. I bought it from a fellow who'd let it go to hell. All my friends told me I was crazy to pay good money for such an old wreck of a place, but I saw the potential behind those crumbling walls, and in the end everyone admitted— Hello, what's happening?"

The dance wasn't over but the music abruptly stopped. "What's wrong? What are they doing?" Haddom demanded from left to right, but the other dancers were as perplexed as he, everyone standing on tiptoe in an effort to see.

Whatever it was was happening at the far end of the room. Sarah watched as dancers halted in midstep and hushed speculation filled the room. She stood on tiptoe but she couldn't see because everyone between her and the doorway was doing the same. Then suddenly the crowd fell away and there, across the dance floor, she saw Zeke Brownell.

He was standing in the doorway with two of the other Boys. One was red-haired Remember, the erstwhile judge.

She recognized the other but didn't know his name. She glanced behind her at the garden doors and saw that two Boys had appeared, no doubt to make sure that no one left. Boys stood at the other windows—at least a dozen men in all. In contrast to the satins and silks that filled the room they were wearing their trusty homespun, decorated by their sprigs of green.

"What is this?" Haddom demanded, but in a lowered voice. Sarah didn't answer; she suspected the marquis would have his answer, and all too soon.

She was right. From his post in the doorway, Zeke surveyed the room slowly and with the air of one who expects to be amused. His brows rose a little higher with each frill and furbelow, each excess in headdress, each unrestrained frothing of lace he regarded. He surveyed the party with the same sort of look he might survey the members of some exotic East Indian tribe. Sarah watched the guests react to his look: some swelled with indignation while others shrank back, abashed. Fingers toyed with ruffles or patted rolls of hair. Pampered hands fluttered nervously to décolletage.

She herself stood motionless as Zeke's eyes moved slowly but surely toward her. She braced herself in preparation.

Then his eyes found her. She felt her body jolt in reaction as their gazes met and locked, and for the first moment the room disappeared and they were as alone as they'd been that night in the stormy woods. She knew she wasn't breathing but she couldn't help herself. If he looked at her much longer she knew that she'd faint.

She could see the effort it took for Zeke to drag his eyes away from her and on to the marquis. Contempt and maybe anger filled them for a space. Then suddenly he was smiling his most maddening smile.

"Good evening," he said, turning to address the room. "We got your letter and here we are." When nobody responded, he spread his arms out wide. "Aren't you going to arrest me? Isn't anyone interested in earning one hundred pounds?" He turned in another direction. "What about you—or you?"

Zeke stepped forward and the crowd fell back. "What's the matter?" he chided them. "A man could make a small fortune by collecting the lot of us. What—nobody?" he demanded as they all shrank back. Their cowardice amused him; he threw back his head and laughed. "Well, boys, if we're not going to be arrested then we might as well dance. It would be a pity to let good music go to waste!"

When Zeke waved, the windows opened and more of the Boys stepped in. "Half of you stay at the windows in case any of our friends here get it in mind to leave before the party's over. The rest of you best choose up partners to dance."

He turned to the musicians, who were watching him agape. "Close your mouths," he commanded, "and play us something that lets a man kick up his heels. None of that mincing popinjay tripe you were playing before. When the Green Mountain Boys dance, they like to dance!"

The musicians glanced at one another, then one of the violinists struck a tentative note. The other joined him and the rest followed. They started with a wobble but quickly hit their pace. "There you go!" Zeke applauded. "Let's do 'em justice, boys! Let's show these lucky ladies what a real party is like!"

Grinning and shoving one another, the Boys fanned out, selecting their partners from among the frightened guests. All of the women asked accepted, and most of the men acquiesced, except for one stout man in a red velvet coat. He swore that Remember would not lay a hand on his wife, whereupon Remember hoisted him up by his stock and deposited him, red-faced and choking, into a chair at the back of the room. Then Remember claimed his lady, who was still in shock.

Almost every Boy looked at Sarah as his eyes circled the crowd but none made a move to ask her to dance. She understood this as Zeke's directive. She could almost hear him saying, "But not Sally, boys, I'll take her myself."

Take her, would he? Did he suppose she'd submit as meekly as those women on the floor who were stumbling through the first steps of a schottische in the enthusiastic grip of Remember and the other Boys.

"The effrontery!" Haddom raged beneath his breath as he watched the spectacle.

Sarah glanced at him. "You heard what he said. Why don't you arrest him? You all outnumber the Boys more than two to one, and by the looks of it, none of them have guns."

"You can't tell," muttered Haddom. "They might have them beneath their coats."

"Not the dancers," said Sarah, which was true, for they were swinging with an abandon that raised their coattails in the air and would have shaken loose any hidden gun. Most of the ladies were doing their best to be prim, but one of the Van Rensselaer daughters was giggling.

At her side she felt Haddom stiffen, and when she turned her head she saw that Zeke had left the door and was crossing the room to them.

When he arrived he ignored Haddom as he greeted her, not with a courtly flourish but with a familiar grin. "Evening, Sally."

She nodded coolly. "Good evening."

Zeke's grin broadened. "Tut-tut, Sally. Where have your manners gone? Here I am waiting for you to introduce me to your friend."

She was about to snap, "Introduce yourself!" when she realized that if she said that, Zeke would only laugh. So she said in the same cool tone, "May I introduce the Marquis of Haddom. Mr. Zeke Brownell."

Zeke whistled. "Marquis, eh? Well now, Sally, you haven't done half-bad." His gaze swept over Haddom, but before the marquis could speak he added, "I hope his lordship has no objection to my having this dance with you."

"He may not, but I do," Sarah said, and felt a flash of satisfaction at Zeke's start of surprise. But of course in the next instant he threw back his head and laughed.

"That's what I like about you, Sally! You don't give in. You put up your nose to my invitation and it doesn't matter that I've come all this way just to have this dance with you."

"I thought you'd come here to thumb your nose at us."

"Not at you, Sally, and even if I have, that doesn't change the fact that I am here and I'm pretty well set on having this dance with you. So what will it be—will you come on your own or will I have to help you out like I did the last time?"

She knew what that meant. If she wouldn't go willingly he meant to sling her over his shoulder and carry her onto the floor, and she knew that this roomful of people watching wouldn't bother him. To the contrary, the crowd watching would make it more fun. She had a sudden vision of the faces of the watching guests if Zeke did upend her as he was threatening to, and suddenly, despite her anger, she was seized by the urge to laugh.

Zeke's eyes sparkled as if he'd read her mind. She tossed her head and answered, "Have it your way. I don't really care."

"I see you took my advice, Sally," Zeke said when they'd joined the other dancers and were cantering through the schottische.

"About what?"

"About finding a wealthy man. His lordship looks like he can afford to pay a good price for the land, though I can't say he strikes me as a worthy adversary—not for my talents, at least."

"You're insufferably conceited," she said breathlessly as Zeke's hands gripped her by the waist and almost lifted her off the floor as he spun her around. "Haddom's the one who got the warrants for your arrest. He's also written to the governor about sending the army after you."

Zeke glanced around at Haddom, who seemed on the verge of a fit. "He won't," he said briefly.

"How can you be so sure?"

"Because I know what men like your marquis want. They want to turn free land into another New York, with lords of the manor getting richer every day from the sweat of tenant farmers who'll never own their land. But they won't do it," he said with sudden bitterness. "I give you my word on that. I'd die before I'd see the Grants turned into another New York." He spun her around so hard she couldn't catch her breath, and by the time she caught it, his bitterness had vanished and his eyes were twinkling again. "You're a fine dancer, Sally."

"You're not," she replied, trying to fill her lungs with enough air to keep up. Haddom would have taken umbrage if she'd said that to him, but Zeke only threw back his head and laughed the great full laugh that nobody else could match.

The sound of it was infectious. She'd forgotten how big he was, how solid and unyielding, how masterful his grip. She felt a wave of something that was both weakness and strength. Confused by the force of the feeling, she looked away.

"I don't see Eli."

"This isn't his kind of caper. Besides, he's our lawyer, and if he gets himself arrested, who'll be left to argue us out of jail?"

"Are you worried you'll be arrested?"

"Terrified." He laughed.

"You could be yet," she told him, turning her face away so that he wouldn't see the spark of humor in her eyes. "How did you get in?"

"Just like you—came up the front steps. We wanted the butler to announce us but he seemed to have lost his voice. Sam and Jasper are helping him with the door. They're letting in all comers but nobody gets out. Besides, who would want to leave a fine party like this!"

Turning his head, Zeke cast a glance around the room. Unsure of direction and afraid to stop, the musicians were repeating the schottische, much to the apparent delight of the Boys. Unlike the gentry, who weren't so used to exercise, they seemed to gain spirit as the dance progressed.

Their partners were not having quite so good a time. Headdresses tilted as pads were jarred out of place, while hoop skirts twirled like particolored tops and every lady was bright red in the face. Although most of them looked as though they'd prefer to be sitting down, the Van Rensselaer daughter was still giggling and one stately looking matron was dancing a jig while her outraged husband watched helplessly.

In spite of herself, Sarah laughed. "They won't let you get away with this."

"They won't have any choice—for all your beau looks as though he wants to murder me."

"He's not my beau," she said sharply.

"All right, then, your friend. Whatever he is, he's certainly got murder in his eyes. But what makes me so certain that if I challenged him to a duel he'd flop like a fish out of water trying to wriggle out of it?"

"Probably because of the way you'd try to bully him into it."

"I'd rather be a bully than a fake, like your marquis. But of course he's got money—you can tell from the cut of his clothes."

"What do you know about clothing?" she asked, bristling at the way he kept referring to Haddom as hers.

He grinned, delighted as always to have raised her ire. "Enough to know that this blue you're wearing is the color for you. It turns your eyes the color of the hills behind Lake Champlain just after sunset. I don't know the name of the color. I don't think it has a name."

She felt herself blushing with pleasure and also with surprise. Men had been paying her compliments since she could recall, and mostly she didn't believe them and was offended or bored.

Of course Zeke noticed. He leaned close to her and murmured, "Careful, Sally, you shouldn't look so pleased. The marquis is watching you and he'll get the wrong idea. You'll make him think that you've developed an illogical weakness for me."

His closeness made her skin burn and she pulled away. "You are insufferably conceited!" she said for the second time. Then she asked, "Where are we going?"

"For a breath of fresh air. Isn't that what they call it in polite society?" As he spoke he was guiding her toward the garden doors with a firmness she couldn't have resisted if she'd thought to try.

The Boys who were guarding the doors winked as she and Zeke danced past and into the coolness of the early summer night. Zeke was right about the air here. It was pleasantly cool and full of the scents of the flowers blooming unseen in the dark.

"Mmm. This is better." Zeke took a deep breath and the pace of his dancing slowed. "I start feeling suffocated when I'm in a place like that. Too many people too close together—my skin starts to feel too small. I don't know how you can stand it."

"It's better than lots of things. Such as being carried upside down over someone's back," she answered, glancing back at the house. She could see the guests through the windows, including the marquis, who'd moved to the doorway and was arguing with the guards. "Look—Haddom's seen us and he's ready to have a fit."

"Let him," Zeke said shortly without bothering to turn. They had stopped dancing but he still held her hand, though he held it between them where Haddom couldn't see. "You were wrong about me coming here to thumb my nose. I don't think I'd have come here if it hadn't been for you. I think about you, Sally. Do you ever think of me?"

Her heart, which had slowed when they'd stopped dancing, had begun to race again. "Sometimes," she said, her tongue darting out to lick her lips, which had begun tingling. From the way he was looking she knew what he had in mind; she felt a wave of longing and also one of shock. "Zeke . . ." she murmured. "People are watching."

His fingers tightened on hers and his eyes wouldn't let her go. "Does that bother you, being watched and talked about? Do you really care so much what people say?"

For the first time since she'd seen him in the doorway that dark fear returned as she remembered that he'd been arrested for murdering his wife. Before she could stop herself she stiffened and pulled away.

Zeke frowned. "What is it, Sally?"

"Nothing." She turned her face toward the darkness, away from the open doors. "Nothing at all. Don't—don't you want to dance anymore?"

He drew a long breath and released her hand. "No, I don't want to dance. I don't mind being insulted but I can't stand it when people lie."

She began to deny it, but there was no point. She knew him well enough to know there was no use: he'd keep at her until he had the truth. Or worse, she realized, he'd give up on her. She said, "I heard . . . something."

"Tell me what you heard."

"I heard that you were arrested for murdering your wife."

She'd turned back when she said it so that she could see his face, and from the way his features contorted she thought he might lash out. Instinctively she cringed sideways before she could catch herself.

Zeke saw. His face flattened with the shock, and despite the darkness she could see his pain. "You believe that I would hit you?"

"I—no." She shook her head. Their eyes were locked together and suddenly she was filled with a dread that had nothing to do with fear. She knew he wouldn't hit her but she thought that he might leave. Indoors the schottische had finally ended and a contradanse had begun. The guards must have threatened Haddom because he was no longer at the doors.

Zeke glanced toward the mansion, then back at her again. "Do you believe I would do such a thing?"

She looked down and answered, "Not intentionally."

"But I might have killed her out of anger—is that what you mean?"

"I—I don't know." She could feel the tears stinging her eyes. She knew how her words sounded but she didn't want to lie. "I suppose I thought it must be some sort of accident." She shook her head. "I'm sorry."

Zeke didn't answer and when she glanced up she saw that he was looking at the mansion again. She expected that he'd walk away and leave her standing there, but instead he murmured, "You shouldn't be. I'm the one who ought to apologize for interrogating you. I asked you to tell the truth and that's what you did. Besides, after what you've seen of me, what else could you think?"

"I could think you had a kind heart."

Her words hovered in the air as Zeke turned to look at her harder than she'd ever been looked at in her life. She knew he was searching for any sign of a lie and she knew he wouldn't find one.

At last he relaxed and a glint of the old humor stole into his eyes. "You wouldn't be trying to flatter me out of the land, would you now, Sally?"

She relaxed, too. "What do you think?" Then, before he could turn the whole thing into a joke, she said, "Is that why you keep Archie up in the woods and don't let him go to school, because you're afraid of what people would tell him about you?"

"I'm not afraid of people!" He drew back.

"I didn't mean—"

He cut her off abruptly, gesturing toward the house. "What makes you so sure that living like this would be so good for the boy? What do you think he'd learn here that he can't learn where he is?"

"That people are people," she said quietly. "That you can't condemn them just because of how they dress or where they live."

"In other words you'd like to turn him into one of you. A Yorker," he said with the same bitterness she'd heard before.

"You know very well I'm not a Yorker." She matched him tone for tone. "And I know Yorkers who are every bit as brave and honest as you. That's what Archie needs to learn so he doesn't have to grow up weighed down by misconception and hate. So he can have a real choice about what he wants from life instead of telling himself that he's got all he wants and then making enough racket to drown out his own doubts."

"You're talking about me, aren't you?"

"No, I'm talking about your son."

"I don't see why you care so much about one back-woods boy."

"Because he's a child and he ought to be more than an accomplice to his father's schemes."

"Was that what you were, Sally?"

"That's none of your affair. I don't care what people are saying but I want to go back in." She turned away before Zeke could read the truth in her face and thus gain one more weapon to tease her with.

Too late. He caught her by the arm and turned her back to him, and as he did she raised her head, preferring to have him see the truth than to have him believe her too ashamed or frightened to look him in the eye.

"What if I was?" she challenged, but he didn't reply. He held her there and looked at her until she stopped being angry and began to be afraid, not of Zeke and those rumors but of herself, of the way his and only his presence could make her feel.

He said, very softly, "Sally!" and she shivered at the sound. The world shrank for a moment till it hung reflected in Zeke's eyes.

The moment ended. He raised his head and said, "I guess we've had enough dancing for one night," loudly enough for the Boys at the door to hear, and when he let her arm go, Sarah turned and walked back to the house.

Haddom was waiting as she came through the garden doors and grabbed her so hard he almost knocked her off her feet. She gasped, "What are you doing?" but he didn't answer because he was waiting for Zeke. Thrusting her behind him, he faced Zeke as he came in.

"You backwoods hoodlum! You immoral cur! Don't imagine for a minute that you'll get away with this! If it weren't illegal, I'd call you out and fight you one-on-one!"

A slow smile spread across Zeke's lips as his eyes surveyed Haddom's silk and lace as they'd done before. "So you say. But if it were my lady whose honor was involved, I don't think I'd let a little thing like the law stand in my way."

"Obviously not!" snapped Haddom. "You've got no respect for the law, you and your ruffian friends! Then hear me, because I intend to teach you that respect. I intend to bring you to justice for everything you've done. For everything," he repeated in a tone that made Sarah cringe for fear he was about to mention the rumor about Zeke's wife.

But Zeke wasn't cringing. He looked even more amused. "I'll look forward to the lesson," he said genially. "As my grandfather used to say, a body's never too old to learn. Mistress Meade—" he bowed to Sarah "—I wish you a good evening and thank you for the dance. I won't wish you good luck with the land, since you've got his lordship's help, and with help like his lordship's, why would a person need luck?"

He didn't wait for her answer before he turned to the rest of the room. "Ladies and gentlemen, on behalf of all the Boys, I want to thank you all for entertaining us—especially the ladies. We'd always heard that Yorkers were uppity but I guess you folks changed our minds, taking us into your home this way and giving us so much fun. I can't think of when we've had such a fine time. Isn't that right, boys?"

The Boys, most of them still short of breath from the dancing, agreed that it was.

"I'm sorry to say we have to be going, but like they say, all good things have to end. Maybe we'll do it again in the future, or maybe next time we'll do something else." He winked at the Van Rensselaer girl, whose parents had reclaimed her and looked ready to eat her alive as soon as they got her home. Despite this, she winked back and giggled into her sleeve.

"One last thing," said Zeke. "We don't want you to stop the party just because we have to leave. We want you to keep on dancing and enjoying yourselves, so Jasper and Remember here will be staying behind in case any of you take it into your minds to come after us—to show us the way out of town or thank us or some such thing. Jasper and Remember will be right outside the door. Oh, and one more thing—they've both of them got guns."

As quickly as they'd come in, the Boys disappeared, leaving behind a silence that lasted until the hoofbeats faded outside in the street. Then everybody began to talk at once.

Haddom whirled on Sarah. "What did he say to you? What were you talking about when he took you outside?"

She opened her mouth, reconsidered, then said, "Child-rearing techniques."

"Child rearing!" Haddom stared as though she'd gone mad. "I've never seen such an outrage!"

Throughout the ballroom other men were saying the same, exclaiming to one another and glaring at the door. Sarah didn't see her father anywhere and guessed that he'd taken shelter as soon as the Boys had come in and wouldn't show his face until they were all safely gone.

"If you want them," she said to Haddom, "why not go after them now? Two men posted at the door can't stop all of you."

"And why should we believe him when he said two? For all we know there might be two dozen waiting outside and all of them armed, whereas we have nothing but what there is in this house. You heard his warning—people might get hurt. Women," he added, looking around the room.

Sarah didn't answer but she stared at him thoughtfully. So this was the knight in shining armor who was to help her get her land—a man who'd rather rant and rage in safety than risk danger in pursuit. All in all it didn't bode well for the fight ahead. Neither did the effect Zeke's touch had had on her, nor her relief in believing he hadn't killed his wife. Those things were supposed to mean nothing and she and Zeke weren't supposed to meet. Things were definitely not going the way she'd intended them to.

Chapter Nine

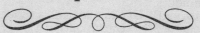

The next day all of Albany was atwitter about Zeke Brownell's appearance at the Van Kalms' ball. Men were offering to add to Haddom's hundred-pound reward and women were swearing that they'd never go out unprotected, not even to the market in the middle of the day. The Van Rensselaer daughter had been confined to her room and was rumored to have told her parents that she didn't care if they kept her in for a year because she'd never had as much fun in her life.

Sarah had been right about her father. He'd been playing cards in the parlor when the Boys had arrived. When the others had rushed out to see what the fuss was about, he'd hidden himself in a cupboard and remained there so long he'd actually fallen asleep, and if he hadn't been snoring, she would never have discovered him.

Haddom had ranted all the way home and in the morning he had awakened to rant some more. He'd gone off to see the sheriff after breakfast and had returned sometime after noon to report that, in the sheriff's opinion, last night's escapade would make it more and not less difficult to enlist recruits willing to ride to Bennington.

"Would you go?" the sheriff had demanded to Haddom's utter disgust.

"Of course I would!" Haddom had snapped in retort. "I'd go on a moment's notice—given sufficient support. You can't expect me to go there on my own."

The sheriff had assured him that he expected no such thing, after which Haddom stormed back home to write yet another letter to his friend the governor.

The worst news for Sarah was that George Mason had been called away on another business trip. He had to leave that very morning for New York.

"I'll be gone two weeks at most," he assured her, and she did her very best to act as if she didn't mind. "I wouldn't go if it wasn't necessary, but I'm afraid it is. I've instructed all the servants to lock the doors at night and not open them to anyone. The night watch has been alerted and they'll look out for you."

"No one will try to harm us," she answered honestly. She wouldn't miss Mason's protection; she'd miss his guidance and steadying influence. Speaking to herself as much as him, she added, "I've managed things with Father for ten years and I guess I can manage with Zeke Brownell for two weeks."

At that Mason smiled. "When you put it that way, I guess you can. Is there anything you need before I go? A letter of credit...?"

"No. Nothing at all," she told him firmly as if she weren't almost broke. But she was so used to that condition she hardly noticed it. Besides, she had deeper concerns on her mind. Zeke for starters—and not just as he related to her need to sell the land. In the past week she'd managed to convince herself that the night they'd spent together had been a fluke and best forgotten since neither of them had any place in the other's life.

But last night something had changed. Lying awake in the early hours after she'd come home from the Van Kalms', she'd made all sorts of excuses to herself. She wouldn't have enjoyed dancing with Zeke if she hadn't been so bored. In fact, she hadn't really enjoyed the dancing at all, since dancing with him was more like galloping on a horse. But then she'd remembered that, when she'd told him so, he'd thrown back his head and the sound of his laughter had made her feel alive.

The truth was that she was attracted to him. The very things that should have repelled her had the opposite effect: his size, his manners, his resolution to keep the land. He was bold, fearless, exciting, like no one she'd ever met. He could roar like a lion and be gentle as a dove, and when he touched her he made her feel things she'd never felt with any other man.

What did it signify? Everything. Nothing. After a total of three hours of sleep, she was too tired to think. She'd think tomorrow after she'd had some sleep. For now the important thing was not to lose sight of her goal, which was to find a surveyor and then to sell the land.

She drifted through the day like a sleepwalker in a fog, went to bed very early and immediately fell asleep. She was so tired she didn't even dream. She was floating in velvet blackness when the maid's hand on her arm rudely shook her awake.

"Heaven preserve us! He's back, Mistress Meade, and he's asking for you!"

"Who's back?" Sarah muttered drowsily, burrowing into the bolster and away from the maid's urgent words.

"Zeke Brownell, that's who! He's right outside the front door and he's asking for you!"

"Zeke!" She bolted awake so fast that she knocked her forehead against the maid's. "But why? What's he doing?" Was she dreaming? She rubbed her head.

The maid was too frightened to rub hers. "Just standing there and calling for you to come out. When I told him I wouldn't open the door he told me to fetch you. Mistress Meade, I'm scared!" Her fingers clutched at Sarah again.

Sarah pried them loose and pushed the covers back, swinging her feet to the floor. "What about the others? My father and the marquis?"

"I came to you first. Should I wake them?"

"No, don't," Sarah said. The last thing she wanted was another scene between Haddom and Zeke. "Go back and tell Mr. Brownell that I'll be right down."

"I can't! I'm scared!" the maid sniveled. "What if he knocks down the door? What if he grabs me and takes me away?"

"He won't grab you," Sarah answered impatiently as she reached for her robe. She didn't want to take the time to get fully dressed for fear Zeke would get impatient and start making noise. She'd stop only long enough to put on her robe and brush her hair. "Go!" she told the maid.

"I can't, mistress! You can do whatever you want to but I can't go down there alone!" She was clinging to the bedpost and trembling.

Sarah dropped the brush on the table. "Oh, never mind. Whatever I look like, he's seen me looking worse. Go to your room and stay there, just don't wake the marquis— and don't worry about Mr. Brownell. He doesn't want to hurt anyone, he only wants the land."

She lit a candle from the maid's and started down the stairs. The hall was so quiet she thought perhaps he'd gone. Moving close to the front door, she called softly, "Zeke?"

"I'm out here." He spoke in a normal tone.

She leaned her forehead against the door and closed her eyes. A voice in her was warning not to open the door, less because she feared him than because she feared herself.

"Open the door, Sally."

So much for the warning voice. She opened her eyes, threw the bolt, turned the knob and pulled.

Zeke was standing on the stoop. Archie was with him. So was Thumper, Archie's dog.

"But why?" she murmured.

"Here's the boy," said Zeke. "You think you can do a better job? Go ahead and have your try."

"My try?" she repeated, struggling to understand.

"You're so keen to civilize him. I'm giving you a chance." Then before she could answer, he turned and strode down the path, vaulted onto his waiting horse and galloped away.

Sarah stood where he'd left her, gaping at the empty road. At her feet Thumper sat down to scratch a flea.

She turned slowly to Archie as a door opened some-where upstairs. "He isn't joking?"

"No, ma'am," Archie said.

"But—" began Sarah, when a voice from the hall cut her off.

"What is going on here?"

It was Haddom, dressed in a velvet robe and with a tur-ban on his head. He must have heard Zeke's arrival but taken time to dress. He looked at Sarah in her night robe; he looked at the boy and the dog. "What's going on?" he repeated.

"This is Archie," Sarah began, and stopped herself just short of adding Archie's last name. "He's the, uh, son of an acquaintance of mine. His father has to be away on business, so he's left the boy in my care." Thumper was scratching loudly. "He's also left his dog."

"I can see that," snapped Haddom as his eyes swept Archie up and down, from his bump-toed farm shoes to his homespun shirt. "What sort of acquaintance?" he de-manded. "And what's his father's name?"

"Brownell," said Archie before Sarah could think of a lie.

Haddom recoiled. "Brownell! You can't be serious! You don't mean to tell me that he's Zeke Brownell's son?"

Sarah might have denied it if she hadn't been certain that Archie would tell the truth. Cornered, she nodded. "Yes, he's Zeke's son but there's no use waking up the whole town to tell them he's here." She beckoned to Archie. "You'd better come inside."

"He had better not!" Haddom sprang forward to block the door. "I forbid it! I will not allow you to harbor a criminal's son. He must be turned over to the authorities. We'll send for the sheriff or, better yet, I'll take him there myself."

"You'll do no such thing!" Instinctively, Sarah moved to stand between Haddom and the boy. "Whatever his fa-ther might have done, Archie is only a boy. Besides," she added firmly, "this is Mr. Mason's house and it's up to him to decide who can stay."

"In his absence I'm deciding."

"Oh no you're not." She hadn't in her wildest dreams imagined Archie here, but now that he was here she felt an obligation to keep him safe—beyond which she was fed up with Haddom's attitude. When there was no chance of acting, he made a lot of noise, but when it was time for action, he could only make an excuse. She didn't mean to let him do to the defenseless son what he didn't dare do to the father. "I've got every bit as much right to decide as you."

"You might," agreed Haddom, "if you were in your right mind. But to consider keeping this creature—creatures..." he amended, glancing disdainfully at Thumper, who was deep in combat with the flea. "No," he concluded firmly. "These two will not stay."

"They will," Sarah said in a tone that even Thumper recognized. "If you'll move out of the way we can go inside."

Haddom stood where he was. Reaching out, he took her hand and, to Sarah's increasing annoyance, laid it upon his chest. "My dear Mistress Meade. You know I am your devoted servant in all things, but I cannot let you indulge in this foolishness. I cannot believe you are even considering it." He paused, then added, "And at the risk of appearing ungallant, may I remind you how little chance you have of successfully disposing of your land without my help and my connections?"

He spoke with the conviction of a man used to having his own way, but in her mind Sarah could hear Zeke roaring about where Haddom could take his connections and what he could do with them. Glancing at Archie, she wondered if he heard the same.

"Mistress Meade," Haddom repeated, tightening his grip on her hand.

"You may remind me," she said calmly. "But it won't do any good. I'm not turning the boy over to the authorities and I won't let you do it, either, and if you try I promise I'll make a scene that will embarrass you in front of the entire city of Albany. The boy is staying, and if you don't like it, you can leave. While you're about it, you can also let go of my hand."

Haddom's face turned pale then red, and he released her hand. "This is madness, Mistress Meade," he said in a strange strangled voice. "I shall inform Mr. Mason of your shocking behavior as soon as he returns. I shall also inform your father!" From the way he was looking, Sarah half expected him to threaten to tell the governor, too.

He didn't. He spun away from the doorstep and stalked across the unlighted hall and back up the stairs. The sound of his door slamming echoed through the house.

Archie let out his breath. "Jumpin' Jehovah! You sure told him, didn't you." He was staring at her in admiration. The dog was staring, too.

"Yes, I told him. And I'll pay for it."

"That don't count," said Archie. "What counts is principle. If you believe in something, you got to take a stand."

She looked down at Archie, at his shaggy hair and stubborn jaw, at the way his eyes were shining with his belief in principle, a belief he had certainly learned from Zeke—Zeke, who had just deposited him at her door. "Doesn't," she corrected. "That doesn't count. Come inside, Archie, and let's find you a place to sleep."

"What about Thumper?"

She'd forgotten about the dog. "We'll leave him in the backyard or in the barn."

"We always sleep together."

"Then you'll learn to sleep apart." She saw Archie's eyes open at the sudden edge in her voice. She was sorry but she couldn't help it. She'd had enough for one night: first Zeke, then Haddom and now a flea-bitten hound. "You take him around to the stable then I'll let you in through the back. What have you brought with you?"

"Just this." Archie held up a bundle wrapped in a knotted cloth. A bundle, for heaven's sake.

"I'll take it," Sarah said. "See to the dog quickly so we can all get to bed."

Her first thought was to put Archie in the kitchen, but she didn't want the cook to find him in the morning and have a fit. Besides, despite his appearance, he'd come to be civilized, so she took him upstairs to the bedroom next to hers—and across from Haddom's, but that couldn't be helped.

As she lighted a candle for him, she realized that she had no idea in what sort of a place Zeke lived—a shack with a dirt floor or a proper house. She wouldn't have put it past him to live in a cave in the woods, but Archie made no comment about the room and even allowed her to tuck him into bed. As she blew out his candle, she heard a strange eerie noise.

"That's Thumper," said Archie. "He's accustomed to being with me."

"He'll learn to be without you."

"I don't know."

"Well, I do. Good night, Archie."

"Good night, ma'am."

An hour later Sarah heard Archie's door creak and the soft pad of his footsteps in the hall. A few minutes later the footsteps returned, accompanied by the telltale padding of four paws. She didn't get up to tell him that the dog had to sleep outside: she was only grateful that the awful yowling had stopped.

She was awakened from a deep sleep by a commotion outside her door. The maid's exclamations and Archie's protests were almost drowned out by the barking of the dog. Without pausing to put on her robe she opened her door and found the maid doing her best to drag Archie toward the steps while Thumper had a mouthful of Archie's breeches and was pulling the opposite way.

"Let him go," Sarah ordered.

The maid stopped in midstruggle and turned. "But, mistress, I caught him prowling in the hall!"

"He wasn't prowling. He slept here last night."

"Slept here, mistress?" the maid said, aghast.

"Yes, slept," Sarah told her. Her eyes were on Archie, who was staring at the floor with all but his stubborn jaw hidden by his hair. He was barefoot and dressed in his familiar homespun shirt and breeches, from which the dog had just torn out a sizable chunk. Through it she could see the dingy nap of woolen underwear. She stared at him for a wordless moment, by now awake enough to decide that as soon as they'd had breakfast she would take him directly to the barber shop and then to the tailor to have him fitted for a decent set of clothes.

"And the dog, mistress?" asked the maid, who had stopped looking dumbfounded and was now looking annoyed. Thumper had also released the boy and was going after a flea, his busy hind leg beating a tattoo on the floor. Sarah watched him scratching, then she heaved a sigh. No barber could help Thumper but he might improve with a bath.

"The dog came with the boy. Why don't you take him outside, Archie, until it's time to eat."

"Everywhere?" asked Sarah as they walked down Market Street, Thumper's thin whine fading in the distance behind them. Sarah had insisted that the dog remain back at the house.

Archie shrugged in answer. "He's used to me. Ain't no reason he can't come with me, places I usually go."

"He'll learn," muttered Sarah, wondering to herself what the neighbors must be thinking by this point. So much for not advertising Archie's presence to the world, but the alternative was to have Thumper trailing them down the street, and people were already turning to watch as they passed.

"He ain't a bad dog," said Archie.

Sarah didn't reply. She told herself that things would be better once she had Archie cleaned up and looking like everyone else.

She deposited him with the barber her father used, along with the most basic description of what she hoped to achieve. Then she went off in search of the next surveyor on George Mason's list. She finally found the man's house, only to learn that he was out but that if she cared to see him she might return later on. She noted the address, then went back to the barber's shop to find a half-shorn Archie waiting in the street. When he caught sight of her approaching he set his jaw.

"What happened?"

"Goddamn Yorker devil was scalping me!"

She took a deep breath, counted to ten and let it out. Then, taking hold of Archie's arm, she led him back into the shop.

"Don't bring him in here," warned the barber as soon as she opened the door. "Lest you've got a muzzle!"

"What are you talking about?"

"Ornery whelp bit me!" The barber held out his nand to show her the arc of Archie's teeth marks across his thumb.

Sarah looked at Archie, whose mouth was mutinous. "He won't bite you again," she said grimly.

"No, ma'am," the barber declared. "You can have your money so long as you spare me the boy."

She tried to argue but the barber was adamant, so she finally found another barber a couple of streets away. This time she laid down the law with Archie before they went in, and she stayed with him to be sure that he behaved.

It was just as bad at the tailor's. Archie twisted and turned and grumbled that the man was intentionally poking him, while the tailor glared at Sarah as though it were all her fault. She ordered him two pair of breeches, a coat and two shirts, and promised the tailor extra if he'd have them ready soon. Walking home with Archie, she felt as though she'd spent the morning on a battlefield. But at least the dog had stopped howling in the two hours since they'd left.

They found Haddom waiting for them at the door, his expression ominous, something grayish and raveled clenched in his fist.

"Look at this!" he commanded, thrusting the object at them. Looking more closely, Sarah saw that it was a wig, or rather the remains of one. Whole patches of hair had been pulled out and what remained was tattered and torn. "That bloody dog did this!" Haddom fumed, shaking the wig at Archie with such menace that the boy stepped back.

Haddom turned on Sarah. "You see! I warned you not to do this!"

"I'll buy you a new wig."

"Damn new wigs! I'm giving you one final warning to get rid of that boy!"

Without waiting for her answer, Haddom stormed past them and out the door, still clutching the battered wig in his hand. There was a moment's silence, then a familiar yowl.

The servant, who'd been watching the scene from the parlor door, said, "We tried to keep him outside but he made so much noise that finally we locked him upstairs in the boy's room."

Sarah followed Archie upstairs to his room. Thumper was so glad to see him he almost knocked him down. She closed the door behind her.

"Archie," she began, when, to her surprise and horror, she began to laugh. She tried to stop herself but it was no use, not with the image of Haddom so vividly in her mind. Thumper stopped lunging at Archie and turned to watch, no doubt concluding that he'd been brought into a household of lunatics.

When the fit of laughter ended she wiped her eyes and said, "Archie, things can't go on like this. You've got to control Thumper. Do you understand?"

"Yes'm," Archie muttered, looking at the floor.

"I doubt that you wanted to come here, but here you are, and there are things I mean to teach you before you leave. You may not believe it, but these are worthwhile things and I intend to teach you them the best I can. You will find me fair and reasonable if you are fair with me. I may not roar as loud as your father but I know how to hold my own. Do you understand what I'm saying?"

Archie inclined his head.

"Good. I'm going out now, and when I get back I want to hear that you and Thumper were perfectly behaved, because if you aren't, Thumper is going back to Bennington. Do we understand each other?"

"Yes'm," Archie said.

Chapter Ten

Despite Archie's agreement, she left with a sense of unease that followed her as she retraced her steps to the surveyor's. He was in this time and received her cordially—that is, until she told him the location of her land.

"No. No, thank you! The job ain't for me. I've got a wife and children and I can't go around getting caught in cross fires and whipped by those Green Mountain Boys. No, thank you, mistress. I'm not your man."

She knew there was no use in arguing but she was desperate, so she asked if he knew anyone else he could recommend.

"To go up there after what happened?" He shook his head. But as her shoulders were slumping, he said, "Just a minute. You might try Willie Gow. William Gow. I'd best give you the direction—you won't find it otherwise. Yes, Gow might do it, depending . . ."

"Depending on what?"

He dipped his pen and paused. "On how drunk he happens to be when you ask him. Don't look so distressed, mistress. No man in his right senses would agree to do what you want sober, and in his time Willie Gow was the very best."

She followed his direction, which led her to the south, past the crumbling palisades left over from the last of the wars with the French. A half dozen chestnut trees grew over the lane, creating a leafy green tunnel from which she emerged into a small, sadly derelict settlement. William

Gow's house was the most derelict of them all; her heart sank at its sorriness, but she knocked on the door.

She got no answer, so she knocked again. Finally she pounded.

"Coming!" someone called, and after a minute she picked out sounds from the far side of the door: a shuffling like footsteps, then a crash followed by a few moments of silence, then shuffling again. The shuffling came closer, then Gow opened the door and stood squinting and blinking, almost blinded by the sudden light of day.

He was wigless and badly in need of a shave. The stubble of his hair covered his scalp just as the stubble of his beard shadowed his sleep-creased face. The sunlight from behind her picked out flecks of gray. All in all he looked like something someone had crumpled up and thrown away.

"What do you want?" he queried. Then he said, "Never mind, come in." And before she could protest, he pulled her through the door.

"Damned sunlight!" he muttered, giving the door a shove that sent it flapping shut and plunged them into a gloom created by the fact that all of his curtains were drawn. But the dimness didn't hide the state of the room in which they stood. Sarah supposed it was his parlor, though she couldn't really tell since piles of books and papers covered everything. A little bit behind him a chair lay on its side; she guessed it accounted for the crash she'd heard—either the chair falling or Gow falling over it.

Gow blinked experimentally before he opened his eyes all the way. When he got a good look at Sarah he blinked hard and looked again. "What vision do I see before me? A houri sent down from paradise, or an angel of mercy come to lead me away from my life of sin? No, don't tell me—you've made a mistake and come to the wrong address. The door's right behind you, go ahead and let yourself out, but please do it quickly. I can't stand the light."

As he said this he lifted his arm in order to shield his eyes, but he dropped it when Sarah asked, "Are you William Gow?"

"What's left of him. And who are you?"

"My name is Sarah Meade. I need a surveyor and someone suggested you." She supposed it was a minor scandal to be in this room with him, unchaperoned and with all the curtains drawn, but if she stood on ceremony she'd never get anything done. Besides, Gow didn't look the least bit dangerous. If anything, he looked as though one good shove would be enough to bring him down.

"Suggested me, did they? I can't imagine who."

Sarah repeated the name and added what the man had said about him having been the best.

Gow nodded. "Cut my teeth on surveying. I've probably seen more of the land around these parts than anyone else." He stopped and squinted at her more closely. "You here about a job?"

Hesitantly she nodded. "I've got six thousand acres of land lying to the east of Lake Champlain. I want it subdivided so that the lots can be sold. If you are willing to consider—"

"I'll do it," said Gow.

She stopped, startled and uncertain. "You will? Just like that?" She addressed the question to his back, since he'd turned away with no explanation and begun poking about the litter of papers and books.

"Why?" he asked, still poking. "Should there be something more? I said I'd do it and I'm a man of my word."

"You heard where I said the land was—on the east side of the lake?"

"I heard." He unearthed a pewter tankard and turned it upside down. "I could have sworn..." he muttered and dropped the tankard, which rolled under a chair. "When do you want it done?"

"As soon as possible." She paused, then added, "There will also be a guard."

He stopped his rummaging to glance back at her. "You don't trust me?"

"Oh, no," she said quickly. "I mean to protect you against the Green Mountain Boys. They've been causing some—uh—trouble in those parts."

She thought that the mention of trouble would change Gow's mind, but he only shrugged. "Whatever you want, Mistress Meade. When do you want me to go?"

"When could you go?" she asked, feeling ridiculous, since it was clear that Gow had nothing else to do except stumble around in the semidarkness tripping over furniture and muttering to himself. Even more ridiculous was asking Gow at all, since she couldn't imagine him doing the job. But she had no choice, so she asked him.

He shrugged again. "Whenever you like. I'd just need a day or two to track down my chainman and collect my things."

He could leave the day after tomorrow. She was tempted to tell him to go, but she knew that if he went alone Zeke would find him and chase him off. She'd have to wait until Haddom had obtained his troop. "I'll have to settle certain things first, then I'll let you know. I'll send word when I know the date, if that's all right."

"Nothing better." Gow had given up on his rummaging. "Is that all? Because if it is and you're leaving, do you suppose you could stop in next door and ask them to send around some spirits—a bounce or a bowl of punch? Tell them to charge it to my account. And don't worry, I'll mark your land for you."

It was slim reassurance, but she accepted it gratefully. She said goodbye, let herself out and went around to the tavern to order him his punch. The barman took the order willingly until he learned who it was for, then he told her he'd be damned if he'd send Gow over a single swallow unless somebody paid him first. So she paid him and fled, wondering whether William Gow would remember her name tonight, let alone his promise to survey her land. And if he did remember, could he do the job? And then there was the troop to be sent along with him. With a sinking heart she thought about her row with Haddom last night and his fury over the wig today. She wondered if she could still count on his support or whether she'd have to come up with a guard herself.

Lost in thought, she had entered the tunnel of chestnut trees and had come halfway through them when suddenly the shadows moved, and with no more warning than the rustle of leaves, Zeke appeared.

She gave a little yelp of surprise, which made him smile. He touched his forehead in greeting as his eyes swept her up and down. "Afternoon, Sally. Did you get your man?"

"My man?" she repeated. Then, her hands on her hips, she demanded, "Can't you come and go like other people instead of landing on doorsteps and dropping out of trees?"

He grinned at her irritation. "I didn't drop, I stepped. I thought the ladies liked a little excitement in their lives. Next time I'll send my card first. I suppose that's what your friend the marquis would do?"

"If he did he'd be showing good manners," she retorted. His reference to Haddom irked her. "What are you doing here? I thought you'd be long since back in Bennington."

That seemed to surprise him. "Did you really think I'd desert my own son with no more than a fare-thee-well?"

"That's what you did last night," she pointed out. "Anyway, I hadn't really given it a thought. I have more important things to do than sit around thinking where you might be."

"I'll bet you do—such as hiring Willie Gow. What about it, Sally? Did he agree to survey the land?"

She'd forgotten Gow for the moment but now she recalled him with a sinking heart. Before Zeke could read her expression, she drew herself up and said, "As a matter of fact, he did." She said it very calmly and looked Zeke right in the eye, as though William Gow were steady as a rock. She should have guessed that Zeke would know better—damn him, he knew everything.

He rubbed his beard skeptically. "I guess Willie Gow's enough of a fool to go up there. The question is whether he'll be sober enough to stretch a chain once he arrives."

"He'll be sober if I have to go up there with him and see to it myself. Besides, if you hadn't frightened off every other surveyor I wouldn't have had to resort to Mr. Gow!"

"You didn't have to resort to him. You could have just given up." Before she could retort to this he said, "Speaking of things to do, how's the civilizing going—as easy as you thought?"

"I never said it was easy," she returned with a toss of her head. "And if you've been spying on me since last night you ought to know." She hated the way that he always managed to stay two steps ahead of her and the way he was always so cocky and made everything into a joke. There was no point in trying to beat him in an argument, but when she raised her skirts to move past him, he moved along with her.

"I guess I should have warned you about cutting Archie's hair. He never did care for that. As for the dog, I'd have left him behind but I knew he wouldn't have given me a minute's peace, and as soon as he could slip out he'd have come here on his own. Thumper's a hound and he's Archie's. He'd have tracked him down. I guess he's stirring up a little bit of ruckus at the house."

"Nothing I can't manage."

"I didn't think it would be, but I don't reckon your friend the marquis would agree."

"Stop calling him my friend," she snapped, moving the other way. "If you're done making fun of me, I have to get home." She tried to get past him but he blocked her way again.

"What else can I call him if you won't let me call him your beau? By the way, what was that he was holding when he left the house today?"

"His wig—or what was left of it after Thumper was through."

"Wig!" His eyes opened as he digested this, then he threw his head back and roared with laughter. "Are you telling me that Thumper ate his lordship's wig! Ho—I couldn't have done any better if I'd thought of it myself! What's this, Sally, don't tell me that you're amused?"

"If I am I shouldn't be and neither should you," she answered, trying not to smile, but all the time the laughter was tickling her chest. She knew she shouldn't let it out, especially not with him, but she couldn't help herself. His high spirits were infectious and the day was so fine and she was glad to see him, no matter what she told herself.

"That's a girl, Sally!" Zeke patted her on the shoulder and beamed approvingly. "Laughter does you good. It makes you look even prettier—if that's possible."

He said this smiling down at her, the greenish shade of the chestnuts turning his eyes a deep warm brown and his hair blue-black. The way he looked made her breath come strangely, turning her laughter into gasps. "It's not funny at all," she scolded, doing her best to look stern. "Especially since Haddom thinks we ought to turn Archie over to the authorities."

With the swiftness of lightning, Zeke's good humor disappeared. "The hell he will!" he swore, reaching out to grasp her arm. "You wouldn't, would you, Sally?"

The strength of his fingers hurt, but she made herself ignore that. "I ought to," she said, "after the way you dumped him off like that."

"I thought it was what you wanted."

"Oh—were you thinking of me? I didn't get that impression."

They were standing chin to chin and anyone passing in the lane would have seen them there. But nobody was passing, and the trees shadowed them so that they could probably stand there for an hour without being observed.

"Would you do it?"

"What do you think?"

At the sharpness of her retort some of Zeke's anger drained away and a spark of humor gleamed in his dark eyes. "You're a tough one, aren't you, Sally? You're not afraid to stand right up to a man."

"With a man like you, Zeke Brownell, a woman has no choice. And now if you've done with pinching my arm, do you suppose you could let it go?"

His fingers loosened but they didn't let go. She heard him draw his breath in a different way and that was all it took to start the same thing happening between them that had happened before—the night of the storm, for instance, and the other night at the dance.

"Let go, Zeke," she said softly.

"Is that what you really want?"

"We're standing here in public. Anyone can see."

"And if we were in private?" His face was very close, so close that he could have kissed her anytime he pleased. Her heart was pounding and her face was tingling as though she could already feel the rough heat of his skin.

She whispered, "Please, Zeke."

"Please what?" he whispered back.

A voice called out a little ways off—calling a child home to dinner, or perhaps even calling a dog. As Zeke turned to glance behind him Sarah felt a flash of fear.

"You know if they catch you they'll throw you in jail."

"What if they did?" He turned back. "Would you mind if they did, Sally?"

She was afraid to answer his question so she said, "If they did you'd deserve it," with what tartness she could manage, which wasn't very much.

He chuckled deep in his chest. Her own chest echoed his chuckle, they were standing that close. Then he drew her even closer, until his beard brushed her cheek. "Sally," he murmured as he'd murmured that night at the dance.

"You mustn't!"

"Yes. I must."

He moved a few steps backward until he was touching the trunk of the tree, and when he pulled her along with him she murmured in protest but she went anyway, and her lips were waiting when his found them and gently nudged them apart.

Her entire being responded to his touch. It was as though they were picking up where they'd left off. Every lesson his body had taught hers was instantly recalled, and by the time his hand came up to cup her cheek she was already melting from the nearness of him. His palm was familiar with its planes and calluses; she turned her head sideways to cradle her cheek in it—turned to inhale the scent that was his alone, and which held a promise she longed to have fulfilled.

His tongue coaxed and tickled, stroked and thrilled, while his arms slipped around her to raise her up, sliding her breasts slowly over the hard muscles of his chest. He held her there for a moment, then he slid her down and caught her snugly against his hips.

"I like that robe," he murmured, his breath tickling her skin.

"What robe?" Every place his hands touched felt instantly wonderful. She was amazed that she could feel the heat of them through all the layers of her clothes.

"That one you were wearing last night when you came to the door. I'd have liked to undo the fastenings and watch it slip away." His hands slipped down as he said this to illustrate his words.

She shivered and whispered, "I had my nightgown underneath."

"Mmm, I saw it. I'd have liked to unfasten that, too. Would you have liked that, Sally?" he breathed against her throat.

"Right there on the doorstep for the whole city to see—not to mention Archie and Thumper!" Her pulse was leaping wildly and her body trembled in response everywhere he touched. "Zeke, don't," she pleaded, trying to twist away.

"Why not, don't you like it?" But he knew she did. He could feel it in her responses, in their sweetness and their force. As much as concern for Archie had kept him here, Sally had kept him, too. He'd never felt this for a woman, not even his wife. She'd also been a beauty and he'd wanted her, but not with the single-minded madness that seemed to have crept into his blood. When he wasn't with Sally, he was thinking of her, telling himself to leave her alone, thinking about the lushness of her body and the loveliness of her face until he began to feel like a rope in a tug-of-war.

She twisted in his arms and murmured, "What if someone comes?"

"No one will come, don't worry." His tongue traced the outer then the inner curves of her ear. "Do you let his lordship see you in your robe?"

"Zeke, what a question!" Her breath was coming fast.

His was coming just as quickly. "Do you?" he asked. "If I was him I swear you'd drive me mad. I couldn't stand it, having you so near. I'd sneak into your room, Sally, when you were asleep. If you woke up and found me, would you make me leave?"

"Zeke!"

"You wouldn't, would you? Oh, Lord!" he groaned. "You'd better stop me before it's too late."

She couldn't. A thrill of panic flamed up along her spine and blended with the madness that was engulfing her. He had his back against the tree so if someone did come by she was the one they'd see, but all she could think of was where he'd touch her next.

"You're so damned sweet," he murmured just as the voice called again—only this time it was much closer than it had been before.

Sarah could feel the warring forces as Zeke's body tensed. Someone was coming. He couldn't stop. He had to. He didn't want to. She heard him groan again, then in the next moment he was pushing her away, pulling up her bodice and pulling down her skirts. When he released her she swayed dangerously to the side so that he grabbed her by the shoulders and held her there until her legs were ready to do their part.

"I've got to go," he told her, his face close to hers.

"Go where?" she asked dazedly.

"To Bennington. As you said, I'd deserve it if they caught me here. Take good care of Archie." He kissed her one last time—it was meant to be a brief kiss, but when his lips touched hers they couldn't let go. His hands gripped her shoulders, pulled her close, then thrust her back. "Goodbye, Sally."

"Wait!"

But he was gone, blending with the shadows behind the trees. She took a step in that direction but then she stopped, knowing she'd never catch him if he didn't want to be caught.

Whoever was coming had nearly reached the trees. She patted her hair, tucking away the trailing curls Zeke's fingers had worked loose. She'd hardly had time to smooth her skirts before she came face-to-face with a broad-faced Dutch farmer driving his wayward cow.

"Good day, mistress." He touched his hat as he passed and she nodded, turning her face away so that he wouldn't see her and guess exactly what he'd interrupted when he'd come along.

She went straight home, homing like a pigeon toward the privacy of her room. She wanted to see no one until she'd recovered from being with Zeke, and she prayed that Archie had stayed out of trouble while she'd been gone. She didn't believe she could cope with a new disaster in her present state of mind.

The house looked peaceful enough as she approached; she heard no shouting or barking and no one flung open the door as she came up the steps. But when she reached the hallway she found her father waiting for her, and from the way he said, "We've got to talk," she knew what it concerned.

He didn't say another word until they were in the library with the door shut behind them. Then he turned on her and demanded, "What do you think you're doing, taking in that boy? Please tell me he's not really Brownell's son!"

Tired, still shaken and angered by his tone of voice, she answered, "I'll tell you whatever you want."

"Then it's true!" He stared at her as if she'd gone mad. "You must have lost your reason, taking in Brownell's son! You, of all people—when Haddom told me I thought he was dreaming. You must know he's fit to be tied."

"I don't care what Haddom thinks. I'm tired of him and his tempers."

"His tempers!" her father exclaimed. "Do you know where you'd be without him?"

"Happier," Sarah said. "And since we're on the subject, I've found a surveyor willing to do the job."

He'd been about to remonstrate but he forgot about that and gaped. "You have? Who is he?"

"A man named William Gow," she said as coolly as she'd said to Zeke, though fortunately her father couldn't know the truth. "The man who recommended him said he was the best and he's promised to do the job with or without a guard."

"Then he must be as mad as you are."

"Not necessarily. Maybe he's just not a coward like some people I could name."

He shrugged off her innuendo; he'd never claimed to be brave, only worldly and shrewd. "You'd better send a guard all the same. If the governor won't help us we'll have to hire one ourselves."

"And pay them with what?"

"With credit against the money you'll get from the land. If you make up with Haddom, maybe he'd bear the cost. Now, to get back to where we started, what about the boy?"

"His name is Archie."

"All right, Archie. What is he doing here?"

She didn't want to tell him but she saw she had no choice if she wanted to keep him from joining Haddom in insisting that Archie be turned over to the sheriff.

"His father brought him for me to civilize. When I first met him in Bennington I questioned the conditions in which he was growing up. Two nights ago at the Van Kalms' I questioned them again. I must have expressed myself rather strongly because last night Mr. Brownell brought his son here as a sort of challenge to me to prove that I could do a better job than him."

When she finished her explanation her father shook his head. "You really must be mad—unless there's more between you and Zeke Brownell than a struggle over the land. After what's happened he ought to be your worst enemy, but instead, here you are dancing with him and playing nursemaid to his son."

"There is nothing between us," she answered icily, but despite her tone she couldn't make herself meet his eye. "I've already told you why he brought the boy, and as for us dancing, there are fifty eyewitnesses who can tell you it wasn't my choice. Plenty of other women danced with the Green Mountain Boys—as you would have seen if you hadn't been hiding in a cupboard."

As she'd expected, he didn't respond to that. She turned and found him staring out the window with an expression on his face she'd learned to dread.

"No," she said quickly. "Whatever it is, just no. Remember that you promised you wouldn't interfere."

He turned from the window. "You know that Haddom thinks we ought to turn the boy over to the authorities."

"I told him I wouldn't let him."

"Yes. I totally agree. We'd be fools to give up the goose that guaranteed us the golden egg."

"What are you saying?"

"It's simple, don't you see? We hold the boy as insurance for Brownell's not interfering until we've sold the land. Once we've sold it, we let the boy go."

Now it was her turn to stare. "Are you suggesting we hold Archie hostage?" Even knowing her father as well as she did she could hardly believe her ears.

Undaunted, he nodded. "Of course. Don't you see? Thanks to you, Brownell's played right into our hands. All you've got to do is to tell him that so long as he leaves you alone he'll get his boy back safe and sound—as soon as you've sold the land." Suddenly his face clouded. "He does want him back? The plan won't work unless he cares about the boy."

"Of course he cares about him!" she exclaimed with disgust. "Not every father sees his child as a pawn!"

He ignored the insult; he was concentrating on his plan. "Chances are Brownell will come after the boy, so we'll have to let the sheriff know. Then, if Brownell did come, they'd be ready for him and they could grab him and throw him into jail. It's absolutely foolproof. Either way we win."

"No!" Sarah repeated. "Absolutely not. And if you even try it, I swear I'll return the boy myself. I'll even warn Zeke that you're setting a trap for him. I may want to sell the land, but I'm not so desperate that I'd play with the life of a child!"

"You're not playing with his life. You're just doing what you meant to do anyway—teach him his manners and whatever else he needs to learn. And in the meantime, you're ensuring being able to sell the land in time to pay our debts."

He looked so complacent she actually wanted to cry. "No! I've told you no. I won't let you do it. Anyway, do you honestly imagine that it would succeed? After everything else Zeke Brownell has done, do you really believe that if he wanted Archie he couldn't get him away? My God, he comes and goes from this town as though he were the mayor!" She stopped herself just short of adding that she'd seen him less than an hour before.

"Clever men get too cocky and in the end they get caught. And as much as he might come and go, he's not the mayor. He's a criminal, Sarah. He's also a murderer."

"No, he isn't! He didn't do it—he was unjustly accused!"

Her father's eyes narrowed. For several moments he looked at her, and when he came toward her she fell back a step or two, less in fear than in confusion about what he had in mind. When he reached her he gripped her shoulders in a way he'd never done and she'd never seen him look so serious.

"Listen to me, Sarah. I may have lost more than I gained over the course of the years, but I did win that land. It was mine and I didn't have to sign it over to you. I did because you asked me and because I wanted what was best for both of us and because I never doubted you'd turn it into cash.

"I want my share of that money as much as you want yours, and I don't mean to give it up because you get it into your head to form some sort of bizarre attachment to Zeke Brownell. You're very smart in some ways, Sarah, but in others you're naive, and behind his country-bumpkin act Brownell is sharp enough to take advantage of you.''

''What are you saying?'' she demanded, her cheeks beginning to burn.

''That I wouldn't put it past Brownell to woo you into giving up your right to the land.''

''He wouldn't do that!''

''Of course he would. From the way you're acting, I'd say he's already begun. But I won't let that happen. If you can't stop him, I will. That land's my last chance and I don't mean to give it up.''

''I won't give it up,'' she answered, twisting away from his grip. ''I want that land sold as much as you do, and no man is going to trick me out of it. But I'm not going to take advantage of an innocent child.''

''You wouldn't be taking advantage of the boy. You'd probably be doing him a favor to have his father put in jail.''

''No, and that's final! I won't be fooled by the father and I won't play games with the son—and if you try to do anything behind my back, I'll see to it that you don't see a penny beyond what it takes to pay your debts. I will do that, Father. Do you understand?'' But before he could answer, she turned and flung out of the room.

She couldn't have said what made her seek Archie out. After she'd left her father she'd run upstairs to her room, shut the door and leaned against it, awaiting the storm of tears that threatened. When no tears came she went to sit down on the bed, then got up and walked to the window and saw Archie down in the yard. He was sitting on the back steps tossing pebbles at the garden well with Thumper lying contentedly at his feet. She watched him for several minutes, then she splashed water on her face and went downstairs to join him without really knowing why.

He glanced up when she came out, but if he noticed the signs of emotion on her face he kept it to himself.

''Are you hungry?'' Sarah asked him, thinking with dread of facing her father and Haddom at dinner when she was still so upset. Then again, she couldn't leave Archie to face them alone.

"I dunno." Archie shrugged. "Guess that would depend on the company."

For an awful moment she thought he'd somehow overheard her father's plan, but then she realized he was thinking about Haddom and the wig. She sat down on the steps beside him. "You know what I think? I think we should have them send a tray up to my room. We could eat up there together. What would you think of that?"

Archie's grin was his answer. "I guess I wouldn't mind."

The morning's events had taken away her appetite but Archie must have been famished; he put away more food than she'd seen most grown men eat—and with manners that made her glad she'd decided to eat in her room. At one point he paused in attacking his food long enough to look up and observe, "Zeke always did say I got his appetite."

She started almost violently at the mention of Zeke's name, but Archie didn't notice because he was busy eating again. Her father's accusation repelled her and made her feel unclean, but when she tried to dismiss it she found that she could not. Had Zeke been trying to take advantage of her? The possibility disturbed her more than anything else had done, including the rumor about his murdering his wife. Or was the idea only a figment of her father's unscrupulous mind?

When she looked at Archie she saw a lot of Zeke. She saw his gusto for life and his open face as well as the vulnerability she'd glimpsed from time to time. When Archie paused to slip Thumper a scrap of meat she saw his inherent kindness and his mischievousness.

Had Zeke's kisses been designed to weaken her? She recalled that just today he'd complimented her by saying she was tough enough to stand up to a man. Did a man who was trying to weaken a woman praise her for being strong? She remembered Eli's comment about Zeke liking a good fight. When Zeke wanted something he didn't sneak around. He stood right up and claimed it for all the world to see, whereas her father was a master of stealth. Her father wanted to hold Archie hostage. Had he intentionally planted the seed of doubt in order to trick her into agreeing with his plan?

Archie paused in his eating to belch resoundingly. At Sarah's stern expression, he grinned and mumbled, "Good vittles," through a healthy mouthful of cherry pie.

Sarah pushed her own plate away and said, "When you've finished your dinner we'll start teaching you to read."

She had intended to hold the lesson in her room, but when the maid came for the tray and reported that Haddom and her father had both gone out, she changed her mind and decided to go down to the library.

Thumper came along and collapsed with a contented grunt at Archie's feet while she spread the primer on the desk. She pointed to the first letter. "That's an *A*. It also happens to be the first letter of your name. I want you to write it." She handed him a pen. He wrote it without comment. "Very good," she said.

They went through the letters in very little time and progressed to simple words. They went over a dozen, then Sarah left Archie to copy them while she went upstairs in search of her needlework. When she came back she found that he'd gotten up from the desk and was in the process of browsing Mason's shelves. As she watched he took a book down, opened the cover and studied the title page. When he flipped to the text she said, "Why didn't you tell me that you knew how to read?"

Archie started at her question. He'd been so engrossed in the book he hadn't realized she'd come back. Discovered, he said gamely, "You never asked. Besides, I got the feeling you wanted to teach me yourself."

"Who did teach you?"

"Zeke in the beginning. Eli all the rest."

"You don't call Zeke 'Father'?"

Archie shook his head. "Mrs. Williams claims that's disrespect, but Zeke says respect has nothing to do with a name, and if I can't call him Zeke and respect him, he doesn't figure I respect him much. 'Sides," he concluded, "everyone calls him that."

Zeke had told her the same thing the first time they had met. *Nobody calls me Mr. Brownell, leastways nobody I trust.* She looked at the book in Archie's hand. "Is that something you'd like to read?"

"Yes'm. I reckon so." He held out the book to her and she saw that it was the *History of the Six Nations of the Iroquois*.

"You think you can read it?"

"I reckon I could try."

"Then why don't you read for a while and afterward we'll discuss what you've learned."

He nodded in agreement and dropped into the nearest chair; curling himself up like a hound, he began to read. She sat down with her needlework to occupy her hands and the events of the day thus far to occupy her mind. She thought of her father's accusations, William Gow, Haddom's wig, but in the end her thoughts returned to Zeke.

Raising her head she watched Archie as he read, his lips moving as his eyes traveled down the page. She remembered that when she'd been upset she'd sought Archie out. Had Zeke sent his son here to try to weaken her?

"Archie?"

"Yes, ma'am?" He looked up.

"Do you know what made your father decide to bring you here?"

Archie's eyes dropped back to the book and he shifted in the chair. "I thought you'd told him it'd do me good."

"Is he in the habit of doing what other people say?"

In spite of himself, Archie grinned. "No'm. Not usually."

"On top of which he disapproves of civilized society. I can't help but wonder what made him change his mind."

Archie stopped grinning and shifted again. "Beats me," he said. He looked down at the book again but he wasn't moving his lips.

"Archie," Sarah said. "Please tell me what you know."

He didn't want to tell her. The way he struggled against giving in reminded her of Zeke, but he was only ten years old so in the end she won.

"Well, ma'am," he said slowly, "I reckon it kinda was my fault."

"How's that, Archie?"

"You know that night he came here when you were having a dance? Well, the next morning he was taking on something fierce about Yorkers this and that, and I was fool enough to open my mouth and say some Yorkers wasn't so bad."

"Weren't," corrected Sarah, but absentmindedly. "Any Yorkers in particular?"

"Yes'm. I said you, and for some reason that sent him into a proper fit. 'Is that so?' he hollers—you know, in that voice of his. 'Seeing's how you and Mistress Meade are so fond of each other, why should I keep you apart!' I thought he must be joking, but he was serious, and the next thing I know he's got the horse saddled up and we're riding west— and so fast that poor Thumper couldn't hardly keep up."

"I see." She was fairly shaking with relief. He hadn't brought Archie as part of a devious plot. He'd brought him with characteristic impetuosity. She knew that Archie was telling the truth because she could see the whole thing perfectly: Zeke's harangue, Archie's unthinking response, Zeke flying into a rage and bundling them both off to Albany before he had time to change his mind. And even if Zeke had changed his mind he wouldn't have turned back, because once he decided to do a thing, he did it. That was the way he was.

Zeke hadn't brought Archie to try to soften her. In typical Zeke fashion, he'd brought him to prove her wrong. He'd brought him to show her that she had no idea how much was involved in caring for a boy. He believed that once she realized that, she'd bring Archie back home, and he'd be there waiting to laugh at her when she did.

Sarah sat up straight. She had no intention of letting Zeke win this round. He'd said she was a tough woman and she meant to show him how tough. She might not yell as loudly as he did, but she could be every bit as stubborn when she put her mind to it. She'd civilize Archie and then she'd take him home. In this particular battle she'd have the last laugh on Zeke Brownell.

Miraculously, after that things settled down. Although Archie had too much of Zeke's blood in him to conform for more than short periods at a time, after his initial adjustment he did settle into a routine. He did the lessons she set for him and learned to eat with a fork. He hardly cursed the tailor when he went back to try on his clothes, and when he brought them home Sarah caught him admiring his reflection in the looking glass.

Even Thumper learned to behave, once he comprehended what was expected of him. Archie took him for long rambles past the edge of town, and when he was at home, for the most part he made himself invisible. Both he and Archie did their best to stay out of Haddom's way.

Haddom had sulked for the first week after Archie had arrived, relieving Sarah of the burden of his company. On the other hand, he had redoubled his efforts against Zeke. After weeks of impatient waiting, a letter from the governor had arrived, with the assurance that if the decision to call out the army were up to him he'd do it right away, and regretting that it wasn't. It was up to the king's American commander, General Haldimand, and General Haldimand believed that armed intervention against the Green Mountain Boys would cause more problems than it could solve.

Haddom was incensed by the letter.

"Cowards!" he fumed.

"Not necessarily," said Meade, which was as close to contradicting Haddom as he'd ever come. "You've got to keep in mind what's happening in the other colonies. Although New Yorkers and Grants people are too busy fighting each other to care, all the rest of New England is on the verge of rioting against the crown. If Haldimand sends troops to Bennington, people in Boston might conclude that he's about to send them there. That might be all it takes to put them up in arms. That's what he means by causing more problems than he would solve.''

Haddom was unconvinced. "There comes a point at which one must use force to maintain the respect of one's subjects. My mother's first cousin married a Haldimand. I will write to the general myself!"

But while Haddom wrote his letters, time was running out. At Sarah's suggestion her father approached Haddom about paying for a private guard, but Haddom retorted that he saw no reason to waste his own funds when his majesty kept standing troops for just this reason.

"Cheap," her father concluded. "Sometimes the richest ones are."

"I think he's just wise about money, which is probably why he still has most of his."

"If you think that, you ought to play cards with him sometime," Meade retorted unadvisedly, because Sarah then interrogated him minutely on where he'd been gambling. When, to prove he hadn't lost, he showed her his winnings, she made him give her half.

"Thirty pounds," he grumbled.

It was more than she'd had before, and with it in hand, she decided to set out to hire a guard on her own. She got a list of names from the sheriff, who offered the advice that if she wanted recruits she'd better be willing to offer enough gold to counteract their fear.

Taking the sheriff's advice, she offered each man on the list five pounds upon agreement and promised another fifty when the land was sold. Upon hearing the offer, each man turned her down. As one of them explained, "If Brownell's going to kill me, I want to have a little fun before he does. You give me the money in advance and maybe I'll change my mind."

Archie's education was a happier experience. Never having had access to a proper library, Archie fell upon George Mason's like a starving man upon a feast. He whipped through the *Six Nations* and *Gulliver's Travels* in two days each. Sarah suggested *Robinson Crusoe* next.

"Have they got it here?"

"I believe so. I'll go down to the library and look."

"When?"

"I'll go right now."

The library door was shut. Laying her ear against it, she caught the sound of her father's voice. She couldn't hear Haddom's, but she guessed he was in there, too.

Discussing what? She detested eavesdroppers but some instinctive sense warned her that she shouldn't leave before she knew. She turned the knob silently and slowly pulled open the door until she could hear them clearly.

Her father was saying, "Of course it would benefit you. You'd be known as the man who caught Zeke Brownell. Once Haldimand saw that, he'd probably change his mind about giving you troops, and once you have the troops, everything else will fall in place. What would make more sense than putting the man who drove out the enemy in supreme control of the land?"

"I don't know." Haddom sounded skeptical.

"What don't you know?" challenged Meade. "It seems perfectly clear to me."

What seemed clear? wondered Sarah. And what had her father meant about Haddom taking supreme control of the land?

"If it works," said Haddom. "But what about Brownell? He seems to be able to come and go at will, so what's to stop him from sneaking in one night and making off with the boy?"

"We'll post a guard," Meade answered. "No, better yet, we'll put the boy where his father can't find him."

"Hide him?"

"Yes, that's right."

There was a moment's silence, then Haddom said, "What about Mistress Meade? I don't think she'll like that."

"She won't have any choice. We won't tell her where we've put the boy."

"I don't know," Haddom said for the second time. "I don't understand why she agreed to take him in the first place. If Brownell weren't such a barbarian I'd be tempted to think she actually admired him.''

"That's nonsense," Meade scoffed. "I told you she feels sorry for the boy, having Brownell for his father and growing up in the woods. I suppose it's a sort of maternal instinct, if a bit confused. Forget about Sarah for the moment. What we need is to come up with a place where we can hide the boy."

As quietly as she'd opened it, Sarah shut the door, though she kept her hand on the knob as hot liquid anger surged through her veins. Half of her wanted to fling the door open, storm into the room and confront her father with his duplicity. She wondered if he'd have the nerve to deny it if she confronted him face-to-face. And what about Haddom—would he go along with the plan? He had sounded dubious but she was sure that her father would be able to wear him down.

And after she'd sworn not to give her father his money if he plotted behind her back! Clearly he hadn't believed her. That made her angrier yet. She was so furious at his betrayal that she actually thought of riding straight to Bennington to sign the land over to Zeke. All of the land, not just his share, and let them lose everything. That would show him. But of course it would show her, too.

Already her anger was fading, replaced by disgust and familiar sorrow that he would break his word. Her own father. Her shoulders heaved in a sigh, when the sound of a chair being pushed back in the library made her release the knob and beat a hasty retreat up the servants' stairs. She didn't want to confront her father, not before she'd had time to think. But even as she ran silently up the stairs she knew what she had to do.

Archie looked up when she came into his room but his face fell when he saw that she didn't have the book.

"He didn't have it?"

"Have what?" she asked.

"*Robinson Crusoe.* You said you'd look for it." Archie seemed puzzled, since Mistress Meade didn't usually forget. Then he looked at her more closely. "Is something wrong?"

"No, nothing," she said quickly. "At least not yet. Can you keep a secret?"

"I reckon so," Archie said, so she shut the door tightly and told him what she had in mind.

Chapter Eleven

"Archie! Wake up."

To ensure his silence, she laid two fingers over his lips. She needn't have worried. Archie might be backward about many things but his training had included both silence and stealth. He was awake in one instant and on his feet in the next, and since he'd gone to sleep with his clothes on, he was ready to go.

Sarah hadn't slept at all. In the first place she'd been too worried that her father and Haddom might settle on their plot and try to grab Archie before she could get him away. Beyond that, she'd been afraid that if she did doze off she might not be able to wake up when it was time to leave.

Downstairs in the drawing room the eight-day clock had already struck four. Haddom and her father had come in about an hour ago and in another hour the servants would be getting up. She'd debated leaving while the men were still out, but she'd been afraid they might think of checking on Archie when they came back and discover that he was gone. And since she didn't imagine the ferryman would be willing to cross until dawn, that would leave them at the river, waiting like sitting ducks in case the two men between them summoned the courage to give pursuit.

In any event, they hadn't checked. They'd just bid each other a blurry good-night and clumped upstairs to bed. Now that they were sleeping they wouldn't be up until noon, and it would be hours before the maid knocked on her door with her tea. By then, with any luck, she and Archie should be safely across the river and on their way to Bennington.

She had been worried about Thumper giving them away, but he, sage veteran of countless possum hunts, was as silent as Archie going down the stairs. The tricky part was saddling the horses without waking the stable boy, but somehow they managed it, and in an impressively short time they were leading the horses out of the yard with Thumper padding noiselessly behind.

They kept their pace slow until they'd reached the palisades so as not to alert the watch, but as soon as they were in the country they gave the horses their head—riding too fast for the darkness, partly from fear of pursuit but also from the exhilaration of a clean escape. Turning her head, Sarah caught a glimpse of Archie's face, which was shining as brightly as any star. For the first time she realized how glad he was to leave, and that gave her a stab of guilt for having kept him against his will. But when he caught her looking, he flashed her a grin that held no regrets, and followed it with a wink that meant, "Guess we fooled 'em pretty good!"

I hope so, Sarah thought, turning her head to look back, but the road behind them was empty and dark.

"Slow down," she called to Archie. "There's no point in laming a horse getting to the river, since we'll only have to wait."

He obeyed with reluctance, looking back as she had and making a worried face. "They could still catch us."

"I don't think so," she said, but his concern was infectious and she speeded up again. By the time they reached the river, both of their necks were sore from craning backward at the empty road.

By that time the sky had lightened to a placid gray with the first pink line of sunrise gathering in the east. The light gave Archie his first good look at her.

"Hell's fire, Mistress Meade! What's that you've got on?"

"I thought you'd stopped your cursing."

"Mostly." He grinned. "You're wearing britches. Fancy that."

She gave him a reproving look, which didn't quite succeed. "It seemed like the practical thing. I've got a skirt to put over them for the ferryman's benefit. Speaking of whom, if you've finished gawking you might ride on ahead and see if you can rouse him while I stop here to change."

"Yes'm." Still grinning, he spurred on ahead while she pulled her horse up and reached back to fish her skirt out of her saddlebag.

She arrived, suitably clad, to find Archie and Thumper waiting out in the ferryman's yard.

"His wife says he's at breakfast and he's not to be disturbed."

"How long?"

"She didn't say."

In one motion she and Archie looked back toward the road.

"Maybe if I asked." Sarah slid down off her horse, but as her feet touched the ground the door opened and the ferryman appeared, patting his full stomach and looking pleased with the world.

He was a friendly garrulous man, more inclined to stop and gossip than to get under way, so between them Archie and Sarah practically dragged him down to the boat, and Sarah held the horses while Archie cast off the rope. The ferryman recognized Archie as having come over with Zeke and he asked a good many questions, most of which Sarah pretended not to hear, so finally he gave up and passed the time by whistling.

The river was peaceful in the first morning light, gray and lavender, with the mist rising from the surface and playing hide-and-seek in the coves along the banks. Sarah leaned back against her horse's flank and sighed. She felt the peace settle over her, and with it came her fatigue.

"Tired?" asked Archie.

"Just a bit." She glanced at him and smiled. He was watching the eastern shore as if the force of his wanting to be there could increase the ferry's speed. From his expression she knew he was thinking of Zeke, and for the first time since she'd pushed open the library door, she found herself thinking about him, too.

Up until now she'd been too intent on getting Archie safely home to consider what she meant to tell Zeke when they did arrive. She'd told Archie the whole story because she'd needed him to understand why they had to sneak off in the night. But now that she gave it thought, she wasn't entirely certain that she wanted to tell anybody else. It was bad enough having a father who would plot a kidnapping and break his word to her without having to admit it to the entire world. She remembered how humiliated she'd felt when Eli had questioned her at the trial about why she'd forced her father to give her the land. She shuddered with revulsion at the memory.

"Chilly?" asked Archie. He'd been watching her.

"No." She made herself smile reassuringly and she was touched when Archie smiled back. She'd miss him. She'd even miss the dog. The house would seem lonely without them there. Then again she'd be busy organizing Gow's trip north. And dealing with her father and Haddom, she thought with a sinking heart. But she wouldn't think of any of that until she got home; right now she had more than enough with which to concern herself.

The sun was just coming up when they reached the shore. "Will you be staying in Bennington, mistress?" the ferryman asked, using the pole to hold himself against the shore.

"No, I'll be coming back. I can't say when, exactly. Just a little longer than it takes to ride there and back."

The ferryman had other questions, but before he could ask, Sarah and Archie were mounted and riding to the east. The ferryman looked after them and muttered to himself, "Lest I'm mistaken, she's the one with that land. Then what in the devil is she doing with the boy?"

They rode in silence until they'd reached the rise where she and Zeke had parted the morning after the storm. From there they had a good view of the opposite shore.

"No sign of them," said Archie, shielding his eyes as Zeke had done. "I reckon even if they did show up now, by the time the ferry got over and back again we'd be too far ahead for them to catch up.''

"I don't think they'd cross the river," Sarah replied. "My father certainly wouldn't, and I can't see his lordship coming after us alone.''

Archie grinned broadly. "He's a cross-eyed popinjay. Too bad Thumper didn't eat all his wigs so's he'd be a bald one, too!" He grinned at Sarah hopefully, but she was thinking of something else.

"Archie, I've been thinking. When we get to Bennington . . . I don't want Zeke to know why I'm bringing you back.''

Archie's grin faded as he tried to understand. "What do you reckon to tell him?''

"I don't know. Something else.''

"Well'm, I guess it's up to you. But if you don't tell him the reason, he's likely to reckon that I was bad. And if he reckons that, he's likely to have a laugh on you. Then afterward he's likely to take into me pretty fierce.''

"Fiercely," Sarah corrected, wincing inwardly at the thought of just how Zeke would laugh. "I won't let him blame you. I'll tell him something else. I'll . . . I'll say I believed you'd been away long enough and it was time for you to get back. I'll tell him how much you've learned and how proud of you I am so he can't think that I'm bringing you back because you misbehaved. It isn't a lie," she reasoned, as much to herself as to him.

Archie considered this, thoughtfully scratching his ear. "How come you don't just tell him the truth?''

She looked down at the river, sparkling in the sun, the dark square of the ferry anchored to the shore. "Well, Archie, to tell the truth, I guess I'm ashamed to admit that my own father would think of something so low.''

"It ain't so low," Archie protested. "No lower'n what Zeke done himself. Lookit how he kidnapped you that first time he brought you over here.''

"Did," she corrected, "not done. And what Zeke did was different. He took me because I was the one who owned the land. But you don't own anything and you're only a child. That's very different. Zeke would never use a child as bait. When he has a dispute with someone he stands right up to them, he doesn't sneak around grabbing their children behind their backs.'' She paused, then added sadly, ''Besides, my father gave me his word.''

''I'm sorry,'' said Archie, sounding so much like Zeke that Sarah was tempted both to smile and to cry. ''But I still think you should tell him. Zeke'll understand.''

He spoke with perfect confidence. Looking at him, Sarah longed to know how it felt to have a father in whom you could put such faith. Then, all of a sudden, she realized that she knew—not how it felt to have such a father but how it felt to put faith in Zeke.

Hadn't she put her faith in him that night of the storm, when he'd soothed her panic, sheltered her and fed her— and even pinched her toe? The thought of that pinch made her smile. Such a little thing to mean so much, but it did. At that moment she'd been at his mercy; he'd known that she wouldn't have stopped him if he'd chosen to finish what they'd begun. Despite knowing that, he not only had kept them both from making a mistake but had done it with humor and affection and a sense of playfulness that had drained away all the tension between them and allowed her to drift off to sleep with a smile.

Zeke could be boisterous—he could bully and tease, roar with laughter and bellow with anger. But he could also be quieter than any man she knew. And, more than any man she knew, he could understand. She remembered that night at the Van Kalms', when she'd tried to run away. He'd caught her and pulled her back, looking at her so long and hard that she knew he'd seen the truth. For the first time she realized that the attraction she felt for him was more than physical. A bond had been growing between them since that night in the woods, though until this moment she hadn't realized how strong it had become.

Archie was right. She could tell Zeke what had happened and he would understand. She could shrug off some of the heavy burden and he'd help her to shoulder it. Zeke's shoulders were strong enough to handle anything. Raising

her eyes from the river, she turned her face to the sun, and
at the moment that the warmth washed over her, she knew
that she trusted him.

She blinked at the force of the light. It seemed to her that
the sun must have brightened, but then she realized that the
brightness was inside. All the tension and turbulence inside her had calmed. Spaces stretched out within her, un-
cluttered by anger or guilt or pain. She could think of her
father clearly. She could also think of Zeke; she could even
think of a solution to the problem with the land. In the
fresh clear light of the morning she realized that what she
really wanted was to share the land with Zeke.

As if he were beside her, she heard her father's outraged
cry.

*Sarah, what are you doing? You're throwing the
land away! You're hurting your own father to help
your enemy! Your own father, Sarah!*

*Father, it's your own fault. I warned you what
would happen if you tried to use Archie as bait to
capture Zeke, and you ignored the warning just the
way you've always ignored what I've said. You made
a promise and broke it without a second thought.*

Your own father, Sarah!

*Yes, and you'll still be my father if I give Zeke the
land, and maybe if you see that I mean what I say, next
time you won't be so quick to break your word.*

He has no right, Sarah.

*I believe he does. Under the law Zeke's title might
not be as good as ours, but his principles are a lot more
admirable. You won the land at a card game, but he
worked long and hard to pay for it. To him, the land
is more than a means to pay off debts. Working out a
compromise seems only fair.*

What kind of a compromise?

*I don't really know, but once Zeke understands what
I'm doing, we'll be able to work one out.*

Will you? asked a new voice she recognized as her
own. *I seem to recall you and Zeke standing on this*

*very spot that night after the storm, and you bringing
up the possibility of compromise and Zeke just about
laughing in your face. What makes you think he'll be
more willing to listen to you now?*

She winced at the memory. *Because...because, she
thought, what I offered that day wasn't really a compromise. It was me acting as if the land were all mine
and I'd pay him a little something out of sympathy.
This is different—and things between us have changed
since then. Now I know I trust him and I believe he
trusts me, too. He brought Archie to me and now I'm
bringing him safely home. When Zeke sees that, I
know he'll understand.*

"Ahem . . . Mistress Meade?"

While she'd been debating with silent voices, Archie had
been watching her and waiting impatiently for them to be
on their way. She was surprised to find them both still by
the river; she felt as though she'd traveled such a long way
in her mind.

He looked worried. Sarah smiled. "You're right, Archie.
I will tell Zeke the truth. Shall we be going?"

"Yes'm, you bet!"

Zeke stayed in her thoughts as they rode into the woods.
She wasn't thinking about the land now, she was thinking
about other things—the things she'd been so careful not to
think of before, because thinking of them might cloud her
resolution about the land. But if she and Zeke could settle
their differences about the land, wouldn't all those other
things come within their reach? Even the possibility sent
shivers down her spine and made her heart beat faster.

Archie spurred his horse to keep pace. "Where are we
headed for?"

"Where?" She turned blankly. "Why, to Bennington!"

"Bennington's a big place. What part are you headed
for?"

Something else she hadn't considered. "Wherever you
think Zeke would be."

Archie thought for a moment. "Most likely at Eli's farm."

"Is that where you stay when you're down here?"

"No'm. That's where we live."

"Live?" she repeated, slowing her horse in surprise. "But I thought you lived up north. I thought you lived on the land."

A guarded look crept into Archie's eyes. "We go up there sometimes, but mainly we live down here. That's where you'll find Zeke most likely, 'less he's at the Catamount."

Surprise faded to distaste at the thought of meeting Zeke at the tavern, surrounded by the Boys. "We'll try the farm," she concluded. "You lead the way."

The way followed the road for another hour, then branched off on a lane to the left. They followed this for some miles until the forest gave way to fields and Archie turned past a trim farmhouse and into a tidy yard.

"We're here," he announced briefly, and raising his voice he shouted greetings to Eli and Zeke.

His call echoed unanswered through the peaceful yard. A sly-faced goat tethered beneath a tree turned its head and the chickens paused in their pecking to gawk. Thumper, revived by the sight of home, was sniffing everywhere, trying to catch up on everything that had happened since he'd been gone.

Archie slid down from the saddle. "Could be they didn't hear me. I'll check the house." He started at a dead run, then recalled his manners and skidded to a halt. He trotted back to Sarah to help her down from her horse. She'd been in the saddle since they'd crossed the river, and when she landed, the ground seemed to be rocking back and forth beneath her feet.

Archie was squirming with impatience. "Go ahead," she said. "I'll follow at my own speed."

"If you're sure," he answered, already on the run. He was in the door and out again before she'd reached the steps.

"Nobody's home. Eli's likely gone on business, but I can't say about Zeke. I'll check the barn for horses. You want to come?"

This time she declined. She wanted to see the house, so she let Archie scamper off alone while she opened the door and went in.

She entered through the kitchen, which was as tidy as the yard, with pots and pans hanging neatly from their hooks and cups and dishes all stacked on their proper shelves. It was a big room with broad beams, an enormous hearth and a two-legged bed projecting from the wall. Next to the bed was a ladder leading up to a loft, and just beyond that was a door to another room. She hadn't done more than look through the door when Archie reappeared.

"It's a nice house."

"Yes'm. Zeke built it himself."

"Zeke? But I thought it was Eli's."

Archie's pride vanished and the guarded look returned. He jerked his head toward the open door. "There wasn't a sign of either horse out in the barn. I reckon they're both off the place. If you want to see Zeke, you'd best try the Catamount."

"The Catamount!" Her heart sank as she forgot about who owned the farm.

Her distress made Archie grin sympathetically. "We got ink and paper—you could always leave a note."

"We have."

"Have what, ma'am?"

"We have ink, not we've got. In any case, I'm afraid writing a note won't do. How far is it to the Catamount?"

"Not long from here. Maybe if we're lucky we'll meet him on the road."

They weren't, of course, and forty minutes later they rode into the tavern yard.

"I could go in to get him if you wanted to stay outside," Archie suggested.

Sarah shook her head. Anything hinting of cowardice had never been her way; besides, she could imagine the

Boys crowding out into the yard to gawk at her and Zeke. It made more sense to use the parlor, where at least they'd have privacy. Then, afterward, maybe they'd go back to the farm....

Between them, she and Archie managed to open the door, and this time he remembered his manners and let her enter first. She paused on the threshold to look around: a dozen pairs of curious eyes looked back at her, then a dozen smiles blossomed as recognition dawned. She returned the smiles resolutely as she scanned the room for Zeke.

He was sitting with Eli at the far side of the bar. He was talking when she saw him, his face half-turned from the door so that she saw the moment at which he realized she was there. His jaw dropped and his eyes opened with astonishment. Stifling the urge to giggle, she crossed the room to him. By the time she arrived at his table, he'd recovered enough to greet her with his usual aplomb.

"Well, Sally!"

"Hello, Zeke." She gestured behind her. "I've brought Archie back."

His smile of welcome broadened. "Mmm. So I see. I guess the civilizing business was harder than you thought."

"No, not really. The fact is—"

But Zeke wasn't listening. He was looking past her toward Archie and he was still smiling. "At least he's got himself a haircut and some damned fine clothes. Damned fine!" he repeated as his eyes swung back to her. "If you're not careful, Sally, you may find the rest of these homespun beggars knocking at your door at midnight and begging you to civilize 'em, too! I can just imagine what your marquis would say to that!"

The image struck him as so amusing that he threw back his head and laughed. "You might even find me, Sally!"

She smiled tolerantly. "Zeke, if you don't mind, could we talk alone? There's something I'd—"

For the second time in two minutes he cut her off.

"What's this, Sally? Are you afraid to admit your failure in front of the boys? Tut-tut, girl—I'd have expected more of you. Besides, none of them could do better with

Archie—isn't that right, boys?'' He looked around the room.

Eli was watching Sarah. "Zeke," he said quietly, "I think you should take Mistress Meade into the parlor to talk."

"What's this, Eli!" Zeke waggled a finger at him. "Don't tell me you're taking Sally's part again? Next I suppose you'll be wanting to try her case all over again! Not that I've got anything against talking to Sally alone. The truth is I'd like nothing better—" He turned to grin at her. "Off to the parlor we'll go, just as soon as she 'fesses up here in public and admits that she was wrong. What do you say, Sally?"

Sarah had nothing to say. Or rather she had a great deal she couldn't articulate, mainly because of the anger that was clogging up her throat. Zeke was kind and reassuring? Zeke would understand? God in heaven, what had she been telling herself? Had she been so tired she'd forgotten what he was like—this overgrown juvenile, this loudmouthed tyrant who'd never encumbered himself with the burden of pausing ten seconds to think!

Zeke was still grinning. "What about his schooling, Sally? Did you teach him his letters, too?" That struck him so funny he slapped his thigh and let out a loud guffaw.

Her fist curled like a hammer and she brought it down so hard on the top of the table that Zeke's glass began to dance. The violence released the flood dammed up in her throat. "You know damn well I didn't!" she snapped.

She leaned across the table to put her nose only inches from his. "He already knew his letters, since you'd taught him those yourself. But there are other things I'm certain he'll never learn from you—such as respect for other people. Such as discretion and tact. Such as thinking about feelings—such as knowing that feelings exist! Such as generosity and simple tolerance.

"What kind of a father treats his child like a pawn to be dragged hither and yon to satisfy his whim! I may have been talking about my father that night at the Van Kalms', but now I'm talking about you. I wasn't much older than

Archie when I understood, and Archie's a fast learner, so I don't think it will take him any longer than it took me. This time he came back, but maybe the next time you send him someplace he doesn't want to go he may surprise you and stay away!''

She pulled back from the table and stood glaring down at him. "You know what makes me angriest? That I was stupid enough to believe that you might be capable of working out a compromise! You're as bad as my father or Haddom—you only care about yourself and you think that if you yell and threaten you'll get what you want. Nobody's feelings matter! Nobody else's rights! It's all just what Zeke Brownell wants.

"Well, I'm here to tell you there's one thing you'll never have. You'll never get an acre—not a square foot—of that land! That land is mine, Zeke, and I mean to have every inch. I mean to sell it where and when I please, and I mean to have it surveyed if I have to survey it myself—and if you try to stop me, I swear I'll get a gun and shoot you down! Laugh all you want!" she concluded. "And you'd better do it now, because one day very soon I'll be laughing at you!"

Zeke wasn't laughing. He was staring at her in shock. So was Eli, but she was too angry to notice or to care. She stood there another moment but she had nothing more to say, so she whirled around from the table and stalked back to the door.

None of the Boys moved a muscle as she swept past, but Archie sprang forward and obligingly lifted the latch, and she managed to fling the door open by the force of her anger alone. Archie followed her out of the tavern to where the horses were tied. "Shall I ride along with you to show you the way back home?"

"No, thank you," she managed to say calmly, though what she really wanted was to scream at the top of her lungs. Her whole body was shaking and Archie looked abashed. "I'm not angry with you, Archie."

"I know that," Archie said. "Zeke does that to a body."

"He most certainly does! Take care of yourself, Archie. I'll miss seeing you every day."

"Yes, ma'am." He helped her to mount and when she was in the saddle he handed her the reins. "I'll tell him later," he offered, "after he's quieted down."

"Don't bother," she said bitterly. "You were wrong. I'm sorry. He wouldn't understand. Goodbye, Archie."

"Take care," he said, stepping back to avoid being trampled as she wheeled the horse around and took off out of the yard as if she were chasing the devil or the devil were chasing her.

She rode hard, keeping her body low and her shoulders hunched forward against the inevitable assault of Zeke's bellow thundering from behind. Damn him, damn him, damn him! she chanted to the beat of the horse's hooves. He'll have to drag me out of the saddle this time if he wants me to stop, and this time I'll fight him with every ounce of strength. Damn him, damn him!

Tears of anger stung her eyes and she didn't realize how far she'd ridden until she felt the horse slowing on its own. To her surprise she realized she'd already passed the turn-off to Zeke's farm. Zeke wasn't coming. He didn't mean to come. She pulled the horse to a stop and turned back toward the empty road.

The horse was grateful for the rest and stood with its head down, cropping grass from the side of the road. The sight of him made her realize how tired she was: bone-aching tired, weary through and through. She'd been traveling since before daybreak, and who knew how late it would be when she finally got home—where Haddom and her father would be awaiting her.

Never mind the future, the present had trouble enough; she had a long way to go and wouldn't get there by standing still. Pulling the horse's head up, she got him moving again, then she felt in her saddlebag for the last of the bread and cheese she and Archie had eaten on the road. She hadn't brought dinner, assuming they'd eat in Bennington. Had she imagined a cozy meal with Zeke? The thought of it made her angry all over again. She was angry at him and she was angry at herself for fooling herself into believing that he was different from other men.

She ate while she was riding, chewing woodenly, and if the food made her feel better, her own thoughts made her feel worse. With pain she remembered all the sweet things that Zeke had said and how his words and caresses had melted her. As recently as this morning, she'd trusted in those things. Now she realized that they were meaningless.

Her father had suggested that Zeke had been using her. Now she saw that he had been, but not in the way that her father had meant. Her father was calculating but Zeke was the opposite. He was as impulsive about women as he was about everything else: if he found a pretty one within reach, he'd reach for her as thoughtlessly as a child grabbing for a sweet. Zeke lived for the moment and to amuse himself, and when the moment was over, he moved on to the next. He'd pursued Sarah as long as she looked sweet, but now that she'd turned sour, he'd find someone else. Probably at this very moment he was back at the Catamount, drinking with his comrades and laughing at her expense.

Poor Archie, she thought, recalling the way he'd looked when she'd snapped her goodbye and bolted from the tavern yard. She hated to leave him to be brought up by Zeke, but he was Zeke's child and there was nothing she could do. At least she didn't have to feel guilty about the land. She'd fight Zeke for every acre, no matter what it took.

The sun had set when she reached the river but by luck she found the ferry still on her side. The ferryman was fishing off the edge and smoking his pipe. "My missus was of the opinion that you'd determined to spend the night, but I thought I'd come over just in case." He pulled his line in and stowed his rod.

"I don't know how to thank you," she told him, remembering what Zeke had said about his staying on this side of the river in order to avoid his wife. Zeke probably blamed everything on women, that's how he saw the world. Probably at this moment he was blaming things on her.

Damn him! she repeated for the millionth time, sliding out of the saddle to totter on the ground.

The ferryman helped her with her horse, then untied the rope. "So you got the boy home. I suppose you saw Brownell. He's a wild one, he is. I'm surprised you'd go back there after what he did to you."

She practically shouted, "Well I won't go again! Zeke Brownell can drown in the river, for all I care!"

The ferryman's mouth opened. For a minute he stared at her, then he closed it and muttered, "Well now, I reckon there's a heap of folks that would agree! Me, I run my ferry and mind my own affairs."

It was long past midnight when she pushed open the back door to Mason's house, and despite her apprehension, no one was waiting for her as she tiptoed upstairs to her room. She stripped off her dusty clothes and fell into bed, dreading how her body would feel when she woke up. She hoped that wouldn't be for twelve hours at least.

"Hellfire and damnation! Why didn't she say so in the first place instead of letting me make a damn cursed fool of myself?"

Archie ducked closer to the cow's side as Zeke gave the stable wall a vicious kick.

"Because," Eli said calmly, "you didn't give her the chance. She said she'd brought Archie back and you lit into her." He didn't add "as usual," but that was what he meant. "She did her best to stop you but you were too far gone by then. When you got to the part about his knowing his letters, I guess she'd had enough."

Eli had his back to his brother and was spreading straw with a fork while Archie did the milking and Zeke paced and roared. He'd been pacing and roaring since they'd gotten back from the Catamount—and Archie had explained the real reason why Sarah had brought him home.

"Hellfire!" Zeke muttered, and kicked the wall again. He glared down at Archie, who kept close to the cow's flank. Most of the animals were used to Zeke's ways and didn't spare the effort to look up from their feed, but the hens roosting on the crossbeams peered down indignantly.

"Damn biddies!" Zeke muttered, shaking his fist at them. "You could have done something," he said to his son.

Archie ducked down farther.

"Like what?" Eli asked.

"Waved his hands or something—or stopped her so she couldn't leave. But he had to help her out to her horse, and by the time he got around to telling me the truth it was too late for me to go after her—even if I'd wanted," he added belatedly.

"He couldn't have told you sooner," Eli pointed out. "You were too busy drinking and laughing with the Boys."

"And you—" Zeke pointed at Eli. "No doubt you knew. No doubt you were laughing behind your sleeve the whole cursed time!"

"I wasn't laughing," said Eli.

"No, but you probably knew. You knew and you didn't tell me. It's the same damn thing."

Eli set down the fork. "Why are you so angry?"

"Why! Why do you think? Or maybe you think I enjoy making a fool of myself?"

"Is that all? You're only angry because you made a fool of yourself?"

"Isn't that enough?" Zeke growled, but he wasn't yelling now.

Eli shrugged his shoulders. "I suppose it could be."

"What's that supposed to mean?"

"It means that maybe it's about time for you to stop and figure out just what you want out of this."

"What I want out of it—you know damn well what I want! I don't want any Yorkers messing around my land, or yours, or any of ours!"

"What about Sarah?"

"What about her?" Zeke snapped. When Eli didn't answer, he raised his foot to kick the wall again. But before he could kick it he caught sight of the cow watching him over her shoulder with big placid brown eyes—and the horses, and the chickens, and his brother and his son, all of their expressions saying what he knew damn well enough.

"Damnation!" he muttered, and stormed out of the barn.

Back in the barn, the door flapped behind him. When it had stopped flapping Archie looked at Eli over the cow's broad back. "What do you figure he'll do?"

Still leaning on his pitchfork, Eli shook his head. "I don't know. But for once in his life I hope he thinks about it first. What about you Archie? What do you think of Mistress Meade?"

"Who, me?" Archie flushed scarlet and ducked his head again. He recommenced his milking almost frantically, but gradually the pace of his fingers slowed back to a steady rhythmical pull. Finally he looked up. "She ain't no Yorker," he said firmly. "And that's a god-honest fact ."

A moment or so later he muttered, "isn't" to himself.

Chapter Twelve

It was a good deal less than twelve hours after Sarah had fallen asleep when her father's outraged voice jolted her awake.

"I can't believe it! I cannot believe it is true! When they told me yesterday morning, I could not believe you'd gone. Why did you do it?"

Sarah dragged open her eyes. Her body was aching. Even her eyelids ached. She blinked at her father, who was up and fully dressed despite what she perceived to be the very early hour. Or maybe she perceived that because the curtains were still drawn.

"Why!" he demanded.

She sighed. "You already know. I overheard you talking to Haddom—Father, you gave me your word."

"My word!" With a gesture of impatience, he brushed her recrimination aside. "I told you that the boy wouldn't have been harmed. If you weren't so wrapped up in your misguided morality, you'd realize that what I suggested is a good deal less dangerous than sending a bunch of armed men to do battle in the woods!"

"At least they'll be grown men who've chosen to go."

"Oh, really!" He threw his hands up. "I don't know what you want."

"You know what I want, Father."

"I'm not so sure I do. When they told me you'd run off with the boy to Bennington, all I could think was that you'd gone there to be with Brownell. Is that why you went, Sarah? Have you made some sort of a deal?"

That stung her badly. "I've made no deals with Zeke Brownell," she said bitterly. "We're as much enemies in this as we've ever been—more, if anything. And I'm as determined to sell the land."

"So you say, Sarah, but after this I don't know. First you estrange Haddom, then you return the boy—at this point I'm not sure you care about the land."

Last night she'd been too tired to braid her hair, with the result that this morning it was streaming everywhere. Her father could read her anger in the way she shoved it back. He was right, she was angry, but it wasn't the same anger that had erupted yesterday with Zeke. This anger wasn't explosive, it was slow, steady and white-hot, and it burned with a clarity that had been lacking before. She recalled what she'd decided about her father and the land, and she remembered what she'd sworn to Zeke. From there it was a short step to what she meant to do next.

She pushed herself up against the pillows. "You're wrong if you think that, Father. I do care about the land. Shall I tell you how much I care? Enough to go up there myself with the surveyor and the guard. Enough to make sure they stay there until the surveying is done, and that no one succeeds in frightening them away."

His eyes opened with shock. "You could be killed!"

"That's a risk I'll have to take because I mean to go."

"I'm afraid we'll both regret this." He shook his head. "If you'd done things my way, no one would have gotten hurt."

She opened her mouth to tell him how very wrong he was, and how much he'd already hurt her with his scheming and his lies. But there was no point in trying to tell him, since he'd never understand. He didn't care about feelings—in that way he was like Zeke. If she kept his share of the profits after paying their debts, she knew he'd accuse her of greed. The fact that she'd sworn to do exactly that wouldn't matter a bit to him. She was fed up with all men—

and she hadn't seen Haddom yet. And Haddom was certain to have a tirade of his own.

"If you approach him the right way, Haddom might still buy the land."

"No, thank you," Sarah said, knowing all too well what "approach" he had in mind. "I said I'd have that land surveyed and that's what I mean to do."

"You'll regret this," her father warned darkly.

"Maybe I will. But at least this time I'll have only myself to blame."

She avoided Haddom all morning, mostly by staying in her room, but when they finally met at dinner he took her by surprise, reacting to Archie's return almost philosophically.

"It's probably just as well," he observed, to her father's profound chagrin. "When you start taking hostages there's always the chance of someone getting hurt, and as obnoxious as the boy was, he was still a boy." Fluffing his lace, he added, "Besides, I wouldn't want it said that the Marquis of Haddom hid behind a child because he was afraid of facing Zeke Brownell!"

"I'm not, you know," he declared for Sarah's benefit. "Let him come. I'm ready to face him, but man-to-man and not with him barging through windows with two dozen of his friends."

Meade gestured toward Sarah. "Speaking of confrontations and people getting hurt, why not ask my daughter about her plans for going up north?"

"Up north where?" demanded Haddom.

"Never mind," Sarah said.

"To the land," explained her father. "She's going with the surveyor—or so she says."

Haddom gave her the sort of look he might give to an overexcited child. "Of course you won't go there," he said dismissively. "And neither will your surveyor until General Haldimand agrees to send a troop."

"But he won't do that," said Sarah, her patience running out.

"I say he will. Let us say no more about this. My mind is made up!"

Sarah said no more, not because she had the faintest intention of giving up her plan but because there was no point in arguing with Haddom, and even if there had been a point, she was too weary to argue. She was almost too weary to raise her fork to her mouth, though it had been two days since she'd eaten a decent meal.

At first she thought the weariness came from lack of sleep, but as afternoon drew into evening she realized that the fatigue she was feeling was very much spiritual, and that the deep pain in her spirit was all related to Zeke. Yesterday beside the river she'd recognized the strength of the bond between them, but she'd believed that once she'd discovered her mistake the bond would dissolve. But today, far from dissolving, the bond seemed stronger than before. It held her captive as firmly as Zeke had ever done, and it brought her face-to-face with all the things she'd been denying since that first night in the woods—things touching love and her future; things about hopes and dreams.

Apart from her father, she had never loved a man, and after loving her father it came as no surprise that she envisioned love as a deep and terrifying hole into which a woman would fall if she ever relaxed her vigilance with a man. Life with her father had taught her to be a realist. It had taught her the importance of controlling one's own destiny. For her, heaven had always been the chance of throwing off the grinding burden of her father's debts and living independently.

Since she'd turned sixteen, countless men had offered her marriage as the means of escape. Many had even offered to pay her father's debts, but she'd refused them all, seeing marriage as a different sort of trap in which she simply exchanged the known for the unknown. Her suitors had tried to woo and argue her out of her belief, but none of them had ever convinced her to change her mind.

It wasn't that she hadn't wanted to be convinced. Even the most hardheaded realist has her secret dreams—and often the harder the head, the more passionate th dreams—and Sarah was no exception to the rule. In a deep secret place she hardly acknowledged herself, she yearned for love as deeply as any woman on earth. The more strongly she built her defenses, the more she longed for a man strong enough to storm them and lay claim to her heart. She wanted to be taken and she wanted to be loved.

Until she'd met Zeke no man had ever come close. But then, as she'd grown closer to Zeke, down in the depths of that secret place hope had begun to stir. She'd felt the first faint stirring in the cabin that night, and again when he'd claimed her at the Van Kalms' dance. She'd felt it clearly yesterday at the river when she'd turned her face to the sun. When she'd admitted she trusted Zeke, she'd laid the door open to love. The door had remained open all the way to the Catamount—where Zeke had slammed it point-blank in her face. At least, she told herself, staunchly, Zeke would never know. But that reassurance did nothing to ease the pain.

Perhaps aware of the melancholy into which she had sunk, or perhaps worried that she might run off again, Haddom and her father decided to stay in that evening. They brought out Mason's chess set and sat down to a game, while Sarah took her needlework and settled herself in a chair where she could feel the breeze drifting in through the open garden doors.

She worked desultorily, hardly able to focus on the color of the thread as memories of Zeke rose up to mock her with the vision of what she'd lost. Touching the bit of cloth in her hands, she could feel Zeke's fingertips and the breathless wonder of his lips brushing hers. Above the murmur of the men's voices, she could hear Zeke's in her ear, sighing and groaning and whispering that she was sweet, the warmth of his breath raising gooseflesh up and down her arms.

She could remember the bitter way he'd looked when he'd asked her if she believed he'd killed his wife. He'd said that he hated liars and she'd taken that to mean that he never lied. But hadn't he been lying when he'd whispered in her ear, and when he'd touched her and looked deep into her eyes? Hadn't he been lying when he'd called her sweet and when he'd sworn he couldn't stay away from her? Hadn't he been saying whatever he thought she'd like to hear—whatever he'd thought would sound pretty and get him what he desired?

Spurred by a flash of anger, she drove the needle hard, straight through the linen and into the ball of her thumb.

"Ouch!" she protested, and both men turned.

"What's wrong?" demanded Haddom.

"Nothing. I pricked my thumb." She sucked on the sore spot.

"Your move," her father said, and with a sigh of reluctance Haddom returned to the game. Her father must be winning, she thought. Her finger had stopped bleeding. She blew on it to be certain, then bent back to her work.

Zeke had deceived her—or had she deceived herself? After all, he'd never promised anything. When he groaned how much he wanted her, that was probably what he meant, right then, at that moment, in his usual impulsive way, and she'd been weak and foolish to tell herself otherwise. When you put your faith in a man you were asking to be let down.

To her horror, her stitches blurred. She, who never stooped to self-pity, was on the verge of tears. In a moment she'd bawl like a baby, then Haddom and her father would look up and Haddom would ask, "What's wrong?" and her father, disgusted, would tell him to get back to the game. There were no knights in shining armor. All men were the same.

She thrust her work aside and stood. "It's warm in here. I believe I'll step out into the garden for a breath of air."

Haddom's head swiveled. "I should go with her."

"Of course you shouldn't!" her father said. "You can't just get up and leave when we're in the middle of a game."

"We can call an intermission. After what's happened, I don't think she ought to be out there by herself. Brownell could appear at any time."

Sarah could have laughed at that with a short bitter laugh. "He won't appear," she said flatly. "If he does I'll scream and you can rush to my aid. In the meantime, you can go on with your game."

"You see," said her father, tapping Haddom's arm. "You've got plenty of good moves, but you've got to watch the board."

Sarah heard Haddom's sigh as she stepped through the doors.

She'd thought the fresh air would alleviate her mood, but instead it did the opposite. The night was balmy, almost sultry, the air soothing in its softness and fragrant with perfume. The air made her feel like crying; it made her feel empty and low. It made her regret things, which was something she never did.

She looked up for distraction, but the stars were hidden beneath a gauzy haze. When she looked back down at the garden she saw something move. Something in the shadows at the end, near the wall. Something was moving. A person. The person was Zeke. Zeke was standing in the shadows, beckoning to her.

Without thinking she stepped forward before she caught herself. What was she doing—running straight to him when she'd just been telling herself that he didn't care?

But he was here! He wouldn't have come if he didn't care.

Care for what? her rational mind demanded.

Oh, Lord!

As if he'd read her mind through the darkness, Zeke reached out his hand. From across the garden she could feel its pull, hard and insistent. Her heart began to pound and waves of sensation rippled down through her limbs. In her mind she saw herself running across the grass to him; she felt the thud of their collision and the rough heat of his arms. Her body was vibrating.

She turned away, clenched her fists and slowly walked back into the lighted rectangle of the drawing room doors.

At her reappearance, neither of the men looked up. Haddom was about to move and her father was watching the board with such concentration that he didn't see her in the doorway. From behind she could feel Zeke pulling.

He's here!

Look up, she urged her father. Look up and break the spell. Haddom fondled the black pawn. Sarah turned and fled.

Into the emptiness. The garden was deserted. Zeke had disappeared. He hadn't really been there—she'd just imagined him. Cruel, cruel illusion! Tears came to her eyes and she moved into the darkness just to be alone. When she reached the shadows she heard him speak her name.

Zeke felt as if he were in a dream, a dream composed of soft air and visions dressed in white. Sally was wearing a white dress cut low in the front. He wanted to press a soft kiss to the valley between her breasts. He wanted to drop to his knees with his arms around her waist. He wanted to run his hands up and down her legs and hear her moan and feel her quiver with pleasure at his touch.

He'd been watching her through the window since she'd sat down to sew and the whole time he'd been watching he'd been wanting her, until he'd had to clench his fists and press his back to the garden wall so as not to barge straight in through the open doors, snatch her up and carry her off as he'd done before.

Even from that distance he'd seen that she hadn't been concentrating on her work. When she'd pricked her finger he'd known for sure. He'd wanted to kiss it and suck away the blood. He'd wanted to ask her if she was thinking of him.

God knew he'd thought of her. He hadn't thought of anything but since she'd stormed off yesterday. And not only yesterday, but the days and weeks before. Over the weeks since he'd met her he had gotten to the point where, like the catamount over the tavern sign, he was pointing toward New York. He was always facing Sally. He was always wanting her. At night he'd lie awake while Eli and Archie slept, remembering that night in the cabin; remembering other things. Last night he'd remembered the anger

in her voice when she'd called herself a fool for ever believing in him.

Eli had asked him what he wanted and the truth was he
didn't know—it was all complicated by the goddamn land.
He smiled with faint irony; imagine him cursing the land.
He had it bad for Sally. He had it very bad.

He'd stood in the shadows watching and wanting her
until the force of his wanting had pulled her from her chair
and into the garden. Then he'd beckoned her, holding his
breath and hoping that she wouldn't turn and run—or
worse, that she wouldn't sound the alarm to the other men.
Not that they could catch him; there wasn't a breath of a
chance. But it would hurt him to know that he'd sunk that
low in Sally's eyes.

He'd felt his chest collapsing when she'd turned away.
He'd told himself it was for the best, but he'd known that
was a lie. He'd fallen back into the shadows and covered his
face with his hands, and when he'd dropped his hands and
looked, she'd been coming to him. In thanks, in fear, in
disbelief, in longing, he spoke her name.

"Sally!"

She faced him in the shadows, waiting for him to speak.
All the light came from behind her so he couldn't see her
face, but maybe that was a good thing, because if he didn't
know what she was feeling he could always hope.

"Hello, Sally."

She didn't reply. She just stood there waiting, her body
tense as though if he said the wrong thing she'd turn and
bolt for the house. It didn't make things easier but he
hadn't expected her to.

He stuffed his hands into his pockets. "I came to apologize."

"For what?"

"For doing the things you said. Leaving Archie the way
I did…not letting you explain. I also wanted to thank you
for bringing him back."

Her shoulders moved in a faint shrug. "I did it for him,
not for you."

What hurt most was her tone of voice, because it told him he'd let her down. He wanted to say he was sorry but the words just wouldn't form, so instead he said, "Even so, you were good to Archie. I want to thank you for that."

"Why shouldn't I be good to Archie? He's a wonderful boy. I would have kept him—" Her voice broke off and despite the darkness he saw her bite her lip.

"I know," he said softly. "I'm sorry about that. Archie told me about your father—"

"Leave it!" She spun away and might have bolted if he hadn't caught her arm.

"Let me go, you brute!" she cried out, struggling against his grasp.

"Hush!" He used his free hand to cover her mouth. "Be quiet or they'll hear us."

She made a noise that meant "Let them hear!" But at least she stopped struggling so he took his hand away. "If I let you go, will you promise to stay?"

"I don't know," she muttered, turning her head away and using her free hand to brush back the hair that had come undone. They were close enough that he could have embraced her easily. He was longing to embrace her but he knew it would do no good. The way things were between them she'd only fight him off.

"Listen to me, Sally," he said, his head near hers. "If you don't want to talk about your father, we won't. We'll talk about something else—we'll talk about you and me."

"You and me?" She pulled against him. "What about you and me?"

"Everything!" he answered, keeping her where she was. "For instance, the reason I can't stay away. I can't stay away, Sally. You must know that by now. You're like a flame, pulling me, and I'm the bewildered moth, bumping up against the window, trying to get close to you. The more I try to hold back, the worse I fail. I've worn down a set of horseshoes riding back and forth.

"Take last night, for instance. I didn't fall asleep. I just lay there thinking how much you must hate me and how you probably never wanted to see me again. I kept telling myself that the best thing I could do was to leave you alone, but all the time I knew that, come sunrise, I'd be on the road again. I've never felt this for a woman—I wonder if I've ever felt it for anything."

"Let me go!" she whispered.

"Don't you see I can't?"

"You've got to!" She was shaking.

"Please, Sally—"

"No!"

Let her go, a stern voice commanded, but he paid it no heed. Instead he pulled her to him and caught her with his other arm. He felt her stiffen, then shudder, as her body melted into his. Then his head came down hungrily in search of her mouth.

He found it and claimed it with a force that made her writhe. He knew he should be gentler but he couldn't stop. He hadn't been lying when he'd said he'd never felt so much for a woman. It was as though he were starving and she were food and drink. When he held her he knew he had been starving all his life, and though he didn't want to be greedy he couldn't help himself.

She was better than he'd remembered. It was like this every time. Other women had always been the same or less, but Sally was always better, lusher and firmer and hotter, more pliant in his arms, her hair tangled in his fingers, her breasts hard against his chest. Everything else ceased to matter, including the land. If he'd been made to choose now he couldn't have let her go, not when she moved that way against him, not when she opened her mouth as though she could never get enough of him.

"No, oh no!" she groaned when he lifted his head.

"Why not, Sally?" he whispered.

"Because you don't care!"

"Don't care—how can you say that?"

"Because it's true!"

He saw the glint of silver and he realized it was tears. "Sally, you're crying!"

"Damn you, no I'm not!"

"I told you I hated lying." But his voice caught on the words, and this time when he pulled her close, his embrace wasn't so rough, though it was deep or deeper than it had been before. It wasn't enough to hold her. He wanted to swallow her—to draw her inside so deeply he'd never have to let her go.

Clothing became an obstruction; his hands pushed it away, seeking for the finer texture of her skin. When he found it she shuddered but she didn't protest. He thought she'd stopped crying but he wasn't really sure. The world was spinning around them, whirring in his ears, insulating them from danger in a bright shining cocoon.

"Don't leave me, Sally."

"No, never!" she swore.

She couldn't, he knew that. The spell between them was too strong. The world could crumble around them and they'd never even know. Her petticoat was muslin and gave way easily. Beneath it her thighs were satin and her buttocks round and firm. Her hands had found their way up under his shirt and her nails dug sharply into his naked back. He welcomed their sharpness, reveled in the pain, as it only increased the pleasure. It only increased the—

"Let her go this instant or you'll be dead in the next!"

Haddom's voice exploded behind them. Zeke's whole body tensed and he cursed—but before the curse was completed, Sally had been torn from his arms and Haddom was staring at her dishevelment in shock.

"My God! What has happened here!"

But the question was rhetorical, and Haddom had seen enough. Grasping Sally by the forearm, he thrust her behind his back, and she went like a puppet, her face ghostly white from the shock. As soon as she was out of range, Haddom turned on Zeke.

"You!" The word split the soft air like thunder. "You swine—you savage animal, you deserve to die! I ought to kill you here and now!"

The hand that was not holding Sally waved violently at Zeke, which was when he noticed that Haddom was holding a gun; a long-barreled pistol, its barrel leveled at his breast.

Haddom's voice rose in triumph. "I've got you this time, Brownell! When I heard the lady cry out I guessed it might be because of you, so I took the precaution of arming myself before coming out. I've also sent for the sheriff—he ought to be here soon. You're trapped this time, Brownell! You're headed straight for jail, and after what you've done tonight, I'd bet even money that you'll never get out alive. I wonder if the good people of Albany have enough restraint to let you live long enough to be tried. I wouldn't blame them if they don't!"

Zeke's eyes were fixed on Sally and he scarcely heard Haddom's words. He didn't give a damn about Haddom or his bloody gun. What he cared about was Sally—if only she'd look at him and stop staring at Haddom's back, her face so pale, as if she were already feeling ashamed of what they'd done. He spoke her name.

"Sally."

"Don't you dare!" Haddom raged, thrusting her farther behind him. "You may have fooled the lady, but you don't fool me. From the first minute, I've known you for what you are. You may act hotheaded, but your blood's as cold as ice. Cold enough to have figured out how to take the lady in, right down to bringing her that wretch of a son of yours. Taming the lion cub—ladies like that sort of thing, don't they, Brownell?"

Zeke's eyes shifted from Sally, who still hadn't moved. "The devil take you, Haddom. What the hell are you getting at?"

"Hell is where you're going before I'm through with you!" Haddom's eyes gleamed at the thought. "You've been seducing this lady in order to steal her land. Do you deny it? Do, and I'll laugh in your face! I'll bet if I were to search you, I'd find the deeds tucked inside your coat, all drawn up and ready for her signature." He glanced away for a moment to the shrubbery near the wall. "Have you brought your witnesses and notary along, or did you mean to carry her off the way you did before?"

"You bloody bastard!" Zeke gritted, moving forward instinctively.

By the same instinct Haddom yielded ground, taking Sally with him to keep her out of reach. "You hate me, don't you, because I've found you out!"

Zeke kept moving. "You bastard—let her go!"

"Ha! Never! You must think I'm mad."

"Let her go," Zeke repeated. "Or you'll wish you had." Taking another step forward, he spoke her name again.

"Sally."

The word echoed in Sarah's mind, clashing with the others: "ladies like that sort of thing," and worse, "seducing this lady . . . to steal her land."

This must be a dream, a nightmare, painful and violent. In one moment her body was melting into Zeke's; in the next it was gripped by Haddom, who was also holding a gun. Her bodice was still open—she could feel the soft air on her skin. The softness of it shamed her, but she couldn't raise her hand. She could only stand frozen, listening to Haddom's words—words that served as lodestones, attracting the worst of her fears.

Haddom's words were harsh and hurtful. She longed to call them lies, but although she struggled, she found that she could not, not pushed and pulled as she had been in these last two days. Her feelings for Zeke had shifted back and forth so violently that she no longer knew what to believe.

She needed Zeke's reassurance, needed it desperately. She moved around Haddom as far as his grip would allow, until she could see Zeke. Words seemed beyond her, but her eyes held her naked plea plain for him to read. Their eyes met and she watched as he read it.

As he did, his whole body changed. To her horror, it seemed to harden and draw away. "You believe what he says?" he murmured.

She opened her mouth in protest but Haddom answered for her.

"Why not, it's the truth! Deny it if you dare!" Sneering, he pulled her against him, encircling her with his arm—

as if mocking Zeke with what he wanted but could not have. Sarah tried to pull away but her body had turned to lead, for her entire will was concentrated in a struggle with Zeke.

"You believe it," Zeke repeated, accusatory now. His eyes shifted disdainfully from her to Haddom and back.

"Shut up!" Haddom snarled, crushing her closer to him.

She stumbled, thrown off balance. She could hardly breathe. A word, that was all she needed—just a word, a sign. "Please—please, Zeke!" she whispered.

"Please, what?" Zeke bit out. "Please will I debate his lordship over just how bad I am? Is that what you want, Sally? Knowing the two of us as you do, you'd credit him over me, after—" He finished the sentence with a bitter shake of his head.

Before she could speak his eyes narrowed and shifted again. "Or am I missing something? Am I—is that it? Did you decide to take my advice on making your future secure?" His gaze lingered on her and Haddom and his lip curled in a cruel mockery of a smile. "Were you misleading me, Sally, while I was misleading you?"

"What's that supposed to mean?" Haddom demanded.

Zeke didn't answer, but Sarah knew. Zeke meant that she'd lied to him about what Haddom was to her. She'd asked him for reassurance and he'd slapped her in the face, jumping to conclusions the way he always jumped. Was he being cruel on purpose or had Haddom been right? One possibility was as bad as the next, and even if neither was true, the unjustness of his reaction chased away her lassitude and restored her voice. She straightened as she answered, "After the way you've acted, I would have been more than justified if I had taken your advice."

"Did you, Sally?"

"Do you have to ask?"

Their eyes met and locked together, hers angry and hurt, his hard. They held but neither yielded. Slowly Zeke nodded his head. "If that's the way you put it, I guess maybe I do."

She released her breath slowly. "Then maybe the answer is yes. Maybe I did take your advice. Maybe that's just what I did."

"Did what?" snapped Haddom. "What is this all about?"

At his demand, Zeke looked at Haddom as if seeing him for the first time. Gone in an instant was the coldness, replaced by a white burning heat of such fury that Haddom instinctively moved away, releasing his grip on Sarah though keeping tight hold of the gun.

But Haddom didn't move quickly enough. There was a flurry of motion, and the next thing Sarah knew, Haddom was flat on his back and Zeke was towering over him, breathing in deep gulps and holding the gun.

"I demand—" blustered Haddom.

"Shut up!" Zeke cut him off. "Don't push me, your lordship, or, savage animal that I am, I might lose all control and blow out your brains. I ought to do it anyway, for what you said, but I've always had a strange savage taste for an equal fight. And I suppose you've done me a service, if not a pleasant one. You once promised to teach me a lesson, and it looks like you have—and not one I'm ever likely to forget."

His breathing was more even as he glanced toward Sarah, and the heat of fury had drained out of his eyes. They met hers briefly before turning to Haddom again. "You were right about one thing, your lordship. I do mean to keep my land, and anyone who wants it will have to take it from me by force. I believe the lady is fool enough to try. She said she meant to yesterday, when she brought back my 'wretch' of a son. I don't suppose you can stop her—she's not the stopping type—but if she were my lady, I wouldn't let her go alone. That is, unless you haven't got the guts to go along."

"I'll have you—" began Haddom, but Zeke shut him up with a wave of the gun.

"Goodbye," he said to Sarah. "I guess if I were a gentleman I'd wish you luck."

"I don't want your wishes."

"Suit yourself." He shrugged and, gripping the gun by its barrel, held it out to her. "I'll leave this behind. Both you and your lordship have threatened to shoot me and you'll need this to try."

She took the gun without speaking and without touching his hand, and when their eyes met it was like stone meeting stone. No sooner were her fingers curled around the wooden butt than he had vanished up and over the wall. She heard the muffled thump as he landed on the far side, then his running footsteps, which soon disappeared.

"Bloody swine!" cursed Haddom, struggling to sit up. His wig had slipped sideways and was half covering one eye. "Damn it! Meade, where are you?" he shouted toward the house.

"I'm here." There was a rustling, then Henry Meade emerged from the bushes, where he'd been hiding all along.

"What the hell!" cried Haddom. "You were supposed to back me up! We could have had him between us!"

"I doubt it," said Meade. "Besides, I told you, it's not my sort of thing. Your wig is on crooked."

"Damn it, don't you think I know!" Shaking with frustration, Haddom straightened his wig. "And what about the sheriff? You were supposed to have gone for him."

"I sent the maid."

"Confound it, man, where is he! He could ride in pursuit!"

"It's too late," Sarah said. Her voice was flat. She was no longer angry, but hurt and embittered. That Zeke could touch her that way, then accuse her as he had—

"Damn it!" cursed Haddom, shaking his fist at the wall. "Does that man believe that he can mock me at his will? He says I've taught him a lesson, but he'll find out I haven't begun to teach him yet!" He looked at Sarah, who was still holding the gun. "Does he think I'm afraid to go up north? If he does, he'll see that he's mistaken. If Haldimand won't send a guard, I'll hire one of my own, then we'll see just who's teaching whom! Give me the gun," he commanded, before Sarah could reply.

She held it toward him. "Don't you think you'd better stand up?"

Meade came forward to help Haddom to his feet. Once up, he snatched the gun from Sarah and strode off toward the house.

"I'm going," said Sarah. "And I don't want him along."

"I can't see how you'll stop him," her father replied. "Besides, if he'll pay for a guard, at least you'll be able to go." He paused, "Did Brownell hurt you?"

Sarah laughed bitterly. "Thank you for asking. What would you do if he had? Tell me, Father—would you have defended me?"

He started to answer but then he gave up. "Probably not," he admitted in a voice she had never heard before.

She glanced at him in surprise. His shoulders were slumping and suddenly he looked old. For the first time in many years she felt sorry for him. Truly sorry.

She patted him on the arm. "Well he didn't," she said flatly. "So never mind. Come on, Father, there's no point in staying out here." Taking his arm gently, she led him back into the house.

Chapter Thirteen

After that, Haddom forgot about the governor or General Haldimand furnishing a troop and determined to spend his own coin on a private guard. Mincingly imperious, he demanded that Sarah give him the list she'd gotten from the sheriff, then brushed aside her explanations about which men she'd already seen.

"Men are far more willing to listen to another man," he informed her smugly, though it would have been closer to the truth to say that men were willing to listen to money, which Haddom was able to pay. Speaking in pounds and guineas, he hired six men on the first day alone. He said that he'd be satisfied when he had a dozen more.

When he wasn't out hiring men, Haddom devoted himself to lambasting Sarah to force her to stay behind. He fumed and expostulated, and her father explained and begged, and when George Mason returned home from his trip, they enlisted his aid, as well, but all of them together couldn't shake her resolve. When her father brought up the lack of a chaperon, she dryly replied that she doubted her reputation could be tarnished any more than it had been already by her various trips to Bennington.

"If you're worried, find another woman to go along," she said, but of course they couldn't find a woman—it was all they could do to find men—so finally they gave up.

Sarah felt no triumph in the victory. She felt almost nothing at all—nothing but the blankness that Zeke had left behind. His hot caresses seemed like scenes from another life. Whether or not he'd seduced her for the land seemed irrelevant. What mattered was that in the end he hadn't cared. When she'd asked him for understanding, instead he'd chosen pride. He'd spoken to Haddom of lessons, and she'd learned one of her own. She'd learned that only a foolish woman would put her faith in a man.

Then why was she so determined to go up to the land, the one place she was almost certain of seeing him again? There were several reasons and one had to do with pride. Just as Zeke had his, she had hers, too, and she wanted to show him that she wasn't afraid to face him again. Besides, what did she have to fear? How could he hurt her more than he'd already done? He couldn't, if she didn't let him, and she wouldn't—not ever again.

And there was something else, an almost superstitious need to see the land that had turned her life topsy-turvey and caused her so much grief. She couldn't say why she had to see it, she only knew she did. So, as full summer turned the days hot and the nights full of hazy stars, she prepared to leave. Then one day Haddom announced that since nothing else seemed to dissuade her, he'd decided to buy her land.

"To *what?*" They were drinking tea in Mason's garden, where an occasional breeze cooled the air.

"To buy your land," he repeated. "I'll pay you a good price, perhaps not so much as you'd get if you sold it in lots, but certainly more than enough to cover your needs." He sipped his tea with satisfaction, his little finger crooked. "So you see, there's really no need for you to come along."

"No, thank you," she replied.

No longer so contented, Haddom set down his cup. "You are speaking hastily and without giving the matter thought. The truth is, you can't do any better than sell to me. You'll have your money and I'd be free to take on Brownell, unburdened by any worry for your safety." He paused before he added, "I know your father agrees."

"That may be," she said calmly, "but it's not my father's land. Thank you for the offer, but I prefer to wait."

Tea forgotten, he snapped open his painted fan and worked it with a vigor that reached to where she sat. "You're being foolish—and ungrateful, if I do say so myself. Without my help you'll never get rid of Brownell, and until he's gotten rid of no one will buy the land. If you're worried about the money—"

"It's not money," Sarah said. "Your lordship, I am grateful, but I can't sell my land to you."

"You'll regret this," repeated her father, when he'd heard what she'd done—from Haddom, as she'd expected, as soon as he'd finished his tea.

"I thought you were the one who wanted to hold on to the land until Haddom had raised the value by chasing away the Boys."

"If he can chase them away. But what if he can't? Take the money, Sarah, and let's go home."

Home? "I can't," said Sarah, "I know you can't understand it, but I have to go up there."

Her father shook his head. "As you'd be the first to tell me, I've made some mistakes in my life. But the biggest one may have been signing that land over to you. I hope you know what you're doing."

Although she didn't say so, she wasn't sure she did: as she'd told her father, she only knew that she had to go.

But before she could do that there were other crises to brave, such as the one that followed Haddom's visit to Gow. He came home from the meeting on the verge of apoplexy, ranting at Sarah for hiring a drunk and vowing to replace Gow before the day was done. But even Haddom's money couldn't buy a better man, and only his desire to get at Zeke kept him from calling the whole trip off.

"I'll hold you responsible," he warned Sarah, "if he shows up drunk." Whereupon Sarah went to call on Gow herself.

She found him at home, unshaven and wigless and inclined to make snide jokes about the marquis, which, on another occasion, she might have found humorous. Not today, however.

"Mr. Gow," she said. "You've promised to survey my land, and if you do that, I'll see that you have enough credit with your friends around the corner to keep you in drink for a year. But if you fail me, this is what I'll do. I will have you bound, gagged and set adrift in a boat without oars in the middle of Lake Champlain. Do you understand me?"

"And blindfolded?" Gow asked. "I'm afraid of the dark." When she didn't smile, he sighed. "You can tell his lordship not to worry. Even drunks have dignity."

"It's not his lordship, it's me."

"In that case, Mistress Meade, I think we'll all be fine."

They left at the end of the week, twenty of them— counting Gow's chainman—in two boats, which took them up the river until it veered to the west and degenerated into a series of impassable falls. At that point the boats left them to return to Albany, and the party spent the night in a little settlement at the river's bend. The next morning they traveled up over the height of land that separated the river valley from Lake George. Haddom, Gow and Sarah rode, and the rest of the men went on foot. Haddom fussed over details and was the worst sort of company. Gow, who was sober, looked decidedly pale and pinched, but he was able to maintain his seat, and as the morning progressed he was even able to comment on the scenery.

The scenery was worthy of comment, especially when they crested the final rise and saw the lake in its serene beauty stretching away from them below.

"What do you think, Mistress Meade?" Gow asked as they started down.

"I think it's very pretty."

As for Haddom, he hardly glanced at the view, muttering to himself about the chances of finding enough canoes. "I was assured there would be, but people in the country are not always dependable."

"In my opinion," Gow said blandly, "people generally live up to one's expectations of them."

"Do they?" asked Sarah with such sudden intensity that both men turned to her. Realizing how she'd sounded, she shrugged and looked away, but after that the scenery wasn't quite so beautiful.

It was early afternoon when they reached the trading post at the foot of the lake. Sufficient canoes were waiting, but one of them had a leak.

"Just as I suspected!" Haddom cried, almost triumphantly, and stormed off to complain to the master of the post. The other men seemed unperturbed about the delay. Some found comfortable spots in the sunshine while others went inside to have a drop to drink.

Gow cast a longing glance in their direction. "A drop would be lovely."

"No it wouldn't," Sarah said. "Remember your promise."

"Yes, I remember." Gow sighed. "I suppose that these matters are best resolved by extremes." Settling himself on a stump in the shade, he produced a mouth harp and began to play as Haddom reappeared in pursuit of a narrow-faced Indian, who'd been charged by the trading post's owner with repair of the leaky canoe.

"He'll stand over him," said Sarah, watching the two move off. "He'll fuss until that poor Indian goes mad." She looked toward the edge of the clearing. "There must be a path along the lake. Maybe I'll go for a walk."

Gow nodded in confirmation, setting aside the harp. "Just be careful you don't run into Brownell."

She froze; her heart nearly stopped beating. "You think he's here?"

"Heavens no, I was only teasing. Brownell won't waste his time trailing us up the lakes. He'll take the direct route and be waiting for us at the land."

"How can you be so sure?"

"Because it makes sense. It's his land he's defending—his, from his point of view. Take your walk if you want to. God knows, you've got plenty of time."

Still shaken by Gow's warning, she started toward the lake, but Haddom's voice stopped her before she'd taken a dozen steps.

"Where do you think you're going?"

Addressing her from a distance, he'd practically shouted the words, as one would at a bad servant or a prisoner. The urge struck her to keep walking, but she knew he'd shout again, so she turned back slowly.

"I'm going for a walk."

Haddom goggled as though she'd lost her wits. "As if I haven't enough to deal with, trying to coax this red savage to work! You'll stay here with the others," he snapped and turned away, leaving Sarah with her mouth open and her cheeks flaming red.

Before she could draw breath, she heard a snigger from behind. She whirled around in time to catch two of the men laughing at her. Red flares of anger exploded in her mind as she strode to where they stood. Their smiles slowly faded as they watched her come, but their eyes still held traces of their amusement as she confronted them.

"You're fired," she blurted.

Both of their jaws went slack. "Beg pardon, mistress?"

"You heard me. You're fired. Gather your things and go!" She stood with her arm pointing south until they began to move. Then she let her arm drop and stalked away before the shaking in her legs gave way to furious tears. Damn Haddom! This time he'd gone too far, and only the presence of the men kept her from telling him so. He might be the one with the money, but that didn't mean—

"What do you think you're doing, firing my men?"

She turned, and there was Haddom, hands on his wool-clad hips. He'd given up his silks for the journey but his manners hadn't changed. "What do you think you're doing?"

"They may be your men, but they were impertinent to me," she answered with a calm she did not feel. Not quite so calmly, she added, "Then again, so were you."

Haddom's face reddened as he fought for control. When he had it, he answered, "I told you you shouldn't have come. The master of the post is going to Albany tomorrow and I shall have him escort you home."

"You shall *have*?" She was so angry she almost screamed. "I'll tell you what you shall have—eighteen men with nothing to guard, if you don't change your tune! The troops may be yours but the land is mine, and I'll go there alone with Mr. Gow before I'll let you treat me like a half-wit with two left feet!'' Only the fear that the men might hear her forced her to keep her voice down. ''Do you understand me?''

Haddom's face was scarlet and he could barely speak. ''Madam, you are impossible!'' he gasped, and whirled away.

Seething with anger, Sarah watched him mincing off. His snipping and his snapping would surely drive her mad. If Zeke had been here he would have laughed the whole thing off. ''Boys will be boys. Sally,'' he would have told her easily. If Zeke had been here, he'd have fixed the canoe himself or left it to the Indian and joined her for a walk. If Zeke had been here—

''Oh, damn him!'' she swore, as if it were Zeke and not Haddom who'd gotten her into this state. ''Damn him!'' she repeated, but cursing didn't help.

Haddom must have paid the two men to apologize to her, which they did with a slyness that made her want to scream. Her anger lingered until they started up the lake, but it was no match for the beauty or the pleasure of the trip. Gow, who hated paddling, played his mouth harp instead, and the men were glad for the music, which made them forget their toil. During the breaks in the singing the men swapped tales. A couple of the older ones had come this way in the French and Indian War and gave stirring descriptions of the battles they'd seen at Ticonderoga and especially in Quebec. As long as she steered clear of Haddom, Sarah enjoyed herself.

They reached the fort at Ticonderoga early the next afternoon, snaking through the narrow channel that connected the two lakes. A lone sentry saluted and they saluted back, their voices echoing from shore to shore.

That night they camped on the east shore of Lake Champlain, which was wider and, if possible, more beautiful than Lake George. Standing at the water's edge look-

ing at the mountains to the west, Sarah remembered what
Zeke had said about her eyes being the same color as those
mountains at dusk and that color having no name. Now
that she saw them she knew what he meant. She couldn't
put a name to what the mountains made her feel, towering
sentries in the distance above the broad waters, which
caught and reflected the light of a million stars. One moment she felt achingly empty, the next full to overflowing,
and even her willpower could not turn her thoughts from
Zeke.

The next day the wind dropped and they sweltered, unprotected from the sun. It was so hot they stopped long
before dark, and no sooner had they beached the canoes
than the men disappeared to the next cove for a swim. All
except Haddom, who settled down for a nap and was soon
snoring, his chin resting on his chest.

Sarah listened wistfully to the shouts of the men. She
could just imagine how Haddom would carry on if he
opened his eyes and found her with her skirts hitched up,
splashing in the lake, but she was hot and sticky and longing to be cool. Then let him not find her, she thought,
moving away, not in the direction where the men were
swimming but the other way. Haddom was still sleeping
when she reached the end of the cove and ducked through
the trees that divided this cove from the next.

The neighboring cove was small and hooked around at
the far end, creating a pretty little pool. Walking around to
that little pool, she pulled off her shoes and stockings, then,
on deeper impulse, she pulled off everything else. Less than
a minute later, she was gloriously wet and cool, splashing
and ducking like the most carefree of seals.

When she'd had enough of swimming, she flipped onto
her back, blinking through beaded lashes at the summer
sky. On a branch above her perched a bird, watching her
with its head cocked, as if wondering what sort of strange
creature had invaded its private domain.

"A human one," she informed it. Her voice sounded
very loud. She must have startled the bird, for it took wing
and flew away. Then, suddenly and surely, she knew that

she wasn't alone. All of her senses told her that someone was watching her.

"You're torturing yourself," Eli had said when Zeke had announced his intention of splitting off from the others to track Haddom's party north. Zeke had justified his decision by saying he wanted to see for himself what kind of a guard they had, but Eli had seen through him as though he'd been made of glass.

"As you yourself have said many a time, if you've seen one Yorker posse, you've seen them all. You're torturing yourself," Eli had said.

Zeke had growled, "Well, if I am, it's me I'm torturing, so it's none of your damned affair!"

He watched Sarah glide through the water easy as an eel. Her skin was the color of moonlight and the water had turned her hair dark. He knew what her hair would feel like—he'd felt it soaking wet. He knew how her skin would feel, too. He knew too damn much. Eli was right about why he'd come but he couldn't help himself. He had to feed his resentment and rub salt into his wounds. He was a hound for punishment just like his father had been.

Eli was right about the guard, and as for Haddom, he was a joke. That was the worst part, that Sally had gone with him just because he had money and could help her sell the land. He wondered if she intended to marry him afterward or whether she meant to drop him once he'd served her needs. Too bad he'd never know what Sally had in mind, since she was never going to sell the land, and before this trip was over Zeke intended to expose his lordship for the quivering coward he was. He wondered what Sally would do then. Maybe marry Haddom for his money alone.

She was gliding through the water, wriggling like a fish. Just watching the way she was moving turned him to liquid inside. In his mind he saw himself tearing off his clothes and diving in to join her, swimming out to her and taking her in the water, all slithery and wet. She'd be cool on the outside and hot as fire within. Zeke shuddered violently and swallowed a silent curse as Sally stopped swimming and flipped over onto her back.

That was worse. The sight of those full breasts—his arms began to ache with the strain of not reaching out to her. He'd twist the long fall of her hair around and around his hand and pull her head backward until he had her mouth, then he'd drive down into it and he'd yank her hard against him, flesh to glorious flesh. She'd struggle but she'd want it, the same way she always did. She might marry Haddom but she wanted Zeke, and she made him want her until he forgot all sense. She looked like an angel but she was the devil in disguise.

She floated on the water, then suddenly she froze. In the same instant Zeke heard what she had. Someone was coming. Slowly he sucked in his breath and began to move.

Shivering in the water, Sarah looked up at the bank. She was stark, jaybird naked and her clothes were lying across the pool at the top of a steep muddy bank. Straining against the shadows, she searched the shore, and though she could see nothing, she knew someone was there. Zeke was her first thought, but she wasn't sure. Who else? One of the men? An Indian? The men claimed that the Indians around here were all peaceful, but at the moment she didn't feel so sure.

What should she do, then? She turned toward the shore. Call for help from Haddom? Make a mad dash for her clothes? Swim back to the camp? Her mind flipped through the options, then she saw another one. What if she swam out and around to the next cove, then sneaked back through the cover to the spot where she'd left her clothes? If whoever was watching thought she was just taking a swim, wouldn't he stay where he was, waiting until she swam back? She'd still have to figure out how to get back to the camp, but at least if her plan worked she'd be dressed.

She pushed off from the bottom and began to swim—languidly as she'd done before, until she'd cleared the cove. Then she struck out for all she was worth.

Minutes later, she was scrambling over brambles and roots. By a stroke of good luck she found her clothes on the very first try and yanked them back with her into the undergrowth, pulling them on as quickly and as silently as she could. She'd just begun to lace her bodice when a twig snapped a little ways off. She froze, crouching lower and peering through the leaves.

Someone was coming, step by stealthy step. He was coming straight for her. He must have seen her swim off and guessed what she had in mind, and now he would catch her. She had to call for help. She opened her mouth to do so, but no sound came out. She was too frightened and she was crouched too low. A wildcat? An Indian? She caught a glimpse of gold.

Gold? She found herself eye to eye with the row of buttons on the hem of Haddom's coat.

Without thinking she reared up from the underbrush so unexpectedly that Haddom gave a queer little yelp. She found herself staring down the barrel of his gun.

Sarah found her voice first. "What are you doing?" she demanded.

"Well, you should ask that—I'm coming to rescue you! Wh-what have you been doing?" He lowered his rifle to stare at her.

"I was swimming," she replied, which was when she realized that her bodice was still undone. No wonder he was staring. She reached up to pull it closed. As she did, Haddom stepped forward and, brushing aside her hands, slipped his arm around her and pulled her close to him. "What—" she managed, before his mouth swallowed her words.

He must have put his gun down because now he was using both hands, one inside her bodice and the other around her back. It was all so sudden that at first she didn't react, she just stood there and let him have his way with her. She still wasn't thinking clearly when he pulled her around and pressed her against him in a way that warned her exactly what he was about. Acting by instinct she braced herself with both hands on his shoulders to keep her steady on her feet; then she brought her knee up as hard as she could.

Her aim was perfect. Haddom grunted and folded neatly in two. He went down into the bushes with a resounding crash and stayed there, moaning, while Sarah looked on in disgust. He was still moaning when she had her bodice done up, and she left him while she wrung the water from her hair and twisted it into a knot. She'd have preferred to leave him and return to camp alone, but then she thought of what would happen when the rest of the men found out.

She tapped him on the shoulder. "Come on. Get up."

He stopped moaning and lifted his head, staring coldly at her outreached hand. He took it with reluctance but released it as soon as he was up, brushing the dirt off his breeches and straightening his coat. "You, madam," he said coldly, "have some sort of nerve."

"Me!" She almost choked. "I have nerve! What about you, creeping around here spying on me, then leaping on me like some sort of demented animal."

"It was no more than you deserved, flaunting yourself as you did."

"Flaunting myself—I was swimming!"

"Where anyone could see. You're lucky that it was I who happened along. It might have been one of the men." He paused, then added, "For all you know, it might have been Brownell."

At the mention of Zeke's name, Haddom's face went hard. "He swaggers and he threatens but he has no idea the way things really stand. He sees himself as lord and protector of this whole province. Lord and protector—ha! I'd like to see his face when he hears New Sussex declared!"

Zeke's name had worked a change in Sarah, too, so that she almost missed what Haddom said. Almost, but not quite. "New Sussex?" she asked. "What is New Sussex?"

"For the moment, just a name, but soon enough it will be a royal colony, embracing the land from this lake to the Connecticut River and ruled by me as governor."

"You!" Sarah stared at Haddom, aghast.

"Yes, me." Haddom smiled. "Don't look so distressed. You ought to be elated—just think how it will benefit you. Once Brownell and his gang are dealt with and there's peace and stability, the value of the land will shoot sky-high and you'll be able to sell your lots for whatever price you choose."

"But that's not—" she began, then stopped.

"Not what?" Haddom raised one brow.

"I don't know." The truth was that she didn't, nor did she know why she was so upset. "How will you run it?"

"Run it?"

"The government. Will it be town meetings, like New Hampshire, or manors and lords, like New York?"

His smile became arch and chiding. "Now, now, what do you think? Do you imagine I'd allow Boston fever to infect this virgin land? Town meetings, indeed!"

"But you can't!" murmured Sarah.

"Yes, of course I can. It's what I've intended from the very first—if the scheme was plausible, and now I see it is. After I've finished with Brownell there will be no impediments." His eyes rose to future glory, then descended back to her. "If we've finished here, I believe we should get back to camp before the men miss us and form conclusions about where we've been."

Sarah made no protest. She didn't know what to say.

Chapter Fourteen

It was midafternoon the next day when Gow pointed to the eastern shore and said, "That cove over there. Bring the boats in to the north end of the beach."

The cove was a large one with a long flat shingle beach bounded by meadows that rolled up to a wooded bluff. Beyond the bluff and the meadows rippled ranks of forested hills, which merged at the horizon with the steep blue mountain peaks.

They unloaded the canoes at the water's edge, then pulled them onto the beach, while Haddom fired orders, pointing here and there. "We'll strike camp in those trees." He waved at the crown of the bluff. "The height ought to give us a good view." He didn't say a view of what, but everybody knew. The men stopped working to scan the meadows, searching for some sign of Zeke—as if he'd be standing in full sight waiting to welcome them.

"More likely hiding in them woods," one of the men muttered darkly, "waiting to ambush us."

"Then you'd best look sharp," rapped out Haddom, "so he knows whom he's dealing with!" In honor of their arrival Haddom had strapped on a sword with a jeweled scabbard and an impressively gilded hilt. "Oh, and one more thing. Whoever catches Brownell will get one hundred pounds."

"One hundred pounds!" Gow murmured, appearing at Sarah's side. "Just think of the bowls of punch a hundred pounds could buy."

She'd been looking at the meadow, along with the rest of the men, but she alone hadn't been distracted by the promise of Haddom's reward. "Can I see it from here?" she asked Gow. "Is part of this land mine?"

Gow swept his arm from north to south. "It's all yours, Mistress Meade. The bluff, the meadows, the first ranks of those hills." He grinned at her shocked expression. "More than you thought, I guess."

She shook her head, speechless, her eyes moving back and forth. "I've always lived in the city."

"Well, you're not in the city now. You're in God's country—your country, that is—at least until you sell it."

"Oh, yes..." She let her eyes make a full circle across the glittering breadth of the lake so she could feel the impact of seeing the land once again.

No longer grinning, Gow watched her. "You had no idea, did you? That's the thing about wild land. People buy it for investment—and why not, since it's the only real investment in the colonies? England won't let us trade freely or manufacture our own goods, so how else can a man get ahead unless he invests in the land—or a woman," he amended, in deference to her.

"But most people never lay eyes on the land they own. The closest many come is when they send a surveyor up to mark it out. Of course, when the surveyor comes back they ask him questions—but what questions do they ask? Is the land well drained for farming? What access does it have to the main water routes? What of the standing timber, or levelness for fields? I could tell you all those things and you'd still have no picture of what this land's really like."

"No, I wouldn't," breathed Sarah. "I had no—"

"Taking time out for chitchat?" Haddom's voice broke in on them. "Mr. Gow, I believe you'd do better to be unpacking your tools."

Still too awed to be offended, Sarah turned to him. "Mr. Gow says this is all mine. All of it—just imagine!"

"Hmm...yes." Haddom glanced around. "Fine natural harbor, good access to major ports. Land looks to be quite fertile...plenty of trees. If the lake freezes in the winter, you could ship south all year round. You'll turn a pretty profit—after I've dealt with Brownell.... Mr. Gow, are you coming?''

Sarah watched them walk away. Harbor access, year-round shipping—Haddom had no soul!

Gow spent the rest of the day trampling wildflowers in the meadow with his chainman tramping ahead, while Haddom arranged and rearranged his line of men. He advanced, wheeled and pulled in like a sergeant with his first troop of cadets, until the merciful sunset put an end to the exercise. At supper Sarah wondered aloud to Gow how long the men would put up with Haddom's regimen, but Gow had another view.

''It keeps them busy, which keeps them from brooding. It gives them the sense of doing something aggressive instead of sitting around and waiting for Brownell to strike.''

Certainly the men's behavior bore out Gow's belief. They ate supper in high spirits, joking among themselves about how they'd given Brownell something to think about—if he was even around. Some of the men went so far as to boast that when Zeke caught sight of Haddom's troop, he'd turn tail and run. However, as sunset faded and darkness encroached, Sarah noticed that their predictions became less rash and that the men drew closer to the fire, casting wary glances into the gathering night.

She didn't feel afraid. Fear seemed a foreign emotion amidst so much magnificence. The splendor of the sunset had filled her with a new awe, which had deepened as the cool grays and blues of twilight had eased away the oranges and pinks, smoothing out the mountains and the waters of the lake, above which floated a thumbnail sliver of the crescent moon.

As her eyes feasted on the splendor, her thoughts slipped around to Zeke. For the first time she understood his determination to keep this land. It wasn't only principle, it was also love. She could imagine—no, she knew how Zeke must have felt seeing what she had this afternoon for the first time. He wouldn't have thought about year-round shipping first; that much was clear. With a contracting heart, she realized how he must have felt if he had been watching their arrival on the beach. They were the invading army from whom this land must be defended at any cost. It was a new and a disturbing thought.

As darkness became total they built the fire high until it roared and leapt, and every time a branch snapped, all of the men would jump, then settle back down more slowly, grinning sheepishly.

"'Course they've never killed anyone," one of the men pointed out. "Mainly try to scare 'em so they run away."

"Their scaring's plenty bad enough," another man replied, and launched into a story about a man he knew who'd been caught surveying a Yorker title by the Green Mountain Boys. They'd stripped the man naked, doused him with honey, blindfolded him and tied him to a tree. Then they'd left him.

"Pretty soon along comes this big old bear. Lumbers right up to the fellow; starts grunting and nudging him. Even so, he's not too worried till he hears this high-pitched grunt. Wouldn't you know it—this bear's brought along her cub!"

"That can make a bear mighty testy," one of the men put in.

"Mighty," the narrator agreed. "This fellow's starting to get nervous, when he feels something wet and rough kind of scraping across his skin. Then he feels the same thing scraping somewhere else. Damned if the bear and her cub ain't both licking him! He's trying to hold still, but he ain't doing too well between being nervous and being tickled half to death. Then, all of a sudden, someone begins to laugh!"

"The bear is laughing?"

"There ain't no bear at all! Just Brownell and his cronies having their type of a joke! They left him hanging where he was until they'd laughed themselves sick. Then they untied him and sent him running all the way back to Albany!"

There was silence for some minutes as the men took this in. Then somebody muttered something about one hundred pounds.

* * *

That night there were noises beyond the edge of the camp, the hooting and rustling of some small creature—or maybe it was Zeke. The noises woke Sarah, and through the canvas of her tent she heard the men stirring as they reached for their guns and the muffled clicking of hammers being cocked. She froze in the darkness, her skin clammy with fear, listening to Haddom's orders as he posted men all around the edge of the bluff.

She listened to the feet tramping, filled with a sense of dread. Gone was this afternoon's blissful ignorance, replaced by grim reality. These men were preparing for a battle she didn't want to see, yet which she'd done as much as anyone to cause. She could tell herself that no matter who owned the land, Zeke wouldn't have let them claim it, but perhaps another owner wouldn't have gone so far. And now it was too late to stop, because until he'd met Zeke in battle, Haddom wouldn't leave.

She shouldn't have come here. She should have followed her father's advice to sell the land to Haddom, take the money and leave. If she'd done that, at this moment she'd have been in Philadelphia settling her affairs and putting all this behind her—which was where it belonged. If she'd listened to her father, she would never have seen this land, and if she hadn't seen it she never would have known.

Known what? she wondered. But that she couldn't say. The guard had stopped tramping and all was silent once again. Whatever had been hooting and rustling must have withdrawn, and somewhere toward morning Sarah fell back to sleep.

The morning was as lovely as the night had been, the lake a sheet of brightness and the meadow heavy with dew. Sarah got up early to watch the mist rising from the lake and the last of the morning stars shooed away by the sun. When Haddom emerged from his tent, she beckoned for him to join her, which he did willingly.

"You're up bright and early."

"The birds woke me up. I was thinking...I know how you feel about not wanting Zeke to get away with things, but is it really worth risking all these lives? Right now General Haldimand is worried about disturbances in the other colonies, but in time those will settle down and then he'll probably be willing to send troops up here—enough troops that even Zeke will realize he doesn't have a chance.''

''What are you saying?''

''I believe it would be better to wait until then to try to take possession of this land. In the meantime I believe we ought to pack up and go.''

''What about your money? How will you pay your debts?''

''I don't know,'' she said honestly. ''But I'll think of a way. The main thing is for us to leave as soon as possible.'' She glanced back toward the camp, which was fully awake.

''Absolutely not,'' said Haddom. ''If nothing else, it's a matter of principle. Besides, in case you've forgotten, I have an interest independent of yours.''

''You won't be deserting that interest if you leave now. What I said about General Haldimand is—''

''No. There is no question.'' Haddom shook his head. ''If we leave now, Brownell and his rabble will assume that they've won.''

''So what?'' demanded Sarah.

Haddom turned to her and fixed her with the sort of look he'd have given an idiot. ''I fear your courage has deserted you. I warned you against coming, but now that you're here, you'll just have to stay near camp and do the best you can. I believe breakfast is ready. Why don't you come and eat? No point in letting your health suffer over a fit of nerves.''

''It's not—'' Sarah began, but Haddom was already up and offering her his arm, and from his expression she knew it would do no good to try to explain. She'd made her decision and now, as Haddom had said, she'd have to make the best of it.

She found that increasingly difficult as the morning wore on and she had nothing to occupy her other than sitting in the camp under the vigilant eye of her personal guard. She looked across the meadow to where Gow was at work. By this afternoon he would have penetrated the woods, where, according to popular wisdom, Zeke was most likely to strike. Would Zeke strike today or tomorrow? In daylight or at night? If she spent many days like this one she knew she'd go mad. She needed a diversion.

"I'm going to take a walk."

Her guard instantly objected. She'd heard Haddom's command.

"Yes, I heard him. He said to stay close to the camp. But he didn't say I had to sit in one place all day. I'm going to pick wildflowers in the meadow and the rest of you can come or stay as you wish."

Two came, following at a respectful distance, while the third one stayed behind. She wandered through the grass, filling her petticoat with flowers, and so glad to be distracted that she didn't mind when the dew drenched her hem so that it smacked wetly against her calves. Her shoes got so wet they started squelching, and she was tempted to pull them off, but at that moment she saw Haddom waving at them with both of his arms.

The men had also seen him. "He's telling you to go back."

"I'm not his hireling and he can't order me around."

"He can try pretty hard," one of the men pointed out.

Sarah knew that he was right. She could envision Haddom storming at her, shouting and waving his sword. She sighed with resignation. "I guess I've picked enough."

Back on the bluff, she carried the flowers to a spot just beyond the camp where she would have a bit of privacy. She spotted a low flat stone sticking up from the grass and decided it would make a decent seat, but as she approached it she tripped over something else and went down face forward, scattering flowers everywhere.

"Damn!" she muttered as tears of pain sprang to her eyes.

"You all right, mistress?" called the men.

"I'm fine, just fine! Thank you," she called back before they could come to see for themselves, and to prove it, she struggled to her feet.

The thing she'd tripped on was another rock—one of a number that seemed to have been laid out in a line by an accident of nature or by an act of man. The rocks ran along in a straight line then turned to the left, leading right up to the stone she'd been headed for.

A wall, in this wild land? Who could have built it here? Did Indians build walls? She didn't really know. She looked from the rocks to the lake, stretching below the bluff, and thought that she could understand why someone had put these here. This would be a perfect spot for a house, with the shade of the birch grove and wonderful views on every side. If it were her house, she'd build it with a porch on either side so she could watch the sun rise over the mountains and set behind the lake.

Without warning Sarah shivered. She sensed someone nearby. She sensed Zeke—she was certain. Her heart began to pound and her hands were shaking as she searched the shade of the trees. But although the birch must have been growing on this spot for some time, none of the trunks was broad enough to have concealed a man as big as Zeke. But she felt him, she was certain. What did it mean?

She turned toward the meadow, but all she saw was the line of Haddom's soldiers strung out to protect Gow. Should she warn them—and if so, of what? She could imagine Haddom's reaction if she told him what she'd felt. He'd probably attribute her intimation to another fit of nerves. No, there was nothing to do but wait until sooner or later Zeke made his move.

The flowers she had gathered were lying scattered in the grass. Kneeling, she collected them with hands that still shook. She carried them to the flat stone, where she sat and wove, and by the time the men came in for dinner she'd finished her chain. They'd seen no sign of the Green Mountain Boys. But they sensed, as she did, that Zeke was somewhere near.

* * *

After dinner they went into the woods, and Sarah spent five awful hours jumping at every sound. When they came in at twilight there'd been no sign of Zeke, but rather than boosting their confidence as it had done the day before, tonight Zeke's nonappearance heightened the tension in the camp. Sarah felt it and so did all the men, though Haddom did his best to bluster it away. He praised the men's performance and strutted about with his sword until Gow could not resist a brief trenchant pantomime of his lordship, which did more to calm the men than all of Haddom's carrying-on.

Sarah went to bed tense and managed to fall asleep, only to be awakened almost immediately by a terrible shriek.

The shriek hadn't ended before every man was up, all rushing about in the wildest confusion so that it was several minutes before they were able to determine what the scream had been.

It had been Haddom, who was still leaping about in his nightshirt, slashing the air with his sword and crying, "I was attacked by a wildcat!"

"A wildcat!"

"It must have been—it crept into my tent when I was sleeping and bit me!"

"Bit you where?"

"Never mind!" snapped Haddom, but from the way he was moving everybody knew.

"Why would a catamount bite his lordship on his ass?" Gow wondered aloud, but before anyone could answer they heard a chilling sound—ghostly laughter echoing through the woods.

"Brownell!" someone whispered.

"That wasn't no catamount. It was Brownell that snuck into the tent! He must have poked his lordship so he felt like he was bit...."

"I'll kill him!" Haddom stormed.

Sarah shivered at his words, staring into the darkness and feeling Zeke's presence more strongly than before. She felt a wave of panic. What was she doing here? How could she stop this madness before it had taken its toll? She looked from the darkness to Haddom's hate-filled face and knew that at this point his grudge against Zeke had nothing to do with the land. She could tear her deeds up—she could give them to Zeke—and Haddom would still want to track him down.

And what about Zeke? What if she could manage to find him wherever he was hiding? What if she promised to give up her claim if he went away? She remembered the last time they'd met how quick he'd been to turn against her and believe that she'd lied to him. She remembered the hate and disgust in his eyes and she doubted he'd be any more willing to believe her if she went to him now. But if there was a chance of avoiding bloodshed, wasn't it worth a try?

After he'd calmed down, Haddom posted a heavy guard and ordered the rest of them to try to get some sleep. As there was no way to measure time passing, Sarah lay still as long as she could. Then she pushed her tent flap open and slowly eased herself out.

Thankfully it was still fully night, and dark from the lack of a moon, though she could make out the shapes of the tents. Less clearly, she could discern the silhouettes of the men on guard. Although the night was warm she was wearing her cloak, whose darkness would hide her as much as possible. For the rest, she'd do her best, and if someone saw her she'd make the obvious excuse.

She moved from tree to tree to the edge of the grove, picking a point of exit between two of the guards. Both of the men were looking toward the woods, though from the way they were sitting she couldn't tell whether or not they were still awake. Where the trees ended, she dropped onto her hands and knees and very slowly began to crawl through the grass. It was high enough to hide her, and though to her own ears she seemed to be making a terrible amount of noise, the guard must either not have heard her or have been asleep.

Crawling was painfully slow business, especially in a skirt. When she thought she'd gone a distance, she cautiously raised her head. She couldn't see the guard so maybe they wouldn't see her. She rose slowly until she was crouched low, then she began to run.

The high grass whipped at her skirts, and the dew, which had already fallen, turned them sodden and wet. She caught them up to keep from falling and ran as fast as she could, all the time waiting for the guard to raise the alarm. Would they shoot if they saw her? She doubted they could hit her at this distance in the dark, but the thought of lead tearing into her brought a wave of nausea. She ducked lower and ran faster toward the blackness of the woods. Just before she reached it, something grabbed her arm.

She spun around from the momentum and she would have cried out if someone hadn't stopped her with a hand clamped over her mouth. It was Zeke.

"What are you doing?"

"Looking for you," she gasped as soon as he took his hand away. "Zeke, you've got to stop this before someone gets hurt. If you want the land, you can have it. I'll give you my deeds if you leave."

"Have you got them?"

She shook her head, glad that the darkness hid the tears that sprang to her eyes. She'd been right; he didn't trust her. "But I'll give you my word. I'll send them to you as soon as I get back."

"What about his lordship? If you're concerned about someone getting hurt, why don't you ask him to leave?"

"I have, but he won't do it—especially after tonight. It's become a matter of personal honor, and besides—"

"Besides what?"

But she couldn't tell him Haddom's plan for New Sussex. He'd never leave if she did. He was looking at her intently, his face inches away, his eyes burning into hers so that she found it hard to breathe. "Besides what?" he repeated.

"I don't want you to be hurt."

He was silent for a moment, and so still that she realized he was holding his breath. He released it slowly, narrowing his eyes. "Couldn't stand the guilt, eh?"

"You can think that if you like."

"What if I don't like? Is there another reason, Sally?"

He still had her by the arms, and as he asked the question his thumbs moved unconsciously in a brief rough caress. Brief though it was, it was enough to make her heart jolt hard against her ribs. But she couldn't be distracted from the reason she was here.

"They've got guns," she whispered. "If they start shooting someone will get hurt."

"You knew that when you started up here, but you came anyway. What's changed, Sally?"

"I was angry then. And I needed the money."

"You don't need the money now?"

"Of course I need it," she replied, tossing her head. She couldn't read his expression but she could guess what she would have found in it if she could—his presumption that she'd agreed to marry Haddom, in which case she could afford to give up this piece of land.

"I need the money," she said bitterly, "but I don't want it at that cost. You may be willing to die for this, but I'm not willing to have you die. Oh, Zeke, can't you be reasonable for once!" Her voice rose in frustration and she was dangerously close to tears—so she thought she was imagining the sudden flash of white. But no, in the midst of this nightmare, Zeke was entertained. She was voluntarily destroying her future and he was smiling!

"Damn you!" she cried in frustration. Bringing her hand back she slapped him across the face as hard as she could.

He reached up to stop her, but she was too fast for him. His beard acted as a cushion, but she heard him grunt and she knew he'd felt it. She would have hit him again if he hadn't grabbed her wrist.

"Let me go, you ogre!"

"Hush—they'll hear you all the way to the bluff, then you'll have your war you're trying to prevent."

"It looks as if I'll have it anyway," she said bitterly. "I was a fool to try to stop it. When both of you want it so badly, why should I stand in your way? Maybe you'll kill each other and then I won't have any more men to bother me!" She twisted hard away from him, but he wouldn't let her go.

"Stay a minute, Sally."

"No!" She pulled away. "I don't want to hear it—I don't ever want to see you again. You asked me if I was worried about feeling guilty and the answer is not anymore. I warned you but you wouldn't listen, so whatever happens now, you'll get what you deserve."

"What about your giving up the land? Are you backing out of that?"

"No, I'm not backing out. But you won't get an acre from me unless you leave right away." She gave up struggling for a moment. "Do you mean you're willing to leave?"

He didn't answer right away. He raised his head to look past her toward the bluff. Then, instead of answering, he asked her, "What do you think of the land?"

She beat back a surge of frustration. "I think it's very nice. Are you willing to leave, Zeke?"

"Just very nice?"

Damn him—didn't he know when to stop? "No. More than very nice. I think it's beautiful. Magnificent. Amazing. Are you willing to leave?"

Slowly he shook his head. "No, I'm not. You've done your best, Sally, and I appreciate your concern. Whatever happens from here on in won't be your fault."

"Why, you—" But she couldn't find fitting words. She'd never felt so angry, so hopeless, in all her life. She spun away from him before she could start to cry, in case he was conceited enough to think that her tears were for him.

He didn't try to hold her this time when she left, and the thing she hated the most was having to drop down onto all fours to sneak back to the camp, when what she really wanted was to march across the meadow to show him and Haddom—and everyone else—that she didn't care. She would have done better to have spent this last hour in bed. Next time she'd know better—if a next time ever came.

*w*ood was to make, before the others knew how him and
Durham ... And even the men that ... did ... one ... she
would ... sleep ... all ... while her hand so frail ... a bed
... line she sipped ... took ... food ... dull, cry ... and ...

Chapter Fifteen

Breakfast that morning was a silent meal. The men ate
slowly, their eyes on the woods, and nobody asked the
question that was foremost in all of their minds.

It was Gow who finally answered, almost offhandedly.
Wiping his hands on his handkerchief, he retrieved his
transit from his tent and, shouldering it, said, "Ten days of
being sober is my limit, and I've already gone a week, so the
way I figure it, I haven't got time to sit around and wait for
Brownell to strike. Come on—" He beckoned to his
chainman.

His chainman rose slowly, looking like a man who was
searching his mind for a new way to say no. Before he could
find one, Haddom was on his feet, crying, "Troop to attention! We're wasting precious time! Everybody check
your gun before we leave."

Every man checked his gun, though he'd checked it ten
minutes before. Hesitantly the men came to order.

Sarah also stood. Ignoring Haddom, she turned to Gow,
clasping his arm. "You don't have to go out there today,"
she said with quiet intensity. "I'll pay you what I promised
even if you don't. The quarrel between his lordship and Mr.
Brownell doesn't concern you, and there's no point in your
risking your life."

"That's not true!" Haddom interrupted before Gow
could reply. "She won't have a farthing if she doesn't sell
this land. She won't be able to pay you—and that goes for

the rest of you men. You won't see a penny of your pay if you don't come now!"

"It isn't the money," Gow said to Sarah. "Believe it or not, it's become a matter of principle. Most folks believe I'm washed up as a surveyor, and the way I see it, this is my one chance to prove them wrong."

"But if that's what you're doing, you have already proved them wrong! As for your surveying, I'll vouch for you."

"I want to finish what I started. Don't worry. We'll be all right." Very gently—the way Zeke could be gentle—Gow removed her hand from his sleeve. "I'm ready," he said to Haddom.

"Attention!" Haddom cried. "Men, stay together and nobody shoot until I give the command!"

If the day before had been difficult for Sarah, this one was impossible. She stared, unseeing, at a magnificent view while she listened for the sound of gunfire, which would come from the woods. Last night she'd told Zeke that if he was killed in the fighting he'd get what he'd deserved. She'd also told him that she didn't care, but as she sat and waited she knew that she'd been wrong. She did care about him. She cared all too much. Damn him and damn Haddom! But damning didn't help.

She and Zeke had no future, with or without the land. They didn't trust each other—he considered her a liar—and the thing that drew them together was something he'd walk away from when he'd had enough. She could tell herself she despised him, she could list all of his faults—he was boastful, pigheaded, selfish, insensitive and insincere, and even his admirable qualities trampled innocent people in their willful path. But despite that, the thought of him dying today could still terrify her more than anything she'd experienced or could imagine. And of everything she was feeling, the helplessness was the worst. She couldn't stop her feelings any more than she could stop the battle about to be fought.

The sun had just passed its zenith when she heard the shots. They sounded like distant popping—such a harmless sound that her first impulse was to feel relieved. How could a little popping hurt anyone? But it could: it could kill them. That popping could kill Zeke.

"No!" She heard a voice scream and recognized the voice as hers. She bolted toward the meadow, but the men Haddom had left to guard her were just as quick. They grabbed her by either arm. She fought them with a passion. "Stop it! Let me go! I have to stop them—"

"You, mistress? You won't stop no one."

"Besides," the second man added, "you'd never get there in time. By the sound of the fire, the fighting's way deep into the woods. Look over yonder for yourself and see if you can spot the smoke."

She searched the treetops and saw nothing, but she could still hear the shots. "Let me go," she pleaded, twisting her arms. "His lordship won't blame you. You can say I sneaked away. I'll pay you—"

"I thought you was broke."

"It's not true. I have money. I'll—"

"Hush!" one of the men said harshly. "Listen!"

The popping had stopped. There was a long minute's silence, then they heard another sound like a distant mosquito's whine. One of the men swatted at his ear, but the sound was coming from the woods. It grew louder by the minute. Sarah stopped struggling and she and her captors stood watching in tense silence at the edge of the bluff.

"Look—they're coming!"

A ragged line of Haddom's men appeared among the nearest trees. Even across the span of the meadow, Sarah could see that they were running, and most of them were waving their arms. Some of them were waving their rifles but some were not. They had just reached the sunlight when a second line burst into view. Something about them was different. She gasped: they were Indians!

"What the hell . . . ?" one of the men muttered.

"It's Brownell," the other one said. "I've heard they've done it before—dressed up like Indians."

Sarah caught a glimpse of the bright paint smeared on their faces and chests and heard their savage whoops.

"Goddamn!" one of her guards breathed. "What's happening out there?"

For no apparent reason, Haddom's men had begun to collapse. The first row went down in a pile among the last scattered trees, and as the second rank reached them, they went down, too.

"What the hell?" her guard murmured.

But Sarah knew. "A rope. They must have strung a rope there after the men had gone. Then they chased them back this way knowing they'd all trip and fall." And knowing, she added silently, that they'd turn tail and run. But before they'd turned tail, had somebody been shot? She scanned the Indians for Zeke but it was too far for her to see, and by now the Indians were hurling themselves onto the pile in what looked from here to be a massive free-for-all.

One of her guards took a step forward. "We'd best go help them out."

The other one gave him a shocked expression. "Are you mad? They haven't got a chance. Look, they're already taking 'em prisoner."

He pointed, and Sarah saw that he was right. Of the contenders standing, most were Indians, and those were soon stooping to haul up Haddom's men and push them into two ragged lines.

"Binding their wrists," one guard murmured. "Wonder what they mean to do. Look, they're bringing 'em this way."

Sarah watched as they began to march. Haddom's men walked in the middle with the Indians on either side, most of them carrying a rifle in either hand. Her eyes raced up and down the line—the first familiar sight was Remember's bright shock of hair. She thought she saw Eli. Finally she saw Zeke. She saw his broad bare shoulders and his beard glinting in the sun.

"Thank you!" she whispered, and felt her legs give way. She thought her guards would catch her, but they had other things on their mind.

"If we stay here they'll grab us."

"You're right—come on, let's go! Come on, mistress."

"No!" Sarah twisted away, but this time they were in a hurry so they let her go. She turned to watch them racing toward the beach, where they pushed one of the canoes into the water, practically capsizing it in their rush to be gone. By that time the procession had almost reached the bluff.

Haddom was in the first rank, wigless and furious and no longer wearing his sword, which she saw strapped to Jasper's skinny hips. Eli walked behind Jasper, looking startlingly handsome in his Indian disguise. His eyes met Sarah's with comprehension but with no apology. I told you, his eyes were saying, and indeed he had.

At first she didn't see Gow, but then she saw him toward the back. Zeke was behind him, strolling along at the very rear, his massive shoulders gleaming in the sun and the dark hair on his chest streaked with red and yellow paint. Like the others he was wearing only leather leggings and moccasins with a fringed breechclout back and front. Whereas Eli had looked attractive, Zeke looked magnificent, the image of a warrior coming home from the hunt—only he didn't look self-satisfied, as Sarah had thought he would. If anything his look was of tension and wariness, as if the hunt weren't over yet.

Some of the prisoners stumbled as they came up the bluff, but the Boys prodded them back onto their feet with the guns until the whole procession had reached the camp. There, they herded them into a circle, while Zeke moved to the front. He passed close to Sarah but didn't look at her.

He nodded toward the water. "There go two of them. Who wants to bring them back?"

Two of the Boys volunteered and set off down the beach. By that time Haddom had struggled through the group until he was face-to-face with Zeke.

"In the king's name, I demand you let us go! We have a full and legal right to be on this land and your attack and detainment of us is against—"

"Shut up, your lordship," said Zeke, and from where she was standing Sarah could hear the threatening note in his voice.

Haddom also heard it but he didn't care. "And now I suppose you're going to beat me, or tie me to a tree, or whatever other sort of thing you cowards do!"

"You're calling us cowards?"

"What else could you be?" Haddom snapped. "You haven't even got the courage to come out and face your opponents like men. Instead you hide behind bushes like the cowards you are. Your disguises suit you well, since you're no better than wild savages! I'm warning you for the last—"

"Is that what you want?" Zeke cut him off. "You want to fight me face-to-face? All right, then. Let's fight."

That stopped Haddom's ranting. "Fight how?" he asked.

Zeke looked him up and down slowly. "Why not with our hands?"

Haddom blanched beneath his angry flush. "You're twice my size!"

"Have it your way." Zeke shrugged. He glanced around the circle. "Jasper, free him and give him the sword."

Reluctant to part with his new toy, nonetheless Jasper obeyed.

"What about you?" Haddom asked. "What will you use as a weapon?"

"My knife." Zeke drew it out of its leather sheath and held it for Haddom to see. "Have you got an objection?"

Haddom shook his head; if he had one he couldn't make it without completely disgracing himself. The men on the bluff fell back while Haddom stripped off his coat and slashed the air with his sword, ostensibly testing it. Pausing, in ready position, he glanced at the watching group.

"How do I know your men won't interfere?"

"They won't. They won't have to. Are you ready?"

"Who will give the word to begin?"

Without turning his head, Zeke answered, "Mistress Meade will give the signal."

"No I won't," Sarah said.

For the first time since he'd come onto the bluff, Zeke turned to look at her. "Yes you will," he said, in the same voice he'd used in Mason's garden when he'd accused her of deceiving him. His voice brooked no resistance, neither did his eyes.

Everyone was watching. Sarah raised her hand. "Begin!" she called out as she brought it down.

The two men began to move, circling slowly, Haddom sideways in dueling position and Zeke facing forward, body low, arms out, holding his knife as though it were an extension of his hand. His paint and Haddom's waistcoat flashed gaily in the sun; both men had the same expression of blank intensity.

Haddom made the first move, lunging to test Zeke's range. Zeke pivoted to avoid him, then pivoted again as Haddom lunged a second time. This time his sword knicked flesh. Drops of blood, darker red than his paint, appeared on Zeke's upper arm. Sarah's hands found each other and began to squeeze.

The cut gave Haddom confidence; he lunged again, and this time his sword's blade encountered the metal of Zeke's knife. The clash rang out briefly, then Haddom disengaged—or he appeared to, but the appearance was a feint, for suddenly he came forward, his sword slashing the air, slicing and thrusting more expertly and swiftly than a knife could repel. Zeke fell farther and farther back—he was headed toward the fire.

"Fire behind you!" one of the Boys called, and Zeke missed it just in time—but in stepping sideways his foot hit a rock. He lost his balance and began to fall. Haddom, who'd been harassing him with every step, instantly saw his advantage and moved in for the kill.

"No!" screamed Sarah, bringing her hands up to cover her eyes. When she brought them down a moment later,

Haddom was on the ground and the sword was in Zeke's left hand and pointed at Haddom's throat.

Haddom's eyes were bulging. "What are you going to do?"

"What if I said I was going to kill you?" Zeke pressed the sword closer until blood beaded on Haddom's skin.

"No! No, don't!" Haddom practically shrieked. "I beg you, spare me! You can have the land!"

"Thank you for your kindness, but it isn't yours to give."

"She'll give it to you—I'll see that she does! Do you want money—I'll give you money, too! I'm a wealthy man, I can give you anything you want. Please, have mercy!" Tears of panic streamed from his eyes, tracing grotesque patterns down his dirty cheeks.

Zeke's expression didn't change. "If I do let you go, I'd need paroles from all your men that they'll never set foot in the Grants again. As for you—if I don't hear you've gone back to England within the week, I'll come and find you and I'll finish what I've started here. Do you understand?"

"Absolutely—yes!" Unable to nod his head because of the pressure of the sword, Haddom bobbed his eyebrows and rolled his eyes. "You have my word as a gentleman!"

There was a dull clatter as Zeke tossed the sword down on the rocks. Sheathing his knife, he turned to Sarah. "There's your hero. What do you think of him now?"

"Nothing I didn't think before," she said, meeting his eyes. "And I suppose after all this I'm supposed to think more of you?"

"I doubt you could think less," he said with dry irony, wiping sweat and paint from his forehead with the back of his hand. He turned to the waiting men. "All right, you heard the terms. Who'll give his parole?"

No one refused, and Haddom managed to stop shaking long enough to produce paper and ink. When the paroles were written, Zeke gave Haddom's men five minutes to pack and leave, and the Boys stood around watching while they rushed back and forth, dragging their possessions down from the bluff and hurling them into the canoes.

Sarah stood with them, refusing to demean herself by rushing around like a chicken with its head cut off. Not that it really mattered, since in their mad rush to be gone, the men snatched up her things with theirs.

Although he was standing near her, Zeke was ignoring her again as he watched the proceedings with evident disgust. She saw now why he had refused her offer last night: he hadn't wanted to give up the pleasure of seeing Haddom crawl. In a way she couldn't blame him, but that didn't stop her from being furious. An hour ago she'd been terrified of him dying, but at this moment she was furious to see him so alive and supremely in command.

She was also trapped in a dilemma she didn't know how to resolve, since she didn't want to run away with Haddom but she couldn't stay with Zeke. She was tempted to refuse to leave with the men on principle alone, but she knew that her resistance would end up with her being toted away like a bundle of wood and she'd had enough of that.

The canoes were loaded in five minutes flat and Haddom led the rush to be off.

"Whoa, there, your lordship," Zeke called, arresting Haddom midway into his canoe. At his call, Haddom turned white, but he managed to stay on his feet.

Zeke sauntered down to the water as Haddom watched him come. "There's one more thing, your lordship. Mistress Meade won't be going with you."

Sarah saw from the way Haddom started that he'd forgotten her. Now he remembered and blanched further. "Y-you can't mean to keep her!"

Zeke nodded. "As a matter of fact, I do. Why—were you thinking of trying to stop me?"

"Oh, no." Haddom shook his wigless head. "That is, so long as you give your word that you won't harm her."

Zeke's lip curled. "I won't give you anything. If you were starving I wouldn't give you a crust of bread. If you were bleeding at my feet I wouldn't waste my spit on you. Get out of here, your lordship. The sight of you makes me sick—and here, take this with you." From somewhere he produced Haddom's wig and tossed it at Haddom's feet.

Haddom snatched it up and slapped it, soaking wet, onto his head. Without sparing a glance at Sarah, he clambered into his canoe, drenching himself completely in his rush to get away.

Sarah watched the spectacle, not knowing what to feel. She was still very angry, but she was also relieved—that is, until she realized that Gow was still on the beach.

Zeke saw Gow at the same time. "Go on, get out of here! You heard the order!"

Gow shook his head.

"What do you mean?" Zeke demanded, bearing down on him.

Though his face was as pale as Haddom's had been, Gow stood his ground. "I'm staying. I made a deal with the lady and I want to see that she survives to perform her part."

Zeke stared at him in amazement. "You must be drunk."

"I'm not," Gow admitted, "but to tell the truth I wish I were."

Zeke threw Sarah an ironic look. "Here's your hero, right here."

Ignoring Zeke's comment, she addressed herself to Gow. "I truly appreciate everything you've done, but you don't have to stay. Whatever Mr. Brownell said to his lordship, I'll be all right."

Gow's eyes moved from her to Zeke. "The way I see it, no matter what happens here, in the end one of you's going to end up owning the land, and when you've got that straightened out you'll need it surveyed. So what's the point of my going all the way back down just to come all the way back up again. Besides," he added, glancing behind him, "as they say, I've missed the boat."

He was right: the canoes were already moving down the lake at a speed that would put them in Albany in half the time it had taken to come. Sarah watched their furious progress, then turned back to Zeke.

"All right. You've proved your point about Haddom. What do you intend to prove with me?"

He didn't answer right away. Instead he looked her over the way he'd done before, except that this time there was no twinkle in his eye and not the faintest hint of humor half-hidden by his beard. His eyes, she noticed, still had that wary look.

He turned to Eli. "I want you to take the rest of the Boys and ride back. Just leave us a canoe, and one of those rifles and a knife and we'll be along." To Gow, he added, "I appreciate your offer but there's not going to be any surveying at least for the next little while. And don't worry about Sally. She'll be fine with me. That's it, boys. Get going."

The Boys were ready to obey Zeke, but Eli held back. He pulled Zeke aside, and although no one could hear what they were saying, they could all see enough to know that Eli was trying to change Zeke's mind. But in the end, as usual, Zeke had his way, and Eli looked troubled when he and Sarah said goodbye.

"I'll be all right," she told him, keeping her back to Zeke and trying to ignore the strange sensation that was building in her chest, a mixture of fear and anticipation, laced with uncertainty.

She kept her back to Zeke until Gow and the Boys had gone. Her heart pounding, she turned to face him. "Now are you going to tell me what we're doing here?"

He gave her the same long look he'd given her before, but instead of answering her question, he said, "Let's go up on the bluff."

Silently she followed him up to the bluff—to the place where she'd stood this morning, listening to the gunfire from the woods. Zeke looked out at the water, then he turned to survey the land and something in his expression made her heart start to ache. As she pressed her hands together, Zeke began to speak.

"It's like this," he said thoughtfully. "There's all this here and we've both got the papers to prove it belongs to us. When I first met you I didn't believe you had a snowball's right in hell to lay claim to it and I guess you thought the same of me. When I found out you were a woman, I figured you'd be easier to scare away. But as it turned out, you weren't."

He paused, and she guessed that if she looked up she'd see him smiling. But she kept her eyes on the forest and after a while he said, "Even so, no matter how hard you held on, I knew in the end you'd have to give up. I knew that because I never would, no matter how long it took. When I heard you needed to sell the land within six months, I figured you'd find someone to pass it on to, and whoever it was, I'd keep on fighting with them. I figured you'd sell it to Haddom."

"Yes, I know you did."

To her surprise he sighed deeply. "You should have sold it to him. Then we could have settled the matter fair and square."

"Is that what you call fair and square—using brute force to frighten him away?"

"He doesn't deserve any better." Zeke's voice was harsh. "Never mind about Haddom. I'm talking about the land. I've said that when all this started I made up my mind to win, and I'm not saying that I've changed my mind. I still mean to win."

"You could have won last night," she said bitterly. "I wasn't lying when I offered you my deeds."

"Yes, I know that. That's what I'm getting to. After you did that and after you'd gone back to camp, I got to thinking.... I had my reasons for wanting to face his lordship, but I appreciated your concern, and I appreciated how far you were willing to go to avoid the risk. It was a brave thing to do, Sally. I may not have said so last night, but I'm saying so now, and after you'd done it I knew I wouldn't feel right about ruining all your chances with this land."

She turned to look at him incredulously. "You mean you're giving up your claim?"

He held up his hands. "Whoa, now. That's not what I said. I said I wouldn't feel right about leaving things this way. Whatever you might say, you and I both know that after word reaches Albany of what happened to his lordship up here, you're going to be lucky if you can give away this land. I know that you're stubborn enough to keep fighting even after your time is up, and that's the other reason I came up with this plan."

"What plan?" she asked him, wary herself now.

"My plan to decide once and for all who should get the land."

"What plan?" she repeated.

"That's what I'm getting to. You say that New York law governs here and I say New Hampshire law does. But there's another law that governs above either of those. Natural law, Sally—the law of right and wrong. So I got to thinking about how we could decide this thing under natural law and I came up with a plan. If you believe the land is meant to be yours, you'll live on it for a week. If you can do that, I'll give up my claim."

"Live on it?" she repeated. "That's all I've got to do?"

"That's all." He nodded. "For seven days. If I come back this time next week and you're still here, the land is yours."

Her eyes narrowed as she searched for the trap. "And how would I leave if I wanted to?"

"I'll give you a canoe. There's one in the next cove, hidden just up the creek. If you give up, you can paddle due south until you get to the fort. Or you can just drift and the waters will take you there. I'll also leave you a rifle and a knife. And shot and powder. Do you know how to shoot?"

"A little. I've done it once or twice. And I suppose that while I'm trying to live here you'll be trying to chase me off—making strange noises and attacking me during the night?"

He chuckled. "I won't have to. Mother Nature will take care of that."

"Where will you be, then? Spying on me from the woods?"

"Maybe I will and maybe I won't," he replied. "Take it or leave it, Sally. That's the deal."

"One week—just seven days—then I get the land?"

"That's right," Zeke nodded.

"I'll take it," she decided, and held out her hand for the gun.

Zeke gave it to her. He also gave her the knife and a flint and steel. "The canoe's tucked beneath a willow about twenty yards up the stream. You can't miss it."

"I won't even look," she said. "I'll be right here in a week. You'll deliver your deeds then?"

"If that's what you want."

"That's what I want."

"Then I'll bring them. Good luck, Sally." He touched his head in salute and, shouldering his rifle, sauntered off down the bluff and along the beach until he disappeared over the rise to the next cove in the same direction in which the Boys had gone.

Chapter Sixteen

Left on her own on the bluff, Sarah noticed for the first time how quiet it was. Very, very quiet. No sounds except for the lapping of the water and the rustling of the trees, and somehow those sounds made it seem even quieter. Funny, she'd been here three days and never noticed before—probably because there'd always been someone else around, whereas now she was all alone.

Alone. The word sent a shiver up her spine as she remembered how dark it was here at night. She'd never been all alone before; she'd always been in easy reach of company, friends or servants, neighbors—somebody. Even the time she'd ridden back from Bennington herself, she'd never been more than a few miles from the nearest farm, whereas here . . . She looked across to the forest and she shivered again.

"Stop this!" she said aloud. Of course she could scare herself, it wouldn't be hard to do. She could probably scare herself right into running away, then Zeke would have the land. What she needed was to look on the positive side of things. Take being alone, for instance. After what she'd been through, she ought to be glad to be rid of people trying to bully and manipulate her. Besides, she still hadn't thought very clearly beyond selling the land, and she could use these next days to concentrate on her plans. That way, by the time she faced her father she'd be able to tell him succinctly what she intended to do. Having these days to herself would be an absolute boon.

And as for being afraid at night, she'd simply refuse to be. She'd build up the fire and make herself snug in her tent. Her tent . . .

With a pang of foreboding, she turned back to the camp—or rather, what had been the camp. Now it was nothing but an empty grove with the slightly bedraggled look of having been occupied recently. Not only had the men taken her tent, they'd scooped up all her belongings in their rush to get away. And as for building the fire, there was hardly any wood and she had no ax to chop more, and even if she had, she'd have probably succeeded in chopping off her fingers and toes.

Never mind; she could gather fallen wood in the forest and along the beach and she could light a fire with flint and steel. And as for a shelter—she could tear the low branches off fir trees and build a crude one for herself. As they'd been coming up Lake George, one of the men had described doing that during the French and Indian War. Who knew, building her own shelter might be fun, and even if it wasn't it would be worth the expression on Zeke's face when he came back in seven days and saw her tidy camp. He didn't believe she could do it. Probably right now he was close by, spying on her and making bets with himself about how many days she'd last.

"Seven," she said aloud. "I'll last seven days."

She was halfway across the meadow when she remembered food. She'd hardly eaten breakfast and it was past dinnertime, but she still had to build her shelter and gather wood for the fire. She paused amidst the wildflowers, debating with herself which was more important, having a shelter or being fed. She thought of the darkness lighted by that crescent moon. She thought of the creatures rustling and creeping up near her. Maybe she'd find some berries while she was in the woods.

She wasted a good deal of time twisting branches and skinning her palms before it occurred to her to use the knife. In her zeal she cut enough branches to house a company, then added bruises to her scratches hauling them back to camp. After much trial and error she managed to build

a crude lean-to that didn't collapse when she crawled inside. She covered the floor with extra boughs and stood
back, nursing her sore hands and admiring her work. By
that point she was tired enough to crawl in and go to sleep,
but she hadn't gathered wood for the fire and the sun was
beginning to set.

By the time the sun had disappeared she'd managed to
gather wood and light the fire, but she was filthy and
starving and her body ached everywhere. It was too late to
look for food but a swim would feel wonderful—if she
hadn't been too tired to walk down to the lake. She was too
tired to do anything but crawl into her shelter and sleep.

Her lean-to collapsed in the middle of the night. She was
dreaming of suffocating and opened her eyes to find her
body encased in a prickly cocoon. She made a halfhearted
effort to free herself but then she gave up, curled up more
tightly and went back to sleep, too tired to be frightened by
the strange sounds outside. The next time she opened her
eyes the darkness was gone and the sun was shining brightly
through the branches beneath which she lay.

"One down," she murmured. "Only six to go."

The fire had enough embers to have cooked a morning
meal if she'd had a meal to cook. Just the thought of
breakfast made her feel faint. Her shelter was a disaster and
she was dying for a swim, but she couldn't think about
those things until she'd found herself some food—which
brought her to her only possessions, the rifle and the knife.

In her various comings and goings she'd seen fish in the
lake. If she had a hook and a line and bait, she could paddle out in the lake. She could dig worms up for bait, but
what would she do for a hook—and a line, for that matter.
Then she thought of the knife.

Using a length of vine she found in the underbrush at the
edge of the camp, she tied the knife to a stick, shucked off
her shoes and stockings and waded into the lake. There
were fish in the water but they wouldn't come near her—
they must have seen her or maybe fish could smell. She
tried throwing her spear at a distance but without any luck.
After what seemed like hours, she waded out, put her shoes

and stockings back on and crossed the meadow to the woods. She'd seen a stream there when she'd been collecting boughs, and she thought if she could find a rock to perch on she'd have a better shot at catching a fish.

On her way into the forest she came across a patch of raspberry bushes and stopped to pick. She guessed it wasn't healthy to eat too many all at once, but she was so hungry that she gorged herself until her hands were bright red and her arms were scraped raw from thorns.

At the stream she spotted three fish hovering in a pool. They darted away when her shadow crossed them, but she knew that if she waited, they'd be back again. She found a rock to perch on facing the sun so her shadow would be behind her, then she sat down to wait.

The stream gurgled cheerfully as the minutes dragged by—the minutes might have been hours, she couldn't really tell. Her mouth tasted sweet from the berries and the sun was warm. She was thinking that she'd be satisfied with just one little fish, when a very large one swam into view.

Her heart froze, then began to pound. Food! She could almost taste the tender flesh in her mouth. She inched forward, her spear in her hand. The fish stayed in one place, as if it were waiting to be caught. She was sure it would dart off when she raised the spear but it didn't, it just stayed there. She said a quick prayer and thrust down with all her might, crying out in her excitement.

There was a splash and the surface of the pool shattered. Without waiting for it to calm again, she clambered down into the pool, grabbing the dry end of her spear and pushing it hard into the bottom so the fish wouldn't get away. Then she reached down to feel the fish.

There was no fish. The spear was empty. She had missed. She stood there, empty-handed, not knowing what to do, and eventually the pool stilled and she could see herself: tangled hair, filthy face, her clothes rumpled, torn and stained. Her shoulders slumped in defeat. How was she going to last?

She was going to, damn it! For emphasis she stamped her foot, which broke the surface of the pool and swept her image away. She'd heard of people who'd gone without food for more than a week, and she had berries and water. She would definitely survive. She'd missed her first fish, but she'd catch the next—or the next: she had nothing but time. Squaring her shoulders, she climbed out of the stream and hiked up along the bank until she found another pool.

Hours later she trudged back to the bluff, stopping to pick more berries, though her stomach was grumbling from those she'd eaten before. By the time she got back to camp the sun was beginning to set, but before she dealt with her shelter, she took time out for a bath in the lake.

The water was as lovely as she'd known it would be. She floated on her back, naked, letting the coolness soak the dirt out and ease her scraped and sunburned skin. As the sun dipped beneath the mountains, the sky turned crimson and orange with great towering sounds of clouds, deepening to purple and bronze, then gradually mellowing to silver and gold.

She might be tired and hungry but this was magnificent, and tomorrow when she woke up she'd have only five more days. Tomorrow, she decided, she'd go out hunting with the gun and maybe she'd have more luck than she'd had today with her spear. The woods were teeming with little creatures, and with even the smallest pinch of luck she ought to be able to bring one down.

She built up the fire and reconstructed her shelter, and since it was dark by then, she crawled inside. Her stomach was grumbling more vehemently than before but her body felt cool and silky from the lake. She curled up among the fragrant branches and quickly fell asleep.

A terrific clap of thunder jolted her awake in time to experience the beginning of the rain. At first she was astonished that her shelter kept the water out, but as the shower increased to a torrent the shelter began to leak. She turned and twisted in an effort to keep dry, but as the leaking became universal she finally gave up. Her stomach was aching as badly as her overused limbs, her clothes were sodden and her skin felt hot and tight. Worse, though she tucked the rifle and the powder underneath her, she couldn't imagine how they would keep dry.

She curled up in a tight ball and closed her eyes and thought about the ideal meal. She decided it would be a breakfast starting with biscuits dripping with melted butter and heaped high with preserves; then smoked bacon, ham and fish, meat pie, cold turkey, hot cider, and lemon pudding for dessert—not because pudding went with breakfast but because she wanted it. For that matter, she also wanted chocolate cake, and fresh bread, very crusty, and salad and terrapin stew—and anything else she'd ever tasted that was hot and could be chewed.

Curling up even tighter, she began to cry. She couldn't help it. She was wet and miserable and at that moment she didn't care if she ever owned the land. If it wasn't nighttime and raining, she'd get the canoe and let the waters take her away. She'd trade this whole dismal place for one decent meal. She hoped Zeke died laughing; she didn't really care.

Somewhere in her misery she must have fallen asleep, because when she woke up the rain had stopped, except for an apologetic dripping from the trees. She was still soaking but at least her shelter had held. She crawled out to face the morning—a gray and cloudy day. The air had a nip this morning; she shivered in the cold and crouched down to check the fire, but of course it had gone out and all of the wood she'd piled up was soaking wet.

"Bury it next time, Sally," a genial voice advised.

Her head snapped up and around and she saw Zeke leaning against one of the birch trees, grinning from ear to ear. He was dressed in his own clothes, which were perfectly dry.

"Got a mite damp last night, did you?" he asked sympathetically. "Don't bother to answer, I can see you did. Not me. I had the sense to sleep inside a cave—though fir boughs can keep the rain out if you place them right. But I guess they don't teach that in your civilized schools."

"You've been spying on me, damn you!"

Zeke shook his head. "Not a bit. As I said, I spent the night in a cave. I just dropped by to see how you were feeling—and if you happened to be ready to give up."

"Never!" she flung at him with all her might. "Come back in five days—I'll still be here."

"Five and a half, Sally," he noted with a wink. "It's still morning and you started in the afternoon. But why quibble over hours when you're having so much fun? Keep up the good work—I'll see you then." With another, parting wink he strolled out of the camp, whistling like a man who's having the time of his life. And he was, damn him! Sarah bit her tongue to keep from calling out to beg him for some food. She might be wet and starving but she still had her pride, and this was one contest she was determined to win.

She didn't bother to try the fire, she just snatched up the gun and the shot and the powder and stalked off toward the woods. Despite her worry the powder had stayed dry, though she wasted a good quarter of it trying to load the gun. She even managed to spot a squirrel, but when she pulled the trigger the gun gave such a kick that she went flying backward, hard into a tree.

The memory of Zeke's goading made her try again. This time she managed to stay on her feet but she missed her mark woefully. In her rovings she found some hazelnuts, which were still mostly green, but she ate them anyway, and even before she'd finished her stomach was aching again. The sun had passed its horizon when she trudged back to camp, and the only thing that kept her from crying was the thought that Zeke might be near. At least she could start the fire, if the wood had dried.

At first she thought she was imagining the squirrel. It was a nice plump one, placed on the stone they'd used for the cooking pot before the men had gone. She sank down on her knees beside it, afraid to reach out her hand for fear that it would turn out to be a mirage. Her hand closed around it. It was real. She closed her eyes and bit her lip hard, trying not to cry. She knew where the squirrel had come from and she offered a silent apology for having ever thought ill of him.

It was all she could do not to gobble the squirrel up uncooked, skin and all, but since Zeke was probably watching, she forced herself to move slowly and with dignity. Dignity or no, she had absolutely no idea how to skin the squirrel and not only made a mess of the carcass trying but cut herself and had to rip her petticoat in order to bind her wound.

She had the squirrel cleaned and spitted before she realized that in her excitement she'd forgotten to start the fire; then she was too impatient to wait until the flames had died down to embers, so the meat was badly charred. It was also the toughest meat she'd ever had, but she ate it with relish, hardly bothering to chew. If she'd had another she would have eaten it, too, but at least her stomach had something besides green nuts and berries to digest.

With food in her stomach she fell asleep easily, but as she had the previous night she awoke in the dark. She opened her eyes and listened. There was no storm, just the crackling of the fire and the waves lapping at the beach. Then she heard a faint rustling crunching sound. A wildcat! was her first thought. Her second thought was Zeke.

The sound was nearby, not only rustling and crunching but grunting, as well. She remembered the story about the Green Mountain Boys tying a man to a tree, smearing him with honey and pretending to be a bear. She wasn't quite the idiot Zeke expected her to be. Besides which, after two days on her own she was developing a sense about this way of life. Last night she might have panicked without thinking, but not tonight.

Tonight she took time to reason that there couldn't be an animal eating since there wasn't anything to eat. There was only Zeke standing beyond the fire's light, crunching and gurgling and doing his best not to laugh as he imagined the look on her face when she discovered that tonight's threat was none other than him. It would serve him right if she shot him right through her shelter, and she might have if there had been room to aim. But that would deprive her of seeing the look on his face when she turned his own joke back on him.

Moving carefully so he wouldn't hear her, she reached out for the gun, then slowly, very slowly, she eased her body out through the opening. Zeke must have heard her. He paused for a moment, so she paused, too, drawing her knees up to keep her legs out of view. When he recommenced grunting and crunching, she slid her body around. Then in one motion, she pushed herself up and out, sending boughs flying, but she didn't care. She casually planted the gun at her side and before he could steal the scene, she said, "Very funny, Zeke."

The grunting halted abruptly as a furry head came up and a pair of yellow eyes fixed her with the hardest stare she'd ever seen.

It wasn't Zeke. It was a cat like the one she'd seen on the sign at Bennington. A wildcat—the dreaded catamount— and until she had appeared it had been chewing on the innards and bones of the squirrel, which she'd tossed down beside the fire and forgotten—like a complete idiot. Now instead of chewing, it had fixed her with its gaze, and although it wasn't moving she could feel the force contained in the powerful muscles bunched beneath its skin. It could reach her in a single bound and she had nowhere to go. There was no shelter. She didn't know what to do. The gun she was holding wasn't loaded, and she'd be dead long before she'd finished fumbling with the powder and shot.

For the first time the cat blinked. She felt a thrill of fear so sharp and powerful she almost cried in pain. This was the real thing. She was about to die. Her life didn't pass before her but everything stopped: she didn't breathe, the fire didn't crackle, the wind didn't blow. The whole world hung suspended, waiting for the cat to spring. Then from somewhere, very softly, Zeke said, "Stand perfectly still."

Had she imagined him speaking? The cat didn't even blink, which made her think it hadn't heard. Was this what happened when you were about to die? But in the next moment she saw him on the far side of the fire. In one hand he held his rifle—why didn't he shoot? Was he afraid that he'd miss and hit her instead—or that the cat would manage to hurt her before it died?

She realized that Zeke was moving, slowly and silently, and had almost reached the fire. "Good girl, Sally," he murmured, and this time the cat turned its head, fixing him with a brief look before turning to Sarah again. She wasn't breathing and pretty soon she'd faint. She'd drop where she was standing and the cat would pounce: sharp teeth tearing through soft flesh . . .

She shuddered despite herself, and at that moment Zeke bent toward the fire and his hand closed around the end of a burning stick. The fire shifted as Zeke pulled it out. At the sound, the cat swung its head to look at him again. When it saw the brightness of the burning stick, it also shifted its body so that it was facing Zeke. For the first time since she'd seen the catamount, Sarah allowed herself to breathe.

The cat was watching Zeke the way it had been watching her. An awful thought struck her. She was holding her gun. Did Zeke expect her to use it?

"No," he said softly as if he'd read her mind. "Just stand there. I'll frighten it away."

He was moving again and as slowly as before, edging around the fire and straight toward the watching cat. As he came nearer, the cat made a noise in its throat and its fur rippled as the muscles in its mighty shoulders bunched. She opened her mouth to warn Zeke, but before she could find her voice, the cat crouched lower and began moving back.

Inch by inch Zeke moved forward and the cat faded back, past Sarah's shelter, past the last of the firelight. Zeke stopped when he reached the edge of the light, but the cat continued to move until it had vanished, merging with the trees and the night.

Zeke stood holding his torch aloft, watching to be sure, and Sarah didn't move a muscle until he lowered the stick and turned. He was still holding his rifle and so was she.

"Why didn't you shoot it?" she asked in a voice she hardly recognized as her own.

"Because it's beautiful."

She shuddered again without knowing why. "Will it come back?"

He shook his head briefly. "Catamounts are shy. If you hadn't surprised it, it would have finished its meal and left." His teeth flashed as he smiled. "I guess it never expected to be mistaken for me."

"You—you were here, watching?"

"Luckily. Are you all right, Sally?"

She had begun to shake. He tossed the stick back into the fire and leaned his gun against a tree, then he came to where she was standing and took her in his arms.

"Hush, there's nothing to be afraid of. It's gone and you're still here."

"Oh, Zeke, I was so stupid—leaving food around. If you hadn't been here—"

"Hush . . . but I was. Next time you'll know better."

Next time. She almost groaned, thinking of more days of hunger and more nights of fear. "Zeke . . . ?"

"What is it?"

"Don't go—not just yet." She nestled more closely against him, snuggling into his warmth. His scent was so good and familiar and she fitted perfectly in his arms. "Just stay for a little while."

Zeke smiled against her hair. "Don't worry, I'll stay as long as you like."

"I want you to stay forever, but then I won't have the land."

"Hush, hush, Sally. Don't think about that now." He lifted his head and smoothed her hair, combing it with his fingers as he'd combed it once before. With gentle affection, he tucked it behind her ears and tilted her head back so he could see her face.

"I look awful," she mumbled, embarrassed and trying to turn away.

"No, you look wonderful. Beautiful," he murmured, running a finger along her jaw. "I would have shot that cat in a minute if he'd come after you."

She shuddered as the image of sharp teeth on soft flesh returned, but when the shudder had passed she smiled as a ghost of her spirit returned. "It's a comfort to know you find me more beautiful than a cat."

"You aren't becoming vain, are you, Sally?"

At that, she frankly laughed. "In my tangles and tatters, and with my skin torn to shreds?" Leaning away from him, she lifted one side of her skirt and held it out for him to see.

"I love your tangles and your tatters," he said, and abruptly stopped. The word had just popped out without his intending it, and now that it had popped out, it refused to disappear. Instead it hung between them, suspended in the air, and in his mind Zeke could hear its echo: "I love...I love...I love..." He hadn't said he loved her, but was that what he'd meant?

He looked down at Sally, who was still holding her skirt and staring up at him, looking every bit as shocked as he felt. And no wonder, after what she'd been through: first a catamount at midnight after two days of misery, and now a big backwoods oaf called Zeke Brownell blubbering about love. Her body had stiffened as soon as he'd said that word: he bet she was already sorry she'd asked him to stay.

"I'll go now if you want," he offered, releasing her.

She stepped free of him, looking down. "Perhaps it would be best."

"Perhaps it would be..." He was already reaching for his gun when he caught himself. Perhaps? That wasn't a word he'd ever used before. Hell, he sounded like that whoreson Haddom, and he was acting like him, too—mincing off into the forest when his arms were still aching for her. His whole body was aching, right down to his goddamn soul.

He let the gun go and shook his head. "No, damn it, Sally. I don't want to leave. I want to forget the land and every other damned thing until morning and stay right here with you, and if you don't want me you'd better say so and say so quick!"

He gave her about two seconds, and when she didn't speak, he opened his arms and snatched her up, tangles and tatters and all.

Chapter Seventeen

He could tell from the way her arms came up behind his neck that she hadn't really wanted him to leave. The way her body met his told him something more: tonight he would know what he'd only imagined before. And how he'd imagined. Never in his life had he wanted a woman as much as he wanted her, and having her here in his arms made him want her even more.

He nudged her lips open wider, taking her mouth with his tongue. At first she opened to him, then she began to explore just as eagerly. Their tongues met and tangled, then as he withdrew she became bolder, tasting his lips, his mouth. Her penetration excited him as no kiss had ever done. His body was already stirring—he knew he'd be ready long before Sally was, but knowing and doing seemed a long ways apart.

"What's wrong?" she murmured when he lifted his head.

"Nothing," he mumbled. "That's the problem. You feel too damn good!" She looked too damn good, too, with her eyes half-closed and her lips half-parted and her hair all tumbling down—and her body; all willing and lush and ripe. He ran his hands slowly up her sides. His thumbs slid over her stomach and up underneath her breasts. At their first contact she sucked in her breath and held it as his thumbs moved farther up, circling languidly.

"Oh..." She let her breath out and her eyes fluttered shut. He kept on drawing circles, closer and closer but never touching the hardened peaks, until he had her digging her nails into his back. When he touched them at last, she went rigid and her eyes opened wide.

He smiled down at her. "You like that?"

For an answer she let out her breath and arched toward him, begging him for more. He gave it to her slowly until she was quivering and tossing her head back and forth, her still damp hair dragging on his wrists. He reached up to unbutton her bodice, smoothing back the material as each button came undone, then sliding it over her shoulders and down along her arms.

Her chemise glowed faintly in the light of the quarter moon. When she arched, he could see the outlines of her breasts. He let his fingers drift up and down her bare arms, around and down behind her and then back along her ribs, repeating the caresses he'd given her before.

"Please, please!" she whimpered when she could stand no more.

"Please what?" he murmured, but of course he knew. Bending down to her trembling breasts, he drew the first into his mouth, slowly and gently, cotton chemise and all.

"Oh, oh!" she cried out, and he had to stop for fear of exploding in response to her cries. "Don't stop!" she whispered, and in a moment he recommenced, pleasuring first one breast then the other, until the cotton was as wet as it must have been last night in the rain. He could see her clearly through the wetness when he lifted his head and looked down. She was breathing quickly, her body restless and fully alive. He reached back behind her and unfastened her skirt, which slid away with the faintest sigh, leaving her clad only in her light chemise.

He slid his hands down over her hips and thighs, tracing the lines of her body, which he already knew by heart. The curve of her buttocks perfectly fitted his hands; he cupped them through the thin cotton and, leaning forward to kiss her neck, caught the first faint seductive whiff of her musky scent. The scent of her drove him wild. He buried his face in her neck, trailing a line of kisses down her throat and back to her breasts, while his fingers drifted up along her thighs, grazing the soft skin in a way that made her jump.

Slow now, he cautioned as his hands slid down again then back up the same trail. She jumped again, but less than she had the first time, and the next time he came up she only jerked a little as she pressed toward him. He stroked and caressed her through the chemise, the fabric's resistance adding to the mounting sensuality. Her hands gripped his shoulders as they'd gripped before, and her movements became restless. Then she was still.

"Zeke?" she murmured.

He almost groaned. Was she about to tell him that she'd changed her mind? He raised his head and saw her eyes shift back and forth.

"I was thinking—shouldn't we go inside?"

"Inside?" He stared at her as if she'd lost her mind. Then her eyes shifted to the shelter. "You want to go in there?"

"I don't know. It seems so open . . ." She glanced at the lake below them, then up at the starry sky.

Zeke looked at the sky, too. "It is open here. Just as you're open to me, Sally—and I to you. That's the beauty of it, can't you see? Who'd want to be buried beneath a pile of branches when they could be out here? Don't tell me you're turning modest," he teased, bending down again to run his tongue lightly over the tips of her breasts.

"Oh!" she gasped softly, melting in his arms.

He chuckled with satisfaction and his chuckle caught in his throat. "I don't want to hide," he murmured. "I want to make love with you beneath the stars! I want to make love in the water. I want to see if lake water tastes sweeter on your skin. Last night when I was watching you swim it was all I could do not to run into the water after you. I kept wondering what you were thinking of, looking up at the sky. I kept hoping that you were thinking of me. Were you thinking of me, Sally?"

Dreamy-eyed, she shook her head. "I was thinking that I shouldn't mind being hungry in the midst of so much magnificence."

"Did you stop minding?"

"Until it began to rain. Then I was so hungry I cried."

"Poor Sally!"

She smiled. "I'm not hungry now. At least not that way—then you were watching me."

"When you were swimming? You bet I was. Eli would've had my neck if I'd let you drown."

"So that's what that conference was before Eli left."

"He made me swear on our mother's grave that I wouldn't let you out of my sight—as if I'd have risked being labeled a murderer again," he added, his body going hard.

Now it was her turn to give comfort as she recalled what had happened after the death of his wife. "Hush," she said, running her fingers through his hair with a tenderness she'd never felt before.

At her touch, his eyes came down to hers with a fierceness that reminded her of the catamount. "Maybe I do love you, Sally," he muttered, and before she could react, he took her face between his hands and then he took her mouth in a kiss that left her gasping and clinging to his shirt.

After that things changed. The teasing mood was gone, replaced by a passion that would have been frightening if she'd been sane.

She wasn't. She was as crazy as Zeke, as wanton and abandoned—as hungry for the same nourishment with a hunger far greater than any she'd known before. She knew what to do without asking—she knew before Zeke asked. She knew where to touch him and she wanted to touch him there, and she wanted him to touch her in the places that he knew. He touched her until she cried out, then he entered her; it hurt for a moment, then it was wonderful beyond her wildest dreams—wonderful and terrible until he cried her name and left her shattered and stunned in his strong arms.

". . . Sally?"

"Hmm?"

They were lying intertwined, with her skirt beneath them and his coat on top. All the stars he'd promised were shining overhead, and if the night air had a chill, the heat from Zeke's body drove it away.

"How did you like that?"

"What do you think?"

She felt him smile broadly. "I think you liked it pretty well."

"You're as conceited as ever, aren't you?" she teased.

"With damned good reason, I'd say. You think another man could make you feel that way?"

She raised herself on one elbow to look around the camp. "I don't know. Shall we find another man and try?"

That made him chuckle in his chest. "There's no other men around here, so I guess you have no choice but to try again with me."

"But I've already tried with you."

"Ha! That's what you think. The truth is, you've hardly begun."

"What are you doing?"

"Running my hand up your leg, starting with your ankle, up past your knee and along your thigh, all the way up to—"

"Ahh . . . You're no gentleman!"

"Not in the least," he agreed. "You like that, Sally?"

"No."

He chuckled. "Liar! What are you doing?"

"Giving you a taste of your own medicine."

"Are you?" He caught his breath. "If that's what you're doing, I'll take the whole dose. Ah, Sally—I don't believe I've ever seen so many stars!"

After they made love the second time they must have fallen asleep, because when Sarah opened her eyes it was light. She could tell without moving her head that the sun hadn't risen, and she didn't want to move it for fear of waking Zeke. She was afraid that if she woke him he might think he ought to leave, and then there was the problem of what to do about the land. He'd said that his staying didn't affect their deal, but after what had happened she knew that things had changed.

She didn't want to think about the land. She wanted to savor the feel of Zeke's arms and the heat that rose from him to envelop her and make her feel more secure than she ever had in her life, even lying out in the open with no house for miles around and no servants to prepare breakfast—and no breakfast to prepare. She wanted to close her eyes and breathe in Zeke's scent and feel the silkiness of the dark hair that matted his powerful chest. His closeness made her remember everything they'd done, and far from making her feel embarrassed, the memory of their lovemaking filled her with delight. He'd made her a real woman and he was quite a man.

Damn! The sun was rising. A long nosy finger of it had insinuated itself through the birch trees and was poking Zeke right in the eye. She was afraid that when he opened his eyes he'd have turned back into the Zeke who would see nothing wrong with putting last night behind them and launching them headfirst into the struggle over the land again.

Moving as slowly as Zeke had moved with the catamount, she slid her right hand up between their bodies to use as a shield against the sun in his eyes. The position wasn't especially comfortable but she figured that as the sun rose it would stop shining on Zeke.

"What are you doing?"

His voice made her jump.

"The sun was right in your eyes and I thought it would wake you up." She drew her hand back quickly as Zeke opened his eyes. He blinked at the sky overhead, then turned to look at her, and as he did, she braced herself for the first sign of change in him.

"If I kept on sleeping, I couldn't be kissing you. Are you trying to tell me that you don't want to be kissed?"

He hadn't changed back after all! To her surprise and horror, she practically wept with relief. Without waiting for her answer, Zeke pulled her into his arms, which didn't take much doing since she was mostly already there. Her breasts felt tender as they pressed against his chest, but the tenderness was exciting—that and everything else.

He kissed her eyebrows, her eyelids, her nose, teasingly and gently. His beard tickled her skin. She reached up and touched it. "Why do you wear a beard?"

"I don't. It just grew there." He stopped stroking her shoulder to run his hand over it. "Why, don't you like it?"

"It's all right," she said. "But I keep wondering what you look like underneath."

"Maybe I'm plug ugly, did you ever think of that? Maybe you wouldn't like me if you saw me without my beard."

"Maybe," she said calmly. When he pinched her, she said, "Ouch! Are you plug ugly?"

"Would you still like me if I was?"

"If I were," she corrected, then started to laugh. "Who says I like you with it?"

"Do you?" He meant to be teasing, but he didn't quite succeed.

Sarah stopped laughing. "Yes," she said softly. "I do. I like you very much." As she said it she remembered that he'd said "love," and the way he'd offered to leave right after he had. She wondered what he'd been thinking and whether he knew himself.

"I like you, too, Sally," he murmured, drawing her very near until she could feel him against her, hard and ready and hot. His hands found her buttocks and gently squeezed. "Very much," he said, his lips tickling her ear. She shivered and pressed closer. They were both beginning to move: at this point the least friction made her ready for his love.

He kissed her and he stroked her, then he pulled away.

"Stop—where are you going?"

"Nowhere. Be still. Trust me, Sally. Do you trust me?"

"Yes."

Her stomach fluttered as his lips moved down her skin. She knew where he was going and she was half-afraid, but by the time he got there her fear was gone. He stroked her slowly—too slowly, she thought, and pleaded with him to go faster, but he only laughed and told her to be patient. Patient! But she had no choice, and when it was over, she knew that he'd been right. When he came back up to meet her, her body molded to his as though she'd become molten iron, as pliant and as hot.

Sometime much later, Sarah raised her head and announced, "I'm hungry!"

Zeke laughed. "I should think you'd be, after what you've eaten these past two days—or should I say after what you haven't eaten! I'll tell you what. You get the fire going and I'll go and get us some food."

"From where?" she asked, raising herself up to look around, wondering if he'd brought something into the clearing last night.

His eyes crinkled with laughter. "Oh, from here or there." Nipping her on the shoulder, he tossed back his coat, stretched himself, then rose to stand, facing the sunlight and scratching his chest.

Despite her best intentions, Sarah couldn't help but stare. He looked even bigger naked than he did with his clothes on, but the most amazing thing was that his body was perfectly proportioned even for its size. Compared to his massive shoulders, his hips were almost sleek, and his dark hair gave him a vivid masculinity.

Of course he caught her looking. "Well, Sally, what do you think?"

"I think you ought to get dressed."

"And why is that? Who do you think will see us?"

"Somebody might come."

He shook his head. "Not likely. Most everyone we know has already left, and as for the rest of the world, I don't think anyone will be too anxious to tussle with Zeke Brownell."

The sun on his body made him so magnificent that Sarah couldn't take her eyes off him. He grinned at her admiration and teased her, "What about you? Do you mean to spend the rest of the day clutching my coat to you?"

"No, I don't," she said tartly. "I mean to spend it decently dressed as soon as you have the decency to turn your back. And if you mean to spend it with me, you'd better get dressed, too, since I don't intend to parade around as naked as Adam and Eve.''

That made him roar with laughter. "Good point. After all, look what happened to them! All right, my girl, you win, but only temporarily. Sometime before the sun sets I mean for us to have our swim!''

From his coat pocket, Zeke produced a hook and a length of line, and by the time Sarah had got the fire going, he'd caught two fish.

"It's all in the knowing how," he remarked, cleaning them on a rock.

"Having a hook and a line doesn't hurt," was her wry reply.

The fish were delicious, and after they'd finished their meal, he took her across the meadow and showed her other things to eat. There were groundnuts, starchy tubers he dug up, and early apples and watercress from the stream. He also shot a rabbit. "I'll make you a stew," he said.

"In what? We haven't got a pot."

"If you'd bothered looking you would have found one in the canoe. You'd have also found a blanket."

She turned on him, prepared to be angry, until she saw his face. "Never mind," he told her. "You'll have your blanket now and a tasty rabbit stew."

He found some wild onions on their walk back to the camp, then he stayed to clean the rabbit while she went to the canoe to bring back the blanket and the pot. After he put the stew on he showed her how to weave the fir branches to make a decent hut. Then, as they were also low on wood, he went off to gather some.

"Shall I come?" asked Sarah.

"No, you stay and relax. Rest up for our swim." He winked as he said it and she felt a little thrill. Far from lessening the sexual tension between them, their being dressed and hardly touching had only served to heighten it. There hadn't been a moment when Sarah had not been fully aware of Zeke, and she knew he felt the same from the looks he gave her and the way he reacted when they happened to touch. When he mentioned the word "swim," her whole body grew warm.

After Zeke left, she wandered along the bluff until she came to the wall she'd tripped over before. When she sat down on the flat rock, she realized how sleepy she was, so she slid down lower, into the grass, and shut her eyes. Before she knew it she was fast asleep.

Zeke panicked when he got back and found her gone. His first thought was that she'd been kidnapped by renegade Indians or that Haddom had returned, but he couldn't find any sign of strangers having entered the camp. Then it struck him that she might have gone herself, and he almost broke his leg sprinting through the underbrush into the next cove to check for the canoe.

It was still there. He walked slowly back to the camp, and by the time he arrived he'd reached the conclusion that she must have gone for a walk. If she were in the meadow he should be able to spot her from the bluff. He walked toward the far edge, so busy looking out that he almost fell over her, asleep in the grass.

She was lying on her back with her knees drawn to one side, one hand curled between her breasts, and the other arm flung out. Her hair, loose and unbraided, framed her face and trailed over her shoulders, mingling with the grass. The sight of her took his breath away and it wasn't just her beauty, it was everything. The curl of her little finger could break his heart, if a heart could be broken from an excess of joy.

Slowly and soundlessly, he settled himself on the rock, shifting his eyes from her sleeping face to the glittering spread of the lake. Once before he'd sat on this same rock and felt joy, and after that joy had ended, he'd sat here and felt pain—more pain than he'd believed it was possible to feel. Just the memory of that pain contracted his heart and flooded his mind with bitter memories and familiar regrets. The summer sun faded and the leaves fell from the trees; the water turned slate gray and the beach was cov-

ered with snow and someone was crying. That someone was
him. . . .

Even before she opened her eyes, Sarah knew that Zeke
was near. She was filled with a sense of well-being warmer
than the sun. Somehow she'd wandered into the midst of a
miracle and she hoped she'd never leave. He was out of her
line of vision when she opened her eyes, so she shifted her
head and saw him sitting on the rock, looking out toward
the water with a strange expression on his face. The joy and
wonder had given way to a haunted pain.

"Zeke, what's wrong?" she murmured, sitting up. He
didn't seem to hear her so she asked the question again.
When she laid her hand on his knee, he jumped as if he'd
been shot. His eyes came to her as if he were seeing a ghost.
Gradually they focused.

"I saw you sleeping and I didn't want to wake you up,"
he explained.

"I liked waking up with you here." She touched his face.
"You look unhappy."

He sighed. "I was remembering things that happened a
long time ago."

"Tell me about them." Leaning back, she rested her head
against his knee. A minute later she felt his hand in her hair,
gentle as a child's despite its strength.

"It's such a long story, I don't know where to begin."

"Why not at the beginning? I'm not in any rush." And
there was nothing on earth that she wanted to do except
help him banish his sorrow and rediscover their joy.

He sighed again. "The beginning . . . I guess that was in
New York, on the manor where Eli and I were born. We
had other brothers and sisters but they died, so did my
mother eventually. My father was a miller. He ran the mill
for the lord of the manor, but he didn't own it. He didn't
even own our house or the few acres we farmed. He was a
good miller and he managed to put a little money away over
the years. He had the idea that one day we'd all move farther west, where a man could own his own land. But things

kept happening to put off leaving so somehow we never did, and then one day my father was killed in an accident.

"I was there and I saw it myself. They were moving a new stone in and the rope got loose and he was crushed. We took him home to lay him out and the lord came dressed in his finest to pay his respects. He said he was very sorry. He was sorry, all right, since my father was as good a miller as he was likely to find. Now that he'd lost my father, the lord wanted me to take his place. Since I had less experience, he wanted to give me a smaller share than my father had gotten, but I refused. I would have refused no matter how much he'd offered me. All I wanted was to get out of New York.

"Eli, too. For years he'd wanted to go to school, but my father didn't believe in that. But now he figured there was nothing stopping him, so we sold everything we had and I took Eli down to New Haven and enrolled him in Yale. When he was settled, I went off to fight in the war. That's when I saw this land. We passed this way on our trip up to Quebec, and the moment I saw it I knew this was the place for me. As soon as the war was over I set to buying it. I had money from my soldier's pay and I trapped and traded furs until I had enough—but I guess you already know that part."

"Yes, I know," Sarah agreed, thinking of the trial at the Catamount. "Then did you come to live here?"

"Not quite. By then Eli had finished at Yale and had begun to read law in Northampton, in the Bay colony. It had been a while since I'd seen him, so I thought I'd better stop by there before I went up north—though, all in all, we'd have both been a hell of a lot better off if I'd never stopped."

"Why—what happened?"

"What didn't?" Zeke's hand twisted deep within her hair and held tight before he let go. "At the time Eli was reading law with this lawyer and he was also boarding at his house, and when they heard I was coming they said I could share his room. This lawyer had a daughter. She was only seventeen and she was considered the prettiest girl in

Northampton. To put it mildly, she was the apple of her father's eye. . . .

"To make a long story short, I fell in love with her. We fell in love with each other. It all happened so quickly that before anyone realized what we'd started it was already too late, so I went to her father and asked his permission to marry her.

"Her father said no. He liked Eli well enough and he had no objection to me, but he didn't want his daughter living in the wilderness. He told me I could have her if I'd live in Northampton and take up a useful trade. Well, of course I didn't want to do that. I was dead set on this land. I was also dead set on Louisa—that was her name—and she was dead set on me. None of us was willing to give an inch, so Louisa and I eloped. We left a note for her father on our way up north, and by the time he'd set the law on us, Archie was on the way and it was too late for him to get Louisa back."

"You were living up here then?"

He sighed again and nodded, looking at the lake. "We were living in a lean-to over in the camp, and meanwhile I was building us a proper house right where we're sitting now."

"These rocks—"

"Were the foundation. I had the whole thing planned. A kitchen and parlor downstairs and a loft above, and a porch out front so we could sit an evening and watch the sun set on the lake."

"I thought a porch in back, too," she murmured against his leg.

"What do you mean?"

"When I first saw this wall. I thought if it were my house, I'd have porches on both sides so I could see the sun rise off the mountains in the east."

She turned to look up at him and he looked down at her, but after a while she saw that his eyes had changed and knew that he was traveling back into the past.

"What happened then?" she asked.

"Then...when Louisa got pregnant, I changed our plans. The baby was due in December and I didn't think I'd have the house finished by then, so I decided to take her back south before the bad weather came. We were going to leave in September, but then she got sick and so we stayed until she was well. Then there was an early snowstorm, so I delayed us leaving again. That was my mistake. The snow wouldn't have hurt us as much as staying did."

"What happened?"

"The day we were leaving, her labor began. It was almost two months early by my reckoning and I never expected that the baby would live. It was a terrible labor—it went on and on forever and the baby wouldn't come. I'd done my share of birthing and I knew what to do and I did it, but nothing seemed to help. Louisa was so worn-out when the baby finally came that she couldn't even open her eyes to look at him. She never did see him. She died two days later without ever once opening her eyes."

Sarah realized that she was crying. "What did you do then?"

"Then?" he repeated vaguely. "What could I do? I had the puniest scrap of a newborn you've ever seen and no one to care for it, so I did the only thing I could do. I loaded us all in a canoe and I headed south as fast as I could. When I got there, by some miracle, the baby was still alive. I left him with someone who could care for him, then I took Louisa's body back to her father's house.

"I found him waiting for me. I'd sent a message on ahead so he already knew. He'd gotten the judge to swear out a warrant for my arrest."

"But it wasn't your fault!"

"He didn't care. In his mind I'd killed her by taking her up north. And in a way, I had. If we'd have stayed in Northampton, maybe she would have lived. Maybe a doctor could have saved her."

"You can't know that."

"No. But they did arrest me and lock me up in jail. I stayed there for eight months—until Eli found another judge willing to get me out."

"What happened to Eli?"

"My running off with Louisa had already ended his relationship with her father. My being charged with her murder lost him his girl. Since I'd left with Louisa, he'd gotten himself engaged. The girl's family hadn't been too happy with their daughter marrying the brother of the man who'd run off with Louisa Chandler, but when it turned out he'd also killed her, they insisted she break off the engagement, so she did."

"She wasn't as brave as Louisa—or she didn't love him as much."

"Whatever it was, Eli took it pretty hard, but even so he never blamed it on me—not that he had to, since I already blamed it on myself."

"And that's why you never came back to live up here—because you felt you should be punished for what happened to your wife?"

"You could say that. I was also afraid that my father-in-law might try again. I was afraid he might try to take Archie if I lived up here. I guess I was also afraid of how I'd feel if something had happened to him. I brought him here, hunting and fishing, but never to live. I figured one day the wounds would heal and we'd start up here again."

She said softly, "Poor house, waiting all this time to be built." In her mind she saw the house exactly as it would be—she and Zeke sitting on the porch just as they were sitting now. She blinked hard to banish the image but it refused to go.

"It will be built one day," Zeke said, his voice growing strong. "It will stand right here on free land—never in New Sussex, whatever his lordship thinks!"

It took Sarah a few moments to realize what he'd said. When she did, she looked up sharply. "But how did you know?"

"What—about New Sussex? I heard Haddom telling you that day after you'd gone swimming in the cove."

"You—then you were there, too?"

"From the very first. His lordship didn't come until you'd already gotten out." His eyes crinkled with amusement at the memory. "I saw what you did to him—better him than me!"

"You were spying on me then, too!"

"You could call it that. I like to think of it as watching over you. You could have drowned that afternoon and no one would have known."

"In four feet of water?" But in truth she was touched. Then another thought struck her. "Then you knew all along! You knew about Haddom wanting to make this a separate province with him as governor!"

Zeke nodded slowly. "That's why I wouldn't leave when you asked me to. I wasn't about to leave his lordship up here alone, knowing what he had in mind. You guessed I wouldn't if I knew—that's why you didn't tell me. You started to that night when you snuck out of camp, but then you caught yourself."

She remembered the sharpness of his question when she had. "Did you hate me for lying?"

He shook his head. "It wasn't a lie and I knew you were trying to help."

"But you knew more—as always."

"Not always, no. I'm a fool sometimes."

"Oh, really—such as when?"

"Such as believing you'd marry Haddom for his money, when, if I'd thought for ten seconds, I would have known otherwise."

That night in Mason's garden when he'd turned on her. She remembered all too clearly and her chest contracted with the pain. Without thinking she turned her head away from him, but he put his fingers beneath her chin and gently turned it back. He tilted her face to his and pulled her up to her knees. Nudging her lips apart, he kissed her, his hands running down her sides.

"Forgive me for that," he murmured.

"I already have."

She slipped her arms around his neck; it had been too long since they'd kissed, and now with the first contact, their bodies were springing to life. Her bodice was already unbuttoned and his shirt was off when he lifted his head and chuckled. "Before we waste the whole day lying around up here, how about that swim?"

They undressed each other on the beach and walked in hand in hand, but when they got up to their knees, Zeke scooped her up and started running.

"Stop—let me down!" she squealed.

"If that's what you want, Sally!" he agreed, and the next thing she knew she was sailing through the air to land, bottom first, in the water.

She came up, blowing like a whale. "Why, you—" She dived in and swam toward the spot where he was standing, sleek as a seal and laughing at her. Still laughing, he saw her coming and began to swim away.

He made his escape too late; she managed to catch his foot and cling to it until she could stand. Then she hoisted it as far up in the air as she could, which forced his shoulders underwater. He splashed wildly, keeping himself up with his arms. Twisting around, he managed to grab her and pull her under with him. She had to let his foot go to beat against his chest so he couldn't grab her and toss her in again. In the midst of the struggle she realized that he was kissing her.

They were still underwater, but Zeke pulled them up without letting her go. Her feet weren't touching, but between Zeke and the water they didn't need to be. She and Zeke came up plastered together from their mouths to their thighs. When Zeke raised her higher, she curled her legs around his waist and he slid her back down slowly until he was deep in her.

The sensation was indescribable—the cool of the water, the heat of where they were joined. He sucked her mouth hard then released it to lick the water off her skin as he'd told her he wanted to. His tongue stroked her neck and her shoulders. She shivered and squirmed in his arms and his hands on her buttocks began to move. Her arms around his neck, she moved with him at first consciously and then in single-minded pursuit of the pinnacle of pleasure she'd already learned to expect.

She felt like a mythical creature, half human and half fish, and Zeke with his beard was like Neptune, as powerful as a god. The water increased their freedom and passion. He rocked her faster and faster, she was whimpering in her throat. When she felt him stagger she was afraid that he would fall, but somehow he managed to keep them up as they reached the summit and exploded over the top, crying out wordlessly and calling each other's name.

He kept her with him afterward, holding her more gently and letting the water cool them down, until finally he kissed her and let her go. They swam together, as loose and supple as fish, twining around each other with their arms at their sides so that their bodies touched in passing until they were both aroused. Then he carried her out of the water and up to the camp, where they made love on the blanket, then lay together, spent.

By that time the sun was setting and the stew was cooked. "Sally," Zeke said, "I'm hungry."

"Then let's get up and eat."

"In a few minutes. I've got to do something first. I've got to get something out of the canoe."

"But there's nothing left in it," she said drowsily. She'd been reduced to two states in his presence: either sleepy or aroused.

"I meant near it. Stay here, I'll be back." Kissing her on the tip of her nose, he pushed himself up, and she lay watching as he pulled on his breeches and shoes.

The sun had disappeared completely by the time he came back, and she'd taken the stew off the fire and was letting it cool. She was also starving. "It's about time," she said, crouching to lift the kettle. "Since we don't have any plates, I thought we'd set this on a rock between us and both eat from it. I thought—"

She stopped abruptly as she caught her first good look at Zeke. She screamed and almost dropped the pot.

He leapt forward to catch it and burned his hand.

"Look out!"

"Look who's talking!"

Between them they managed to get the kettle down onto the rock. Then Sarah stood to inspect his clean-shaven face. "You shaved your beard off," she said, still in a state of shock. She raised her hand to run it along his cheek. It felt strange, almost naked.

He watched her closely. "Well, what do you think?"

"What do I think about what?"

"About my face? Now that you've seen it, are you going to change your mind?"

She brought her hand down and looked at him instead. His face was broader than Eli's, the line of his jaw straight and long. His lips were full and sensuous, though right now they were drawn in a frown. She realized that he was nervous and couldn't resist the urge to give him just a little dose of what he'd given her.

She frowned. "How long do you think it would take to grow it back?"

"What—grow my beard back?" There was real panic in his voice.

"Mmm-hmm." She nodded, struggling to keep her face straight. "I'm not saying that you have to, I was only wondering ..."

Damn! She couldn't help it, she started giggling. As soon as Zeke realized, his face broke with relief.

"Sally, you devil! You know you had me scared!"

"Why, Zeke, you've got dimples!" Deep ones in both cheeks, and laugh lines around them. She looked up at him and thought that she'd never seen a more handsome man—though she had no intention of telling him as much.

"Then you still like me?"

"I guess, a little bit. And if you've finished preening, can we please eat the stew?"

Chapter Eighteen

The next morning Sarah woke before sunrise again. They were sleeping in the shelter, which, thanks to Zeke's remodeling, was roomy enough for two, and whose leafy green fragrance made her imagine they were sleeping in the trees. From his even breathing, she knew that Zeke was still asleep, so she closed her eyes and nestled closer to him, waiting for the next wave of sleep to catch her and float her gently into the coming day.

Despite her expectations, sleep didn't come. For the first time since that night he'd taken her in his arms, she felt fully awake. She also felt alert, as if she were waiting for something to happen.

Waiting for what? she wondered. She opened her eyes to find herself looking at the powerful swell of Zeke's arm. That arm was distracting, since it made her remember things they had done together—things he had done to her. She smiled to herself, drifting; then the alertness returned. Something was happening inside her. What? She wished she knew. Her heart started beating faster and she felt a flash of fear. What was this feeling?

As though he'd sensed her fear, Zeke shifted against her, moving away a few inches, then fitting back next to her as perfectly as if their bodies had been made to go together. She breathed in the warmth of his presence. As she did, she knew she never wanted to sleep apart from him—and in that moment she knew what she'd been feeling before. Love. She loved him. She loved Zeke. The words brought a warm rush of secret delight, deeper and more stirring than any she'd ever felt.

She loved Zeke Brownell! The truth of it soared skyward like a bird taking wing. She smiled at his arm. She loved that arm—loved it, and loved the shoulder it was connected to, loved the neck, the hand, the chest. She loved Zeke's wonderful body but she also loved his soul. She loved the way he bellowed and how gentle he could be. She even loved his teasing. She loved him. She loved Zeke.

It made her want to laugh to think of other men she'd known, and how she had sometimes wondered if she could make herself fall in love with them. Love wasn't something that you made yourself do. Love was something that happened whether you liked it or not, and if it happened with the right person it was the most magical thing on earth. She smiled at Zeke's arm. It was the right arm for her, and if she could wake up with it around her every morning for the rest of her life, she'd never ask for anything more. She'd be absolutely happy if she could marry Zeke and live right here on this bluff in the house he meant to build.

But what about Zeke? she wondered. And what about everything else? The land, for instance, and all the creditors who were waiting for her to pay her debts. All she wanted was to stay here with Zeke and go on and on, but what would happen to her father if she didn't pay those debts? And what about George Mason? What would he do when he heard that Haddom had run off and left her here? And what about Archie—there were a thousand whatabouts. But she thought that if Zeke loved her, everything else would work out.

She studied his arm. Did he? He loved her physically. He thought she had spunk and he cared about her. He loved certain things about her, but did he love her the way she loved him? And if he did love her, would he be willing to try something that had hurt him so badly when he'd tried it ten years before? Would he be willing to risk loving her, knowing from experience that love often brought hurt? But it also brought joy and pleasure—that's what she'd learned

from him. In these past days he'd given her more of both
than she'd known in all her life, and she was fairly certain
she'd given him the same. She was certain enough that she
didn't mean to give up without what Zeke would call "a
damn good fight." She wouldn't give up Zeke Brownell
without the fight of her life.

Between her and her heart's delight lay the unpaid debts.
Of course they weren't really hers, they were her father's,
and someone else might argue that she shouldn't risk her
happiness to pay them off. Ironically, she could imagine her
father arguing just that about someone else. But she wasn't
her father, she was herself, and she couldn't start a new life
on avoided obligations and a dishonorable past.

Then she had an idea. Maybe she wouldn't have to sell
her land. Maybe Zeke would be willing to sell his—that is,
to sell under the New Hampshire titles in a way that would
guarantee that whatever he sold would be settled the way he
wanted. Since she held the New York grants, no one would
ever challenge the right to what he'd sold—and he'd only
have to sell enough to pay her father's debts.

She didn't think Zeke would mind. Six thousand acres
was a lot of land, and besides, it would be nice having
neighbors if they were living here. There would be children
for Archie to play with, and to support a school.... Her
mind raced ahead eagerly as the plan took shape, and she
snuggled into Zeke's big warm body, thinking what she
could tell him when he finally woke up.

Actually, Zeke was awake and had been for some time,
thinking about his seventeen-year-old bride. He'd told Sally
that she'd been pretty and he'd fallen head over heels for
her. That's what he'd believed at the time it had happened,
and he'd believed it over the years. Louisa had been damn
pretty and he had fallen in love, but compared to these days
with Sally, even their elopement had been pretty tame.

Take this moment right now. At this moment he was
wishing that Sally were awake so he could roll over and
make love to her. They'd made love last night before they'd
gone to sleep and it had left him so sated he'd sworn he'd

finally had his fill, but here he was as eager as a rutting bull, and if he thought about it another two minutes he'd roll over and start to pleasure her while she was still asleep. He smiled, pleased by the notion of waking her that way.

He'd never have his fill of Sally and it wasn't just the lovemaking. He thought of their fight in the water, how she'd struggled and grabbed his foot. He thought of her efforts to spear a fish, how her shoulders had slumped, then straightened, as she'd found new strength. He thought of her long gold hair and her blue eyes, her remarkable loveliness. He thought of her biting tongue and the way she wasn't afraid to say what she thought. He couldn't imagine loving any woman as much as he loved her.

Love. There was that word again, but this time the sound of it made him want to laugh. He did love Sally, he loved her with all his heart. He'd be perfectly happy if he could spend the rest of his days living right here with her. If Sally was here with him no one would try to take Archie away, and he'd build the house just the way she wanted, with porches in the front and the back. He'd give her anything she wanted—anything on earth.

He felt a surge of yearning that was too strong to hold off. With a groan he rolled over—and found Sally awake.

"I thought you were sleeping."

"I thought you were, too. No, wait a minute," she said as his arms enveloped her and he began to touch the places he knew would make her moan.

"Wait for what?" he asked. "Are you getting modest again?"

"What do you think?" She chuckled, but nevertheless she wriggled away. "Zeke, I was thinking . . ."

"Later . . . I want you now."

"You'll want me later! Just listen, this won't take long."

He sighed with a lover's tolerance. "All right. What were you thinking about?"

"Well, the land for one thing. I have a plan."

"I have a plan, too, Sally," he teased, running his lips along her arm.

She pulled her arm away. "Not yet, Zeke. I'm serious. Just listen for a minute. What if I gave you all my deeds and you could keep them or destroy them, whichever you preferred, and in exchange you'd sell just enough of your land to pay my father's debts. You wouldn't have to sell the part on the lake. You could sell the far meadows or the forest, whatever you wanted, and that way you'd be sure they were settled the way you want. It wouldn't matter that you were selling under New Hampshire grants since there wouldn't be anyone to enforce the New York claim." She stopped, looking hopeful. "Well—what do you think?"

What did he think? To tell the truth it was hard to think with this awful falling-in feeling inside. Here he'd been thinking of loving Sally and wanting to give her everything, and all the time she'd been thinking of a way to make sure she still got her share of the land. She'd been thinking of business while he'd been thinking of love. Curled up with him so close he could feel every part of her, she hadn't been thinking of him—she'd been thinking of herself. He'd been thinking they were close together but really they were miles apart.

He remembered how when he'd told her he wanted to stay, she'd asked him what his staying would mean about the land. Scared out of her skin by a wildcat, and still she'd been thinking about the land. Why, she'd probably been thinking of it all along! Lying in his arms at night, maybe even when they'd been making love—all that time she'd been plotting how she'd still get the land. As if who owned the damn land even mattered to him anymore! But it mattered to Sally—it mattered more than his love. He felt like some big brute of a giant had set one foot on his chest and was pinning him down and laughing at how pathetic he looked.

He felt pathetic. He felt like a fool, and his voice sounded strange and choked when he managed to answer her. "Is that what you were thinking about just now? About the land?"

His voice must have sounded strange to Sally, too, because when he spoke she stopped looking hopeful and began to look puzzled instead. "Well, yes," she admitted. "Among other things."

"Other things such as what?" he demanded, holding her away. "Such as how fast you'll be able to get Gow back up here, and how much you could get per acre—"

"Of course not!" she cried. "Please tell me what's the matter—why you're looking at me like that! For goodness' sake, Zeke, it was only an idea. If you don't like it, we can think of something else. All that really matters is that we—"

He jerked away violently as she lifted her hand to his face. He didn't want her to touch him—no, never again.

"Take it all!" he bit out. "If it means that much to you, I want you to have every foot. Maybe when you count your money you'll think of me—then again, maybe you won't!"

"Stop! What are you doing?" Sarah cried, catching hold of his arm as he pushed back toward the shelter door. She caught him but he twisted loose.

"I meant it, the land is yours. Free and clear, just like you want it. I'll send you the deeds. Will that make you happy, Sally?"

"Zeke, please!" she cried, but by then he was already out, so roughly and quickly that the whole shelter shook and Sarah imagined it was about to come crashing down.

The shelter didn't come crashing down: Zeke had built it too well. It stayed and so did Sarah, lying rigid with shock. What had happened to set Zeke off? Was he still so sensitive about the land that just the mention of it would cause him to explode that way? But this explosion had been different from the others she'd seen. Other times he'd exploded with anger, but this time he'd been hurt. How had she hurt him?

Miserably, she shook her head, too upset to think. She'd been afraid of the sweet dream ending, but she'd never imagined this. If Zeke had been only angry she would have known that after he'd calmed down they would work things out, but at this moment she really didn't know. She knew it wouldn't do any good to go after him, since he'd never hear her when he was this upset. Without his warmth beside her she felt hopeless and terribly alone. She felt like curling up into a little ball and lying here until she died. At least she knew he wouldn't leave for good, since he'd left his clothes right here.

Or did she? If Zeke didn't want to see her, he wouldn't let a thing like clothes hold him back. He'd go naked—he had no compunctions, she'd seen that well enough—or he'd find something else. He'd find that Indian garb he'd been wearing when he'd attacked Haddom in the woods.

Panic brought her to her hands and knees. She stuck her head out of the shelter. Zeke was nowhere in sight. Was he gone? Cold fear gripped her and she reached for her chemise. She'd just pulled it down over her head when she heard shouts.

Shouts? She froze, listening. They were the shouts of men and they sounded as though they were coming from the direction of the cove where he'd left the canoe. Who could be coming? She immediately thought of the Boys. Had Eli decided to come back to be sure that Zeke was keeping his word? Or had the Boys guessed what might have happened between her and Zeke and this was their idea of a practical joke? That seemed the most likely. Gritting her teeth, she imagined them swarming up the bluff, full of jokes and good humor—to find her half-naked in the shelter with all of Zeke's clothes.

She reached for her bodice, then on second thought, she snatched up Zeke's clothes, wadded them into a ball and tossed them in the direction of the lake. Maybe they'd believe that he'd been sleeping outside and had gotten up early and gone for a swim. She wondered what Zeke would tell them in his present mood. He'd probably bite their heads off for coming back. She paused to listen, but the shouting had stopped. What were they doing now? She reached for the rest of her clothes.

She was dressed and groomed after the crudest fashion by the time she heard their tramping feet, and she emerged in time to see them coming up the bluff. Zeke was among the front ranks and her eyes went to him first. He was as naked as when he'd left her, but now he was filthy, too, as if he'd been rolling in the mud, and his lip was split and bleeding and one eye was swollen shut. He was walking strangely because his ankles were shackled with ropes and his hands were pulled behind him and obviously bound.

Her mouth dropped open and she stared at him in shock. Then she saw Haddom striding along in front, wearing his blue silk waistcoat and his fancy sword. Belatedly she realized that these were not the Boys. Haddom had broken his word and come back in order to ambush Zeke. With him were the men who'd run away, as well as a dozen more Sarah had never seen.

Her eyes swung back to Zeke to find his unswollen one on her, as cold and unyielding as it had been before. He paused as their eyes met, then stumbled and fell as one of the men behind him prodded him with his gun. He sprawled out face forward and the men dragged him to his feet, kicking him when he resisted and clubbing him with their guns. Sarah's stomach convulsed in horror and only the memory of Zeke's expression kept her from crying out. He'd hate the sight of her weakness as much as he hated the rest of her right now. Oh, dear Lord, what was happening?

Haddom's lip curled with derision at the sight of Zeke on the ground. "Maybe you should leave him down. Maybe we should let him crawl, like the animal he is. I had in mind that we'd set up a court right here and treat him to one of his own brand of trials, but you don't try animals. When they've gone bad you butcher them. Maybe that's what—"

He stopped as he glanced up and saw Sarah standing ahead of him on the bluff. The rest of the men saw her and they also stopped, all of them gaping at her, except for Zeke. He was keeping his eyes averted as though the sight of her made him sick, and she could feel the force of his hate coming at her in waves.

She steeled herself to ignore him and swallowed her nausea. "Why did you come back?" she demanded of Haddom.

Whatever he'd expected as a welcome, he hadn't expected that. For a moment he faltered, then he recovered himself. Turning to the men behind him, he snapped, "The animal is offending the lady's eyes! Find something and cover him."

He turned back to Sarah as the men searched for something to wrap around Zeke's waist. "If you ask that, you must be in shock. We came to rescue you and to deal with Brownell." He glanced at the crowd behind him. "As we were coming down the lake we met a troop from the fort, and after they heard our story, their commandant very kindly agreed to give us a dozen men. Where are the others?" he added, looking around.

"They've gone," she said briefly. "I want you to leave, too. I want you to untie him and go."

A look of incredulity rose in Haddom's eyes. "Don't tell me... It isn't possible! I assumed that when we caught him, he'd been for a swim and left his clothes behind...." His eyes swept over Sarah with unutterable disgust. "I've heard of women developing strange tastes, but this is beyond strangeness. This is—"

"This is my land." She cut him off, hiding her hands in the folds of her skirt so he wouldn't see her fists. Her heart was pounding so hard with anger she could hardly speak, and if she'd been Zeke she'd have slugged Haddom in the face. She would slug him gladly if it would get him off the land, but she realized that it would do just the opposite.

"I have no idea whether Mr. Brownell was swimming or not. I was in my shelter alone," she said, her eyes daring Haddom to dispute her word. "Mr. Brownell is here because we have made a deal. I'm to live here for one week, after which he will transfer the title to me. I fully plan to stay here until that week is up. Besides, I thought you gave your word that you'd never come up here again."

Haddom's lip curled again. "One's word to an outlaw hardly counts. And as for you making deals, that won't be necessary anymore. I can assure you that Mr. Brownell will never bother you again." Without turning, he barked, "Tie him to a tree, and tie him tightly. We don't want him to escape.''

Sarah moved to stop them, standing in front of Zeke. "No!" she said loudly. "I meant what I said. This is my land and I decide who stays. I demand that you release him and leave immediately!"

Haddom gave her an almost pitying look. "My dear Mistress Meade, these are his majesty's men and they have every right to come here in pursuit of a criminal. When they find him, they have the right to do with him as they please. And as for your land, I don't think you need to worry about Mr. Brownell trying to assert his right. On second thought," he added, taking out his snuff box and opening the lid, "there's no point in wasting time. We may as well start back. Men, take him down to the boats. Mistress Meade, have you anything to pack?"

"What could I have?" she asked dryly, watching him dip out a generous pinch. "When you and the others ran away you took everything. Besides, I'm not going."

Haddom sniffed deeply and sneezed. "Stab my vitals! Of course you are—if not of your own volition, then, unhappily, by force. I couldn't answer to your father and Mason if I left you here. Go ahead, men," he said over his shoulder as he whipped out his handkerchief.

Sarah watched the soldiers prodding Zeke back down the bluff. There was no point in staying if Zeke was going with them. She had to go with them and free him if she could—though how she meant to do that, she had no idea. She glanced at Haddom, who was busy blowing his nose. He'd seemed to believe what she'd said about her and Zeke. It occurred to her that Haddom hated Zeke so much he couldn't imagine that she'd feel differently. So long as he believed she and Zeke were still antagonists, she'd have some degree of freedom to help Zeke escape. She could only hope that she'd have enough—and that Zeke would be willing to accept her help.

As she'd expected, they put her and Zeke in separate canoes. Zeke rode in Haddom's and she did her best not to think of the abuse Haddom must be heaping on him as they traveled south. She tried to keep her mind calm and to think rationally. Once they camped for the evening they'd probably tie Zeke up somewhere and post a guard. She was still wearing the knife Zeke had given her, since Haddom hadn't thought to take it back. If she could get to Zeke, she could cut his bonds. The real problem as she saw it was dealing with the guards. Maybe if she waited long enough they'd fall asleep. She'd have to see.

At twilight they beached the canoes and set up camp in a grove of fir trees that grew right up to the edge of the lake. At Haddom's direction, they tied Zeke to a tree. As before, he resisted, and by the time he was subdued his lip was bleeding worse than before and so was his nose.

"Not very smart, Brownell," Haddom clucked when they had Zeke tied. "You'll never woo the ladies with a face like that. But I suppose you couldn't have wooed them in any case. If I had a face like yours I'd have left the beard. I can't imagine what possessed you to shave it—perhaps you were hoping to impress Mistress Meade!"

Haddom glanced at Sarah, who was watching from a few feet away, trying to keep her outraged emotions from her face. The sight of Zeke torn and bleeding made her want to throw herself on Haddom and rip his arrogant smile off his face with her fingernails. But if she did that, she wouldn't be helping Zeke, so she stood in silence, trying not to think of how Zeke was ignoring her.

"Obviously you didn't impress her," Haddom concluded, curling his lip, and with one final disdainful glance at Zeke, he strolled away.

Sarah waited until she knew she could speak normally, then she followed him.

Zeke watched her go. His whole body was aching and his eye hurt like hell, but the truth was he didn't mind. Concentrating on what was hurting let him forget the other pain. Let Haddom try him and hang him, he didn't really care. Probably Sally would be happy, because then she'd know he'd never bother her about the land. Maybe that was what she was saying to Haddom right now—suggesting

they hold the trial and be done with it. The devil take her!
He turned his head away. The thought of her betrayal hurt
worse than all his injuries, and just the sight of her talking
to Haddom that way could still break his heart.

There was the story his mother had told him about a man
named Samson, whose strength was in his hair. His enemies sent a woman to bewitch him and she cut his hair, after which they captured him. It was the same thing with
Sally. He'd shaved his beard to please her and he'd walked
into this trap—the sort of trap he'd normally smell a mile
away. But he'd been blinded by Sally this morning and he'd
stumbled straight into Haddom's arms. Let Haddom abuse
him, he didn't care. Haddom couldn't say worse about him
than he already thought of himself.

She'd finished her talk with Haddom and was walking
down to the water alone. Watching her walking made him
remember last night when he'd carried her into the lake. He
didn't want to remember but he did despite himself—how
she'd felt, how she'd tasted when he'd licked her skin.
Damn her—he'd never forget her until he was dead. He'd
never look at a woman without thinking of her. Let Haddom kill him but let it be quick.

She'd turned from the water and was walking back up to
the camp. She had a cloth and a canteen and she was coming toward him. He didn't want to see her. He turned his
head, but he could still feel her as if she'd seeped through
his skin.

"Zeke." She was standing before him.

"What do you want?"

"To wash your face." He heard the slosh of water as she
uncorked the canteen and poured some on the cloth.

"Never mind."

"It must be painful."

"Some things hurt worse. Much worse," he added,
turning his head so he could see her with his one good eye.
A mistake; he looked away quickly.

"Do you mind?" she said to the guards, who were
watching her every move. "I appreciate your concern, but

he's not going to hurt me with his arms tied to a tree. Can we have a little room please?''

Zeke knew that voice and he wasn't surprised when the men obediently moved away. At another time, in another place, he knew he would have smiled. But there was no part of him that wanted to smile today.

She crouched beside him and touched him with the cloth. The cool of it felt wonderful but he jerked his head away. ''Leave me alone. I've already told you, you can have the land!''

''Zeke, please!'' she said, too softly for the guards to hear. ''How can you think that matters to me more than you!''

At that he did smile, a bitterly ironic smile that made his face feel as though someone had hit him with burning coals. ''I don't think it, I know it, so spare me your lies.''

She raised the cloth again. ''Don't push it away until you've heard me out. I still don't understand what happened today, but whatever it was, I want to help. Later tonight when the men are asleep, I'll come and cut your bonds. Maybe the guards will have fallen asleep, but if they haven't, I'll think of something. You probably won't have much of a head start, but it's the best I can do.''

''Don't put yourself to the trouble,'' he said in a normal voice. ''I said to take your cloth away. I don't want your help.''

''Zeke!'' Her voice was low with muffled urgency.

''Don't Zeke me!'' he rasped. ''You goddamn witch! You've got the land already so what else can you want? If you're missing a man in your bed, why not try his lordship? He may not be as good a lover, but think of what else he's got.''

At his words she drew back and her face blanched with shock. ''How can you say that?'' she asked in a shaking voice.

''How?'' he repeated. ''How? Because it's true. Now take your stinking cloth and get out of here!''

Despite the days she'd spent in the sun, her face was the color of Haddom's shirt. ''I will get out,'' she spat back.

"I'll get out and I won't come back. You're a cruel stupid man, Zeke Brownell, and I'm sorry I ever told myself that I was in love with you!"

Before Zeke could think of a fitting response, she'd whirled away and stalked off, clutching the canteen and the cloth.

"Good riddance!" he muttered, and shut his eyes before he could let himself grasp onto that spiteful word "love."

Sarah sat with her back to the camp and her shoulders hunched forward, staring at the lake. A high veil of clouds hid most of the stars but not the moon, which was still less than half full. Her body was aching with hurt and anger at Zeke. After a stint of lying in the tent the men had strung for her, she'd given up on sleeping and come out to watch the lake, hoping it would soothe her as it had at other times.

How could he be so hateful? She still couldn't understand as she cast her mind back over the course of the day to the morning. It seemed like years ago that she'd woken up in the shelter, curled into Zeke's body and enveloped in his warmth. She'd lain there feeling happy, then she'd realized that she loved him and wanted to spend her life with him. She'd been so eager to tell him how she felt, then he'd rolled over and wanted to make love with her, but she'd told him that she wanted to talk to him first. And then she'd told him her idea about the land and he'd turned icy cold and accused her of caring more for the land than she did for him.

How could he think that, after all that had happened? She shook her head sadly. How could he not believe that she loved him when she told him she did?

Sarah raised her head. She hadn't told him she loved him. She'd thought it, but when she went to tell him, she'd begun with the part about the land and he'd jumped to conclusions before she could finish. If she'd told him everything he'd have understood, but he'd pushed her away and rushed off before she could. He didn't know that she loved him—he thought she only loved the land. No wonder he'd acted the way he had!

Her shoulders straightened as a rush of hope filled her, but then they sagged again. It was the same old story. Whenever he had the choice, Zeke always chose to think the worst of her. If he didn't have faith in her, how could they build a life together? Because, she thought slowly, he would learn over time. He was a man of strong emotions. He loved and he doubted with more force than most people dreamed about, and if she wanted to keep his love she'd have to struggle with his doubt.

They'd have to struggle together, she thought to herself, recalling the awful hurt she'd seen in his eyes. As much as he'd hurt her, he'd also hurt himself. He hurt because he loved her. He loved her that much.

She shook her head slowly. He wasn't like other men, but he was the man she loved, and at that moment she knew that he was worth every bit of struggle it took to prove her love. He was—

Her thoughts were interrupted by a shout. Light flashed behind her along with another shout, then the whole camp was alive as men poured from the woods and fell upon the soldiers, who were trying to unwind themselves from their blankets and find their guns. Sarah jumped up and would have run forward but someone held her arms.

It was Eli. "Stay here," he said briefly. "It'll all be over soon."

And so it was. In less than a matter of moments, Haddom's force had been subdued and was being tied to the trees, while Jasper used his knife to cut Zeke loose.

Someone held a torch up so they could see Zeke's face. "Jumpin' Jehoshaphat!" Remember muttered. "Look what they done to you! They shaved you!"

"No, they didn't. I did that to myself. They did the other."

"I'd say that's bad enough." Remember cast a glance at Haddom. "I thought he gave his parole not to come back again. In my book that's about as big a crime as there is. I say we call court and try him right here."

Zeke shook his head briefly. He was rubbing his wrists to restore the circulation. "No, just leave him and let's get out of here."

"Just leave him!" Remember's eyes practically popped out of his head. "At the least we ought to give him as good as he gave to you."

"Do what you like. I'm leaving." Zeke began to move away.

Eli stopped him. "What about Sarah?"

"What about her?" Zeke swung around to face his brother, his eyes hard and challenging. Before Eli could speak, he said, "Leave her. She belongs here with them."

"Zeke, wait!" Sarah cried out as he began to move again. She lifted her skirts and ran to him. "You don't understand. What I said this morning wasn't what I meant. I didn't mean I didn't love you. I—"

"Forget it." He cut her off. "Tie her up if she won't stay put and let's get out of here. We'll take their boats with us—that'll hold them for a while."

"Zeke, please!" Sarah pleaded, watching him walk away. She turned to Eli. "Please, you've got to make him listen to me!"

From the way Eli looked at her, she knew that he understood, but he could only shake his head sadly. "You know I can't make him listen if he doesn't want to hear."

"Then at least take me with you!"

"I said let's go!" Zeke's voice cracked from behind. "If you can't do it, I'll tie her up myself."

Stooping down, Zeke picked up a length of rope from the ground and tossed it to his brother.

Eli tossed it back. "Tie her up yourself. I've helped you make enough mistakes in your life."

"He's right," Sarah said softly. "You are making a mistake."

"No, I'm not." Zeke's head came up and he looked her in the eye. "I've made my mistake already. Now I'm being smart. Goodbye forever, Sally. Have a safe trip home. I'll send you the deeds in Albany—I know the address."

She could have called out to him, but she knew there was no point. The canoes were already in the water, they were just waiting for Zeke, and as soon as he joined them they were gone. She stood watching their silhouettes in the light of the moon, but Haddom was already bellowing for her to cut them free. And because there was no point in refusing, she went to obey his command.

Chapter Nineteen

"What I don't understand," Remember was saying as he and Zeke and Eli sat in the Catamount, "is why you gave her the land after only five days. According to Eli here, it was supposed to be a week. I know that popinjay Haddom forced her to leave when she was set on staying, but I don't see why that should count against you—especially knowing how partial you were to that land. To up and sign it all into her name like you did... I just don't understand." Remember shook his head in such profound bafflement that he completely missed Eli's warning look.

"'Course there are other grants you could buy," he went on in the same vein. "If you're considering it, I've got some nice land I'm looking to sell. Nice lake frontage—"

Zeke slammed his tankard down. "No, thanks," he said shortly, pushed back his chair and left.

"He doesn't like talking about the land," Eli said mildly as Zeke slammed out the door.

"He don't like talking about anything these days! Ever since he came back from up north, he's been in the devil's own mood. Just look at him the wrong way and he'll snap your head clear off! And giving up his claim to a Yorker..." Remember shook his head mournfully. "If it wasn't for who he is, I'd call that straight-out treasonous."

"She isn't a Yorker," said Eli, but Remember remained unconvinced.

"And you helping him do it, Eli. You drawing those deeds up for him."

"He asked me and I'm a lawyer. Besides, his mind was made up," Eli added, wishing that he knew what exactly had happened between those two up on the land. Maybe it was better that he didn't know, though partly he could guess. Despite what he'd said to Remember, he had tried to change Zeke's mind. When Zeke had first asked him to draw up the deeds conveying his interest to Sarah, he'd asked Zeke if he wouldn't regret it when he'd had time to think.

"I won't regret it half as much as I'll regret other things," Zeke had said. "Besides, even if I kept the land I'd never go back up there. Too many bad memories. Let her have it."

He hadn't even said Sarah's name, but he'd stared at it for a long time when he'd seen it on the deed. Then he'd signed his own name and sent the whole thing to Albany. That left any hope of reconciliation between them up to Sarah, and since she hadn't made her move yet, Eli was beginning to doubt that she meant to make one at all. Which was a pity, he thought to himself. Those two belonged together in their own crazy way. He'd sensed it from the beginning—from the day of the trial—but what could he do? If the horse was Zeke, you couldn't even lead him to water, let alone force him to drink, and by now he realized that Sarah was just as bad.

Zeke ran into Archie throwing sticks for Thumper out in the yard. When they saw him coming even Thumper cast him a wary look, which didn't help his mood.

"I'm going back to the farm. You want to stay here or come?"

"I reckon I'll stay. Eli said he'd take me fishing." Archie glanced at Zeke to see how he took the news. He took it frowning, as he took everything these days. These days he hollered so often Thumper had taken to sleeping in the barn, and every so often Archie slept there, too.

"If that's your choice," Zeke muttered, looking so down that Archie hated to think of him going home alone—even though these days Zeke wasn't what you'd call good company.

Still, if Archie had been down, Zeke would have tried to cheer him up. "Come to think of it," Archie said, "I just went fishing the other day. I guess I'll go with you."

"If you gave your word to Eli..."

"Naw, that's okay. It's more like he gave his to me. I don't think he'll mind, and I'd just as soon go with you. I'll go tell him so he knows I've gone."

Zeke was mounted and ready by the time Archie came back out. He waited for Archie to mount, then they trotted out of the yard. As Archie had suspected, Zeke didn't have much to say—he rode hunched forward and frowning at the road as if it had done him a wrong. But Archie knew damn well that Zeke's problem wasn't the road.

"Zeke?"

"Hmm?"

"Do you reckon she's gone?"

"Who's gone?" Zeke shot Archie a suspicious look in case he'd suddenly developed a knack for reading minds. But he could tell from Archie's expression that he'd been thinking for himself. "How'n the hell should I know?" he growled in response. "If she's sold the land, she'll be long gone by now. Why should she stay?" It had been a full month since he'd sent her the deeds and he hadn't heard a word from her—not a single word. Not even a thank-you. Not even an acknowledgment.

Archie shook his head. "I don't know... Zeke?"

"What is it this time?"

"Nothing. Never mind...."

Zeke held his temper until it got too big to hold. Then he exploded. "Goddamn it, boy, why don't you do us all a favor and just forget it and let it go? I'm sick and tired of your questions and she's not worth thinking about!"

Before Archie could point out that he'd never asked before, Zeke kicked his horse sharply so that it plunged ahead, thundering down the dirt road until he was gone from sight.

Archie narrowed his eyes to slits as he rode through the dust Zeke had left, and sure enough, five minutes later when the dust had cleared, he came upon Zeke pulled up and waiting under a chestnut tree.

"I shouldn't have blown up like that," Zeke muttered, falling in at Archie's side.

Archie shrugged. "That's okay. I'm used to it by now."

Zeke raised an eyebrow. "I've been that bad, eh?"

In spite of himself, Archie grinned. "That bad and worse." Taking his life into his hands, he said, "Did you ever think of going over there?"

"Never!" Zeke snapped. "Never," he repeated with finality. "Why should I go over there? There wouldn't be any point. There was nothing between us except that goddamn land."

"It was good land," Archie said sadly. "The best land there is. You reckon she sold it?"

Zeke shook his head slowly. "I can't rightly say."

Thinking about Sally selling the land was like taking hold of a long knife and twisting it into his gut. He couldn't have said which hurt worse, losing Sally or losing the land—except that he'd never really had Sally, he'd only believed he had.

He knew what everyone was saying behind his back. He knew they thought he was crazy to have given her the land. He'd believed that giving the land to Sally would somehow ease his pain—a sort of suicidal killing two birds with one stone. But it hadn't turned out that way. The truth was that he couldn't forget about either one. He kept thinking of little things they'd done, things he'd hardly even noticed at the time, like the way she had of looking up with one eyebrow raised. Like the way she sometimes pouted when she was asleep. He kept thinking about Sally, just twisting that knife in his gut.

The worst part was that little nagging voice that kept suggesting that maybe it wasn't too late. Maybe he had misunderstood her, the way she'd said. If he had, it wouldn't be the first time, heaven only knew. Maybe she did love him, or at least maybe she had, and maybe if he went to see her it wouldn't be too late to make some sort of peace. When that little voice started talking, the knife twisted deeper yet, because he could feel how much he was longing to believe what it said.

What was holding him back? Doubt, for one thing, and for another thing, his pride. In his imagination he knocked on Sally's door and she and Haddom greeted him as man and wife. Or else she opened it herself and said she'd sold the land. Or she said that she'd loved him but she didn't love him anymore.

Hell! It wasn't doubt and pride that were holding him back—the truth was, it was fear. He was afraid to find out the truth, which would either give him a chance for Sally or silence forever that little nagging voice. He was as bad as goddamn Haddom, moping around Bennington instead of facing facts.

Archie said something.

"What?"

"I said we're here."

They'd come to the turnoff that would take them to their farm. Zeke had been thinking so hard he hadn't realized. Now he stopped at the crossroads.

"What's wrong?" Archie asked.

"Nothing. I want you to go on home by yourself."

"Where are you going?"

"There's something I have to do. I may be a while, but Eli will be along. Go on, now."

"I'm going." Archie turned his horse and set off down the lane. He kept on going until he heard Zeke ride off, then he turned back and saw that Zeke was riding west to the river and Albany. From the sound of it, he was riding pretty fast. Archie grinned broadly. "Well, it's about time!" he declared. Then his grin faltered and he added, "I just hope it ain't too late."

Zeke rode very fast, in part because he was thinking the same thing Archie was, and in part so he didn't have to think. There were a million reasons for not doing this, and now that he was doing it, he didn't want to know what those reasons were. He was riding so fast as he came around the turn that he didn't see Sally and almost rode her down.

He would have ridden her down if she hadn't heard him first and pulled over to the side. He recognized the color of her dress as he flashed by, told himself he was dreaming, glanced back and saw her again. It was either Sally or a damn lifelike ghost.

She waited calmly until he turned his horse around and trotted back to her.

"Hello, Zeke."

"Hello." He cringed at the sound of his voice but Sally ignored it. "Where are you going?"

"Where do you think?"

"I guess that's for you to know." Damn, it was good to see her despite everything. She'd lost most of the color she'd gotten up north but she still had the freckles scattered across her nose. "You could be going anywhere. You could be lost."

"I'm not," she said flatly. "I was coming to see you. What about you, Zeke?" To her own ears, Sarah's voice sounded very calm, which was amazing, since she'd practically fainted when she'd seen that it was him. It had taken every bit of her courage to ride over here today, and meeting him unexpectedly had shaken her nerve.

Zeke reached down to scratch his horse's neck. "I was just out riding. The horse needed exercise, so I-thought—" He broke off and shook his head. "No, that isn't it. The fact is, I was coming to see you."

"You were?" Her hands were shaking from pure nervousness. He hadn't grown his beard back. She'd imagined that he had, and the fact that he hadn't made her feel strangely faint. "About what?" she managed.

"For one thing, about the land. I—I wanted to know if you'd sold it."

She swallowed hard. "Yes, I did."

"You what?" His head snapped up and his voice broke with pain. "Sally, you didn't!"

"Yes, I did. You said you didn't want it and I took you at your word."

He shook his head. He couldn't believe it. Sally had sold the land. "I suppose you sold it to his lordship?" he asked bitterly.

"He offered a pound an acre."

"How could you resist?"

"I thought about New Sussex."

"You—I don't understand."

"I didn't sell to Haddom. What do you think? I wouldn't have sold to Haddom if he'd been the last buyer on earth. In any event, Haddom left the day after we got back."

The relief he felt was fleeting. "Then who did you sell to?"

"George Mason and someone else."

"Mason." For a moment, Zeke couldn't recall who he was. He frowned at a spot halfway between his horses's ears. Even when he remembered Mason, he kept frowning at the spot. He kept frowning and frowning.

"Zeke?" Sarah said finally.

Slowly Zeke looked up. She'd expected the same bitterness she'd heard in his voice, but instead his face was suffused by a look of wonderment.

"I don't care," he said softly.

"Zeke?"

"I don't care. I don't care who you sold the land to—I don't care about the land. I thought I did, but I don't. Oh, I care about it, but not the way I did—not compared to the way I care about you. I was trying to remember Mason, then I realized that I really didn't give a damn who Mason was or whoever else you sold to—what I cared about was you. I love you, Sally," he said, his eyes on her. "I'd sell the whole of the Grants in a minute if it meant I could have you back. Is there a chance, Sally?"

Her hands were sweating and the world had begun to turn. She clutched the reins tighter and said, "Yes, Zeke. There is."

"Is that why you were coming here?"

She nodded once. "In part."

"Do you love me, Sally?"

This time when she bowed her head, she kept it bowed. Zeke watched her for a minute, then, with a wordless groan, he reached out with both hands and pulled her off her horse to gather her in his lap. "God, I missed you, Sally!" he groaned against her hair. "I missed you so badly I thought I'd die from missing you! Promise me you'll never leave me again!"

"Zeke, I didn't leave you."

"I know. I know. I was blind and stupid and I wouldn't listen to you. When you were trying to tell me you loved me, I thought you meant the land. I can't say why I did it. I guess I was so afraid of being hurt that I ended up hurting myself, if that makes any sense."

"It does make sense." Sarah closed her eyes and tried to remember all the resolutions she'd made about going slowly and making sure. But it was hard to remember with Zeke's arms tight around her, when she'd been wanting him so terribly all these last awful weeks.

"What is it, Sally?" He stroked her arms, her hair.

"Oh, Zeke, I do love you, but I'm afraid what happened that morning will happen again. There's no other man I want to spend my life with but you, but I can't spend it trying to earn your faith! If I don't have it by now, I'm afraid that I never will."

He held her tighter, breathing in her scent. "You've got my faith, Sally. You've probably had it all along. If I lacked faith in anyone, I lacked faith in myself. I guess deep down I've been afraid of turning out to be my father's son—always planning what to do but never getting it done. Saying I meant to move up to the land but never moving up there. And always making a mess of things for the people I love. Eli and Louisa and Archie, and now you...."

"You do make messes," Sarah said, and felt herself smile. "You make the biggest messes of anyone I've ever known."

"I'm sorry," Zeke murmured, then he pulled away. "You're smiling, Sally. Why are you smiling?"

She shook her head. "I don't know."

"I think you do."

Her smile broadened. "I think you're right."

Holding the reins with one hand, he used the other to cup her chin, turning her toward him so he could kiss her mouth. It was a kiss of possession, strong and masterful, and she felt her body responding, molding itself to him. The kiss deepened and then he pulled away.

"Zeke—where are you going?"

But he was already gone, leaving her in the saddle to spring down to the ground. He scanned the side of the road until he spotted a good-sized rock, which he scooped up as if it had been a pebble and deposited in her lap.

"What's this for?"

He grinned up at her. "For you. Next time I start running off half-cocked, I want you to use this to knock some sense into me." Taking her hand from the rock, he held it between his. "Sally," he murmured, "will you marry me? I'll live anywhere you want—even Philadelphia, if that's what you want. Now why are you laughing?"

"At the idea of you in Philadelphia! I'm also laughing because I'm so glad. Oh, Zeke, I'm so happy!"

"I'm happy, too!" He reached up and swung her, rock and all, into the air. He swung her around until she begged him to let her down, then he let her down slowly in just the way she loved. He took the rock out of her hands and put them around his neck. "You haven't answered."

"In a minute," she said. "First I have something to give you." Reaching up, she unfastened her saddlebag and took out a sealed packet.

"For me?" he murmured.

She watched as he broke the seal, opened the paper and read. When he'd finished, he looked up. "The other four thousand acres. You deeded them back to me."

She smiled. "I only sold Mr. Mason enough to pay the debts. He took the New Hampshire titles and that's how they'll be resold. All our neighbors will be free men who own their own farms."

"Our neighbors, Sally?"

She nodded her head. "I'll marry you on one condition—that you build me the house on the bluff. That's where I want to live, Zeke."

"Sally, are you sure?"

"Absolutely positive. With two porches and you—and Archie and Thumper," she added with a smile.

"Archie!" Zeke remembered. "He's waiting back at the farm. Shall we go tell him?"

"Right away!" She laughed.

"I love you, Sally!" He kissed her, then grabbed her around the waist to swing her back into the saddle.

"No, wait—I've forgotten."

"Forgotten what?"

"The rock." The rock he'd given her to help maintain his good sense. She stooped down and retrieved it from where it lay in the dirt. "You wouldn't want me to leave it behind, would you?"

He grinned. "Perish the thought. Though something tells me you won't be needing it after all."

"Maybe not." She smiled. "But I'll keep it to show to our grandchildren in fifty years when I tell them the story of how you proposed to me."

"You can keep it on the mantel."

"On the table beside the bed."

"Now wait just a minute, Sally—" Zeke began, then he laughed. They were both still laughing as he swung her onto her horse, then swung himself up to ride side by side back down the country road that led to Eli's farm.

* * * * *

AUTHOR'S NOTE

Given the intensity of feelings between the Green Mountain Boys and the Yorkers, the two groups probably would have gone on fighting each other forever had not other events intervened. On April 19, 1775 American Minute Men turned back a line of British soldiers at a small Massachusetts bridge; with this "shot heard 'round the world," the Revolutionary War began.

The Boys dropped their local squabbles to rush to their country's defense, but the more they thought about it, the more they realized that the same independence Americans wanted ought to apply to the Grants. In July, 1777 the people of the Grants petitioned Congress for recognition as the sovereign state of Vermont. When Congress—at New York's urging—turned them down, Vermont declared herself an independent republic instead. As such she continued until 1791, when she was finally admitted to the Union as the fourteenth state.

COMING NEXT MONTH

#131 TEXAS HEALER—Ruth Langan
Morning Light, sister of a great Comanche chief, had vowed
never to trust a white man. But Dr. Dan Conway's soothing
touch soon healed her bitter, lonely heart.

#132 FORTUNE HUNTER—Deborah Simmons
Socialite Melissa Hampton and impoverished Leighton Somerset
both profited from their marriage. Yet, was Lord Somerset the
one plotting Melissa's demise—or had he truly fallen in love
with her?

#133 DANGEROUS CHARADE—Madeline Harper
Beautiful Margaret Hanson had told Steven Peyton a pack
of lies. Why should he believe her now, when she claimed
he was a missing prince and begged him to save his tiny
European country?

#134 TEMPTATION'S PRICE—Dallas Schulze
Years ago Matt Prescott chose adventure over the girl
he'd been forced to wed. Now he was back—and one look at
sweet Liberty told him that *this* time, she wouldn't be so easy
to dismiss....

AVAILABLE NOW:

COMING IN JULY
FROM HARLEQUIN HISTORICALS

TEMPTATION'S PRICE
by Dallas Schulze

Dallas Schulze's sensuous, sparkling love stories have made her a favorite of both Harlequin American Romance and Silhouette Intimate Moments readers. Now she has created some of her most memorable characters ever for Harlequin Historicals....

Liberty Ballard...who traveled across America's Great Plains to start a new life.

Matt Prescott...a man of the Wild West, tamed only by his love for Liberty.

Would they have to pay the price of giving in to temptation?

AVAILABLE IN JULY WHEREVER HARLEQUIN BOOKS ARE SOLD

HHTP

Harlequin's Ruth Jean Dale brings you
THE TAGGARTS OF TEXAS!

Those Taggart men—strong, sexy and hard to resist . . .

There's Jesse James Taggart in **FIREWORKS!**
Harlequin Romance #3205 (July 1992)

And Trey Smith—he's **THE RED-BLOODED YANKEE!**
Harlequin Temptation #413 (October 1992)

Then there's Daniel Boone Taggart in **SHOWDOWN!**
Harlequin Romance #3242 (January 1993)

And finally the Taggarts who started it all—in **LEGEND!**
Harlequin Historical #168 (April 1993)

**Read all the Taggart romances!
Meet all the Taggart men!**

Available wherever Harlequin books are sold.   DALE-R

BIG SUMMER READ

Summer Reading At Its Best

In July, Harlequin and Silhouette bring readers the Big Summer Read Program. Heat up your summer with these four exciting new novels by top Harlequin and Silhouette authors.

SOMEWHERE IN TIME by Barbara Bretton
YESTERDAY COMES TOMORROW by Rebecca Flanders
A DAY IN APRIL by Mary Lynn Baxter
LOVE CHILD by Patricia Coughlin

From time travel to fame and fortune, this program offers something for everyone.

Available at your favorite retail outlet.

BSR